"Carol McCleary's *The Alchemy of Murder* is rollicking good fun. The idea of starring the great Nellie Bly in a novel of suspense is such a natural that it's a wonder it hasn't been done before. But if it had, I doubt any other writer would have done it better. A historical period that includes Joseph Pulitzer, Oscar Wilde, Jules Verne, Toulouse-Lautrec, and Jack the Ripper requires an artist of McCleary's talents to do it justice."

—Loren D. Estleman, winner of two American Mystery Awards, four Shamus Awards, finalist for the National Book Award, and author of *The Branch and the Scaffold*

"What a great idea for a novel. Nellie Bly is one of my favorite characters. This book more than lives up to the drama and suspense that are still part of her aura."

—Thomas Fleming, president of the Society of American Historians, winner of the Lincoln Prize in History for Lifetime Achievement, and author of the *New York Times* bestseller *The Officers' Wives*

"Gripping, atmospheric, and exciting, *The Alchemy of Murder* takes Victorian mystery and science beyond *The Alienist* by having one of the most amazing women in American history put together a Victorian era *CSI* to battle a deadly plot: Nellie Bly, the world's first investigative reporter, teams with the great microbe hunter Louis Pasteur, Jules Verne, who invented science fiction, and Oscar Wilde, who shocked even the scandalous Vic-torians to combat a threat more menacing than that in

ional bestselling author whose books have been ed into thirty languages

NELLIE BLY
circa 1890

THE
ALCHEMY
OF
MURDER

Carol McCleary

A TOM DOHERTY ASSOCIATES BOOK
NEW YORK

THE ALCHEMY OF MURDER

A Forge Book
Published by Tom Doherty Associates, LLC
175 Fifth Avenue
New York, NY 10010

www.tor-forge.com

Forge® is a registered trademark of Tom Doherty Associates, LLC.

ISBN 978-0-7653-6175-2

First Edition: March 2010
First Mass Market Edition: March 2011

Printed in the United States of America

0 9 8 7 6 5 4 3 2 1

ACKNOWLEDGMENTS

To Hildegard Krische, who was sent to me by the heavens
above—she is my guardian angel—you will never know
what you have done for me and what you mean to me. . . .

To Doctor Pasteur, who saved my life—
as a child I was bitten by a rabid dog. . . .

To Nellie Bly, who gave me life. . . .
and
To Cenza Cacciotti, my incredible soul sister,
who keeps me sane and very happy, and
I truly don't know what I'd do without you. . . .
Thank you very much.

As always, there is a host of people who deserve to be
acknowledged for their help and support and just being
fabulous friends who understand and put up with me.
The list would be endless, and I hope there will be more
books so I can give each of them their just deserve. With
this first one, I want to thank Ghyontonda Mota for giving me immense support, encouragement, and, most important, helping me survive this crazy journey—thank
you a million times. To David Young, who kept my
hands and body functioning, Nellie might have not been

written if you hadn't spun your magic—thank you. Harvey Klinger, an amazing man who has always given me a chance and believed in me—thanks for not only being my agent, but also an extremely true-blue friend. My sis, Gen-Foxey, who gave me faith in fairy tales—love you. My mother, who not only gave me the opportunity to write Nellie, for which I will always be thankful, but also a deep, precious understanding of life. I will always be extremely grateful to Bob Gleason, my editor, who made this happen—thank you. And to Ashley Cardiff, who kindly kept me on track—you're a real trooper—and Eric Raab, who took a helpful interest in Nellie. Then there's my copy editor, David Stanford Burr, who did an absolutely incredible job—wow! Linda Quinton, I wish I could say the right words to let you know how much I appreciate you—you are not just a wonderful person who took a bold chance with me, but someone I consider a true friend, always. Last, but by far not least, Tom Doherty, a gentleman and a man who has given countless opportunities to so many writers whose voices would never have been heard—thank you for letting Nellie's voice be heard again.

P.S. I feel it's very important to acknowledge people who give you a smile when you so desperately need it and a kind word that keeps you moving forward. They are little gestures that turn a crappy day into a happy one. This is to some very special people in the village of Dennis, where I live, who did this for me when I most needed it—thank you from the bottom of my heart. . . . Sarah Humphrey; Brad Tripp; Tony Itri; Paulo Murta; Laurie Desso; Lorraine Steele; Stephany Hutchinson; Maureen Costa, who always had such a beautiful smile on her face; Emily Hennigan; Roseanne Smith; Dr. Kristine Soly; Dr. Jamie Nash; Sasha Reljic; Suzie Maguire; Deb Leo; Cathy Connolly;

Su Pratt; Barbara Wells, our incredible librarian; Dr. Blake and Judy Blake; and my new friends at Pilates Plus, Michelle Mashoke, Kerstin Holve, and Chrissie Mashoke. And a couple of people not on the Cape, but who need to be here, Carlo Trinidad and Elvin Alvarez.

PREFACE

Journal of Nellie Bly
Paris, October 27, 1889

"I have never feared any man as much as I fear the man in black. His is an evil that seeks blood in the darkest places of gaslit streets and forgotten alleys . . ."

Until the discovery of the manuscript containing this passage, these words written by Nellie Bly, the world's first female investigative reporter, were kept secret. The French government decided over a hundred years ago that knowledge of gruesome deeds and a diabolical plan should die with her and others who shared her secrets—Jules Verne, the creator of science fiction, Louis Pasteur, the great microbe hunter who battled deadly creatures invisible to the naked eye, and the wonderfully flamboyant and witty Oscar Wilde.

We are confident that once the reader is acquainted with the contents of this manuscript, they will appreciate the reason for the secrecy.

While the editors of this work wish first and foremost to protect the reputation of Nellie against the baseless accusations that she has not been entirely candid in this "lost manuscript" about her adventures in Paris, and about the serious events that took place, we are also forced to counter accusations that we had in some manner "concocted" this tale from Nellie's previous writings and a liberal use of historical facts. As the ensuing litigation over the ownership of the manuscript revealed, it was found in a metal box during demolition of the building that had housed the newspaper that employed Nellie Bly, the *New York World*.

The editors admit to having made modest corrections to the manuscript before submitting it for publication (Nellie was a terrible speller), but we want the reader to rest assured that they may compare our truth and veracity to that attributed to the lioness of literature, Lillian Hellman, by none other than Mary McCarthy.

THE EDITORS

I

Paris, October 27, 1889

I have never feared any man as much as I fear the man in black. His is an evil that seeks blood in the darkest places of gaslit streets and forgotten alleys. The Alchemist, is how I've come to think of him—like a medieval chemist trying to turn lead into gold or seeking the elixir of life, he has a passion for the dark side of knowledge, mixing murder and madness with science. What purpose he has for the broth he's brewing I've yet to discover, but in an age where many young doctors are following the footsteps of Dr. Pasteur in searching for benefits to mankind in their laboratories, a man who uses his microscope to concoct evil . . . well, I fear his ambitions are of the most preternatural sort.

My name is Nellie Bly, though it isn't my birth name. I had to adopt a pen name because the common wisdom is that newspaper reporting is no job for a lady. As an investigative reporter for Mr. Pulitzer's *New York World*, I've chased many strange tales and written of things that seared my soul, but on this night I'm questioning my own sanity as I set out to track a killer at Montmartre, a notorious hillside overlooking Paris.

Through intuition, a little information, and perhaps a

great deal of imprudence, I've followed his gruesome deeds from New York to London and now Montmartre—the hillside Parisians call "La Butte," noted for artists and poets and its Jezebel streets, where men buy empty shouts of pleasure and women lose the shine on their souls.

As a carriage carries me down dark cobblestone streets on my hunt for a madman, I can't help but worry about the task I've set out for myself. No matter how hard I try to find good sense in my plan, nothing comes to mind. Thinking about what I may face this gloomy night gives me the shivers. "A goose walked over your grave," my mother always said whenever I got cold chills. Not a pleasant thought on this dreary night.

Streets wet from an earlier drizzle glisten where sallow glow from gaslights reach. Now the night air tastes damp as a fine gray mist falls.

Had Mr. Dickens wrote about Paris today, he would no doubt find that this is not the best, but the worst of times. The City of Light is racked with attacks by anarchists out to destroy civilized government while a deadly pestilence sweeps in from the East, striking down people like the Grim Reaper wielding his bloody scythe.

With the city besieged by a plague of violence and sickness, no one will listen to my warning that another evil stalks the city. I am left with no other choice but to go out alone to bring the beast to bay.

The German doctor. That's what we called him at the madhouse on Blackwell's Island because of his accent and clothes, although we knew nothing about his background or nationality. What I do know is that he's evil, a depraved monster lusting for the blood of women.

Since his preference for victims are prostitutes, I've dressed the part.

I boldly bought from a Montmartre streetwalker a jaded black dress that plunges immodestly at the neck, with the hemline a scandalous six inches above my naked ankles. Despite a vigorous washing, it still bears a scent of cheap rose water. A wool shawl, trashy red lipstick, and a vulgar swish that would erupt fire and brimstone in a Baptist minister complete my costume. Having donned many disguises—from ballet dancer to elephant trainer, servant girl and thief—I pride myself on authenticity.

I've learned a great deal about the Alchemist since my first encounter with him in New York. For a time I thought he was simply a rabid beast who murdered women for satanic pleasures, but now I believe his acts of madness cloak a diabolical plan and the test tubes and microscopes in his laboratory play a sinister role.

My carriage pulls to a curb at the destination I gave the driver. The time has come to test my plan—along with my courage and resolve.

The cabby has a lumpish face devoid of sensibility. He leers at me and does a vulgar half whistle-click sound with his lips and teeth as he takes my money. "Good hunting, Mademoiselle."

He thinks I'm a streetwalker. Good. I've passed the first test and this gives me a bit more confidence, but as I step down from the carriage I find myself praying for my nerves to hold.

I'm in an area I've gauged the man in black will be hunting for his prey. Normally it would be filled with people, but because of a fall carnival at Place Blanche, I'm walking up a deserted street. The damp chill closes in on me and I pull my shawl snugger.

Paris is an ancient, urbane city with graceful, curving streets and wide boulevards, but its bastard child Montmartre is a cranky old woman with bulges and lumps; streets are narrow and crowded with small shops, sidewalk cafés, and the cheap hovels of artists and writers. Roads accommodating carriages stop halfway up the hillside, then blend into a maze of narrow alleys and stairwells shaded with moss-covered weeping willows and clusters of creeping vines.

Nothing about the Montmartre is considered respectable by decent society; the immorality and depravities of its bohemian inhabitants is a scandal known throughout the world. Its reputation is further tarnished by the crimes and social ills of the *marquis*, an area of dank shacks in which the phrase "unwashed masses" is not a literary allegory but a description of the inhabitants.

Paris is spread out below. Mr. Edison's newfangled electric street-lights line the main boulevards, while the pale yellow glow of gas lamps are on lesser streets. The heart of the city is ablaze with the sparkle from the magnificent World's Fair celebrating the centennial of the French Revolution. The marvels of nature and technology from around the world are on display, including an entire North African village, an amazing horseless carriage that operates on gasoline, and an electric submarine like Jules Verne's *Nautilus*, which can plunge hundreds of feet beneath the sea. Buffalo Bill is even there to thrill visitors with his Wild West show.

The most stunning and controversial monument of the fair—Mr. Eiffel's thousand-foot, gangling steel tower—is the tallest manmade structure on Earth, twice as tall as the Great Pyramid at Giza. The nation's art community fought bitterly to stop building of the tower, calling the crossbars of steel a betrayal of French art and history, scornfully dubbing it the Tower of Babel. Construction was approved only because the tower would stand for a limited time and then be dismantled.

I wish I was at the fair right now, safely ensconced in the gay crowds rather than trudging down a dark and lonely street in an area that carries more social taint than even San Francisco's infamous Barbary Coast.

I'm told that Montmartre received its name because some sixteen centuries ago St. Denis got his head chopped off at the foot of the hill. The saintly Denis picked his head up off the ground and carried it to the top of the hill, inspiring the name *Mons Martyrum*, Mount of Martyrs. For centuries the district was a rustic village with windmills that ground flour for the bread of Paris. But Paris finally grew out to the Butte and the hill became part of the city.

As the old windmills stopped grinding flour and awoke to find lewd jokes in their staid cabarets and dance halls, scandalous cancan girls, artists and poets, bohemians—with their long hair, rebellious minds, and shameless attitudes about sex—abandoned the Latin Quarter for this little village with its grand views and low rent.

My ruminations about the Butte and my feet come to an abrupt halt when a man wearing black steps out of a doorway twenty paces in front of me and stops beneath the glow of a street lamp. I pretend to be interested in a store window display in which the storekeeper has left an oil lamp burning to advertise his stock of lamps. I brought a Chinese fan to hide my features and use it now to cover most of my face.

My body goes cold to the bone as I observe the man out of the corner of my eye. "My God," I whisper. It isn't possible that the very man I'm hunting would suddenly appear in front of me.

Too scared to run back down the dark street I'd come up, I freeze in place as he lights a cigarette. I can make out shaggy, dark hair sticking out below an unfashionable box hat, baggy trousers, and a long, cheaply tailored frock coat.

Even though the clothing isn't exactly the same as the man I tangled with in New York, it all adds up to the same impression: a poor Eastern European immigrant fresh off the boat onto Ellis Island.

He turns to look directly at me, revealing a beard and heavy, round, gold-framed eyeglasses.

I reach into my pocket and palm a rubber bladder of acid. Besides my police whistle, I've armed myself with an unusual weapon I learned about from prostitutes in the slums of Mexico City. They have a small, palm-size rubber bladder filled with hot pepper and their urine to spray into the eyes of men who get too rough. Modesty forbids me from using my bodily fluid and instead I filled the flask with plumber's acid obtained from a maid at my hotel.

The man in black turns and walks in the opposite direction.

Beyond him I can see the lights of Place Blanche. Keeping my panic in check, I follow slowly, thankful that he's heading for the celebration at the square.

Thoughts whirl in my head like ghosts in an attic. *Could I have actually found him?* It seems impossible that I traveled thousands of miles, spent a week in Paris trying to track him down, only to have him suddenly appear in front of me.

As I near Place Blanche, the night glows with bright lights and gay people. Time has rolled back the curtain of centuries, ancient cemeteries have yielded up their dead, and living ghosts pack all the bright cafés as costumed revelers crowd the square.

The recently opened Moulin Rouge is ablaze with crimson lanterns on windmill blades that turn in imitation of the old flour mills. Cafés and cabarets lining the square are dizzy with merrymakers. Happy shouts, sparkling laughter, and a bewildering kaleidoscope of people in strange costumes greet me.

As I follow the man in black, a Roman senator wearing a bedsheet for a robe and a crown of laurel, crosses my path. Queen Victoria strolls by, in white lace and black wool. Not only is the queen taller and broader than her pictures, but "she" has the beard and impish grin of a bohemian poet. Charlemagne has escaped his statue in front of Notre-Dame and strolls along with a golden crown and breastplate and an enormous goblet of wine in hand. He's surrounded by prancing cocottes—those particularly French tarts, dressed as forest nymphs—or undressed, I should say, since they have less on than off. All this intensified to electrifying cancan music and the cheers of the men surrounding women showing their lace as they kick up their heels.

The nation's president told the city that merrymaking is most important this year because of the doom and gloom created by terrorist bombs and the deadly influenza. His personal awareness of the city's plight was highlighted by an attempt to assassinate him on the eve of the grand opening of the World's Fair.*

I try to get a better look at the man in black as I follow him through the maze of merrymakers. His gold-framed glasses have a red tint. I don't recall a tint to the German doctor's lenses. And his bushy hair and beard are longer and more unkempt than I remember.

Still, I think it's him . . . or am I fooling myself into seeing what I want to see? After all, the preference of men everywhere is for beards or mustaches. One significant difference in appearance is obvious: he wears a red scarf, the mark of a radical and revolutionary.

The scarf begs a question: if he's trying to hide his identity, why bring attention to himself by wearing a red

---

* A second attempt didn't fail. President Carnot was murdered by an anarchist in 1894. President McKinley of the United States, Czar Alexander of Russia, Empress Elizabeth of Austria, King Umberto of Italy, Prime Minister Canalejas of Spain, King George I of Greece, and countless others were also assassinated by anarchists. —The Editors.

scarf that identifies him as a radical? The answer, of course, is that this is the Montmartre, not New York. Wearing the color of a radical is no more a fashion statement on the Butte than wearing a watch on a gold chain is on Wall Street.

He stops and turns around, appearing to look for someone. Avoiding eye contact, I pretend to be interested in a ragged young woman holding a black cat while she sings a sad song about life on the streets.

> At night I stroll along the Seine
> In the moonlight,
> I take men under the bridge
> And sell my love for a few sous.
> When there's not enough to eat,
> I bite my lip and keep on walking,
> down the lonely street.*

I've been given the opportunity to be his proposed victim, but my courage wavers. I have to remind myself I didn't come all this way to be a coward. That said, I muster my courage and turn to give him my harlot's smile, but he's already moved away. The girl singing the song of sorrow speaks to me as I start to follow.

"Here." She takes money out of the bonnet that holds the alms she has collected. "Take this and don't sell your body tonight."

I smile my thanks as I rush away, warmed by her charity. I have found that people who have endured hardship seem so much more willing to share their worldly goods than those who have spent their lives in well-padded nests.

---

* This is a song by Aristride Bruant, Montmartre's poet-songster. —The Editors.

Dodging around musketeers in gay red uniforms and plumed hats, I keep my eye on the man in black. What a strange place to be shadowing a killer—surrounded by the profane and the grotesque: Socrates with his mug of hemlock, a headless Marie Antoinette arm-in-arm with a black-masked executioner carrying her head, Héloïse

THE MOULIN ROUGE ON THE NIGHT OF THE BALL

and Abelard holding hands, two round balls hanging from a string around the latter's neck, my own good breeding refusing to speculate on the symbolism of the balls.

A drunk dressed as an Elizabethan nobleman gropes me and I roughly knock away his offending hands. I'm not a big woman but as a small-town girl with six brothers, I learned early to put up my dukes to a masher.

"*Slut*!" His voice is British.

I quickly move away from the fool, using my Chinese fan to hide a smile of pleasure. In my hometown if a man used that kind of language on a lady, he would be horse whipped. But on this night in Paris the insult pleases me, for it confirms my disguise is working.

Shouting breaks out off to my right and a champagne bottle flies at a wagon that's being drawn into the square by a team of horses. Men and women on the flatbed of the wagon yell:

> Give us bread!
> Give us freedom!
> Death to those who deny bread and freedom
> to the people!

They wear the red scarves of radicals. From the words and the curses hollered back from the crowd, it's obvious they're anarchists urging violence to gain a better life.

The words strike home with me. My days as a factory girl were marked by strikes, injuries to workers, and layoffs. I don't like to think about what happens to families when factories close and workers are turned out into the streets. Losing one's job ultimately has one consequence: desperation. Often times, starvation sets in.

In these bad times, the ranks of the anarchists have swollen. Their aim is to destroy organized government by terrorizing the public with bombs and eliminating their leaders with assassination, believing that if organized governments are abolished, the people will rule themselves in a utopian society.

While my heart goes out to the workers, I don't condone violence. And I can see that these anarchists are deliberately appealing to the wrong crowd. The merrymakers are not unemployed factory workers who retch at the sight of their hungry children, but bourgeoisie who enjoy meat and a bottle of wine at every meal. The radicals are obviously here not to enlighten, but to stir up trouble.

Stepping back to avoid a collision with a very tall thin man walking on stilts, I bump into a fat Indian maharaja and my fan is knocked out of my hand.

As I bend over to pick it up *something pokes me in the derriere.*

2

I freeze in place, stunned. The intruding object is removed as I straighten up to the sound of laughing behind me.

With the fan hiding my features, I turn around.

The man with a British accent who called me a slut grins as he holds the offending cane. His three companions, all dressed in Elizabethan costumes, find his insult to me amusing. With their generous paunches, the foursome look rather like caricatures of Shakespearean actors.

Rage explodes in me and I shake like Mount Vesuvius ready to erupt. Had I a dagger I would have plunged it into his heart.

"She should roger us all!" one of my assailant's friends bellows.

Roger us all! The swine is proposing I conduct coitus with them.

My assailant's short jacket falls to the waistline of his tights. His private parts rudely bulge. I stare at the swelling as I struggle to keep my anger from exploding.

A woman steps between us and grabs the arm of my assailant.

"Mi'lord! Choose me, Mi'lord." She is a real prostitute—sadly one who has said good-bye to innocence long before. She speaks the words in English, the limits of that language known by most of the street girls. "Mi'lord" is a street name for any man from across *La Manche*.

With an unkind hand, my assailant pushes her aside and steps closer to me.

"I'll give you ten francs for the four of us."

His friends howl with laugher.

I stand rooted in place, confused. I've been in many terrible situations, fought off drunks and turned the tables on pimps, but I've never been touched offensively before.

Swaying drunkenly like a ship at sea, he moves so close I can smell curdled whiskey on his breath. For a second I see the cruel man my widowed mother married, a drunken scoundrel who beat her and dealt lewdly with personal matters before us children.

"Did you hear me? Ten francs for the four of us."

His friends double over with laughter.

The devil grips my heart and I edge closer to him, the fan still in front of my face. With trembling lips, I ask, "Do you want to get hot, Monsieur?"

"Yes, yes." He moans and smacks his lips.

I squeeze the rubber flask of acid onto his bulging male parts.

Wide-eyed, he stares down at the wet stain between his legs.

"*Bitch*!" He reaches for me and I quickly step away as he bounces off Attila the Hun. I dodge and dart through the crowd with his wails of agony erupting behind me—the acid has seeped into his private parts. The hotel maid assured me that the acid is painful but not permanently disfiguring, but at this point I hope his private parts are fried.

Damn him. I fear I've lost my man in black.

Then I spot him moving through the mass of people. He stops and looks to three prostitutes standing next to the wall of a cabaret and gestures to the woman in the middle. As she hurries toward him, it's easy to see she's a real streetwalker—she has that tart's swish that only a true prostitute possesses. The poor woman has not a clue that the price will include her life.

Wondering what I should do, I watch them walk away. If I had evidence that a policeman would accept, I'd have him arrested on the spot.

Cleopatra with a live snake around her neck steps in front of me, blocking my path. Nubian slaves, looking suspiciously like Frenchmen with bootblack, follow behind her. Hopping up and down to keep my quarry in sight, I struggle through the throng, wishing I am six feet tall instead of five-foot-one.

They move toward the Moulin Rouge. He turns and looks in my direction and I feel that goose walk over my grave again.

Slipping into a group of men watching two women doing the cancan to music provided by street musicians, I pretend to watch, but keep an eye on the man and the prostitute, who have stopped to watch tumblers perform.

The dancers lift their legs high with a froth of petticoats and swirling lace as the men cheer. It quickly becomes clear to me that not only are the women showing bare legs, but they are completely naked under their petticoats.

Really! Women showing their private parts when a man is only privileged to see a little lace above the ankle. And men! It always amazes me how grown men transform into young boys experiencing the rush of puberty when they see a bit of flesh on women *other* than their wives.

The man and the prostitute enter the Bal du Moulin

Rouge and I shoot across the circle, breaking through the other side and hurrying toward the dance hall, puzzled by their destination. Why would he want to take her into the busiest cabaret in Montmartre? The establishment has only been open a few weeks, but the daring cancan show put on by Monsieur Zidler is already the talk of Paris. Hardly the place for a murderous rendezvous with a prostitute.

As I quicken my pace toward the Moulin Rouge, I let the rubber flask slip to the ground. The flask is empty and I don't want it on me if the police start rounding up street girls to find out who burned a tourist with acid.

Music, shouting, and a blast of body heat assault me as I enter the cavernous ballroom. Good Lord, it's the size of a railroad station, perhaps two hundred feet long and half that in width. In the center is a dance floor, flanked by two stories of alcoves with tables.

Off to the right an orchestra plays frantically, filling the vast hall with pounding music. Thor couldn't make more noise with his thunderous hammer than the orchestra performing a Jacques Offenbach tune played with the ferocity of a Dakota war dance. Slide trombones, brass drums, cymbals—what bedlam!

Out on the dance floor, two women and a tall, thin man are doing the cancan with rubber legs, performing splits and kicks that defy gravity and anatomy.

From a hanging banner I quickly grasp that the music hall has been taken over by art students from the Latin Quarter for a ball celebrating the autumn harvest. "Harvest" of what, I don't know, but the decadent art students of Paris don't need much of an excuse to drink and have fun. With their long scraggly hair, silly hats, pointed beards, three-foot-long tobacco pipes, the students give the city character. Debating Life, Love, and Liberty and plotting revolutions while sipping *café noir* in boulevard cafés, students are the pets of the city, tolerated as long as the revolutions they plan never progress further than a café table.

The man in black moves toward the end of the hall with the prostitute behind him. I'm still baffled . . . why would he come into this huge dance hall? Certainly he doesn't plan to murder the woman to the tune of the cancan. And the red scarf still bothers me. Am I pursuing the wrong man? Is he just a café radical planning to have pleasure with a tart? I never got a good look at the man's face when he tried to kill me in New York.

As I follow, barnyard doors to the right suddenly fly open and cheers fill the hall as a stunning parade enters. Leading the procession is Montezuma, followed by Aztec warriors, a dozen strong, dressed in the bright feathered capes and headdresses in brilliant greens and reds and yellows. The warriors are carrying a platform on which four buxom women, scantily clad, lie on their backs with their feet holding up a small round table top. Standing on the table top is a well-proportioned woman who is stark naked except for a turquoise band around her forehead.

Shouting threatens to blow off the roof. I gather that the naked woman has been elected queen of artists' models for the carnival. She should get an award just for keeping her balance.

To these students who paint nudes as part of their learning, I'm sure flesh is not equated with sin, but I find it a little disconcerting to be in the midst of hundreds of drunken students shouting about a naked woman.

A student paws me and I knock away his hands.

The killer and his chosen lamb reach the rear door and I hurry to intercept with no thought as to what I will do or say after stopping them. Running is impossible in the crowded dance hall and they vanish through a door before I reach them.

Undecided as to what my next move must be, I stare at the closed door as if it will give me an answer. What danger might I find behind it? Is he waiting for me with knife in hand?

I can forget about getting the attention of anyone in the music hall. The men are completely out of their minds in crazed delight, hailing their new queen. The puny police whistle around my neck wouldn't be heard five feet. And if I did manage to gain their attention, what am I to tell them? Exclaim in my poor French I'm an American detective reporter who, after encountering a maniac while I was a patient in a New York insane asylum, followed him to Paris?

I grab a champagne bottle from a table where men are on their feet yelling toasts to the naked queen and her ladies—I could have cut off their beards and they wouldn't have noticed.

Opening the door, I peer out to a patio with tables and an enormous replica of an elephant that appears big enough to hold a small orchestra. The patio is dark, cold, and deserted. Beyond is an alley shrouded by fog and darkness.

I can't shake my heart's conviction that I'm following the right man and that the poor woman is in mortal danger. Summoning my courage, I prop open the door with the bottle and hurry across the patio.

As I stare at the alley, trying to make out whether I see two people or figments of my overworked imagination, I hear something behind me and spin around to see a waiter holding my champagne bottle as he shuts my door to safety.

Running back, I try the handle. Locked! Banging on it does no good, it remains closed.

Staring at the fog-shrouded alley, I pull my shawl tighter to keep out the chill but in truth it's not the night air that's making my blood run cold.

THE GRAND CAVALCADE

Too much of a coincidence.

I should have known. It's too convenient that the man I am searching for suddenly appears purely by chance. I'd be a fool to think otherwise. Obviously he's found out that I've been in Paris hunting for him.

It's no accident that I find myself alone in a dark place.

The hunter has become the hunted.

It's a long way from Cochran Mills, I think as I step into the lonely night. That's my home town, Cochran Mills, Pennsylvania, population exactly 534. The little town was given my father's name after he built a mill on the river nearby, turning the sleepy town into a thriving community.

Elizabeth Cochran is my birth name, though my family calls me Pink because of my mother's preference for dressing me in that color when I was little. My father passed away when I was six, leaving our family in a bad state of finances. Unable to afford finishing high school, I lived with my mother and worked as a factory girl, making half the wage of the men working beside me.

Defending working women is how it all started. It began with a newspaper article that criticized women who earned their daily bread.

After that I was committed to a madhouse in New York . . .

*I've always
had the belief that
nothing is impossible
if one applies a certain
amount of energy
in the right direction.
If you want to do it,
you can do it.*

—NELLIE BLY

3

Nellie, 1885

On January 15, 1885, I read an article entitled "What Woman Was Made For" in the Quiet Observations column of the *Pittsburgh Dispatch*. The writer, Erasmus Wilson, had the cheek to say:

> Man was made the highest of God's creation and given dominion over all. Woman retains the same relation to man that Eve did to Adam—a helpmate, a partner, an assistant, a wife.
>
> Whenever woman is found outside her sphere, whenever she assumes the place of man and makes him her complement, then she is abnormal. A man-woman—that is a woman who ignores her mission, denies her station and usurps the place of man—is a monstrosity, an abnormal creature, a lusus naturae.

Can you believe such utter nonsense!

This was an attack upon women, not a brutish one by a masher, but done with pen and paper. Mr. Wilson had no understanding of the plight of women who either refused to give up their freedom and legally prostitute themselves in marriage—sex for board and room and a twenty-four hour workday—or for those who were turned out onto the streets to sell their bodies for their daily bread. Had this foolish reporter but opened his eyes, he would have seen that there are thousands of women working in factories and shops, doing just as good a job, if not better, as their male coworkers—*for half the pay*.

This man was repeating the conventional wisdom that a woman should stay away from the rigors of employment and devote her life to husband and home. The fact that many women had neither husband nor home and had to subsist minimally on beans and bread at a workers' boarding house from the pennies earned in a factory or retail shop, had been completely ignored by the columnist.

I, for one, was brimming with ideas and ambitions, but because of men like him I was unable to express myself. Mind you, I know what I speak of, for I was a factory girl grinding out a meager subsistence in a Pittsburgh sweatshop working ten and a half hours a day, six days a week, and living in a boarding house with my mother. What held me back was not my poverty, but this conventional wisdom about the "weaker sex."

Weaker, indeed. I worked as hard as the men around me, yet there were no opportunities for me—or any of the women I worked with, except a lifetime of the same menial labor.

One could argue that I held a lowly position because my education had been cut short by a heart condition that forced me to leave high school just prior to getting my three-year diploma.* But there were men at the fac-

---

* Nellie is not being candid about her education. The story about leaving school because of a "heart problem" was told after she became a famous reporter. School records state Nellie left before completing the *first year* of high school due to financial problems.—The Editors.

tory that had less education and received better pay and promotions.

It all boiled down to one thing: *I was a woman in a man's world.*

Emboldened by my anger—for I knew this Mr. Wilson would just think of me as a hysterical woman if I barged into his office and gave him a piece of my mind—I sat down with pen in hand, determined to educate this newspaper about the plight of factory girls. However, I was not entirely ignorant of how my employer might react if he found out one of his worker bees held the radical belief that she should be treated as fairly—or at least not more unfairly—than men.

For fear of losing the job that put food on the table, I signed the letter to the editor, "Lonely Orphan Girl."

To say the least, I was more than surprised when a few days later I read a cryptic message in the "Our Mail Pouch" column in the *Dispatch*:

> LONELY ORPHAN GIRL
> If the writer of the communication signed
> "Lonely Orphan Girl" will send her name and
> address to this office, merely as a guarantee of
> good faith, she will confer a favor and receive
> the information she desires.

Concerned over what action to take, I finally decided that the best course was to take the matter in hand and present myself at the newspaper office.

I arrived in a black ankle-length dress and black coat, an imitation Russian silk with a circular hem and false fur turban. The coat and turban I borrowed from a woman at our boarding house who had received it as a "present" from her shopkeeper employer after she worked "overtime" for him. While the outfit might have appeared flamboyant for a girl of eighteen, I hoped it added a degree of sophistication and feminine poise.*

As the doorman took me into the news room and pointed out Mr. Maddox, the editor, I couldn't help but smile for I'd expected a big man with a bushy beard who would look over the top of his specs and snap, "What do you want!?"

Instead, I found a pleasant-faced, boyish individual, wearing suspenders and an open collar, who was mild-mannered and good-natured. He wouldn't even kill the nasty roaches that crawled over his desk.

He told me I wasn't much for formal writing style, but what I had to say I said it right out regardless of paragraphs or punctuation.

"I could tell you wrote that Lonely Orphan Girl stuff with your heart, not your head, and it's just right, too." He also added that with guidance, I could learn the newspaper craft quickly.

"Miss Cochran, I am looking to bring something fresh to the new Sunday edition. Would you compose an article on 'the woman's spheres in life'?"

I was rendered speechless. I'd never dreamed I could be a reporter, it being the consensus that newspaper reporting in general was not a fit job for a woman. However, I've always had the belief that nothing is impossible if one applies a certain amount of energy in the right direction. I believe this state of mind emboldened me to obtain a job reserved for men.

---

* Nellie subtracted three years off her age to keep a "girl reporter" image. She was twenty-one at the time. Her charade has been successful. Even the *Encyclopedia Britannica* lists her birth date as 1867, rather than the actual date of 1864.—The Editors.

"The Girl Puzzle," my very first newspaper piece, was prominently placed at the top of page 11, on January 25, 1885.

To make life better, I received five dollars—*five dollars* mind you, more than a week's wages earned at the factory. I could only conclude my article was well received because Mr. Maddox not only asked me to write another piece, he suggested I choose my own subject.

"Young lady, your grammar is still rocky, but you do manage to get your facts straight, so why don't you select a subject that interests you."

I'm impassioned to write exposés of the terrible wrongs people suffer—especially women. That being said, I chose the subject of divorce.

Not only are divorces rare and difficult to obtain, most people have no idea how awful it is for a woman to be trapped in an unhappy or even brutal marriage. After witnessing what my mother had endured with my stepfather, I became in favor of divorce, especially when there is abuse—physical or mental—in the household.

At fourteen years of age I offered this testimony for my mother concerning her divorce:

> My stepfather has been generally drunk since he married my mother. When drunk, he is very cross and cross when sober. He often uses profane language towards her and calls her a whore and bitch. My mother is afraid of him. He attempted to choke her. This was sometime after they were married. The next time was in the Oddfellows Hall New Year's Night 1878.

I decided to take my own experiences, along with my father's old law books and case notes, and report on why I felt divorce was proper when the circumstances demanded it. The following week when the article appeared

I became infuriated, to say the least, when no one believed a woman had written the article. Everyone thought it was a man using a woman's name! Imbeciles.

Mr. Maddox, however, decided I should have my own byline, but because reporting was considered unladylike, I had to write under a pseudonym. When he threw out to the men in the news room the question of what my byline should be, someone started humming and the whole gang sang a popular Stephen Foster song:

Nelly Bly, Nelly Bly, bring de broom along.
We'll sweep de kitchen clean, my dear, and hab a little
song . . .

"Nelly Bly!" was shouted in the news room and Elizabeth Cochran from Cochran Falls, Pennsylvania, was laid to rest, R.I.P. But I spelled it Nellie, not Nelly. As Mr. Maddox was so fond of saying, my spelling and grammar were "rocky."

I bid farewell to my factory friends, but I would never forget them. I was determined to help them gain better working conditions and wages. To that end, I did a hard-hitting story on sweatshop conditions in the city.

The day my story appeared, I was indoctrinated into how the system really works, and I didn't like the taste of it.

A delegation of businessmen paid a visit to Mr. Maddox and advised him that working conditions were too rude a subject for a woman. Just like that I was assigned to the society page to report: "On June 1st *the* Mr. and Mrs. Snot-Grass gave their daughter, Amanda, to Brian, the son of *the* Mr. and Mrs. Blue-Nose. The bride wore . . ."

Poppycock!

Anarchists were planting bombs, factory workers

were battling for rights, courageous women were demanding the right to vote, empires were clashing around the world, but all the newspaper women in America—and there were only a few in such a lofty position—were pigeonholed into reporting news about weddings and gossip.

Unbelievable, yet depressingly true.

To become a detective reporter, and investigate crime and corruption, or a foreign correspondent sending dispatches from wars and revolutions at the far ends of the world, one must be a man.

Rubbish. I was not going to spend my life writing about liver pâté, especially after my article was so well received. I had to do something to change management's rules.

The question was "what?"

I considered traveling to the West and wiring stories of desperadoes and boom towns. Stagecoaches rumbled where the tracks didn't reach and encountered fearsome Apaches where the cavalry didn't dare go. But the Wild West had been covered by male reporters. To be noticed, I had to do something different. Mexico fit the bill—it was wild and dangerous and virgin territory.

With my mother in tow and my meager savings in hand, I bought train tickets for the land of the Aztecs.

What a marvelous country it turned out to be—ancient and beautiful and exotic, but also a place of political unrest and tyranny. Not long after I started sending dispatches focusing not only on the color and charm of the sunny land but on the poverty and injustices I saw, I was informed that the Mexican government no longer desired my presence in the country.*

---

* Nellie's Mexican adventures were later published in a book as *Six Months in Mexico*. Always for the underdog, Nellie, while visiting a

When I returned home I discovered that my feat didn't convince the paper's management that being a foreign correspondent was a fit job for a woman. To the contrary, they considered it pure luck I had not been raped and murdered by bandits and ordered me back to covering card parties attended by horse-faced society women.

Unacceptable! Pittsburgh was too confining for a woman overflowing with ideas. On March 23, 1887, I left a note on the desk of Erasmus Wilson, the Quiet Observations columnist and my dear friend:

> *Dear Q.O.—I am off to New York. Look out for me.*
>   *Bly*

I left for New York with my poor mother once more in tow, but a bit wide-eyed at my exciting dream of being a real news reporter so I could change the world for the better.

---

graveyard in Mexico, saw a tombstone with no name and no epitaph except the initials T.M. Feeling the "loneliness" the grave's occupant must have felt at having been forgotten, she surreptitiously carved "R.I.P." on the headstone. It turned out to be the grave of General Tomás Mejía, who bravely faced a firing squad alongside Emperor Maximillian.—The Editors.

*Accuracy is
to a newspaper
what virtue is
to a woman.*

—JOSEPH PULITZER

4

Upon arriving in Manhattan I went straight to the *New York World*, my newspaper of choice for a job. Its domed citadel was on Park Row where the city's papers gathered to make it easier to spy on one another.

The guard protecting the *World*'s newsroom off the main lobby refused to let me in after I told him I'd come to see Mr. Pulitzer about a reporting job. "You should be home cooking and cleaning for your husband," he told me.

I left fuming. Pushing my way in would have been futile because the guard also told me Mr. Pulitzer was out of the country.

I soon found out it made not a bit of difference to the newspaper gods of Gotham that I had worked for the *Dispatch*, had quite a few good stories to my credit, and had been a foreign correspondent in Mexico. All the determination of a mule did me no good.

After nearly four months of no job, I was almost penniless and losing weight.

I'm ashamed to admit, but this city really put to test my stamina. I was on the verge of giving up after my purse was stolen in Central Park and I found myself stranded and about to face eviction and starvation when a picture of Mr. Pulitzer entering the *World* appeared on the front page of the paper. He was back. It's a day I will never forget— September 22, 1885.

This time nothing was going to stop me from seeing him. He was going to hire me and that was that. Besides, my parents constantly told me, "It's not how many times you get knocked down, its how many times you get back up."

I borrowed streetcar fare from the landlady who was running the brownstone boarding house on Lexington Avenue where we were staying and mustered up the last of my courage for another assault on the *World*.

BEFORE I APPROACHED Mr. Pulitzer for a job I decided to take my mother's advice—society would not be ready for a woman warrior like me; I would have to work twice as hard as a man and knowledge would be my strongest power. So, I stopped at a library to learn all I could about Mr. Pulitzer.

Other newspapers claimed that the *World* was lurid and offensive in its reporting, but they just didn't have the intestinal fortitude to expose political corruption and do hard-hitting stories the way Mr. Pulitzer did. He was a reformer and had a flair for news that no other newspapermen had.

He believed the paper was a watchdog against privilege, a friend of the people. As long as society was kept ignorant of what was really happening, change would never happen. And he had a strong belief in crusades against wrongs. When he began to receive threats on his life, it didn't stop him; he just started carrying a pistol. To him, the threats only proved he was hitting home.

When I discovered how he had obtained his first job as a newspaperman, I knew I was destined to work for this man.

Mr. Pulitzer, at the age of seventeen, was rejected from the Austrian, French, and British armies because of his poor eyesight and fragile physique. At six feet two and one and a half inches tall he looked like an emaciated scarecrow. But these obstacles didn't stop him. He went to Hamburg and signed up with bounties looking for people to enlist in the U.S. Army during the Civil War.

Once the war was over he headed to St. Louis to obtain a job, only to run into another obstacle. In order to get to St. Louis he had to cross the broad Mississippi River. Even though he was penniless and hungry, he approached the operator of the Wiggins Ferry, who also spoke German, and worked out a deal where he paid his fare by firing the boiler.

After working jobs as a mule hostler, deckhand on a packet to Memphis, construction laborer, and a waiter, Mr. Pulitzer, along with several dozen other men, paid five dollars each to a fast-talking promoter who promised them well-paying jobs on a Louisiana sugar plantation. To get there, they had to board a small steamboat. Some thirty miles south of the city they were let off through a ruse. When the boat churned away without them, they knew they had been swindled and had no other choice but to walk back to St. Louis.

Infuriated by the fact that this person could so easily rob a group of honest, hard-working men and get away with it, Mr. Pulitzer wrote an account of the fraud and submitted it to the *Westliche Post*. Not only did they print it, they gave him his first job on a newspaper.

Mr. Pulitzer stood up for men; I stood up for women.

Soon he was running newspapers. When he gained control of the *St. Louis Dispatch* and the *Post* and merged them as the *Post-Dispatch* they soon dominated the city's evening newspaper. After purchasing the *New York World*, a morning paper that was failing, within three months the circulation doubled.

He wasn't afraid to be innovative—like covering sports and women's fashion with illustrations. He believed a paper shouldn't just be informative, but entertaining. Not everyone agreed. A reporter for the *New York Times* said, "How can anyone take the *World* seriously when it prints such silly things like comics?"

Obviously, the public did.

I also found it interesting he considered ten his lucky number. He made it a point to purchase the *World* on May 10, 1883. Maybe I could use this to my advantage. I didn't know how, but it was good information to have.

The *World* was the leading journalistic voice in America and I was going to be a part of it, come hell or high water.

KNOWING MOST MEN would hesitate to physically remove a lady, I decided my plan of attack was to be polite, but firmly inform the guard I wouldn't leave until I met with Mr. Pulitzer.

After three hours of ignoring the copy boys who tried to shoo me home as I badgered everyone who entered the building with desperate pleas to get me in to see Mr. Pulitzer, I was surprised no one called the police and had me arrested as an anarchist or Free Love advocate.

An older reporter who watched me from his desk with an amused grin on his face raised my ire. I was a hair's breath away from giving him a tongue lashing when he suddenly helped me slip inside before the gatekeeper could stop me.

I swept across the editorial room with the grace of a

lady of quality, careful to lift my skirt off the floor to keep the bottom from being fouled by the tobacco juice that didn't reach spittoons. Newspapermen pride themselves on being a special kind of intellect who hang around smoky bars for five-cent beer and the free lunch, and believe they are entitled to foul editorial offices with chewing tobacco juice and cigar fumes.

I felt the animosity of the men as a woman invaded their territory, and that put my chin up an extra inch.

I quickly knocked, then threw open Mr. Pulitzer's office door without waiting for an answer. Facing me was Mr. Pulitzer and John Cockerill, his managing editor. Both frowned for a moment before Mr. Pulitzer removed a pipe from his mouth and said, "Since you insist, do come in, young lady, and close the door."

I put my clippings from the *Dispatch* on his desk and collapsed in a chair. I blurted out I'd been robbed of my last penny and needed a job. I don't know if they were impressed or just speechless because a young woman had the nerve to barge in and demand a job. Either way, they seemed much amused by my wanting to be a newspaper-*man*.

Mr. Cockerill handed me twenty-five dollars but declined to give me a response as to whether I was being hired. I realized the money was charity because I was broke and it was their way of brushing off an annoying child.

I wanted a job, not a handout.

"I have a great story," I stated boldly. "The type of newsworthy reporting the *World* is famous for."

"What is this newsworthy story?" Mr. Pulitzer asked with a hint of humor in his voice that irritated me.

"An exposé on the scandalous conditions at the madhouse for women on Blackwell's Island."

"Young woman, every newspaper in town has already

done a story on that notorious insane asylum." He scoffed. "It has a worse reputation than Bedlam."

He was about to have me evicted from his office. I had to do something quick or I was finished, not only in New York but in the newspaper business. To accept a position on a lesser paper was not in my blood.

"No one has done the story the way I will do it."

My mind was flying. I hadn't really thought out how I would do the story, but I had to say something that would impress him. I researched stories about conditions at the asylum and felt they ranged from too maudlin, to little more than what a *man thought* conditions for the unfortunate women must be like. I wanted to write a more personal and realistic story. And I knew how he was drawn to sensationalism.

Desperate for a job, I realized there was only one way to really impress him.

"I'll get myself committed to Blackwell's Island as a mad woman." And then, thank God, I remembered his quirk about ten being his lucky number, "And I will stay there exactly ten days!"

Mr. Pulitzer took the pipe out of his mouth and stared at me.

5

It's not easy to act crazy.

I've never been around a person insane enough to be institutionalized, unless you include my stepfather whom I suspect was bitten by one of Dr. Pasteur's rabid dogs. But, I knew from my research that one could not get committed to the asylum without an examination by doctors and an order from a judge.

In the streetcar on my way home, I drew my plans.

I would check into a boarding house for working women. If I could convince a houseful of women I was crazy, they'd stop at nothing to get me out of their reach and into the hands of the authorities.

Once home, I explained to my dear mother what I was about to do. She said I wouldn't have any trouble convincing them I was mad, because I was crazy to even try such a scheme.

In need for a boarding house to enter, I selected from a directory the Temporary Home for Females, No. 84, Second Avenue. As I made my way to the address, I practiced "dreamy" and "faraway" expressions.

Mrs. Stanard, the assistant matron who greeted me at the door, reminded me of an aunt I had—disgusted with life and not wanting anyone else to be happy. She curtly told me the only room available was one shared with another woman and the rate was thirty cents a day. This worked to my benefit. I only had seventy cents. The sooner I was broke, the sooner I would be put out.

That night, I had a less than enticing supper—boiled beef and potatoes, definitely lacking in salt or any spices, accompanied with coffee so thick it smelled like tar and bread with no butter.

The dining room floor was bare; two long rough wooden tables lacked varnish, polish, and table covers, it's unnecessary to talk about the cheapness of the linen. Long wooden benches were on each side of the tables, with no cushions. Mrs. Stanard obviously wanted no dallying, which was understandable—you'd realize how horrible the food tasted.

This place was a mockery of a home for deserving women who earned their own bread. And to add insult to injury, she charged thirty cents for what she called a dinner. One good thing about her ridiculous price, I was now almost broke.

After dinner everyone adjourned to the parlor. Just entering this room made me depressed. The only light fell from a solitary gas jet in the middle of the ceiling that enveloped everyone in a dusky hue. It was no wonder everyone's spirits were down. The chairs were worn and dull in color, no flower prints or spring colors—just dark blue and grey. Above the mantelpiece was a picture of a sea captain. He sat straight as a board in a black leather chair with one hand holding a pipe. His dense black eyebrows shadowed his steel, grey eyes. He had the scowl of a sea captain not pleased with his crew. There were no logs in the fireplace, just ashes from long ago.

I sat in a corner in a very stiff wicker chair that was made with no thought of comfort and watched the women. They made lace and knitted incessantly. No effort came from anyone to share in conversation. No laughter. No smiles. Everyone just sat in their chairs, heads hanging down, as their fingers incessantly knitted. The only sound was the tapping of the needles.

I hated this establishment.

With little cost, the management could easily supply this room with a game of checkers or a deck of cards— simple things that would bring enjoyment to these women who spent their days working like slaves. Even a cheap vase of daisies on the mantel and a log burning would bring some cheer. And remove that sea captain and replace it with a picture of a beautiful meadow—something colorful and bright. And have a cat or two who'd earn their room and board catching mice, which I'm sure lurked about.

I couldn't have picked a more ideal place to become crazy. One thing for certain, once I was done with my story on Blackwell's Island, my next article was going to expose the fraud of these "Homes for Females." But right now I needed to concentrate on being a mad woman.

I began by telling Mrs. Stanard that all of the women in the room "looked loony and I was afraid of them."

Throughout the night I kept up the pretense that I believed everyone in the house was "nuts" and I was going to be murdered by them. Feigning amnesia, I frightened the whole household and tortured my roommate, Mrs. Ruth Caine, with my paranoid delusions. The dear soul tried to calm me as I paced back and forth.

NELLIE IN THE HANDS
OF POLICE WITH
MRS. CAINE

The next morning Mrs. Caine, who barely slept, told me one of the ladies had a nightmare of me rushing at her with a knife. And Mrs. Stanard left the house immediately upon rising to obtain policemen to have me removed.

When she returned with the two large policemen, she asked them to take me "quietly" in order to keep from making a scandal before the neighbors. "If she doesn't come along quietly," responded an officer, "I'll drag her through the streets."

After being processed at the station house, I appeared in court before Judge Duffy. I gave the pretense that I was Cuban. Having learned a good bit of Spanish in Mexico, I threw around enough "Sí, Señors" to sound convincing.

Being told about my strange behavior and amnesia, Judge Duffy said, "Poor child, she is well dressed and a lady. Her English is perfect and I would stake everything on her being a good girl. I'm positive she is somebody's darling."

Everyone laughed and I had to put a handkerchief over my face to choke my own laughter.

"I'm sure she's some *woman's* darling," hastily amended the judge. He suspected that I'd been drugged.

Dear Mrs. Caine pleaded not to have me sent to "the Island" (exactly where I wanted to go) because I would be killed there. The judge decided to send me to Bellevue for the "drugs" to wear off.

A crowd of curious onlookers gathered to see the "crazy girl" in the police ambulance. The doctor dropped the wagon's curtains as a group of children, mudlarks, raced after us trying to get a look at me as they shouted all sorts of vulgar taunts.

At Bellevue the order was given to take me to the insanity ward. A muscular man grabbed me so tight I lost my composure and shook him off with more strength than I realized I had. Seeing my distress, the ambulance doctor interceded and escorted me to the mad ward. Once there I was examined by another doctor who, after a short discourse with me, announced to the nurse, "She's positively demented, a hopeless case."

BEFORE JUDGE DUFFY

My "amnesia" case created something of a sensation at Bellevue and soon the worst possible thing occurred: newspaper reporters were permitted in to question me and my picture appeared in the papers!

Desperate to get to Blackwell's Island before the reporters saw through my act, I eagerly convinced two more doctors I was "hopeless." They removed me from the ward and took me to a city wharf where about a dozen women waited to be put onto a boat.

An attendant with rough manners and whiskey breath half-dragged us onto the boat. It seemed as if we were forever on this bumpy boat ride before we were taken ashore at a landing in New York's East River.

"What is this place?" I asked an attendant who had his fingers dug deep into the flesh of my arm.

"Blackwell's Island," he grinned, "a place you'll never get off."

THE INSANE ASYLUM

6

Blackwell's Island

The name alone sounded depressing.

The small island was grey and gloomy on the chilly day I set foot on it. About a mile and a half long and only an eighth of a mile wide, it sat like a stepping stone in the East River between the boroughs of Manhattan and Queens. Unless you were a competitive swimmer, it was too far to swim back to land.

If I wasn't already quite mad when I arrived, keeping my sanity in the face of conditions that have been frowned upon even at London's notorious Bedlam quickly became a challenge.

The reception area was a long, narrow, austere room with bare concrete walls and barred windows. Nurses sat at a large table covered with a white bedspread in the center of the room. "Checking in" began immediately.

"Come here," a scowling, red-faced woman at the table snapped at me.

AN INSANITY EXPERT
AT WORK

I approached and was immediately assaulted with one rude question after another. The woman didn't bother to look up as she penciled my answers on a sheet.

"What have you on?"

"My clothing."

Another nurse lifted my dress and slips as if I were a child. "One pair of shoes, one pair of stockings, one cloth dress, one straw sailor hat," and so on. When the examination was over, someone yelled, "Into the hall, into the hall."

A kindly grey-haired patient told me that this was an invitation to supper.

"Get in line, two-by-two," "Stand still," "How many times must I tell you to stay in line?" As the orders were snapped, a shove and a push were administered, often accompanied with a slap on the ear.

We lined up in a hallway where open windows invited a cold draft. The shivering, thinly clad women looked lost and forlorn. Some chattered nonsense to invisible people; others laughed or cried.

The grey-haired woman who had been kind nudged me. With sage nods and pitiful uplifting of her eyes, she assured me that I shouldn't mind the poor creatures because they were all mad. "I've been here before, you know," she said. She volunteered earlier that this was her second commitment to the island. Her daughter had managed to get her released but her son-in-law had her recommitted.

When the dining room doors opened a mad rush was made for the tables. Food was already set out for each person—a bowl filled with a pinkish liquid which the patients called tea, a piece of thick-cut, buttered bread, and a saucer with five prunes.

A large, heavy-set woman pushed by me and sat down. She immediately grabbed saucers from other place settings and emptied the contents in one long gulp while holding down her own bowl. Then proceeded to empty two more. As I watched, the woman opposite me grabbed my bread.

The older woman with me offered me hers, but I declined and asked an attendant for another. The attendant glared at me as she flung a piece of bread on the table. "I see you've lost your memory, but not how to eat."

The bread was hard and dry, the butter rancid. One taste of the "tea" was enough—a bitter, mineral favor, as if it had been made in copper.

"You must force down the food," my new friend said. "If you don't eat you'll be sick and who knows, with these surroundings, you may go crazy."

"It's impossible to eat this swill." Despite her urging, I ate nothing.

After dinner we were marched into a cold, wet concrete bathroom and ordered to undress. A patient chattering and chuckling to herself stood by the bathtub with a large, discolored rag in hand.

I refused to undress. "It's too cold."

Nurse Grupe, whose name tag said she was the head nurse, ordered me to undress.

"No. Heat this place first."

She glared at me and I almost obeyed. What a poisonous disposition.

"Undress her."

Nurses grabbed me, pulled off my clothes, and forced me into the tub. As I shivered in the cold water, the babbling woman scrubbed me with harsh soap that rubbed my skin raw. "Rub, rub, rub," she chanted.

My teeth chattered and my lips turned blue as buckets of cold water went over my head. I yelped and Nurse Grupe slapped the back of the head.

"Shut up or I'll give you something to yell about."

While I was still dripping wet, they put me into a short canton flannel slip labeled across the back in large black letters, *Lunatic Asylum, B. I. H. 6.* The letters stood for Blackwell's Island, Hall 6.

As I was led away I looked back and saw Miss Maynard, a poor, sick girl I'd met on the boat to the island. She pleaded not to be placed in the cold bath. It was useless, of course. Resistance simply inflamed Nurse Grupe's poisonous personality.

I was taken to room 28 where a hard cot and coarse wool blanket awaited.

My wet clothes and body dampened the pillow and sheet. I tried to find some warmth with the blanket, but when I lifted it up to my chin it left my bare feet exposed.

As I lay shivering, I heard a rustle to my left. A girl sat on a bed in the dark corner. She came over and tucked another blanket around me. I was too weak and cold to even properly thank her and just muttered my gratitude.

In the morning I discovered that each patient was rationed only one blanket. The girl spent a cold night so I could have her blanket.

Her name was Josephine.

She was a prostitute, but reminded me of a little mudlark. Seventeen years old, she'd left a hungry, abusive home at eleven and did the only work she could find—selling her body on the streets. Despite the unspeakable life she'd suffered, she still reached out to the underdog.

This tarnished angel and I soon became as close as sisters.

I couldn't help but notice that nothing about her indicated she belonged in a mad house. "Why are you here?" I finally asked.

"I was brought to the island suffering from a brain fever. I suppose I showed signs of insanity, but that left with the fever. Now I'm a prisoner. Few without family or friends ever leave this place."

I hated the thought that she believed she'd never get out, so I confided in her. "Very soon you're going to be leaving the asylum with me. I can provide a home and help you get work. You won't have to go back to the streets again. Life will be much kinder to you, I promise."

The poor dear thought I was mad! I wanted to tell her I was a reporter doing a story, but couldn't chance my identity being revealed.

Gossiping with inmates, I found out that the asylum's darkest secret wasn't the cruelty toward helpless women, a horrible crime in itself, but the mysterious disappearance of inmates. Four women had disappeared from the island in the previous five months and the staff never spoke of it.

"They don't care," Josephine told me. "Women throw themselves into the river or drown trying to escape."

My interest was piqued by the fact all four women were prostitutes—an unusual coincidence being that street girls only made up a small portion of the inmates. I quietly probed to get more information and soon found out no one wanted to talk about it—the patients were frightened and the nurses wanted to avoid scandal.

I was sitting on my cot making a mental list of the appalling things about the institution that I planned to write about when Josephine returned excited from a medical appointment.

She sat down beside me and whispered, "I've found a way to get us off the island."

Her appointment had been with a staff doctor named Blum. He told her if she helped him with an experiment, he'd see that she gained her freedom. "I said I'd do it only if you were released, too."

"What kind of experiment?" My first instinct was that the doctor wanted sexual gratifiction.

"I don't know. It has to do with a scientific study. He has a lab with equipment in that shack on the old pier."

I realized I'd seen him on the hospital grounds. He wore baggy clothes and a box hat and had a heavy beard, long hair, and thick glasses. I overheard the nurses refer to him as "the German doctor" because of his thick Eastern European accent. He had a reputation for being a loner and secretive, which wasn't surprising. Many ordinary doctors tinkered with scientific experiments, hoping to achieve the fame a few had managed by making important discoveries.

"I heard nurses talking about him," I said. "He's an odd fellow who doesn't say a word unless absolutely necessary. And he won't let anyone near that shack of his. Nurse Grupe went out to deliver a package and he ran her off."

"He seems a gentleman to me," Josephine said. "I'm sure it will all work out." She nervously worked the ring on her index finger. A cheap copper band with a small heart, the ring had been given to her by a man she loved—and who abandoned her after he tired of exploiting her body.

Seeing her so excited about getting off the island, I didn't want to dampen her enthusiasm. She was usually dispirited and melancholy.

"I'm sure it will. What exactly does he want you to do?"

"Tonight at midnight I'm to tell the attendant that I have stomach pain and need to go to the infirmary, that I've been under Dr. Blum's care. I'm to go to his quarters instead." She squeezed my arm. "Nellie, I promised I wouldn't tell a soul. You won't tell anyone, will you? Promise?"

It occurred to me that there might be another story in

this for my article. If the man did plan to extort sexual favors from her, I'd see that he neither succeeded nor used his position to take advantage of any more poor women at the institute.

"I promise. But don't be surprised if you look behind you tonight and see me."

THAT NIGHT I was dozing when Josephine got up to go to the doctor's quarters. "Good luck," I whispered as she went out the door.

I waited a few minutes to give her a head start before quickly dressing and hurrying to the attendant's station to use the same stomach pain excuse Josephine used. We were locked in at night as if we were prisoners.

When I came out into the reception area, the night attendant wasn't there. *No!* I should have left at the same time as Josephine. I hadn't because I was sure the attendant wouldn't let us leave together. I heard snoring and spotted the crazy old rub-rub-rub woman sleeping, sitting up on a bench. She was covered with a blanket. Poor thing. She probably came out of the wardroom to escape whatever devils came for her in the dark.

I sat down, crossed my arms and tapped my foot and tried to will the attendant to return and let me out. I should have anticipated this—the attendants left their boring night duties to smoke, play cards, and heaven only knows what else.

As the minutes ticked away, my patience evaporated. Staring at the door as I paced back and forth, I was ready to attack the iron door with my feet and fists.

The old woman came awake and stared at me.

"I need to get out of here," I told her, as if she had the key. I patted my stomach. "Stomachache. Have to see Doctor Blum."

She shook her head, rocking back and forth. "Rub-rub-rub, Doctor Blum, rub-rub-rub."

I ignored her and went back to pacing.

"Doctor Blum puts in the water. Rub-rub-rub."

I froze and stared at her. "What are you saying?"

She stopped rocking and stared at me, suddenly fearful. I took a deep breath and smiled. I didn't want to frighten her away. "Tell me," I said, quietly, "who does Dr. Blum put in water?"

She rocked and chanted. "Rub-rub-rub, rub-rub-rub, in the water, he puts them in the water."

I'd seen her stop the nonsense when Nurse Grupe snapped at her and I did it now. "Stop it! Look at me."

She stared at me with wide eyes.

"Now tell me . . . who does he put in water?"

She looked around and then leaned forward and spoke in a stage whisper. "The women. He puts them in the water at night. Rub-rub-rub."

"Stop that. Tell me—"

She flew off the bench and ran back down the hall to the wardroom.

I stood perfectly still, my whole body turning cold, fear crawling on my flesh. Water. Women. Dr. Blum. Had the old woman seen the enigmatic Dr. Blum putting the bodies of women in water?

The door opened and the attendant stepped in. I flew by her, clutching at my stomach. "Pain. Doctor Blum knows."

I hurried in the direction of the infirmary. When I heard the door slam behind me, I veered and ran for the old pier in a panic. My rational mind told me my paranoia was nonsense, that I was panicking for nothing, but I couldn't shake the feeling of dread. When the old woman had chanted about Blum and water it raised the hair on the back of my neck—not a good sign.

I admit that I'm not the most book-learned person in

the world. But if anything, I had good instincts. My brain sometimes failed me but my intuition never did. And my guts were tied in knots thinking about Josephine alone with Dr. Blum.

A rack at the pier entrance held wooden pins that sailors used to tie down lines—when they weren't using them to crack heads during drunken brawls. I grabbed one.

I'd never been on the pier but had walked by it many times. Dry-rotted, the jetty and building on it looked ready to be washed away in a good storm. I was told that Blum used half of the building as his personal quarters while the other half stored kerosene for the asylum. The only light I saw at the shack was a dim lamplight that shone through a cloth curtain at a window to the right of the front door.

I broke my frantic momentum down to a slow walk as I came to the shack. *Now what?* Should I knock on the door and ask sweetly to see Josephine while I held a wooden club in my hand?

What if the doctor really was doing an innocuous experiment . . . and I spoiled Josephine's chance to get off the island? I couldn't guarantee that I'd be able to get her off the island even if Mr. Pulitzer liked my story . . . but a doctor could.

I stopped and stared at the old wood building. I needed to look through a window. Both windows facing the jetty were curtained. A narrow ledge no more than a foot wide ran along the river side. Walking by in the daytime, I'd seen a window and a door in the back. I didn't know if the window had closed curtains. The only way to find out was to get a closer look.

Facing the building, I held my arms out wide for balance and worked along the narrow ledge. The window was dark and curtained. On impulse I decided to try the door. It wasn't a standard house door, but one that slid open sideways to receive cargo from a boat.

Edging closer, I found the door fastened with a heavy padlock. I tested the lock by jerking on it. The nails holding the hasp to the old, dry-rotted wall were loose. I pulled on the padlock, nearly sending myself backward into the river. Getting my balance again, I pulled and jerked the lock, hoping my efforts weren't being heard inside. When the long nails holding the hasp were out far enough, I pried the hasp off with the boat pin.

My heart pumped like a steam engine. I leaned my head against the building, slowing my breathing to get it under control. Putting my shoulder against the door, it slid over reluctantly, making a scraping noise more irritating than fingernails on a blackboard.

I slipped through the door and into a dark room, wondering where I was. Not daring to move without some light for fear I'd knock something over, I pulled the curtain on the window open enough to let in faint moonlight. It was a bedroom, a small one with just a cot not unlike the ones used for patients, but with a thicker mattress and many blankets.

I went across the room to a door. The door squeaked as I opened it and I cringed, ready to explain that I had entered by mistake. I was surprised I hadn't been discovered and chastised already. I put my head through the open doorway and saw a kitchen. As with the bedroom, it was small. No light was in the room but another door was opened. A source of light came from there. I assumed it to be a living room and the light I saw from the outside. My estimation was that his personal quarters ended there because the kerosene storeroom was next.

I listened and heard nothing but the foghorn on a distant watercraft. No talking between Dr. Blum and Josephine, no sighs or grunts of passion—thank goodness!

Nothing. There was hardly enough light in the living room for two people to sit and comfortably converse socially.

Had Josephine misspoke when she told me she was going to his quarters? Could she have meant his office? Not a hundred percent certain I was alone, I slipped quietly across the kitchen to the open living room doorway.

The lamp on the table next to the window put out enough light to see that the doctor used the living room as his laboratory. And that the lab was much more complex than I had expected. A long table in the center of the room was crowded with scientific apparatus—a microscope, a Bunsen burner, stacks of petri dishes, and a forest of glass tubes and bottles. Two other small tables against the wall held more bottles and canisters.

Dr. Blum obviously took his scientific studies seriously. This was more the workshop of a full-time chemist than a doctor hoping to make a discovery with a microscope and some petri dishes.

The only sitting area, other than a work stool at the large table, was a couch across the room with a mound of blankets on it. It appeared blankets were heaped atop something—the "something" being the right size for a small built woman like Josephine bent in a fetal position.

I carefully went to it and pulled the blankets off.

Two pillows. Probably used by the doctor when he sacked out on the couch.

I smelled something, an odor that I didn't instantly recognize. Not a chemical odor, but something different, something more organic. Two dark mounds about the size of a man's fist were on a glass sheet on the table. Getting closer to sniff them, I recognized the scent. Blood. The stench of raw meat—animal innards. What in God's name could Dr. Blum be experimenting with?

A small, narrow, whitish object lay next to the dark mounds. I leaned down to get a look at it and caught my breath.

A human finger with a ring on it . . . Josephine's ring. I screamed.

The door flew open and a dark figure emerged. Dr. Blum wore a bloodied white smock. He held a large knife in one hand and something else in the other, but my brain was too frozen with shock to comprehend what it was.

He started for me and I screamed and threw the wood pin. It flew by him and hit the lamp. The glass bowl exploded in a burst of fire.

With mindless panic, I grabbed his laboratory table with both hands and sent it crashing over, the forest of bottles and glass apparatus flying at him and breaking at his feet.

Flames exploded behind me as I blindly ran back through the same rooms I had entered. I stumbled out the cargo doors into the cold river.

7

Raging flames engulfed the shack and pier when the fire hit the stored oil barrels, rousing the entire island. Patients and staff poured out of the buildings, but there was nothing they could do to stop the huge blaze—the shack and pier were dry rotted and ignited like kindling wood.

I crawled out of the river and collapsed on the ground.

Dear Miss Maynard spotted me and came running. She took off her shawl and wrapped it around me. I told her that Josephine had been murdered by Doctor Blum and that he tried to kill me, but my words were a frantic jumble.

"Hush, they'll think you burned the place."

From out of nowhere Nurse Grupe appeared, grabbed my hair, and pushed Miss Maynard away.

I babbled that Doctor Blum killed Josephine and tried to kill me. She acted as if she hadn't heard a word I said and kept a tight grasp on my hair. As other nurses looked away, she shoved me into a padded room where they put out-of-control women and locked the door.

I screamed and pounded the door until I finally gave

in to exhaustion. I was freezing and my lungs were raw from yelling. There were no blankets, nothing to get me dry and warm. My hair felt like it had been ripped off of my scalp. I curled up in a ball and started to cry.

I killed Josephine.

I sensed something was wrong with the man and chose to ignore my instincts in order to get a story. No matter how I tried to justify my actions, I knew it was my fault. She died because of me.

Josephine and the doctor were both missing and presumed drowned or incinerated in the fire. But an annoying voice tucked away in the recess of my brain wouldn't allow me to believe the doctor was dead. He either swam or rowed to the Manhattan shore. As hard as I tried to shake the feeling away, I couldn't, so I went to the alienist in charge of the ward and made accusations about Dr. Blum. He stared at me for a moment and then wrote something in his log book.

"What did you write?" I asked.

"That you are hopelessly insane and delusional."

AFTER I WAS released from the insane asylum by the *World*, I told Mr. Pulitzer about the mad killer. I was disappointed when he expressed no interest, but I couldn't blame him—the fire had destroyed the evidence. But he was ecstatic about my mad house story. The report blew the lid off the terrible conditions at Blackwell's Island and Mr. Pulitzer called it the most important story of the year. And I was able to get Miss Maynard released, with a job and a place to live.

Best of all, because of the strength of my story, New York City's committee of appropriation provided $1 million, more than ever before given for the benefit of the insane.*

In regards to Dr. Blum, even though my nagging feeling continued that he had survived the inferno, I had to let it go—but the guilt, grief, and anger stayed with me.

BECAUSE OF MY huge success with Blackwell's Island, Mr. Pulitzer assigned me to other undercover stories: I became employed by a doctor as a maid and did an exposé on the cruelty to servants; I posed as a sinner in need of reform, and committed myself into a home for unfortunate women to report on how the stay did nothing but empty the pockets of helpless women.

Mr. Pulitzer even had me go undercover as a prostitute. Nobody really knew the truth about their lives— why they became prostitutes or how many were really single women working the streets at night. It was dangerous, but in a way I did it for Josephine.

My first night out I befriended a woman and asked her, "Why would you risk your reputation and *life* in such a way?" Her response saddened me deeply and I made sure to share it with the public by printing her exact words:

Risk my reputation! [She gave me a short laugh.] I don't think I ever had one to risk. I work hard all day, week after week, for a mere pittance. I go home at night tired of labor and longing for something new, anything good or bad to break the monotony of my existence. I have no pleasure, no books to read. I cannot go to places of amusement for want of clothes and money, and no one cares what becomes of me.

---

* *Ten Days in a Mad-House* was also published as a book under Nellie's name.—The Editors.

I cared.

For my next assignment I went undercover at the factory where I worked during the day and wrote an article exposing the unfair treatment and working conditions to women—how they were doing the same job as men, putting in the same hours, and many times doing it better, while only men got raises and promotions.

To my delight it created quite a stir and Mr. Pulitzer liked it. As long as circulations climbed, he didn't care whose feathers were ruffled. I just prayed it would initiate change.

In time I began acquiring success and fame as my stories kept making the front pages of the *New York World*. The staff jokingly called it the *New York Nellie*.

EVEN THOUGH JOSEPHINE's body was missing, Miss Maynard and I didn't want her to be forgotten like so many tarnished women are, so we had a tombstone made with an inscription that I bastardized from Shakespeare: *"Life is but a walking shadow . . . one day it disappears, but your beautiful smile and kind and generous heart will never be forgotten."*

On the anniversary of her first year gone, we planted the tombstone under a weeping willow—it just seemed fitting.

Then the London slashings began.

8

In the fall of 1888, a series of ghastly crimes, five in all, put London in a panic. The Whitechapel murderer who called himself "Jack" killed women of the streets, mutilating them horribly and extracting body parts with such precision that the police suspected he might be a doctor with an expertise in surgery.

My blood rose. Dr. Blum was no longer a fleeing ghost. He was alive.

I was convinced this "Jack" and my Dr. Blum were one and the same and was compelled to London to investigate. Mr. Pulitzer did not share my enthusiasm. But when I suggested I walk the streets of London's notorious— and dangerous—Whitechapel district dressed as a prostitute to lure the Ripper, he agreed. No doubt he believed that if I was murdered, I would be canonized as a saint of newspaper*men*—and he would sell many papers.

My mother, on the other hand, had a completely different reaction. The poor dear became so upset when I told her what I was going to do, a doctor had to come and administer a sedative.

She was right. The whole idea was ludicrous, especially the notion that I could fend off the Ripper's knife in London or anywhere else. What she couldn't comprehend was something else of singular importance overpowered my fears—the guilt I felt for Josephine's death. He had to be captured so he could never mutilate another woman.

WITH A POLICE whistle in hand and my mother's long hat pin she insisted I wear at all times to use as a weapon, I left for London. Never would I admit to anyone how scared I was—especially to myself.

Upon arriving I met with Inspector Abberline, of Scotland Yard, the officer in charge of the Ripper investigation. At first he told me he wouldn't allow a woman to make herself bait to a mad-killer. It was, as he put it, "Plain out loony!" But once I told him my story and that I didn't cross the ocean to be stopped, he reluctantly agreed.

He took me to the Whitechapel district, helped me find a place to stay and introduced me to the policemen on the beat so they wouldn't arrest me for prostitution. Just before parting we set up times to meet and he gave a police whistle, noting mine was a toy. If any man aroused my suspicion, I was to blow hard.

I thanked him and told him not to fear, I would blow like Joshua.

After I had a couple of stressful nights walking the streets, Inspector Abberline told me about a doctor that had come to their attention. He was of foreign descent, possibly German, Russian, or other Eastern European lineage, and had a laboratory in a cheap tenement right in the heart of the Whitechapel district. My enthusiasm roused the inspector into action and he allowed me to accompany him to the premises to see if I could identify the man as Dr. Blum.

Emotions ran high for everyone as we raced to the location. An electrical charge was in the air as the carriage drivers cracked their whips to speed their horses along. Inside the police wagon the inspector kept drumming his fingers on his knees. I couldn't believe it. I was on my way to identify the man who brutally murdered Josephine and tried to kill me.

The inspector planned our arrival during the early afternoon, based on an anonymous tip that the doctor would be working in his lab. A block before the building the police wagon slowed down, so not to give warning of our arrival.

We had no sooner stepped down from the wagon when an explosion rocked the building and a fire erupted. I can't say if my eyes were tearing from the smoke and powder fumes or from frustration and anger that all evidence was going up in smoke, as with the pier shack.

Defeated, I returned to New York depressed and without a killer or story.

Mr. Pulitzer made it clear to me that my investigation of Dr. Blum was closed. "Against my better judgment I let you go to London to catch the Ripper. *You failed.*"

I hated to admit it, but he was right.

MATTERS MIGHT HAVE stayed at a standstill but for a chance remark from G. Steven Jones, the *World*'s recently returned Paris correspondent. Hearing of my attempt to snare the Ripper in London, he thought I'd be interested in mutilation killings in Paris.

"Mutilation killings in Paris? Are you sure? Mister Pulitzer just returned from the World's Fair. He never mentioned anything of the sort."

"That's because he doesn't want you running off to Paris. Besides, the French government is keeping a tight lid on the slashings to avoid panic. Think about it. Can you imagine what would happen to the World's Fair if news got out that a man is mutilating women?"

"Is there any particular area where the killings are taking place? In London, he targeted prostitutes in the Whitechapel district."

"Montmartre—it's the city's bohemian district and known for the scandalous behavior of the residents, many of whom are artists and writers. Not to mention it's overflowing with prostitutes."

"You're sure a man has been killing women in the same fashion as the Ripper?"

"Yes, but I must warn you, if you plan on going, don't let the boss know I spilled the beans, and don't contact the Paris police and tell them you're hunting a mad killer."

"Why?"

"Paris is already being racked by problems. Terrorism was born in Paris a hundred years ago during the Reign of Terror. Now it's come back. Anarchists, who cast their votes with guns and bombs, are fermenting revolution at a time when the French economy is as black as Newcastle coal. The World's Fair is pulling in millions of francs and the government isn't going to permit a scandal that threatens the revenue. That's why the police have put a lid on the story. If you go to them with your theory that a killer is on the streets stalking women, you'll be arrested."

Money over the lives of people? What kind of world did I live in?

"And besides all the other problems, there's been an outbreak of Black Fever."

"What's that?"

"A deadly influenza. They believe it's caused by miasma from sewer flumes because it putrefies a body until it decomposes and becomes foul smelling."

Ten days in a madhouse was beginning to sound safer than a visit to the City of Light.

I WALKED THE streets of Manhattan digesting what Mr. Jones had told me. Doctor Blum had resurfaced in Paris. The Paris slashings were the work of the same man who had wet his knife in New York and London. I was certain— again. And I was going. Now all I had to do was convince Mr. Pulitzer to assign me to Paris.

With my failure in London and the expense it incurred, I knew he wasn't going to be receptive to my request. Worse, the only clever approach I could come up with was the truth: I was operating off of pure intuition.

"NELLIE, HOW MANY times do I have to tell you you're a good reporter?" Mr. Pulitzer tapped his pencil on his desk. "But you've fallen off the log on this one. Need I remind you that Paris is in a foreign country and you don't even speak the language?"

"My French is adequate."*

"It's too dangerous."

"The French have a saying: *Qui craint le danger ne doit pas aller en mer,*" I said, showing off. "One who fears danger shouldn't go to sea."

"I don't care what the frogs say."

"Then how about the Bard of Avon. 'I must go and meet with danger there, or it will seek me in another place, and find me worse provided.'"

---

* For once Nellie is being modest. During her madhouse caper, a newspaper reported the "pretty crazy girl . . . speaks French, Spanish and English perfectly." (New York *Sun*, October 5, 1887)—The Editors.

"Young woman, Shakespeare doesn't sell newspapers. And neither do wild goose chases to Paris. There've been no reports of a Parisian slasher."

"The police are keeping it under a tight lid. If news got out that the Ripper is there killing women, it would ruin the fair and destroy the economy of Paris."

"Nonsense!"

"Regardless of what's going on over there, I have to go."

"This conversation is concluded." He pointed at the door.

TO EASE PULITZER'S anger, before getting on the boat in New York I sent him a box of his favorite Cuban cigars with a note boldly boasting I would not only return soon, but with a story that would top my madhouse exposé.

With regard to my mother, I told her I was going to Paris to cover the World's Fair. It would have been brutally cruel to put her through that terrible fear again and as selfish as this sounds, I needed a clear head, not one worrying about my mother's health because she's worrying over me.

Once again I was crossing the ocean to hunt a madman who willingly takes a knife and slashes the essence from women. Only this time I had to avoid the police and an invisible killer from the sewers.

At first it seemed quite
a well-behaved epidemic.

Dr. Brouardel, deputed to investigate it
by the public authority, reported that the dis-
order was trifling and that a few days at home
by the fire was all the treatment it required.

This was complacently published in the newspapers
and became a standing joke. "Have you got it?" "Not
yet?" "Well, you will, because we've all got to have it."

In the cabarets they were singing: Everybody's got the
influe-en-za-ah!

But they soon began to find out that it was not a joke. The
death toll began to mount alarmingly and the people got
into a state of panic. It was useless for the Press to pub-
lish reassuring statements; their own obituary columns
gave them the lie. Public services became disorganized,
theatres closed, fêtes were put off, and law sittings
suspended. Under this cloud of panic and depression the year 1889 passed out. And the winter
following was not calculated to reassure
anyone.

—JULES BERTAUT, *Paris*

9

Tomas Roth, Paris, October 25, 1889

W e've come to find a murderer."

The remark was so unlike Dr. Pasteur, it gave Roth pause as they gently rocked back and forth in the carriage. It was after eleven on a gloomy Saturday night as the three of them—Dr. Louis Pasteur, a sewer worker named Michel, and Tomas Roth, Pasteur's assistant—made their way to the dark river beneath the city's boulevards.

Michel—who was to be their guide into this strange world beneath the city's streets—looked askance at the great scientist sitting across from him. Pasteur, caught up with his own thoughts, didn't notice the concern.

"A killer who creeps in dark places and strikes without warning, or mercy."

Pasteur was not talking to his companions, but to the night outside the carriage window.

Just hours ago the Minister of the Interior, the man entrusted with the safety of the nation, had personally come to the institute to implore Dr. Pasteur to leave the security and comfort of his laboratory and make a secret examination of the sewer system.

"No work you're doing for mankind is as important

to France as discovering the source of this contagion. If you do not find and destroy this disease there will be no Paris and perhaps no France."

A compassionate man, the terrible burden placed on Pasteur weighed heavily.

The examination had to be under the cover of darkness and cloaked with secrecy.

"We must not fuel the panic that is already spreading as fast as the contagion." The statesman's voice cracked from the strain as he pleaded with Dr. Pasteur for his help in fighting a microbe so small, it couldn't be seen by the naked eye.

MIST LINGERED IN the night air, creating wet penumbras in the glow of the gas lamps they passed. The cold hand of winterkill was already hard upon the land, stripping trees into skeletons and wilting plants.

When they picked up Michel several blocks back he knew nothing of the reason for the mission, only that he was needed to take them into the sewers.

In the carriage behind them was Dr. Brouardel—the Director of Health—and his assistant. Separate carriages reflected the different stances that the health department and the Institut Pasteur had taken about the contagion.

"A damnable time to be on the streets," Pasteur said.

"The time of the wolf," Roth muttered, using an old expression of peasants.

Roth had been Pasteur's assistant for six months; long enough to know that it wasn't the wintry night that disturbed Pasteur. It was their destination—the Montmartre, the city's tawdry bohemian quarter, a place Pasteur would not visit voluntarily. He would rather be back in the quiet citadel of his laboratory than mingling with the long-haired, shaggy-bearded painters and poets—

purveyors of art and revolutionary plots that smelled of cheap beer and black cigarettes.

Roth leaned back and rested his head against the seat and listened to the murmuring prattle of carriage wheels and the clopping of hooves. With half-closed eyes Roth watched Michel. He was not the two-legged sewer rat Roth had expected.

The sewer worker's beard was scruffy and matched his brown hair that was in need of a cut. Unkempt strands hung from beneath his wool cap, but his clothing was surprisingly clean, if well worn. Black rubber boots that came above the knees were the only evidence of his occupation. With his long hooked nose and deep-set eyes, the man had the predatory mien of a pirate captain. His face, pitted as though shot by a scattergun loaded with pox, was dark, giving him a morose and grisly appearance. For a man who spent most daylight hours breathing sewer air, he appeared robust and surprisingly healthy.

The worker had been hesitant to board the stately carriage the minister sent to carry them to the site. The poor fellow sat stiffly, hardly touching anything around him, except to clandestinely feel the plush velvet side panel beside him.

His reticence came not only because he was in a gentleman's carriage, but because he was in the presence of a man acclaimed as an asset to the whole nation, if not the world. Only this year the grateful French people presented the great microbe hunter with the institute that bore his name.

The carriage pulled to a stop at a curb and Roth lent Dr. Pasteur a hand as he disembarked. The great scientist had suffered another stroke two years ago. At sixty-seven years old, his short hair and beard were white and his agility had limits, but he still looked into places where no one else could see.

As his laboratory assistant, half his age, it was Roth's job to perform the physical tasks his condition made difficult. Roth carried a wood case which contained the sterilized implements to gather samples and glass jars to store them. It would be his task to gather the specimens.

Dr. Brouardel and his assistant stood a bit aside from Roth and Pasteur. It made no difference to Brouardel that they were all here at the bequest of the minister—he carried the burden with ill grace.

Two prostitutes approached as the men gathered on the street. "Out for some fun tonight, Messieurs?" one asked.

Michel shooed them away. "This is official business."

"That's the only kind we do," the other tart said.

With the night wet, the bohemians who gave the quarter its licentious reputation had retreated from the *terrasse* tables of sidewalk cafés. They crowded inside smoke-filled café salons to argue politics and art with the passion most men reserved for their mistresses.

Montmartre had also exposed its darker heart as street toughs called apaches came out of the narrow passageways to hover under the gaslights along Boulevard de Clichy. Two of these criminals—thugs—loitered a few doorways down, eyeing them as the smoke from their cigarettes curled up into the falling mist. Their hats were pulled down close to their eyes to make identification difficult, while their pants legs flared at the bottom to make it easier to get knives out of their boots.

The sewer worker jerked his thumb at the two men. "They spit in the soup so only they can enjoy it. The city should sweep them all into the sewers."

Pasteur gestured with his cane at Michel. "Come, Charon, lead us down to your dark river so we may find a killer."

Michel gave Pasteur a quizzical look as he opened a rusted iron door to reveal damp stone steps leading down to the sewer. The poor man did not know what to think. With anyone else he probably would have thought they had lost their mind, but this was Dr. Pasteur.

He squinted at Roth in the darkness and whispered, "Who's this killer Monsieur Doctor talks about?"

"You've heard of microbes?" Roth asked, already knowing his answer.

He shook his head no.

"Little animals invisible to the naked eye, so small they can only be seen under a microscope. They get inside people and cause sickness and death, like the Black Fever that's inflicting so many."

"Yes, the fever. That I know about, it's killing my neighbors."

"Some people believe that it's caused by microbes from the sewer. That's what we are looking for, those little animals that get people sick."

Michel scratched his eyebrow. "It's God that causes sickness."

GUIDED BY THE yellow light of an oil lamp, they followed Michel down the grim stone steps. Roth was careful to keep an eye on Pasteur and let him lean on his arm. Behind them were Doctor Brouardel and his assistant who followed closely behind him like an unweaned pup. At the bottom Michel turned to Pasteur, "How will we know when we come across these animals you're looking for if we can't see them?"

"We'll take samples of the sewer water back to the laboratory. Billions live in a single teaspoon of water and we have to find the *one* that has singled out mankind to kill. The only way we can do this is with our microscopes. It won't be easy to find the right one—all cats are grey in the dark."

Once again Michel tossed back a look that clearly expressed his belief that all maladies were in the hands of God.

The sewer tunnel was a half-moon vault of blackened stone with the grim ambience of a dungeon. Perhaps the height of two men and a dozen feet wide, the middle of the tunnel was consumed by a *cunette*—a channel of sewer waters several feet wide. On each side of the channel was a narrow walkway fouled by debris left behind when the tunnel flooded.

"How many kilometers of tunnels are under the city?" Pasteur asked Michel.

"Hundreds of *lieues*," he said, using an old-fashioned measurement. A lieue was equal to about four kilometers.

Air in the tunnel was humid. The dankness was expected, but the smell was not. One would expect that a waterway that carried the excretions of one of the largest cities in the world would smell worse than Hades. But the moist air had the smell of damp laundry that had been left to mold.

Pasteur inquired, "How often do the walkways flood?"

"Whenever you don't expect it. Water on the streets becomes a raging river down here. Lost a friend a couple of months ago when he slipped during high water. Found him days later—what the rats left of him."

In an aside to Roth, Pasteur asked, "Do you recall the role the River Styx played in the Trojan War?"

"Yes, of course. Achilles was invincible, except for his heel. The single weakness was created when he was a baby. His mother, the sea nymph Thetis, held him by his right heel and dipped him into the River Styx to make him invulnerable. The magic water covered all of his body except the heel."

Even though Roth was fairly new to the institute he was used to these random queries from the scientist whose mind was never at rest.

Pasteur pointed his cane down the tunnel. "The heel, the vulnerable heel . . . we have to make certain that our city's weakness isn't in the sewers."

For certain, the sewers of Paris held an unusual place in the hearts and minds of Parisians because so much French history—and mystery—had occurred in them. They had long been the lurking place of criminal masterminds and revolutionaries—Jean-Paul Marat hid from the king's men while plotting the Revolution of 1789, suffering a skin disease that he attributed to the sewers; Jean Valjean saved the life of Marius and dueled with the relentless Inspector Javert in *Les Misérables*; and anarchists now crept through them to plant bombs under public buildings.

A fitting place for a killer to hide, the sewer was a netherworld of darkness and shadows, with small islands of hazy light created by feeble oil lamps set no closer than a hundred paces. A lonely place with only the sounds of drips and rushing water.

Grey-green frogs leaped out of their way as the men came down the walkway. Something floated by, a doll-like creature, with tiny hands and legs. Roth saw it for only a second before it disappeared in the dark waters. It was the body of a newborn, or a prematurely born child, thrown into the sewers no doubt because the mother couldn't afford a burial. Roth glanced at Pasteur and knew immediately that he had seen the child. *Nothing* escaped his attention. If the killer was here, Pasteur would find it.

"The frogs, were they here before the recent storm?" Pasteur asked Michel.

"They're always here, they like this area. Been here as long as I've worked the tunnels. And before storm waters swept them away, there were dead rats lying about."

"And how long have you worked in the sewers?"

"Since my father brought me down when I was fourteen."

"Have you ever become sick from the fumes?"

"Never, and the same for the men who work with me. You can ask my work mate, Henrí. He's been working the sewers for over ten years and has never been sick."

The air rising from the sewers, miasmic vapors, was the reason that brought them to this place.

An influenza pandemic called the Russian flu had rolled off the steppes of Asia and across Europe. The contagion stalled in Paris as a deadly strain called Black Fever erupted. Sewer fumes were suspected as the source of the disease.

Hardest hit by the Black Fever were neighborhoods of the poor and downtrodden areas that could spawn food riots even in better times. The black flag of the anarchists had been raised amidst an outcry that the poor of the city were dying as a result of a plot by the rich to rid the world of poor mouths to feed.

IO

Coming behind them, Dr. Brouardel overheard the sewer worker say that he and his coworker, Henrí, had not been sick after years of working in the sewers.

"It's understood that sewer workers are not affected by the miasma." The medical director's irritation bounced off their backs as they continued treading the narrow walkway next to the stream of sewer. His remark carried both a note of authority and vexation because he had determined the cause of the epidemic to be sewer fumes. The basis for the director's conclusion was propinquity: the sewers below were emitting fumes, people above were dying, a fortiori, the sewers were the cause.

The theory that disease was spread by miasmic fumes had become quite popular since the new age of the microscope demonstrated that sewers were a rich soup of microbes. But Pasteur never accepted or rejected a theory until it was tested in a laboratory, and no one had scientifically demonstrated that sewer vapors carried deadly microbes. To the contrary, the smells had been around for thousands of years, since man had built cities.

The fact that Pasteur had not acquiesced to the causation Brouardel opined to the city's newspapers infuriated the director even more than his customary intolerance toward Pasteur. But it wasn't just Brouardel who held ill will toward Pasteur—medical practitioners resented the fact that people believed Pasteur was a medical doctor. In fact, he was a chemist. They were also infuriated at Pasteur's accusation that doctors spread infection from one patient to another by their failure to sanitize their hands and instruments.

"Just as immunity can be acquired to smallpox by exposure to it," the director went on, "the sewer workers are able to resist the miasma."

"There's no proof," Pasteur muttered.

"My clinical examinations are proof!" the director snapped.

Voilá! There it was—the essence of the dispute between the scientist and the medical profession. Doctors believed that causation and treatment were to be determined by their examination and questioning of a patient. The idea that one could place blood or tissue samples under a microscope and determine the course of treatment was alien to them. They did not want Pasteur's microscope getting between them and their patients.

More of the director's irritated words bounced off their backs as they moved down the dark passage.

"Messieurs, you are here at the bequest of the minister. I, of course, will honor his desire to have you view a suspected miasma area. However, I want it understood that you have both been warned to cover your face to protect yourselves from the miasma and have failed to do so."

"Thank you, Monsieur Doctor."

Only Roth's sideway glance noticed that Pasteur's quiet thanks was made with a smirk.

The director's concern about Pasteur's health was, of course, false. Nothing would have pleased him more than Pasteur droping dead in the sewers, thus not only proving his theory of miasmic contagion, but ridding the medical world of its greatest critic.

To Pasteur, the laboratory was a battleground in a war against two enemies—combating the jealousy and ignorance of the medical professional, and a fight against microbes that caused disease and destroyed millions of lives every year. In the past decade, the institute had battled microbes that caused gonorrhea, typhoid fever, leprosy, malaria, tuberculosis, cholera, pneumonia, meningitis, tetanus, anthrax, rabies, plague, and other demons. Pasteur developed vaccines to prevent some of the diseases. The war was a personal one—he lost two young daughters to microbic diseases.

Pasteur asked Roth, "Do you remember what the Bible says about the invisible killer we hunt?"

"I believe so. Revelations speaks of the Fourth Horseman: 'Behold a pale horse, and his name that sat on him was Death, and Hell followed with him. And power was given unto them over the fourth part of the earth, to kill with sword, hunger, and the beasts of the earth.' The beasts of the earth are microbes."

"Last night, one of the radical newspapers depicted the Fourth Horseman riding through an impoverished neighborhood, cutting down poor people with a bloody scythe. Do you know whose face the horseman bore?"

Roth shook his head, but did in fact know.

"President Carnot. His pockets were stuffed with money from factory owners. The radicals accuse our president of masterminding the death of the poor with this contagion."

"Nonsense, of course."

"Yes, but people threatened by the contagion are willing to believe anything. Truly, the wrath prophesied by the Bible has visited us many times, spreading deadly scourges in its wake. God only knows what the world would be like if progress had not been retarded by these invading beasts. Now these creatures threaten us again."

"Do you think we can stop them?"

Pasteur paused for a moment and gazed at the sewer river. "The creatures are in a struggle of survival with mankind. To defeat them we must find their Achilles heel. But we must be on our guard every step of the way. I lost Thuillier when I sent a team to study the cholera outbreak in Alexandra six years ago, hoping to stop it before the cholera took ship to Marseille. One tiny mistake and poor Thuillier was struck down by the bacteria. *Mistakes are deadly.*"

Wearing a nosegay into the sewers was not one of Dr. Pasteur's safety precautions. Those which the director and his assistant wore were scented with perfume and a bit of alcohol, in the belief that the scent destroyed lethal vapors.

"Medieval," Pasteur muttered at the sight of the nosegays.

Michel grinned when he saw the director and his assistant put on the nosegays. He and hundreds like him had spent a lifetime in the sewers without being stricken by the fumes, although he did tell the visitors to tuck their handkerchiefs around their collars. They had assumed it was to keep out the chill but soon found the real reason sewer men wore kerchiefs around their necks: Large spiders and giant centipedes clutched the ceiling and occasionally fell.

"*Mon Dieu!*" Michel stopped and looked at Roth in panic. "If the insects grow so large down here, how big are the invisible animals you are looking for?"

I I

A faint glow broke the darkness ahead as they followed Michel.

"That'll be the lamp of my partner, Henrí," he said.

How these netherworld workers found their way through the dark maze of stone tunnels was a mystery to match the one surrounding the Sphinx. But when they came upon the hanging lantern, Henrí was nowhere to be seen.

"He's been here," Michel said. "May have gone up for a bite." Michel pointed at an opening in the tunnel ceiling. "That's the waste hole."

It was an ordinary round hole above the river of sewage. Paris, being an ancient city, still disposed most of its waste directly through a hole from the ground floor of apartment buildings. Residents carried their chamber pots to the hole to dump. The hole Michel pointed to was the outlet for a tenement house in the impoverished neighborhood where Black Fever first erupted.

"Did any frogs die in this area when the fever broke out above?"

Michel shook his head. "No, Monsieur, not that I ever saw. But I did see dead rats."

The health director came up beside them as the sewer

worker shined his bull's-eye lantern up at the hole. He stepped on a frog and looked down at the bloody mess and grinned to his assistant. "Doctor Pasteur has always professed that microbes attack us like an eleventh plague of Egypt. Now we know he is wrong. It is another plague of frogs that God has sent."

His assistant found the humor appealing, or considered it expedient to do so, but neither Pasteur nor Roth gave it any thought. Pasteur was busy telling Roth where to obtain samples to be placed into sterilized glass bottles in the leather case he carried from a shoulder strap. When Pasteur worked he fell into a deep concentration and was not tolerant to interruptions.

"We should also take one of the frogs," Roth said, grabbing one of the slimy creatures. "Perhaps the miasma is from their bad breath."

Pasteur was concentrating too intently on the environs of the sewer to react to Roth's witticism, but the sarcasm did not pass the director whose look told Roth he wished he could quash him underfoot as he had the frog. Pasteur turned his attention to the sewer worker and asked about life under the city.

"It's dangerous work," Michel said. "When it rains, the waters can roar through the tunnels like flash floods. Even with normal water levels, you can slip into the channel and be swept under in a second." He turned and stared at the *cunette* as if he wondered whether Henrí had been swallowed by it.

"Are the smells worse in the summer?"

"Much worse. Sometimes gas forms that can explode if you strike a match to light a pipe. Factories pour chemicals down the sewers that can burn a hole in your skin or make a fire in your lungs when you breathe."

"But you're not afraid of miasma?"

"Monsieur Doctor, I've been working in the sewers

for over twenty years. If these vermin you gentlemen talk about haven't gotten me by now, I don't suppose I taste good to them."

Twenty years in the sewers. And his father before him. Not an unusual practice to follow one's père into a profession. Even an executioner was a hereditary occupation in France.

Human excrement came through the ceiling opening and plopped into the water. The director pointed down at it.

"Monsieur Pasteur, you should take some of this merde back to your laboratory and examine it under your microscope. Perhaps you will find in it the plague of microbes that you believe threatens the city."

"It's a puzzle," Pasteur said, completely ignoring the director. He had the faraway look of a swami in a trance when he fell into deep thought.

"Merde is a puzzle?" The director raised his eyebrows.

Pasteur stared at him as if he had just become aware of the man's presence. "No, no, the frogs."

"The frogs?"

"Of course!" He snapped. "Haven't you been observing the frogs and the rats, Monsieur Director? Why do the frogs live and the rats die?"

Michel shined his lamp at something down the passageway. He moved toward whatever had caught his attention, then stopped and gasped.

His partner Henrí was lying on the walkway with the upper part of his body propped against the stone wall. His mouth and eyes were wide open. A stream of black blood had run down from the corner of his mouth. A rat was eating away at his face, while other rats had torn apart his shirt and were burrowed into his stomach. His innards were exposed and blackened.

Dead rodents lay beside him.

12

Nellie Bly, Paris, October 27, 1889

The night is dark and thick in the alley behind the Moulin Rouge. The beacon atop the thousand-foot-high Eiffel Tower sweeps across the gloomy sea of fog as a fleeing ghost. Each time it flashes overhead, the blanched fog and mist take on a shivering pallor that gives life to the unliving.

The alley's quiet as a crypt.

Fear sends wintry chills racing up my legs and back. Lord knows what lurks in this gloom. Pulling my wool shawl tighter, I hurry down the passageway to a corner where a street lamp creates a fuzzy hole of misty light. Huddling under the gas-light, I listen to the night for sounds, but only hear the rasp of my own excited breathing. The light makes it even harder to see in the fog and I step reluctantly into the darkness again. There's a movement down the street, a stirring I sense rather than see.

My feet keep moving, one in front of the other as if they have a mind of their own while I fight the urge to turn around and race to the safety of my hotel.

I find myself at an ancient stone wall with an arched entrance wrapped in weeping moss. I've been led to a less than auspicious place to meet with a killer on a murky night—the Montmartre Cemetery.

I've seen this stone garden from a distance in the daylight. Forested with small crypts adorned with cathedral glass and fine sculptures, it's the resting place of many famous bones, but I don't want to add mine to the pile.

A morbid game is being played.

I give the police whistle three good blasts and shout, "Help!"

I should wait for gendarmes but a woman is in danger. I blow the whistle again. "The police are coming!" I shout out as I go through the entrance.

When the Tower beacon flashes, crypt shadows shudder like stone ghosts rising from the ground. Most of the small mausoleums are about six-by-six and a dozen feet high, tiny palaces of the dead. Some larger ones have statuary and other sculptures worthy of a king. Anything could be lurking behind them. Even in broad daylight,

MONTMARTRE CEMETERY

you wouldn't be able to see a person hiding in the crowded forest of stone edifices.

I hear running steps and my courage melts. I get off the main path and kneel behind a crypt. Hovering over me is a stone figure, a melancholy young woman with bare breasts doomed to watch over a grave for eternity. She makes me think of Josephine. The sound fades but I stay crouching, my heart racing.

This is a creepy, creepy place.

I believe in the dead as well as the living and maybe that's why graveyards affect me so. Gathering my courage again, I stand up and blow the whistle as hard as I can.

The tower beacon flashes again overhead. I see the prostitute. Her white dress is ghoulishly radiant. She's standing still with her hand held out as if she's beckoning. The light passes and she vanishes.

"Run!" I shout to her and blow the whistle again. "Run for your life!"

Another figure emerges from the fog—shaped like a giant bat, it's as black as Poe's raven. I turn and run in a blind panic. I stumble over a gravestone, hitting the ground on my knees, in pain, but I get back on my feet to run, stumbling again until suddenly there's nothing under my feet and I fall into a hole, bouncing off a dirt wall and hitting hard ground, the breath knocked out of me.

It's pitch black and my body hurts everywhere. I crawl, feeling dirt wall around me.

I'm in a grave.

I start screaming before I'm on my feet. Footsteps crunch above and I lose my breath. Dirt pours down at me as someone comes to the edge of the grave. A tall dark figure shaped like a giant bat looms above me as more dirt slides into the hole.

He's burying me alive.

13

W ho's there?" A frightened voice asks from above. Thank God it's not the voice of a killer.

"Help me—get me out of here!"

"Don't move." A match strikes and a lantern flares. It's a man wearing the bat-like cape of a gendarme.

My lips quiver and knees shake. "Please help me out of here."

"How did you get in there?"

"I fell in running from a killer."

"What killer?"

"A man chasing me. Help me out and I'll explain."

The gendarme leaves without a word. One moment he is shining his lantern into the grave and the next he is gone.

"*Don't leave me!*"

I can't believe he would just leave me. I vault up and fall back down. After several attempts, I finally grab and claw my way until I get one elbow and then the other over the edge and belly up with my feet kicking air. Although I am weak and shaky and have a terrible urge to vomit, I'm free.

The rumble of steel-banded wagon wheels over

cobblestones and a bell clanging are a welcome sound. A police wagon has entered the graveyard. An officer swinging a bull's-eye lantern materializes in the fog. More bat-caped men are behind him. The gendarme had gone for help.

The officers gather around me, several talking at the same time. Who am I? What am I doing here? What's this about a killer?

On their heels comes a plain-clothes policeman. He rudely flashes a lantern in my face. "What are you doing here, Mademoiselle?"

Shading my eyes with my hand, I tell him, "My name is Nellie Bly, I'm an American newspaper reporter. A woman has been murdered."

"Murdered? Where?"

"Here, in the graveyard."

"How do you know?"

"I was following the killer. He's in black clothes with a red scarf."

"Spread out," he tells the men, "make a search. Stop anyone you find."

"Who are you?" I ask him.

"I'm Detective Lussac from La Sûreté."

"Over here!" a gendarme cries. "A woman. She's not moving."

My heart sinks when I see her. She's sitting on a grave with her back against a gravestone, eyes wide open as if she sees the unspeakable. Blood has dripped down to her chest from the corner of her mouth. Her white dress is stained with large dark blotches of blood.

Detective Lussac pulls out his pocket watch and kneels beside the body. He opens the cover and the inside crystal covering the watch face. He checks her wrist for a pulse and then places the watch next to the woman's gaping mouth as an officer holds a lantern next to him. I pray her warm breath will fog the glass.

"No breath, no pulse, she's dead," Lussac says.

I turn away and sit wearily down on the footstone of a grave. Fighting back tears, I stare down at the ground. I can't help but feel that if I'd been quicker, braver, smarter, or stronger, I might have saved her.

Lussac is suddenly beside me, examining me with the probing eyes policemen the world over possess. He forces a smile, exposing a left incisor that's black. I avoid his eyes and brush dirt from my dress to gather my thoughts. Experience has taught me never to trust a policeman's smile. It only means they are trying to get what they want with sugar before they use vinegar.

"You're a newspaper reporter? *A woman?*"

I'm sure women reporters are an even less substantial species in France than buffalos, if they exist at all. In the best French I can muster, I start to relate my tale of following the slasher to Paris. He curtly interrupts me and takes me out of listening range of the uniformed officers.

"Now tell me your story."

I get started and he interrupts me again and writes a note. He gives it to an officer who hurries away on horseback.

"Continue," he says.

Through tight jaws, I give the most sketchy details possible because my gut tells me not to trust him. As I'm finishing with my tale, the caretaker of the graveyard arrives.

"The grave is an authorized one," he tells Lussac, "for a funeral tomorrow."

While they're talking, another man is directed to Lussac, a conservatively dressed young man wearing a charcoal-colored long coat, high stiff collar, and top hat.

He appears to be about thirty years old, of average height, light hair, and a mustache that falls short of handlebars. He carries the prematurely grave air of a young professional. I hope he's not a reporter—the man in black is *my* story.

I strain to hear the conversation between him and the detective and am only able to pick up the fact that he's a doctor.

The woman's body has been placed on the back of a police wagon and the young doctor examines it under lantern light while the detective stands by. I edge closer and ask, "Detective, have there been slasher slayings in Paris? Besides this one?"

His features turn stern and officious. "These are difficult times. People are out of work and hungry. There are more plots to overthrow the government than radicals to carry them out. The one good thing is the Exposition. Millions of francs are being spent for French products and the whole country shines in the glory of it. A mad killer loose in the city will frighten away people."

The young doctor interrupts. "Monsieur Detective, I've finished examining—"

"Yes, we can talk over here." He takes the man out of earshot.

Kicking myself for not heeding Jones's warning about talking to the police, I perch next to a snarling gargoyle on a gravestone and wait, cold and weary. My nervous system has been galloping like a team of fire wagon horses and I need to be taken into the barn and rubbed down.

The huddled conversation breaks up and the detective starts toward me with a purposeful stride that reads trouble for me. Before he reaches me, the mounted officer he had sent with a message rides up. The messenger jumps from his horse and hands Detective Lussac a piece of paper. I use the officer's momentary distraction to approach the doctor, who's putting back on his coat.

"*Bonsoir*, Monsieur."

He gives a small bow. "*Bonsoir*."

"Are you from the coroner's office?"

"No, Mademoiselle, I'm from Pigalle Hospital."

"The wounds . . . are they horrible?"

"Wounds?"

"The knife wounds."

"There are no wounds, Mademoiselle. No bleeding."

"No bleeding? I saw the stains—"

"Dirt."

"Dirt?"

"Stains from the wet ground. There are no wounds to the body."

"No wounds." My mind is getting as difficult to maneuver as my tight jaws. "Then how did he kill her?"

"He?"

"The—the maniac who killed her."

"Mademoiselle, I don't know what you're talking about. The woman has no signs of violence. An autopsy will reveal more, but I suspect she's the victim of the fever that's struck down so many people."

It's a cover-up! Lussac has told him to keep mum about the horrible wounds. My feet spur into action faster than my mind can keep up with them. In a flash I'm at the body and jerk off the sheet. Close up, under the lantern light, there's no doubt—the dark stains are dirt. There's no blood except the dark liquid she expelled from her mouth.

"She wasn't slashed." I speak aloud to myself and a response comes from Lussac.

"Exactly, Mademoiselle."

Detective Lussac has two officers flanking him. He nods to the doctor. "Dr. Dubois, Chief Inspector Morant will contact you tomorrow. Merci."

The doctor raises his eyebrows. "The Chief Inspector of the Sûreté? For such a lowly death?"

Detective Lussac glares at me as he answers. "The matter has taken on national importance because of wild accusations by a foreigner."

Dr. Dubois raises his eyebrows. "Strange, but of course I will be honored by the Chief Inspector's visit. *Au revoir.*"

Detective Lussac turns to me as soon as Dubois leaves. Whatever instructions he received are ill tidings for me. But I don't waver before his officious glare. "The man in black killed her. He's simply outsmarted you by his clever method."

"And what is that method, Mademoiselle?" He looks to the officers at his side. "Perhaps this imaginary killer called down a bolt of lightening from God!"

"I know what I saw."

"And what exactly did you see?" The detective throws up his hands in frustration. "A man who had similar clothes and beard to someone you saw over a year ago in New York? How many men in Paris wear the same type of clothes and groom their beards in a like fashion?" He steps closer and jabs a finger in my face. "Tell me, what act of violence did you observe? Tell me one single act that you witnessed tonight."

"I . . . I'm an experienced reporter. My instinct—"

"Police operate from facts, Mademoiselle, not the intuition of a woman who should be home caring for babies and her husband's needs instead of causing problems for the police. We know what you want. The truth doesn't matter to your scandal-hungry newspaper that writes its headlines in blood."

That did it. "Detective Lussac, you've been rude. I'll be speaking to your superior." I turn on my heel to leave.

"One moment. Where do you think you are going?"

"Back to my hotel."

"No, you're going to be a guest of the government. You're under arrest."

"For what?"

"The charge? Officer Vernet, come over here."

A gendarme breaks away from the group of officers.

"Officer, you've been patrolling this district for over ten years?"

"Yes, Monsieur l'inspecteur."

"Take a look at this young woman and tell me what you see."

The man gives me a quick once-over. "A Montmartre prostitute, Detective."

"Do you have your flat fish, Mademoiselle?"

"My what?"

"Your *fille en carte* from the Bureau des Moeurs, the document a prostitute must carry that certifies she's registered with the police and is current with her medical examinations."

"You know I have no such thing!"

"Ha! A *clandé*, a casual girl who spends her days as a seamstress and her nights picking up pocket money on the streets. Officer, arrest her for unlicensed prostitution."

14

I'm made to board a police wagon with seven other women inside.

"Another pea in the pod," Detective Lussac says.

With my chin up and my back straight, I lock eyes with the detective. "Your superior will get a detailed report of the treatment accorded me."

This provokes a giggle among the girls and a smirk from him.

"My *superior* ordered you arrested."

"Well, my editor will speak to your president."

"A madman tried to kill President Carnot recently. Anarchist plots to kill him are revealed every day. Let me assure you that the president desires to maintain a very good relationship with the police."

As I take a seat closest to the doors, the women stare at me with wide-eyed curiosity. With a smile, I tell them in French that I am a newspaper reporter from America, doing a story on Parisian night life. "Perhaps some of you have a story that you wish to share with the world?"

They all began to chatter at once, seven prostitutes, seven stories to tell the world, and each is the most important one. I try to listen but my mind keeps returning to the dead woman. *Nothing makes sense.*

I can't accept that she died from the fever. When I watched her earlier tonight she appeared healthy. What kind of fever can act that fast? And who was the man I was following?

A burst of laughter shatters my thoughts. One of the girls is demonstrating what a customer demanded. I can't help but laugh with them. I'm amazed at what they endure and still laugh with such ease. I must stop this mad killer. If I don't, any one of these women could be next. A prostitute makes a remark that grabs my interest.

"Why were you arrested?" I ask.

"A prostitute wearing a black dress threw acid on a foreigner, a mi'lord. The police are arresting every girl they can find with a black dress."

"Really . . ." I realize we're all wearing black dresses.

"They'll hold us until the mi'lord arrives to identify the girl. They took him to the hospital because she burned his Eiffel Tower."

"I hear she did it because he got his treat and refused to pay," another pipes in.

Oh, Lord. Getting arrested on a trumped-up charge of prostitution will get my editor in action and the American ambassador banging on my jail cell, but for maiming a man's private parts, Pulitzer would let me rot in jail. I've no doubt that the "mi'lord" and his friends will be able to identify me.

The girls talk about setting bail bond. One explains to me, "Those with enough francs can set bond and go free. The rest of us will have to stay in jail. It is too late to pick up any more money on the street, so most of us will save our money and spend the night in a cell."

I lean my head back and close my eyes. No possibility Lussac will let me set bond—that's a certainty. Once we get to the police station, he'll make sure I'm locked up.

As the carriage rumbles along cobblestone streets to the jail cell, I realize my quest has taken an aberrant twist.

A dark game is being played.

And I've lost the first hand.

Dr. Dubois

Dr. Dubois curses as he hurries away from the cemetery. He left his umbrella at the hospital and might not reach Place de Clichy and a fiacre before the light rain turns into a downpour. He quickens his step. He must get to Perun and inform him about Nellie Bly before someone else does. The thought of facing Perun makes what's left of his right pinkie burn. Perun had cut half the finger off.

Reaching the square, he flags down a fiacre.

"Left bank by the Pont Saint-Michel bridge," he tells the driver as he climbs in. Dubois knows his request will not faze his driver, even though he's conservatively dressed and obviously a doctor since he still has his medical bag with him. It's not unusual for even a professional man to be at the Seine past midnight purchasing the services of a prostitute working the river quay.

He rests his head back and tries to let his body and mind relax by listening to the steady rhythm of the horses' hooves. It feels like years have passed from the days when he was a foolish young café revolutionist—a gentlemanly scholar who spent evenings with friends, drinking absinthe and smoking pipes as they talked about how they

were going to overthrow the government and bring justice to the poor.

It was nothing but café prattle until a year ago when
Perun approached his table and asked him to join his
fight against oppression. He was honored and his friends
jealous. Perun was a man of mystery in the world of
political anarchy. Better known by reputation than by
sight, he had a tendency for action—the kind that drew
blood.

He never questioned why Perun chose him. He likes to
think it was because there are few doctors whose main
interests are political anarchy and biological chemistry,
but deep down he knows differently—he's someone Perun can control.

Once again his right pinkie burns. He holds it tight,
but the pain stays, along with the memory of how he
lost it. He had balked when Perun gave him his first assignment—to kill a man. It made no difference to Perun
that the man he wanted killed was Dubois' friend. When
he asked why, Perun refused to tell him. Than, when he
told Perun he couldn't kill his friend, Perun beat him
almost unconscious.

"A comrade must put aside his personal feelings," he
told Dubois after the beating. Then—so Dubois would
have a permanent reminder that he had to obey without
question—Perun cut off half the pinkie. Oddly it sealed
his loyalty to Perun. Dubois even feels lucky—he still
has his life.

BY THE TIME he exits the carriage the rain has stopped.
The fog is even thicker than on the Butte—a damp,
heavy cloak over the night. The closest street-light, a tall
metal post with two huge gas lanterns, is a faint glow a

dozen paces from where he stands. He locates the stairway down to the quay and descends mossy stone steps.

"Monsieur . . ."

Dubois almost loses his footing as he recoils from the voice. *"Mon Dieu!"*

A prostitute materializes from a cove along the wall and he waves her off. "Not tonight."

"Not so fast, my friend. What is the color of your flag?"

He understood. Perun always stations a lookout near the river barge. Using a prostitute is clever. Dubois has no doubt she wouldn't hesitate to kill him if he doesn't give the right answer.

"Black." The color of the flag of anarchism.

Without a word she slips back, leaving Dubois to continue on.

The exterior of the barge is like other wooden vessels used to haul farm products and supplies along the river. Low to the water, twenty meters long, seven wide, the only structure rising on the deck is a small pilothouse. No one would ever suspect the boat houses a laboratory.

He goes up the gangplank and walks across the deck, passing rows of damp gunny sacks filled with rotting potatoes. A faint glow from a cigarette is visible from the pilot-house. A man with a sharp knife is inside, watching for intruders. He has a gun, but that would be used only if the police raid the vessel.

Dubois knocks twice and lifts the companionway door. He hopes Perun has not changed the signal since he saw him that morning. He feels honored that he is even allowed aboard the barge. Few people other than those working directly on the project have been aboard.

The laboratory at the bottom of the companionway

isn't a broom closet like the one he has at the hospital, but a research center that would strike the envy of any experimenter. A kerosene lamp hangs from the ceiling above a long stainless steel table that dominates the center of the room.

Dubois knows from his own laboratory work that he is entering a battlefield in a war that has been taking place since life forms first appeared on Earth and began to compete for existence, an invisible war that goes on every moment of every day, a conflict between mankind and animals so tiny most cannot be seen even under a microscope. Yet they are able to kill creatures billions of times larger than themselves.

The combatants are everywhere: in food, water, air, and dirt; even in the very bodies of man and creature. Most are harmless, some help mankind—without them, food could not be grown or digested, waste decomposed. But some of them are the deadliest killers on the planet, striking down millions of people each year.

Perun is sitting on a wooden stool at the lab table, examining a specimen under a microscope. He uses a Carl Zeiss state of the art optical instrument, far superior to the outdated microscope Dubois has at his make-shift lab at the hospital.

Perun's dedication to his work reminds Dubois of what he's read about the great microbe hunter, Louis Pasteur. Both are fanatics about their science, but they differ on their goals. Pasteur's objective is to control the virulence of microorganisms, to stop their spread and devastation to lives. Perun's an anarchist at war with government and it tempers his scientific work.

The aim of anarchism is to unshackle people from the arbitrary dictates of government, to create a free and peaceful society. But the path to a new society is one of violent acts of terrorism.

Dubois stands quietly by the table, his eyes sweeping the array of biochemistry apparatus on the table: petri dishes, bunsen burners, alcohol lamps to boil water for the beakers, glass stirrers, corked-test tubes, thermometers, forceps, and pipettes. A crate from China, slipped by customs without inspection because it bore Dubois' Department of Health insignia, is on the floor under the table. He silently sighs to himself as he looks at the superb selection of scientific apparatus. If only the great man would permit him to work beside him . . .

"Have a bite of sausage," Perun says, without looking up from the microscope.

The "sausage" is spoiled food in a glass container.

"What is it?"

"*Clostridium botulinum.*"

"Ahhh."

Clostridium botulinum is a bacterium that secretes one of the deadliest poisons known to man: botulism. The name is derived from the Latin word for sausage: *botulus.* It was applied after people in Wildbad, Germany, died from eating uncooked smoked sausage. Even with the knowledge that ill-prepared foods are the breeding ground for a microbe that emits a deadly toxic, thousands of people still died every year from the poison, usually from home-canned foods that were not cooked thoroughly.

Perun had bred the lethal little creatures by following the example of the sausage-eating Germans: He allowed food to spoil in a low oxygen atmosphere.

"What stage are you?" Dubois asks. His tone reveals the envy and admiration he has for Perun's ability as a scientist.

"I have a pure culture."

That meant he now had laboratory-grown botulus as opposed to what he obtained from the decomposed food. Dubois knows the first specimens taken from the "sausage" would have contained many different species of bacteria. Perun had to first separate out the botulus from the other bacteria. Once he has a culture of pure botulus in a nutritious medium of simple sugars or perhaps a meat broth, either in a liquid or solidified in agar, it would not be difficult to increase the size of the colony by keeping the bacteria well fed.

As Perun continues to study the bacteria, Dubois steps over to watch a worker inside an "incubator." While Pasteur's scientists would have found the microscope and other items on Perun's lab table familiar, the incubators on the barge were unique. *Not just unique*, Dubois thinks, *but strange and amazing.*

An incubator is an insulated box in which temperature, humidity, and other conditions are controlled so microbes will reproduce. But the three incubators on the barge are rooms the size of walk-in meat coolers.

One wall of each incubator room is clear glass and faces the lab so Perun can observe the worker inside. The other walls are wood, but were also covered with glass and sealed with rubber. The sealing is necessary to ensure that whatever is inside, *stays inside*.

Perun claims that no one on Earth has colonized as many deadly microbes as he. Dubois does not doubt the claim.

The atmosphere in the walk-in incubators is so potentially toxic, no one enters unless they are in a deep-sea diving suit. Perun chose diving suits because material that keeps out water on the ocean floor is also impervious to microbes. The suited workers are supplied air pumped through a rubber hose. Their faces are partially visible in the glass portholes of the big metal helmets covering their heads. They leave the incubator rooms through a door at the back where they are thoroughly hosed off before taking off the suits.

It is dangerous work. They are all anarchist comrades and Perun occasionally loses one to the tiny creatures they are breeding. "Never forget they're hungry and you are their meal," he tells them.

As they toil with the microbe colonies, they remind Dubois of pictures of deep-sea divers harvesting food on the ocean floor in a Jules Verne book he read as a teenager.

"I'm going to test the toxicity," Perun says.

Dubois steps back to the lab table as Perun draws liquid from a culture of botulus into a syringe. He uses a military bullet extractor biologists call a "mouse forcep" to capture a rat from an animal cage. After injecting the animal, he places it back in the cage.

Perun glances at Dubois as he cleans up his work area. "Botulism kills more slowly if you ingest it in food. Putting it directly into the bloodstream will of course speed up the action. The bloodstream will carry it to nerve endings and cause the muscles to contract. In the final stages there will be paralysis and death." He grins at Dubois. "Are you sure you don't want to sample the sausage?"

Dubois rubs his burning pinkie.

Perun's sardonic humor evaporates. "What's so important that you interrupt me tonight?"

"We have a serious problem that must be taken care of immediately."

"Well, what is it?"

"There is a woman newspaper reporter from America who knows about you and has informed the police."

Perun breaks out laughing.

Dubois's fear level soars. He doesn't know how to deal with Perun's mood changes. "She knows who you are. She's determined to catch you. We must stop her before she ruins everything."

"No. Leave Nellie Bly alone."

"You—you know her?"

"She's chasing shadows."

"But Detective Lussac told me that the Chief Inspector of La Sûreté is coming to see me tomorrow to ask questions about the girl you killed tonight."

Perun abruptly stands up, almost knocking over his stool. He comes within inches of Dubois' face. "You're talking about the girl that died *from fever* . . . aren't you?"

"Yes," Dubois looks down afraid, "yes, that's what I meant."

"Good. Then there's nothing to be concerned about, is there?"

"No, but she has raised questions and I'm to be questioned. Questions that would never have been asked."

"You're a doctor. Give them some technical drivel so they think their concerns are being dealt with." Perun pauses, his eyes penetrating deep into Dubois. "You are capable of handling such a simple task?"

"Yes. Yes, of course. I just thought . . ."

"Let *me* do the thinking." Perun paces back and forth. "This is all very good. As a matter of fact, it's perfect. This will be your opportunity to convince the Chief Inspector that all fever victims should be sent to you for examination."

"But that duty belongs to my superior, Doctor—"

"*Change it.*"

Dubois knows he has no other option. He doesn't want to think about what would happen if he doesn't obey Perun's commands.

"Yes, this is very good." Perun picks a scalpel off the table and taps it against his palm. He looks genuinely pleased. "When everything is accomplished, I must thank her for helping me." He tucks the edge of the scalpel under Dubois' chin. "You agree, don't you, Monsieur Doctor?"

"Yes."

Dubois holds his breath.

Perun smiles as he teasingly slides the scalpel back and forth on Dubois's neck. "It will give me great pleasure thanking her as I kill her." He then sets the scalpel down as if he is bored with the game and goes back to his microscope.

"Leave. I have work to finish."

When he is on the street above the quay, Dubois collapses on a bench. His hands are shaking. He touches his neck. No blood, but he can still feel the cold steel against his throat.

16

Nellie

The police wagon and fiacre behind us carrying Lussac and other officers come to an abrupt halt. I push open a wood flap to find we are in the middle of a commotion in Place de Clichy.

Crowds have overflowed from the Place Blanche carnival to watch a group of chanting men and women standing on a flat bed wagon that has stopped in the middle of the square. It's the same group I saw earlier.

"Anarchists," a prostitute says with disgust.

From the curses hollered back from the crowd and the instant arguments that arise from the girls in the police wagon, I can see everyone has an opinion about whether the country needs another revolution.

Without warning a man steps out of a corner café and hurls a beer bottle at the anarchists. A revolutionary jumps down, fists begin to fly, and in seconds there is bedlam in the square as shouts for revolution resound against shouts for death to revolutionaries.

Our police wagon surges forward, but behind us Lussac and his officers with clubs get out of their carriage to join the *mêlée*. The political controversy remains with us as two prostitutes arguing opposite sides turn to hair pulling.

I sit quietly in my corner as the other girls pull the combatants apart, but words of the revolutionaries stay with me. My days as a factory girl were marked by strikes, injuries to workers, and layoffs. I don't like to think about what happens to families when factories close. Losing one's job—whether it be in Paris, New York, or London—ultimately has one consequence: desperation. Often times, starvation sets in.*

While my heart goes out to the workers, I don't condone violence.

The anarchists are particularly violent in their approach to changing the social system, advocating the extermination of all political leaders in the hope their deaths will cause governments to fall. Yet, when the government falls and the new leadership takes over an interesting phenomena happens—they become what they revolted against.

I still wonder why my man in black wears the red of anarchy. It's a disguise? Or is he an active anarchist?

I ask one of the girls why we're being unloaded at a precinct house and not taken directly to police headquarters.

"We'll be processed here. Only those who can't set bond or who are wanted for other crimes will be taken to the central jail."

It seems only fitting that rain starts falling just before we make it up a set of worn stone steps. A policeman leads us into an austere high-ceilinged room and has us

---

* Poverty, hunger, and the rights of workers were subjects Nellie was particularly sensitive about. Besides many news stories showing the plight of the poor, she dramatized it in fiction. In a poignant scene in her novel, *The Mystery of Central Park*, when her heroine visits the morgue, she sees the body of a streetcar driver who, out of work during a strike, killed himself because his family was starving.—The Editors.

line up to be physically measured by the Bertillon method. I'm familiar with the criminal identification method invented by Alphonse Bertillon when he was a young clerk in the Sûreté. Called "anthropometry," it's a system of body measurements. A surer method would be to photograph suspects, but photography is expensive and time consuming.

As soon as a girl is measured, she goes to another line where an officer at a desk questions her about her charges.

When my turn comes, measurements are taken of my head, feet, two fingers, arm span, forearm, and torso. With fourteen different measurements taken, the odds of any two people having the same exact measurements are nearly three hundred million to one. It's a much more improved system of identification than having criminals line up in front of detectives to see if any of the officers recognize them as past offenders.

Another new criminal identification system, favored by Scotland Yard, is based upon claims that each person's fingerprints are unique. In 1880, Henry Faulds, a Scottish physician, proposed the idea of using fingerprints for identification. Faulds fortuitously became the first person to catch a criminal with fingerprint identification. Working in Tokyo, he identified a thief by fingerprints the man left on a cup. Truly amazing. But it's the anthropometry system that's in use throughout Europe.

As my measurements are taken with a tailor's tape, I make a quick assessment of my predicament. Mr. Pulitzer's heart beats with the same rhythm as the circulation numbers for his newspaper. His heart will turn stone cold when circulation drops because his *girl* reporter is humiliated and ridiculed by other newspapers. Especially when they'll have fun satirizing about "mi'lord" and his burned Long Tom. This bogus arrest will not only severely damage my career, but it will get the biggest laugh from those in newspaper circles who want to see a woman reporter fail. I've got to get out of this mess.

My first concern is how to deal with Chief Inspector Morant. Perhaps I should disarm him with my knowledge of the Sûreté. Its history is a romantic one involving a notorious thief, the Emperor Napoléon, and the first detective agency. It began early in the century when Empress Josephine's necklace, given to her by Napoléon, was stolen.

A thief, Eugène-François Vidocq, was in prison. He convinced the police that the best way to catch a thief was with a thief and made a deal with them—he would recover the necklace in return for a pardon. He recovered the necklace and was permitted to create a new police agency—the *police de sûreté*, the "security police." He organized a network of spies and informers that infiltrated the criminal milieu and brought the first women into police work, including the notorious "Violette," a highly paid prostitute.

Vidocq's colorful life was immortalized—Victor Hugo modeled his relentless policeman, Inspector Javert, in *Les Misérables*, after him; Balzac the criminal genius, Vautrin, in *The Human Comedy*. The first detective story, *The Murders in the Rue Morgue*, by Edgar Allan Poe, was inspired by Vidocq. After leaving the Sûreté, Vidocq opened the world's first private detective agency.

"Name?"

My turn has come at the processing desk.

"Nellie Bly."

The officer quickly checks a list without looking up. "I don't find your name. What are your charges?" He looks up with a deadpan face as if this is the thousandth time today he has asked the question.

"Unlicensed prostitution, but—"

"Yes, yes, I know, you're innocent, they all are. Prior offenses?"

"Of course not."

"Then you may set bond. Do you have five francs?"

"Fi—five francs? Yes, I have it." I quickly glance behind me, fearful that Detective Lussac will walk in at any moment.

The officer scribbles on a piece of paper. "This is your receipt. List your address, sign here. If you fail to appear before the court in three days, you'll be arrested and charged with obstructing the work of the police. Next."

Keeping my face blank and fighting my feet from taking flight, I walk out of the station house like someone trying to make it to a toilet. My mind is reeling. When I reach the street, a carriage pulls up and a middle-aged man with the bearing of a military officer steps out. He's dressed in top hat, tails, white tie, and carrying an ivory handled cane. He stares at my harlot's dress as I sweep by him to step into the carriage he just vacated.

"Pardon," I mumble, keeping my head down.

"Mademoiselle." He tips his hat and proceeds to go up the steps.

As my carriage pulls away another carriage draws up and I hear excited British voices. I lean out the window to look—*big mistake*. Eye contact is made with the mi'lord who has the burned Long Tom. I quickly stick my head back in the carriage.

"The Grand Hotel," I tell the driver. "*Please hurry*, my . . . my baby is sick. I'll double your fare"

He gives me a dubious look but gets the carriage moving. As with a hanson cab, the driver of a fiacre is mounted at the rear of the two-wheel carriage with the reins going over the roof. A trapdoor on the roof is used to speak to passengers. He leaves the trapdoor open and stares down at me as if he thinks I'm going to steal the seat.

I smile up at him. "Can you imagine? I dressed as a prostitute for the fair and was arrested by mistake."

His expression doesn't give me confidence that he believes me and I change the subject.

"Who was that distinguished gentleman you dropped off?"

"Monsieur Morant."

He confirms my suspicion.

"Chief Inspector of the Sûreté. He always gets his man." Once again he gives me a look of doubt. "Or woman."

17

As my carriage rumbles along, I think about my next move. I'm a foreigner wanted by the police. Short of me being guillotined, my consequences will be grave. I could lose my career and freedom. Not even the influential Mr. Pulitzer can intervene if I'm tried for flaunting French justice.

I have only one reasonable recourse—to leave the country at once.

"Pull over here," I tell the driver, even though we are several blocks away from my hotel.

After doubling the fare and adding an appropriate gratuity sacrosanct to cabbies everywhere, I enter an all-night telegraph office and send a telegram to my hotel instructing them to arrange passage for me on the morning train to Le Havre and the New York steamer leaving in two days. I also instruct them to pack my bags and forward same to the station.

Satisfied that I have taken the proper steps, I engage another cab to take me back up the Butte to Place Pigalle. My destination is farther up the hill, but I'll tread the rest of the way on Shanks' mare rather than risk leaving a trail for the police to follow.

Obviously I have no intention of abandoning my investigation. It's not only against my principles, but failure is unacceptable. The telegram is a ruse for the police. Since Lussac and the assiduous Inspector Morant know the charges against me are trumped up, I suspect they'll be satisfied if they believe I've left the city with my tail between my legs.

As for the slasher . . . I'll just have to take my chances and pray the gods will continue to watch over me.

Checking into another hotel is out of the question. I'd have to show my passport and use my real name, not to mention my clothes will arouse suspicion. Even though I've brushed most of the dirt from my black dress and my heavy shawl covers it, it still won't fare well under hotel lights. The lack of luggage will also draw suspicion.

I have no choice but to find alternative accommodations. I know of a place that's available, even though it's not to my liking. David Bailey, Mr. Jones's replacement as the *World*'s Paris correspondent, receives a stingy stipend that provides for a Montmartre garret. Since he is on assignment in French Algeria covering a rebellion, the room is mine if I want it.

I had visited the building my first day in the city, but after learning I'd have to climb six flights of stairs to an attic room and that the building lacks a convenience facility—I would have to lug my bedpan down six flights of stairs each day to empty it in a hole above the sewer—I declined the room, sight unseen.

Knowing Paris is an ancient city adds to its charm, except when one considers the lack of elevators and toilet facilities in its tenements and public buildings. The hotel I was staying at is considered the lap of luxury because on every floor, for each ten rooms, there is a water closet. I'm going to miss that place.

Despite the lateness of the hour, Place Pigalle has not gone to sleep. Lounging in doorways and leaning against buildings are prostitutes . . . waiting for customers. As the shifts change at the Les Halles slaughterhouses, workers covered with blood and mud, puffing on cheap cigarettes and keeping warm with wine, will come into the square to buy a few moments of easy pleasure.

Above the Rue de Abbesses there are no gas street lamps in sight, just complete darkness. I pull my shawl tighter and trudge up a narrow alley and steep, slippery stone stairways. I really hate being alone in the dark and pick up my pace. I just want to be in a bed, all nice and cozy and warm and away from any monsters.

When I arrive at Mr. Bailey's tenement, I take a moment to compose my thoughts. I know my entrance will be explosive.

Between ten o'clock at night and six o'clock in the morning you must contact the building concierge for entry. The method is crude, but effective: one pulls on a rope at the front door which rings a bell in the concierge's apartment above. As might be expected, concierges are not fond of having their sleep disturbed by late arriving residents. And I'm told these apartment house managers have an evil reputation in the city.

Parisians complain endlessly of the doings of concierges when you run out of favor with them. If you're out, your friends can be sent up several flights of stairs to discover you're not home—or sent away, assured that you're out, when in fact you're awaiting them. Letters go astray. Malicious rumors about you are spread around the neighborhood.

I had the displeasure of meeting Mr. Bailey's concierge, Madame Malon, during my earlier visit. She was not a pleasant encounter even during daylight hours. Her disposition reminds me of buttermilk—slightly sour. In truth, her pale face is uneven and spotted like buttermilk. I dread to think what I'm going to encounter when I awaken her tonight for admission after midnight—I'll be slapping Medusa in the face.

The only thing that warms the coddles of a concierge's heart, besides the untimely death of a tenant whose apartment can be rented for more money, is demanding gratuities from late arriving tenants. Tonight, I'm sure I will be paying dearly.

I pull the rope and wait for the ill wind. A moment passes before the wooden shutters to the window directly above the door fly open and Medusa pokes her head of snakes out.

"*What do you want?*"

"We spoke the other day. I'm authorized to stay in Monsieur Bailey's room."

"Go away before I call the police!"

The shutters slam shut. With the hardest pull I can muster, I jerk the rope three times. The shutters are thrown open with a vengeance. Water comes out the window and I stumble back. I see red. If I wasn't so desperate, I'd declare war on this monster. Instead, I hold up a franc. "A franc for the inconvenience, Madam."

"Three," she spats.

"Two. And I will not report you to the police for collecting rent while Mr. Bailey is serving the French Army in Algeria."

I have no idea what Mr. Bailey is doing in North Africa, but I have heard that concierges fiercely guard their financial records from officialdom, so the threat slips naturally off of my tongue.

"Let her in, you old bitch, so we can sleep!" a voice yells from the building across the way.

"Ten sous, give her no more, that's all she charges the others!" a young female voice shouts from above.

The door latch controlled by another rope in the concierge's apartment scrapes open and I hurry inside. The entryway is utterly dark and harbors stale cooking smells. And the last person who emptied their chamber pot failed to close the door to the closet that houses the sewer opening and I get an unpleasant whiff of sewer stink as I go up the stairs. I hold my breath. The smell is awful.

LA CONCIERGE

A pale gaslight glows on the concierge's landing and another is farther up the stairway. Glassless window openings are on every landing in theory that they will bring light and air, but on foggy, rainy nights they provide nothing but dampness and chill. I shiver going up the steps, certain that it is colder inside than out.

Madame Malon is waiting at the top of the landing, her pudgy white face twisted in a menacing scowl. In hopes of avoiding any confrontation, I employ my most ladylike smile and the two francs. Frankly, my desire is to throw her down the stairs.

She slams a police ledger book on the railing. "Write your name and sign. Your presence will be reported to the police."

I know for certain it won't. Reporting a temporary tenant will only get attention from the police and tax collector—something no concierge desires. I manage to find an empty space and scribble, "Nellie Moreno, Havana, Cuba." She snaps the ledger shut, begrudgingly hands me a key, lowers her brows and glares at me.

"No noise, no men. The water pump and sewer hole are on the first level and cost an extra ten sous a week."

I throw her a sweet, "*Buenos noches, Señora,*" as she waddles back into her apartment. She mutter's something ugly about foreigners as she slams the door shut so hard it blows the gas-lamp out, leaving me in complete darkness.

So starts the beginning of a wonderful relationship.

18

I wearily make my way up the cold gloomy staircase to Mr. Bailey's garret which, like the rest of Montmartre, is designed for mountain goats. I pause before the final ascent and will my body to continue.

The garret, as expected, is small, but I'm pleased to find it's clean—a *big bug-a-boo* with me. I hate messy, dirty places. The room has a plain wooden table with two chairs and a potbellied stove holding a copper tea kettle. Three wood shelves above the stove are filled with dishes, drinking cups, a cast-iron pot and pan, and a small galvanized pail holding silverware. A huge ceramic pitcher sits in the center of the table.

Against the right wall is a day-bed that looks like its being used as a couch. On the other side of the room is a step-up to a space holding a wrought-iron bed, a nightstand, an armoire, and a wooden filing cabinet.

A "close-stool" cleverly designed to look like a stack of very wide books on four legs, what the French call a *chaise percée*, or "chair with a hole," is next to the filing cabinet. Inside is a pewter chamber pot. The clever design makes it no less repulsive to carry the pot down six flights of stairs to dump. Mr. Bailey has cleverly placed a basket of potpourri under it. He must hate foul odors like I do.

HOURS GO BY and my mind refuses to surrender to sleep. Even counting sheep doesn't help. I plop myself on the couch and start a list—a habit acquired from my mother. First, Dr. Blum knows I'm here. He knows what I look like. I, on the other hand, am wanted by the police. I don't know Paris. I really don't know what Dr. Blum looks like and I can't go around chasing every man that makes the hair on the back of my neck rise. I need help.

This is gong to be a new experience for me—having a partner.

Even Mr. Pulitzer finally gave up on trying to "partner" me with another reporter. But I am going to have to bite the bullet and get myself a partner.

Which puts me to the big question: *who?*

One name crowded my thoughts.

19

Perun

Evette wasn't surprised when she heard the knocking on her door past midnight. Perun came to her at all hours. But tonight, even though he paid well—very well—she was tired. She didn't feel like entertaining him. So she sat on her bed and didn't answer the door. She hoped if she didn't answer, he'd think she was out working the streets and leave.

He kept knocking—harder and louder. She felt the anger mounting in each knock and knew she had to answer. If he found out she was there—well, there were rumors about what he did when he was crossed. She opened the door.

"What took you so long?" He walked in and began undressing.

"Perun, I can't tonight. I'm sick." As soon as she said the words she regretted them. She saw the back of his muscles tense and immediately tried to rectify it. "I want to, I really do, but I'm not feeling well."

He turned around and looked at her, "Evette, come here."

His voice sent a chill down her spine.

She slowly came to him. She flinched as he put his hands to her face.

"You don't look sick to me."

"I . . . I feel sick." She realized her answer was lame and it really didn't make any difference how she felt. He wanted her and he always got what he wanted one way or another. "But, for you . . ." She started to unbutton his pants.

"Evette," grabbing her hands, "I'm no longer in the mood."

His voice frightened her. She had to do something, so she kissed him, long and hard. He let go of her hands and she unbuttoned his pants as she kissed him. She palmed his hard cock. He pushed her down and then held her shoulders so she couldn't come up.

She knew what she had to do.

"PERUN . . ."

He kept dressing and didn't answer her. She sat on the bed and fiddled with the sheet.

"Did Simone tell you where she was going after seeing you earlier?"

Her question stopped him on his way to the door. Without turning around he asked, "Why do you want to know?"

"Because we were to meet up at a café and she never showed. It's not like her."

"I wouldn't worry. She probably met a man." He started to leave, then stopped. Once again he didn't turn around as he spoke, "Come here, I have something for you."

Evette eagerly came to him, hoping he remembered he hadn't paid her.

He reached in his pocket and brought out a scalpel.

20

Nellie

I've never been one to be in a sweet disposition when I wake in the mornings, especially when I've had broken sleep. This morning I'm in a particularly dark mood.

I made a decision of who my partner will be. Sleep from that point on was basically fruitless because I hated my solution. But I have no other options. The only candidate that finally came to me is a man I don't trust.

His name is recognized throughout the civilized world, although I've heard that some malady of body or soul has caused him to retreat from public attention. Without him knowing who I am, I have weaved a tangled web involving him and now I need to turn it to my advantage.

My interest in him was piqued when Mr. Jones, the foreign correspondent, told me about a bizarre incident in which the adult nephew of this noted Frenchman stumbled onto a scene in an alley in which a man was attacking a woman with a knife. The man fled and was never caught, but the nephew became obsessed that the slasher had been his famous uncle . . . and acted out his fixation by shooting the uncle. Fortunately, the man was only wounded.

The nephew is Gaston Verne and his uncle is Jules Verne, the world-famous writer.* Like so many people, I grew up reading his fantastic tales like *Twenty Thousand Leagues Under the Sea* and *Around the World in Eighty Days*.

Staring at a picture of Jules Verne after I arrived in Paris, it struck me that a few alterations by an artist would create a reasonable likeness of the slasher: a box hat, round eyeglasses, shaggy hair, and beard. Of course, the same would be true of the pictures of most bearded men, but it was Mr. Verne's picture that I had when I found a street artist to make the alterations. I had copies of the finished picture printed so I could distribute them to prostitutes.

When I nosed around about Mr. Verne's movements, I was unable to piece together a four-month absence from his home that would have permitted him to play the role of Dr. Blum at the asylum—but unable to eliminate him, either.

At the moment my interest is not in establishing that Verne is the elusive Dr. Blum, but in having him as an ally. And I chose him for two reasons: He is a very important man, literally an institution in the country . . . and I have a hole card to use in making him help me.

I prefer to think of my action not as blackmail, but as a subtle form of persuasion in a situation where the end justifies the means. Not exactly the best way to begin a partnership, but making war on evil is not a game for the timid.

---

* Gaston fired the shot outside right after Jules left his own home. The bullet initially missed Jules, but it ricocheted and struck his left leg, seriously wounding him. Jules carried the pain and a limp for the rest of his life. Gaston had been employed by the Foreign Service at the time. Police attributed the shooting to a mental defect. Gaston was institutionalized after the stranger-than-fiction incident.—The Editors.

The morning sky does nothing to help sweeten my disposition—it's grey and heavy. But I shake off my inclination to crawl back in bed and cover my head for I have rivers to swim, castle walls to scale, mountains to move, and an immediate need for a bath and fresh clothes. It would be very disrespectful of me to approach one of the most famous men in France in a harlot's dress that has recently rolled in a fresh grave.

I'm lucky to find a cape in the armoire. It will do to hide my dress while I go shopping. Mr. Bailey must only be a couple of inches taller than me; his cape doesn't touch the floor when I put it on.

It's my good fortune not to run into Madame Malon on the way out—this is a good omen. Maybe today will work out.

Le Passage, the alley outside, is a busy little thoroughfare of pedestrians and small shops. An old gentleman across the street beating his rug from his window doesn't miss a beat as he yells down, "*Bonjour, Laitier,*" to the milkman below who methodically deposits milk bottles at each doorstep. The milkman doesn't even look up, but returns, "Bonjour, Louis." It must be a daily ritual.

A young girl pushes a handcart loaded with bread down the cobblestone lane, while an older woman opens a flower stand. Concierges drag trash cans out into the court, as droves of ragpickers fall upon them like rats.

These gleaners are a queer lot. Individuals and families each have a distinct purpose. One appears to be taking nothing but bones, glass, and crockery, while another is sifting the ashes for coal; one is taking only paper and rags; another old shoes and hats, and so on, moving from can to can in a hypnotic movement, none interfering with any of the others.

Where the steps end and a wider street begins, small shops and many more street vendors appear—a man roasting chestnuts over hot coals in a metal barrel, a women serving crisp brown *frites*, deep-fried. From a girl with a handcart, I purchase a *café au lait*, dark roasted coffee with hot milk, the favorite breakfast drink of Parisians and a taste I've developed. I get directions from her to an establishment that provides baths and the location of clothing merchants.

"*Un bain*, Mademoiselle? *Mais bien sûr*! I'll make the bath at five o'clock this afternoon," the bath man says, quite obligingly.

"But I must have the bath this morning. I have a very important luncheon date."

"Impossible, Mademoiselle, it requires time to prepare, but it'll be superb, this bath."

"Nothing is impossible." And I slip him an extra two francs to prove it.

From a specialty store, I purchase muslin drawers, chemises, and a corset cover. I choose a used-clothing vendor for my outer garments because it will take too long to have clothes made. With adequate time I might be able to locate shops selling ready-made new clothes in a city the size of Paris, but my need is too urgent.

Fashion, of course, needs no translation. The French haute couture dominates fashion in both Europe and America, and a woman must stay aware of the current trend from Paris. I personally thank the gods that the horrid rear bustle is going out, but a whale-boned corset is required for a fashionable—but anatomically improbable—thin waist, something I refuse to wear. I don't care if my waist is not nineteen niches. At least I can breathe.

I'm surprised to find the used goods are of very good quality.

"Cheap clothing wears out too quickly to be resold," the shopkeeper tells me.

With little fuss I'm able to purchase a dark green suit of dense cheviot wool consisting of a jacket with a rolling collar and puffed sleeves and a full skirt of the same wool. Both garments are lined with black silk serge.

As a backup I buy a flared skirt of dark grey tweed, with two narrow bands of black braid near the hem. It's a serviceable length for walking, just clearing the ground. A white waist shirt and simple black silk clubhouse tie, a tailored jacket of black wool, with long lapels and puff sleeves that gather at the top, complement the skirt. A hat of black lace covering a wire frame with a handsome bunch of silk flowers and pleated ribbon completes my clothing needs and suits my purpose perfectly—it has a Malines net veiling which I can hide behind when needed. Thank goodness I don't need shoes. My black, high-top, laced walking shoes with low heels are quite satisfactory.

I gather up my purchases and make my way back up the hill to the garret.

"MADEMOISELLE! YOUR BATH!"

I just finished putting away my purchases when a pair of legs with a zinc bathtub on top of them appears at my door. How he made it up the narrow steps is a mystery. Another man behind him carries a cylinder of water and bathing accessories.

The tub is placed next to the potbellied stove and a white linen lining is adjusted. Sundry towels and a big bathing sheet, to wrap myself in after the ordeal, are miraculously produced. Then the process of filling the tub begins: two pails, two men, and countless trips down to a handcart that holds a heated tank of water. When it is half-full, hot coals are placed in a pull-out drawer underneath the tub.

The expense of three francs, which I figure to be about

sixty cents, seems more than reasonable, considering the flight of stairs they had to endure, so I give them a generous tip. Arrangements are then made for them to pick up the tub in two hours.

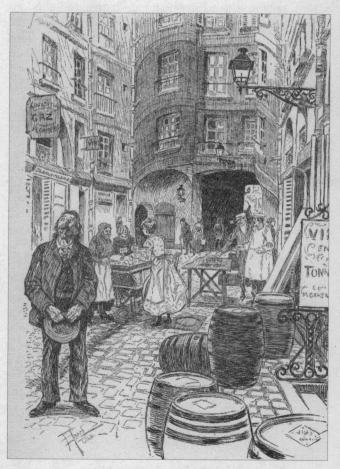

OUR COURTYARD

I can't get into the tub fast enough. *I love soaking in hot bath water.* For me, it's as close to heaven as I'll get. Personally, I've never understood the great number of people who believe that regular bathing is unhealthy. Many Europeans don't bathe fully more than a few times a year, relying instead upon sponge baths, and children often do not experience a full bath until their early teens.

I read an article in *Le Figaro* about an actress who boasted about having taken only two baths a year in order to protect her skin. She received a bar of soap on her birthday along with a note from a drama critic stating that the bar should last the rest of her life.

All too soon the tub men return and I prepare myself for my conquest of a famous man.

21

Café Procope is dimly lit with just a few oil lamps, as if the owner doesn't want to let the world find its way in. I pause in the entryway, soaking in the atmosphere and the strong smell of *café noir*.

Founded a little over two hundred years ago by a Sicilian nobleman, Francesco Procopio dei Coltelli, the place is haunted by the ghosts of literary and political giants who breathed history into its walls.

Procopio provided a place where people of the arts—writers, poets, and philosophers—could work in peace and tranquility while sipping coffee, thus establishing the very first *café* in Paris, the French word for coffee.

In a city where cafés are notorious for blazing with light, noise, and glitter, the Procope maintains the modesty of a quainter and more illustrious age. One can image Ben Franklin, on whose death the café was draped in black, sitting under flickering candlelight, spies and informers lurking about, as he negotiated a secret treaty that would bring French soldiers and sailors to the aid of the colonies in their revolt against the British. Bonaparte, young and unknown, left his hat as security for payment of a drink, having left his pouch at home.

When I visited the café earlier to quietly observe my prey at his table, I was told that the table—topped with dark, reddish marble with pinkish, white veins—had been Voltaire's; a man who prized clear thinking and crusaded against tyranny, bigotry, and cruelty while he drank coffee and argued about life, liberty, and happiness with Denis Diderot, the chief editor of the *Encyclopédie* more than a century ago.

The café staff must know who their distinguished guest is even though he has shaved his beard to hide his identity. The lack of beard provides anonymity and wipes years from his age. I believe he's in his late fifties or perhaps early sixties, presenting a handsome maturity. At the moment he's bent over sheets of foolscap, completely engrossed in his writing. A cup of coffee, a small bottle of vin rouge, hunks of bread, and a plate of cheese are positioned in a corner of the table.

I often find myself attracted to older men. My mother claims it's because of the early loss of my distinguished father, whom I loved dearly. I also think my attraction to older men is because they know what they want in life.

The maitre d' gives me a professional smile. "Table, Mademoiselle?"

"Please inform Monsieur Verne I wish to speak to him."

His eyebrows arch. "*Pardon?*"

"Jules Verne, the gentleman at Voltaire's table. Please tell him that Nellie Brown of New York wishes to speak to him."

The man gets that insufferable look of contempt that only waiters in the greatest city in the world can affect. "I am afraid you are—"

"I know who the gentleman is. Please give him my message." I slap my gloves impatiently in my palm and look him straight in the eyes. I have a great deal to do and have no time for pretense.

The maitre d' leaves with a subtle, but intentional huff and huddles with Verne. The great man looks across the room at me. I meet his eye and give him a small nod and smile. More huddling occurs before the maitre d' struts back to me. I start for Mr. Verne's table and am stopped by a firm grip on my arm.

"I beg your pardon, Monsieur."

With great delight the maitre d' proclaims, "The gentleman does not wish to be disturbed." He propels me to the door. "He suggests you flatter someone else with your unsolicited attentions."

"You have no idea who—"

"My instructions from Monsieur are to call a gendarme and have you taken to Salpêtrière Hospital if you do not leave quietly."

Salpêtrière! It's a madhouse with no worse a reputation than Blackwell's Island. For Mr. Verne to have threatened

INTERIOR OF THE CAFÉ PROCOPE

to have me institutionalized as if I were a crazy girl with romantic intentions is intolerable.

"Tell Monsieur Verne he will regret not speaking to me about Gaston."

I leave in a tempest rather than inviting the police.

To think that the man who wrote stories I thrilled to in my childhood would treat me so callously . . . he'll pay, that promise I make to myself. When the time comes, Monsieur Verne will be at my feet begging for mercy.

As I flag down a fiacre, I chuckle without humor. In a sense I've already started getting my revenge. Wait till he finds out a likeness of him has been passed out on the streets connecting him to a mad killer. He will have a heart attack. I no longer feel guilt, I only hope I will have the entire Atlantic Ocean between us by the time the man discovers my machinations.

With that thought, I direct the cabby to take me to Pigalle Hospital.

22

I have the cab driver drop me a block from the hospital. Pigalle Hospital is three stories of red brick and twelve pane windows. "Hospitals are only for the poor," my mother said when I was a child. What she meant was that doctors usually come to one's home. A doctor carries most of the tools of his trade in his black bag, so there is little a hospital has in the way of special equipment to offer a patient, unless one of the few surgeries offered are necessary. The poor and downtrodden end up crowded together in sick wards because they can't afford home visits by a doctor.

As I approach the building on foot, I find myself hesitating. I lost my father at the age of six and it was a life-altering change for me. I watched a strong, healthy, wonderful man shrivel up and die within months and I couldn't understand why and I hated everyone for letting God take him away from me. That was my first taste of death and I haven't liked the flavor since.

A CROWDED RECEPTION area with an odor of sickness greets me. The large room looks like a shelter for the poor and homeless. Two harried male clerks—one younger and obviously new at the job because he keeps asking the older man for advice—tries to accommodate everyone with little success.

If I wait my turn I'll be parked in the reception area for hours, surrounded by wrenching sickness and sorrow. I boldly cut through the crowd at the desk and in a firm voice demand, "Doctor Dubois?"

The older clerk doesn't even look up from writing down a woman's symptoms. He points down the hall. "Surgical ward. Grab a sponge."

"Merci." There's no sense in asking him what the sponge is for, he's gone back to his world of organized confusion.

The entrance to the surgical ward has large double-doors with a basin full of vinegar-smelling liquid and sponges next to them. The doors fly open and a nurse bolts out. She takes a sponge away from her face and drops it in the basin.

"Doctor Dubois?" I query.

She points behind her. "Down the corridor."

The stench that escapes from the corridor when she opened the doors reveals why a vinegar sponge is necessary. I grab one and enter into a long, drab, empty hallway with doors on both sides.

I choose the third door on my right and flinch back as soon as I open it. Rows of beds fill the small room, with barely enough space to walk between them. There are three and four people to a bed, the feet of one to the head of another. In the bed closest to the door a pale child lies beside a grey-haired man who appears dead. The man's eyes are wide open, staring straight up, never blinking, never moving while a fly is busy gathering something from his teeth. On the other side of the child lie a man burning in the delirium of fever. The fourth person is a man with a terrible disease of the skin; he tears at his skin with furious nails.

I quickly back out of the room, holding the vinegar sponge tighter to my nose. I'm saved from another sick ward as Dr. Dubois comes out of a room.

"Dr. Dubois, may I speak with you? We met last night at the cemetery."

His eyebrows shoot up. "Ah yes, the prostitute . . . who is not a prostitute."

"Exactly. I, uh, suppose the police told you who I really am."

"Yes, a reporter. I have not had an opportunity to talk to the detective again, but his superior, Chief Inspector Morant, has sent word that he will see me today."

"Doctor, I need your help desperately. I'm in terrible straights. I'm a foreigner, and I'm helpless." I must work fast, before the Chief Inspector arrives. I hope saving a damsel in distress will appeal to the romantic nature Frenchmen are famous for. It's obvious that he doesn't know I was arrested and escaped last night.

"I don't understand, Mademoiselle. How can I help you?"

"May I speak to you for a moment? In private . . . please?"

"I'm sorry, I have my rounds—"

"It'll only take a moment, it's a matter of extreme importance. If I tell you it's a matter of life or death, it's no exaggeration."

"Well . . . I suppose I could spare a moment. There's no real privacy in the hospital, but we can use this room."

The stench in the room is worse than the smell from Madam Malon's convenience hole. It smells more of decaying matter, the sort of odor I experienced at the German doctor's shack on the pier. I envision Josephine and have to fight myself from leaving. It gives me the willies.

Hospital supplies, brooms, mops, and buckets are stacked along one wall. In the center of the room is a table with a microscope, metal and glass tubes, various containers of chemicals, and other equipment, along with a coffeepot on an oil burner and some cups. How anyone could take coffee from a room with this smell is beyond me.

On the floor underneath the table is a small wood crate with an *Alexandrie Egypte* shipping label. To my right is a set of white curtains. I can't help but wonder what's behind it.

"As I told you last night at the graveyard, I'm certain that the woman you inspected was killed by a slasher. He's killing women and the police won't help me find him. Now I'm afraid he's after me. I have no one to turn to but you."

The young doctor gawks at me.

"If you will listen to my story, you will see there's more than my own sanity at issue."

I quickly tell him about the murder of Josephine and my suspicions of Dr. Blum at Blackwell's Island. He never takes his eyes off of me as I relate the tale. Perhaps he's decided that I am in fact a madwoman and will lunge at him at any moment with a knife.

"Amazing," is all he says after I finish.

"I need your help in finding the killer of my friend. I swear my only interest is in stopping him from murdering more women. Will you help me?"

"I don't know what I can do to assist you. I'm a doctor, not a policeman."

I take a deep breath and decide to go one step further, a step that might take me straight to the police.

"Doctor, the police believe my accusations about the

slasher being in Paris will hurt the Exposition. Last night I booked passage on a steamship to America. They believe I've left. Please don't give away the fact I'm still here. I need time."

"Mademoiselle, I . . . I can't do that, it would be most unusual."

"Not really. I'm not asking you to lie to the police, merely not to volunteer any information about me. They won't ask if you've seen me, they believe I'm gone."

He shrugs. "Well, I suppose I have no duty revealing you were here, if no one asks."

"Exactly. Now, Doctor, did you do an autopsy on the woman found at the graveyard last night?"

"Yes, this morning."

"Did you find any signs of violence on her?"

"None."

"None at all?"

"Nothing. Her internal organs had decayed and rotted in an extremely short time span. This is a symptom of that strange malady called Black Fever."

"But I saw the woman minutes before she was dead. She didn't appear sick."

"The sickness was inside." He hesitates and looks down as if he is contemplating telling me something of great importance. "Are you aware of what microbes are?"

"Some sort of germ. Doctor Pasteur studies them."

"Yes, little creatures so small we can't see them without a microscope. Do you know anything about the Black Fever?"

"Not really."

"Well, it would take millions of them to cover your fingernail. The only way to know their presence is by the darkness of the blood. It turns black as the microbes consume the oxygen that gives our blood its rich, red appearance. In a way they kill themselves."

"I don't understand."

"They can only live and grow in the presence of oxygen—the blood in our bodies. Once inside they grow and divide. One bacterium becomes two, then four, eight, doubling every twenty or thirty minutes. Billions of them crawl into the lungs, heart, liver, and kidneys. They even make their way to the head, infiltrating the fleshy membrane that encases the brain. Everywhere they go, they multiply, doubling and redoubling, untold billions, a wildfire of growth. It's hard to believe, but if the food supply was unlimited, the incredible doubling process would create a mass of microbes the size of the planet Earth in a few days. Fortunately for us, our bodies die from them eating our oxygen and then they die also."

"That's incredible."

"Yes. As you can see from the microscope here, I have an interest in them. In fact, I have the only microscope in the hospital." He proudly gestures at the instrument. "Because of her strange symptoms and lack of physical trauma, this is a case in which I suspected that a microbe was the villain. But in checking her blood and tissue under my microscope, I detected none, probably because they're too small to see even with my scope."

"Do you have a theory as to what caused her death?"

"Of course. Her condition was derived from miasma."

"Sewer fumes?"

"Yes. Paris has over two million people. Catacombed throughout the city is hundreds of kilometers of tunnels carrying rivers of sewage." He stands up and paces our little space. "Sewage creates noxious gases that can kill when inhaled."

"But all big cities have—"

"Yes, yes, but no doubt a unique combination of virulent matter has come together in the area where this prostitute lived."

"And where might that be?"

"La Poivrière, the Pepper Pot district, one of the areas in which the poor are compressed like Norwegian sardines."

"So you are saying sewer smells kill. But even as I stand here, everything in this room seems to stink of the sewer."

He smiles, as if I made a point. "That's because of the decay."

"Decay?"

"The decay of her internal organs." He pulls back the curtain.

A naked body, cut wide open, is on the table. I stand paralyzed, as if my feet are glued to the floor, staring at the body. It's Josephine all over again and my head swoons and the room spins. The next thing I know he has my arm and leads me into the hallway. After the terrible stench in that room, the hallway smells fresh. He apologizes profusely as I lean against the wall and regain my breath.

"I deal with death so often it's of no matter to me."

"Doctor, is that—the body—?"

"Yes, as I said, I did an autopsy."

"You're saying this woman died from sewer fumes?"

"That is my conclusion, yes."

"Did you find any marks on her body, like a cut or scratch?"

"No."

"How about a needle mark, something, anything?"

"Needle marks? . . . No. Why do you ask?"

"Because I still have a hard time believing she died from sewer fumes. I saw her. She was healthy. Maybe she died from a poison of some sort?"

"Poison?" He looks at me like I lost my mind. "Mademoiselle, as I explained to you, she might have appeared healthy to you, a layperson—but she wasn't. All the signs point to miasma."

"What was her name?

"Simone Doche. Why do you ask?"

"Out of respect. I saw her alive and hate to keep referring to her as just another dead body." I think for a moment. "This Black Fever, is it still raging in the Pepper Pot?"

"Yes, but she could have picked it up anywhere."

He pulls out his pocket watch and frowns as he stares at the time. "Mademoiselle, you should leave. I expect Monsieur Chief Inspector at any moment."

My heart leaps to my throat. I forgot about the police official's promised visit. "Yes, yes . . . I have one more favor to ask. Her home address."

"Mademoiselle, do not even think of—"

"Please, I must hurry."

23

Dr. Dubois insists on guiding me to the hospital's rear entrance where bodies in gunny sacks on the loading platform are being loaded onto a funeral wagon. "Paupers who died of the fever," he says.

I hurry by the impoverished dead with a heavy heart, knowing that but for the grace of God go any of us. After flagging down a carriage, my respectable clothes receive a quick once over after I provide the address.

"Mademoiselle, that is in the Poivrière."

"*Oui*, Monsieur, I do charity work."

"*Mon Dieu*! In the Poivrière? Take care, fair dame, that your good work does not kill you."

As the carriage rumbles along, the driver expounds on a multitude of reasons why a "dame," a lady, should not go to La Poivrière, the Pepper Pot district. He doesn't know that I am not unfamiliar with tough neighborhoods. I've done stories on New York's skid rows of cheap cafés, flophouses, saloons, pawnshops, and dance halls—more appropriately called flesh halls—patronized by criminals and derelicts. The worst of Paris cannot be any more disagreeable than the Bowery and Hell's Kitchen.

I have to admit, the best reason for staying away from

the Pepper Pot was the one given by Dr. Dubois—the dreaded fever gripping the city might still be brutalizing this area. Still, I cannot let fear of a contagion keep me away.

My gut feeling is that Simone Doche knew the slasher for more than the few minutes preceding her death. When I close my eyes and relive the scene at the street carnival, I remember she waved to him as she started toward him. It appeared to be a wave of acknowledgment. Had he befriended her, as he had Josephine? If he had, Simone might have someone—a friend, roommate, neighbor, someone she confided in, like Josephine did with me. Someone I can talk to.

No matter what Dr. Dubois says, I refuse to believe she died from sewer fumes. If she had the fever, she would have looked ill, not strutting about, healthy as a horse only minutes before her death. What could this madman be up to? A new, strange puzzle has emerged and my intuition is screaming that the game he plays has taken on a wicked twist . . . but what?

The carriage stops in front of a tenement and the driver indicates this is the address I gave him. I no sooner step off the carriage after paying when it occurs to me to ask him to wait, but he's already hurrying his horses on.

Down the street, two men come out of a building carrying a body rolled up in heavy cloth. My knees turn weak at the thought that I might be breathing in deadly sickness, but I remind myself there are other people on the street breathing the same air and they aren't dead, or at least not yet.

The street maintenance crews don't favor the area anymore than cabbies—the pavement is pockmarked with ruts and mud holes. Buildings are cracked, trim is often crooked or hanging precariously. Broken windows are stuffed with cloth or haphazardly boarded. In the block where I stand are two taverns, a wine shop, and one small store that sells vegetables and meat—a three to one ratio of demon spirits to food.

The men and women on the street look defeated by life. The stares I get from the men are both crafty and angry and I clutch my purse tighter. These aren't the poor working people I toiled beside in Pittsburgh; they're notches below the working class—performers of odd jobs, small crimes, beggars, and ragpickers. Clothing on both sexes is coarse and worn; shoes are mostly sabots of the cheapest, stiffest leather.

The black flag of anarchy hangs from several apartment windows along the street.

Places evoke feelings in us. I sense sorrow and suffering, anguish and anger. Poverty, strong drink, and violent emotions have left their mark on this street.

At the entrance of Simone's apartment building a little girl of four or five plays with a dirty doll. Her mother sits at the foot of the steps, humming a lullaby while she rocks a baby in arms. She coughs in the baby's face before looking up at me.

"A few sous, *s'il vous plaît*, for my baby." Her plea for a few pennies for her baby brings me to a dead halt.

The little girl skips toward me with a big, happy grin. She might be physically tainted by life, but in her eyes and smile I can see her soul is still pure. Her nose is running and she takes her tiny hand and wipes it before holding it out to me. Her shoeless little feet are hard, crusty, and dirty. I doubt if she's ever worn shoes. Her dress is torn and as vile as her feet. She's skinny, that pathetic emaciation of a gutter child.

I have an urge to pick her up and take her home to bathe, clothe, and feed. She's a victim of unfortunate luck, a bad hand dealt by those mischievous Dark Sisters the ancient Greeks call the Fates, as is her mother and baby sister, for I am certain they all have the influenza and will soon be dead. My heart breaks and I do the only thing I can at this time—I grab money from my purse and give it to her, certain that there's enough for the little family to eat well for a week, and saddened that probably most of it will go for drink.

The entryway is even dirtier than the street outside. The smell is cheap and basic—cooking smells of rancid meat and rotted vegetables mixed in with an odor left by people without soap and hot water. A dungy odor, soiled and unsanitary. To my dismay the building is five stories and Simone's lodgings are on the top floor.

It's uncanny, but during moments like this when I doubt my courage and have feelings of hesitation, for some inexplicable reason my feet have a mind of their own and take the steps one after another.

Coarse laughter coming from men on a floor above floats down as I climb the steps. When I reach the fourth floor I identify the source of the laughter as coming from a flat in which the door is open. The laughter of the men makes my heart race. It's the same laughter of my stepfather coming home after a night out with his drinking pals, disturbing the house with his mean spirit. Often these disturbances would end up with an explosion at my mother, causing me to rush from my bed to make sure he didn't hurt her.

A man appears at the open door. He's almost as dirty as the little girl outside, unshaven, hair uncut and unkempt falls from under a sailor's cap that's greasier than the hair. His neckerchief is stained from sweat and grime, giving only the barest hint that it was once red. He has the look of a street thug, the breed Parisians call apaches.

"Eh, where you going, mon dame?"

I resist the urge to respond, for I'm sure he'd interpret

it as a signal of interest in him. Instead, I quicken my ascent of the stairs. On the fifth floor I find Simone's flat and knock several times. No response. I knock again, harder, causing the door to slip open a crack. Pushing it wider, I poke my head in. "Bonjour?"

It's a large single room. On one side is a messy kitchen counter with opened shelves and a wood stove, on the other side are two small rumpled beds separated by a worn sheet.

"Hello . . . Bonjour?" Two steps into the room I stop. Mother of God!

On the floor next to a bed is the naked body of a woman. Blood is everywhere. She's been butchered, laid open from between her breasts to her female parts. I back out, gagging, biting my fist to keep from screaming.

"What's the matter?"

I let out a scream. It's the lout from downstairs.

"What is it?"

I dart by him, rushing down the steps, nearly losing my footing. My dress prohibits my feet from keeping up with my panic and I stumble and grab the railing. As soon as I get my balance again, I lift my skirts and pedal down the steps as fast as I can. I've gone only a flight when I hear the man yell from above, "Meurtrière!" Murderess!

A group of men come out of an apartment and the man above shouts for them to stop me. They're as startled as I am and stare at me in confusion as I bolt by them, hurrying down the stairs.

"She murdered Evette!" the man above yells down.

The heavy steps of the men are behind me when I reach the second-floor landing. I almost run into the mother that I had given money to. In one arm is her little baby. In the other, a bag filled with food, I think, for bread is on the top. Her little mudlark is behind her eating candy. Seeing my terror, she quickly opens a door and points. It's a connecting door to the adjoining tenement. Without hesitation, I race through the door and she shuts it behind me.

It's another dim landing with apartment doors like the one I just left. On the ground floor I leave by the back door that leads into a courtyard formed by four connected buildings. I enter and exit the building opposite me.

It's only when I'm two blocks down the street and aboard a fiacre that I regain my breath.

24

The death of a prostitute in a big city is of no account to those who run the world, but coming face-to-face with it again has left me cold and frightened. I have the carriage let me off at a café near Place de Clichy. I can't eat anything, but I have a café au lait in the hopes it will melt the hard ball in my stomach.

I am tempted to present myself at the office of Chief Inspector Morant and ask him how many women have to be murdered before a city-wide alarm is made.

I struggle with the impulse to board a train for the port and a steamship home. Finally, I leave the café in a brown study, unsure of my next move except to return to the sanctuary of the garret. Even though there's still a chill in the air, I'm glad to find the fog has slipped away as I make my way toward Place de Clichy. People along the streets seem excited and I ask a woman what's happening.

"The Red Virgin's at Place Blanche."

I can't believe my luck—the famed anarchist giving a speech. I hurry toward the square. I'll never forget the first time I was introduced to the ideas of Louise Michel.

I was a factory girl standing in line, waiting for the

gates to open for work, when a woman came down the line handing out pamphlets. As she came closer I watched the reaction of the people in line—they ranged from being polite, to snapping in anger. By the time she reached me my curiosity was completely piqued and I had to take one. When the girl behind me whispered, "It's the word of the devil," I decided to hide it and wait to read it at lunchtime.

I was shocked as I read the pamphlet. I'd never heard such talk—equal rights for women, the right to vote, to be educated, and to receive the same wages as men when doing the same job—*unbelievable*, until I accomplished things that were considered unsuitable for a woman. Still, there are times when I harbor doubt because there is one reform I am positive will never happen—a world without prejudice. There is just something in human nature that will not allow it to happen.

I was lucky to have a father who respected the abilities of the "weaker sex." He wanted me to understand, to believe I could accomplish anything I wanted. "Pink, in order to have what you desire, you must want it with *all* your heart, then you have to *use your brain* and *never give up*. Success takes time. Always has for me."

I read a quote from Louise Michel that day at the factory that will forever burn in my mind and heart: "Humanity has two parts, men and women, and there will never be equality as long as the 'stronger' half controls a 'weaker' half. Each woman must exert her right to be equal. Molière said women were the 'soup' of men. I refuse to be any man's soup."

These words embolden me many times when I begin to falter.

Louise Michel, nicknamed Red Virgin because of her radical political ideals and her refusal to marry, is the stuff of legends—manning the revolutionary barricades, her hat and clothes full of bullet holes, but her body miraculously escaping harm.

The legend began about eighteen years ago here on the Butte. Louis Napoléon, the nephew of the great Bonaparte, sat on the throne of France as the Emperor Napoléon III. He was tricked by Prussia's cunning chancellor, Bismarck, into a war against the Germans which France was unprepared to fight, enabling the Prussians to storm the gates of Paris.

In the wake of the debacle, the autocratic government of royalists and imperialists fell, leaving a political vacuum. Power was up for grabs and revolutionaries, "reds" of all types—anarchists, socialists, communists, and others—scrambled for control. From the chaos came the birth of the "Commune," an experiment of government by the common people.

Soon troops of the Republican government that controlled the rest of France battled the rag-tag army of the Commune for control of Paris. This final battle took place on the Butte and was won by the Republican forces. But Louise Michel, the fiery leader of a women's Commune brigade, never lost her idealism. When she was finally freed after years in prison, she went back to the streets, urging workers to rise up and kill the factory owners and seize the factories. This is where we differ. I will never believe killing is a solution.

It's nearly dark when I arrive at Place Blanche. I can hear her voice as I reach the outer edge of the crowded square. She's standing on a wagon and wearing her signature clothing—all black except for a red scarf. She claims scarves worn by revolutionaries are red because they've been stained by the blood of the people.

Her raven black hair is cardboard flat. With rather severe looks for a woman—a narrow face that carries a patrician nose and prominent forehead—she's not "pretty" in the conventional sense of drawing room beauty. Rather she has strength—in her voice, her gestures—a fire that radiates from within. I am spellbound as I listen to her powerful and compelling words.

"Factories are closing not because there's no demand for goods, but because the factory owners are conspiring to break the back of French workers! To keep workers from making enough to buy bread, to starve their families until they see their children thin and broken. When the workers are cradling their starving children in their arms, they'll accept slave wages."

Boisterous shouts of agreement rise from the crowd. This audience is much friendlier than the one last night—she's playing to a Montmartre assembly of workers and bohemians.

"Villains that we are, we claim bread for all, knowledge for all, work for all, independence and justice for all! The worse tyrant is not the one that takes you by the throat, but the one that takes you by the belly. Not the one who locks you up, but the one who starves you!"

Shouts of approval come from people in the crowd. "Hang the tyrants!" A woman next to me screams at the top of her lungs, "Kill the bastards! They deserve to die."

"Have you asked yourself why only the poor are dying from the influenza? I'll tell you why—they're being killed by the fumes from poisons put into the sewers in poor neighborhoods. The survivors will be slaves of the rich!"

Someone hands her a flag on a stick. She lifts it so the crowd can see it—the black flag of anarchy.

"The people shall not be free until the factory owners are hanged from the doorways of their châteaux! We'll weave the ropes from the money they've stolen from workers!"

A commotion breaks out as mounted troops enter the

square. As the horses push into the crowd, I'm shoved against a red-faced panicked man. I go down as he strikes me with his flying elbow. Strong hands grab and jerk me to my feet. My body is pushed against a pillar while arms go around me from behind, grasping me and the pillar, as people stampede by like wild horses. My eyes are watery and I'm heaving for air because my breath has been knocked from me. The panic ends almost as quickly as it had erupted, the arms around me release their pressure and I turn to thank my benefactor.

"*You!*"

25

As we make our way from the crowds of Place Blanche I thank Jules Verne and ask, "Will you join me for a bite? I'm hungry."

"Yes." He takes my arm in a manner that warms my heart and guides me to a café on Boulevard de Clichy.

"How did you happen along?" I ask, wondering if he had me followed.

"I was in the area and overheard that the Red Virgin was to speak. I saw you in the crowd."

Even though his answer is credible, something in his voice doesn't settle right with me. I smile and change the subject. "She's quite amazing, don't you think?"

"She's a fanatic who should be rotting in prison."

So much for political small talk.

It's too early for dinner and Mr. Verne orders red wine and a plate of assorted cheese, bread, and olives. I add mineral water to the order.

I smile with innocence. "Montmartre is the most interesting area I've seen. In just the past two days I've seen a colorful carnival, two political riots, two murders, and came a camel's breath away of being murdered myself."

Mr. Verne looks puzzled for a moment. "Mademoiselle, that's a hairbreadth."

"Oh."

"Earlier today I threatened to have you arrested and committed to a mental institution. I suggest you keep this conversation at a rational level or I'll go through with my threat."

"*Rational level!* Who do you think you're talking to?" I slap my napkin on the table and stand up. I had enough with this pompous man. "I came to you in good faith to discuss a serious problem that concerns you and I refuse to be bullied."

"Sit down, you're attracting attention."

I sit down but my temper is still up.

He continues in an irritating tone of superiority and suppressed anger. "You are the only one who can answer that question."

"What question?"

"*Who* am I speaking to?"

"Nellie . . . Brown. My name is Nellie Brown."

"Why did you attempt to contact me today?"

I gather my thoughts while pretending to be interested in two bohemians loudly arguing politics at another table. I didn't dare use the Spanish name or accent that I used with the concierge. Mr. Verne is too well traveled and educated to fall for my Cuban act. His adventure novels are often recommended by American high school teachers for interesting ways to learn geography and the flora and fauna of regions. My research on him revealed that he has an adventurous spirit not unlike the heroes in his books—sailing his own boat to pirate-infested waters in North Africa, journeying to the warring Balkans to research a tale of horror in Transylvania, and trekking to the Arctic Circle to see the maelstrom, the incredible oceanic whirlpool that sweeps ships into its jaws. He has even traveled to America.

I have found that when all else fails, turning to the truth is best. At least a version of it.

"I'm here because of Gaston and the murder of a very dear friend." I don't attempt to hide the subtle threat that underlines my words, nor the anger I feel.

His mood darkens and a bit of temper pulls down the corners of his lips. Perhaps I should have been more subtle. Bright, liquid steel eyes overshadowed with heavy charcoal brows seem to penetrate into my very being.

"Have I the pleasure of addressing Gaston's wife, Mademoiselle?"

"Of course not."

"Then perhaps his lover?"

"Monsieur Verne!"

"His nurse? I think not. Too young to be his mother, a woman I am intimately acquainted with, since she is married to my only brother." He leans forward in his chair, as if he's ready to leap at my throat. "By what authority granted by God or man do you appoint yourself as a spokesman for my poor sick nephew!?"

It is obvious I must carefully select my words. "Mister Verne . . . may I be honest?"

"If that's possible."

A group of policemen come down the street, fresh from the Place Blanche disturbance. Mr. Verne gives them a knowing look and pulls out his pocket watch. With calculated precision he opens the cover, notes the time with deliberation, and places the watch on the table.

"Mademoiselle, you have precisely three minutes to convince me not to turn you over to the authorities. You have even less time if I discover you suffer from the same sort of brain fever that inflicts poor Gaston."

"I'm an American, from New York."

"Of course. One would not expect such improprieties from a French woman."

"Should we call the police now? Perhaps it would be to both our benefit to have a referee in this matter." My heart pounds, but the only way I know how to deal with a bully is with my dukes up.

A pin on his lapel—a small red rose, catches my attention. Red is the symbolic color of the revolutionaries. Is Jules an anarchist? The thought puts me even more on guard. The slasher had sported an anarchist scarf.

He snaps the watch case shut. "Tell me your story."

"*Merci beaucoup.* A little over a year ago I did suffer from brain fever, a nervous condition not as severe as your nephew's, but still requiring a stay in an asylum for a fortnight."

"How did you find me at the Procope?"

"I . . . I went to your house in Amiens and was told you were in Paris and that it's your favorite café."

He nods. "I suspect you're telling me the truth but you left out part of the story. My household staff is forbidden to disclose my whereabouts and my family never would. All of my servants have been with me for years—no, wait, there is one, the girl who comes in as a maid to help the rest of the staff. She has a loose tongue . . ."

I keep my features frozen but the devil take him! Such a quick mind. The servant girl indeed loved to gossip. With a little encouragement, she told me that Mr. Verne had become increasing short-tempered with his family and his staff of late. A few weeks ago he up and shaved off his beard and left for Paris. The staff suspected a woman was behind his sudden flight to the city, a not unlikely scenario in a country where extramarital love affairs are an accepted social institution.

"You were telling me about your mental derangement."

I clear my throat. "During my stay in the insane asylum,

I learned that several women had disappeared. All were prostitutes. The asylum is on a river island in New York City and it was assumed that the women who had drowned were trying to escape or during a period of intense mental disturbance."

I continue expecting my strange tale to stimulate questions from the fertile mind of one of the world's most imaginative writers, but Mr. Verne remains as excited as a mortician.

"As you have probably guessed, Josephine failed to return the night she went to the doctor's quarters." I go on, explaining how I went to the pier and into the shack only to discover a laboratory. My story draws not the slightest response, not even a raised eyebrow.

My throat goes completely dry and the words scrape coming out. "Glass containers were filled with bloody specimens that must have come from Josephine."

I close my eyes for a moment as my mind revisited the ghastly scene.

Without a word, Mr. Verne leaves the table and returns with a glass. He pours wine in the glass and puts it in front of me. I'm not one to imbibe strong spirits, but this is an exceptional moment. I force myself to go on and relate my narrow escape and the fire.

"Everything was wiped out by the fire. All evidence of Josephine, the doctor, his laboratory, and whatever other foul deeds this monster committed . . . it all went up in smoke. Within minutes both shack and pier collapsed into the river and were washed away.

"Because of my temporary brain fever, no one believed my story. Then later that year, last October to be more accurate, I went to London after Jack the Ripper began his killings. I was drawn there because of the newspaper reports about how he killed his victims. His method of slashing was similar to how Josephine was murdered.

"In London I followed the slasher's acts with great interest and was able to make the acquaintance of a lead investigator in the matter. He told me that suspicion had fallen upon a doctor. He described how the doctor fled, leaving his apartment on fire, identical to what happened at Blackwell's Island.

"In the debris of the burned flat my suspicions were rewarded by the discovery of a charred microscope and those small, tall glass vials that scientists use to hold samples, indicating that like Doctor Blum the man had set up a laboratory."

I pause for a storm of questions, but Mr. Verne's features remain stoic.

"In London while cov—uh, investigating the matter, I fell into a conversation with a man who turned out to be a newspaper reporter from Paris. He told me that Paris was having a slasher incident."

Interesting . . . still no reaction from him.

I go on doggedly with my tale, telling him of my discoveries since arriving in Paris and how the man I believe to be the slasher almost killed me. Still no reaction. I include the attitude of the police, but omit the fact I'm a fugitive from justice.

"I'm determined to bring Josephine's murderer to bay and to stop this crazed killer from striking again. Regrettably, the police have other priorities and therefore will not help me or do a proper job."

I pause, twisting my kerchief between my fingers. It's now or never. "Will you join me in this task, Monsieur Verne? Will you help me snare a killer before he kills another innocent woman?"

Finally. I said what I have been dying to say since this morning and I'm positive it will guarantee to provoke a reaction from this man. He raises an eyebrow and I hold my breath.

"You have explained a great deal, Mademoiselle . . . Brown, but you have failed to disclose one critical piece of information."

Oh, Lord, has my arrest last night been reported in the newspapers?

"You have not disclosed your motives for coming to me."

"*Excuse me?*" I am flabbergasted by his response.

"Your motive for approaching me at the Procope . . ."

"Gaston . . ." I offer, hoping that is all I need to say.

"Gaston?"

"A reporter told me of a an incident here, in Paris, several years ago. Your nephew Gaston was on his way home one night when he heard a commotion in an alley. He went into the alley and observed a man bent over a woman lying on the ground. The man fled at Gaston's appearance and Gaston discovered to his horror that the woman on the ground had been slashed."

That moves him.

Mr. Verne's two handsome, bright eyes—what are called laughing eyes—become dark and severe. "My nephew suffers from a mental illness, like yourself!"

I open my mouth to protest but he ignores my objection and continues.

"When questioned by the police, he told them it was I he had seen fleeing the scene. The police recognized that poor Gaston has developed a monomania about me and the matter was *dropped*."

"Which, of course, led to Gaston shooting you."

"These events are well known to the police and my family. The tragedy poor Gaston played out in the grip of his fantasy about me were also well played in the newspapers. It's obvious your intentions are to blackmail me and it will not work. You have come all the way from America and the only thing you will get from me will be a referral to the police."

"*Blackmail you!* That's utterly ridiculous! I came to solicit your help and to give you the opportunity to help yourself."

I pull my trump card out of my handbag and fling it on the table. If this doesn't work, nothing will.

"Perhaps it does not offend you, Mister Verne, that you resemble this mad killer so much that pictures of you are being passed out on the streets by someone seeking information about the killer."

At last, I finally have the great man's attention rather than just his ire. He stares down at the picture. The result is a superficial resemblance, but I must say, the artist did a fine job. I'm quite pleased at the forgery.

Mr. Verne leaps to his feet, sending his chair over backward. "*Who's responsible for this libel!*"

The words blow me back. I jump up, nearly sending my own chair over.

"I—I—" I stumble for words, but nothing comes. For certain, I can't tell him the truth. "I don't know."

"Where did you get this?"

"On the streets, from a prostitute."

The entire café has become still. I look around for an escape route.

"Sit down," Mr. Verne says in a firm tone that reminds me of my father when he became angry at me. He replaces his chair, sits down, and folds his hands on the table in front of him.

"Now, explain exactly *why* you have come to me."

I lift my chin. "I came to you for your help in tracking down the slasher. I thought because of your knowledge of the city, the language, your analytical abilities . . . but, it's obvious that I'm wrong. You apparently have no concern that innocent women are being murdered, or that someone is smearing your good name."

"Mademoiselle, stop trying to throw guilt on me. You

have no idea of how I feel about this libel. Or what I
will do to the person who has instigated it when I catch
him. You claim to have seen two murders in the city in
two days, and you yourself were almost killed." He lifts
his eyebrows. "If that is the truth, perhaps you should
return to America for your own safety."

"That would leave Josephine's murder unavenged.
And your name tarnished."

I decide to make one more desperate plea. He can't
turn away from a damsel in distress. It's not fitting to his
character.

"Mister Verne, I'm a woman, alone, in a foreign city. I
need your help. Together we can track down this killer
and finally have justice served. What do you say? Will
you join me in the hunt?"

"Do I look like a fool to you, Mademoiselle?"

"You strike me as a very angry man, a man who has
spent a lifetime building a reputation as a world-famous
writer, whose books are read on every continent, and
whose name is now being dragged in the mud. This killer
bodes ill for both of us. Together, we can bring him to bay.
Are you going to ignore the libel being perpetrated on
your good name and let the murder of innocent women
continue? How would you feel if I was his next victim?"

"Relief."

I bite my tongue. I'll just learn to live with his sarcasm.

He shakes his head. "It's truly contagious."

"What's contagious?"

"The brain fever that you and poor Gaston suffer
from, it has infected me."

He salutes me with his glass.

"No, Mademoiselle, I do not plan to give up. To quote
a countryman of yours, Monsieur Edgar Allan Poe, 'the
game is not up yet.'"

26

Jules has a noticeable limp as we walk along the boulevard. Not enough to require the support of the gentleman's walking cane he carries, but still a limp. I suppose the source is his nephew's bullet.

A small voice of conscience questions the ethics of how I gained his aid. I push aside the voice and instead tell myself what I'm doing is for the greater good.

As we walk away from our café we can still hear anarchists and police noisily disagreeing over who will run the world. Right now I believe the police have the upper hand and I secretly hope Louise Michel has escaped their grasp. Jules' voice seems to have lost its edge as he asks me about my visit to Dr. Dubois.

"What did the doctor tell you about the prostitute's death?"

I quickly sketch my interview with the young doctor and conclude, "He found no signs of violence on the body of the dead woman. He said there was a strange decay to her internal organs."

"A decay?"

"Yes. He analogized it to what happens to animal and vegetable matter in a sewer. In fact, his theory is that fumes from the sewers are the cause of the condition, the Black Fever crisis. I'm not a doctor, but it did strike me as strange that I saw this woman alive with every appearance of being as healthy as me, and minutes later she's dead of a fever."

"Were there any unusual marks on her? A needle mark or—?"

"Yes!" It just struck me. "I do remember a scratch on her left shoulder. The first time I saw it was when I looked at her body in the police wagon. When he flung back the curtain in that lab of his I saw it again, but I was so shocked I forgot to ask him about it. However, I did ask him if he found any needle marks and he said no."

"A scratch might be an effective way to administer a poison."

"Doctor Dubois doesn't believe she died from poison. He said that if it's a poison, it's the rarest variety, something he's never heard of. He also couldn't find those little animals Doctor Pasteur sees under a microscope."

"Microbes."

"Yes, microbes. I'm familiar with the work of Doctor Pasteur."

"Impressive, Mademoiselle, since there are few trained scientists who can even make that claim."

"I didn't mean—"

"Yes, yes I know."

He's so . . . so condescending, but I decide to bite my tongue again. I need him.

Jules purses his lips. "He must be a very progressive doctor, indeed, if he has a microscope. Of course, you said he's young and it's among the young doctors you'll find modern advances and acceptance of Pasteur's findings."

We walk a bit in silence before he asks, "What is your plan, Mademoiselle?"

"My plan?"

"Yes, your plan."

He poses a good question. Other than passing out pictures bearing a likeness to Jules and hoping lightning will strike, I have no plan.

"Well . . . it's obvious that Doctor Blum is a monomaniac, with a fixation on cutting women's bodies. He kills prostitutes because they provide the easiest opportunity. It strikes me that I've put a crimp in his dirty game by advising the police he's in the city. He has to know I told the police about him since I called them to the cemetery. Also, someone's passing around those pictures. In all, that might keep him off the streets for a while." Then it hit me. "This will probably drive him to a place where he can find prostitutes without having to go on the streets."

"A house of prostitution?"

"Exactly."

"Hardly a place you are equipped to investigate."

There he goes again. I grate my teeth. "I'll have you know—"

"Yes?"

I take a deep breath. "That I have a plan." Here I go again, instantly forming a plan without putting thought behind it. "I'm going to dress as a man and go into houses of prostitution to question women."

He has the bad taste to explode with laughter and once again I have to bite my tongue to keep from boasting of the number of disguises I've used in my past investigations.

"You laugh, but the great Sarah Bernhardt often plays male roles."

He clicks his tongue. "You are a woman who has the scientific knowledge of Pasteur and the acting ability of a Bernhardt. I can see I will learn much from our joint endeavor. With your interest in science and the thespian arts, you're no doubt aware of the findings in Baron von Krafft-Ebing's study, *Psychopathia Sexualis*, that uranism, also called lesbianism, is nearly always suspected in females who wear their hair short, dress in men's fashions, pursue sports or careers as opera singers and in actresses who appear in male attire." *

My will to show restraint goes out the window. He's gone too far.

"*Mister Verne!* I've chased this creature on two continents and have been unable to convince the police of even his existence. Last night I was almost murdered by him. I don't believe I've earned your scorn."

He stops and faces me.

"You're right, perfectly right. I haven't been fair and you deserve credit for your courage and resolve. My reluctance is fed by the fact that I came to Paris for a reason entirely alien to finding a killer. Just the opposite, as a matter of fact."

"What do you mean?"

"Truthfully, Mademoiselle, I came to Paris to kill a man." He tips his hat. "Shall we say tomorrow at one o'clock? The Procope. I'll tell the maitre d' to expect you. Afterward, we shall pay your Doctor Dubois a visit."

---

* The Krafft-Ebing report was one of the century's most influential studies of sexuality. —The Editors.

27

Jules leaves me dumbfounded about his strange pronouncement: *I came to Paris to kill a man.*

He walks away leaving me staring like a fool with my mouth gaping opened. Have I solicited the help of the wrong man? I should chase after Jules and demand an answer, but I need to check with a café proprietor for messages. Besides, I believe Jules wouldn't give me an answer.

As I make my way to Café Lavette, I can't stop thinking about his proclamation. Did a love affair go sour because another suitor intervened? Another man trespassing on his private reserve, the boys in the newsroom would say. Frenchmen are notorious for settling their romantic contests on the dueling field. The fact that Jules is married has no bearing on affairs of the heart. The French middle and upper classes often enter into matrimony for financial reasons, saving their romantic inclinations for love affairs.

I choose the small café as my message center because the owner has a corrupt look and it's frequented by Montmartre prostitutes. I felt that if they come across a man resembling the handbill drawing and/or acting violent, they won't feel uncomfortable leaving me a message there. So far, even with the enticement of a reward, no one has stepped forward, though I have had several false leads. Tonight when I approach the owner, he has other interesting information for me.

"A man asked about you."

"Who?"

"A man with one hand. He claims to be a police detective, but . . ." He shrugs.

"He asked for me by name?"

"No, he wanted to know who was giving the drawings to the prostitutes. He offered me ten francs for the information." He wipes his hands on his apron as if he was wiping away the sin of thirty pieces of silver.

"Did you tell him?"

"Mademoiselle! What do you think I am?"

I dare not express my opinion. "What's his name?"

"I don't know."

"Which hand is he missing?"

"Left."

"Is there anything else about him you know?"

"I know nothing else about him, except . . ." he stops wiping the bar counter and gives me a sinister smirk.

I give him ten francs. The man with one hand had no doubt offered much less.

"He works for someone very important, and he has a reputation of being a very violent man—especially toward women." Once again he gives me that sinister smirk.

"Do you know this *very important* person's name?"

Again he shrugs his shoulders and goes back to wiping his counter.

I give him another ten francs for his loyalty and silence, knowing I can never return to the café. No doubt he'll be contacting the one-handed man for more money. It's a good thing I gave him a false name and never told him where I'm staying. He knows who the man is. He didn't reveal to me his identity because he's playing both ends against the middle.

Thoughts swirl in my head as I leave the café and trudge up the steps of the hillside, bone weary. Who could be responsible for hiring this awful man? I realize Jules was furious when I showed him the drawings, but he seems to be the type of person who would go and find out on his own.

I quicken my pace as I trek up the Mount of Martyrs toward my garret. All I want right now is to curl up in bed and sleep. My problems are still churning in my brain as I come up Le Passage to the tenement when something catches my eye. In an entryway a little ways up to my left I see a man.

I step off to my right and take cover in a doorway and remove the police whistle from my coat pocket. Just as I'm going to blow it, a tenement door to my right opens and a small white dog rushes out and beelines for the man. An anxious old man steps out and yells, "Pierre! Stop you little cur! Pierre!"

A *very* large man darts from the doorway and hurries up Le Passage with Pierre yapping at his heels and the old man trying to stop the dog.

Nothing is small about this man. He's tall and wide— over six feet in height and weighing fifteen stone or more. A large hat is pulled down to conceal his face; a long, billowy cape covers his massive frame. As fast as my feet can carry me, I scramble up the tenement stairs, carrying an extreme case of the jitters with me. No matter how hard I keep trying to convince myself that this man could have been waiting for someone else, with my present frame of mind only the darkest of reasons occur to me.

Once I'm in the security of my garret, I not only lock

my door, I prop a chair against it. I sit on the bed, weighed down with problems and exhausted from a day in hell.

I TRY TO sleep but there is no way my mind will turn off. Dark conspiracies fly at me from every direction. I am really letting my mind run amok. I decide to rummage through Mr. Bailey's secretarial desk for paper to record more thoughts. I find buried under paperwork a long barreled .44 six-shooter. The weapon isn't loaded, nor does a search of the room reveal any bullets. My guess is the gun is a family keepsake Mr. Bailey probably uses as a paperweight. I tuck the weapon under my pillow. I'll use it as a club if the need arises.

Completely disgusted, I blow out my bedside lamp and lie in bed tossing and turning. Sleep once again refuses to come to me. I can't shake from my mind that huge man opening my door and coming to my bed holding a knife high in the air ready to stab me. Then it's no longer him; it's the slasher.

The man in the alley has two hands.

How many men are looking for me?

28

Tomas Roth

Pasteur and Roth were in the laboratory when René, Pasteur's other assistant, entered bearing the card of Monsieur Depierris, the deputy to the Minister of Interior. The minister was in charge of internal security for the nation, including police and spies. His recent visit to the Institut sent them on a mission to the sewers.

"He must have sent his deputy to inquire about our examination of the sewers," Roth told Doctor Pasteur.

Pasteur looked at the government official's card with some reserve and sighed morosely. He did not like to be interrupted in his work. And this was not an ordinary interruption. The government's concern about the Black Fever outbreak had invaded the intense concentration and focus on his work that he maintained.

"Show him to my office," Pasteur said with slight hesitation.

To their surprise, the man who entered was not the deputy—it was the minister himself, with a scarf concealing the lower part of his face.

"I apologize for the masquerade, but the newspaper reporters besieging my office are suspicious that we're covering up the danger of this deadly influenza outbreak.

They're correct, of course. And if they saw me personally visiting you again in the dead of night, hat in hand, on bent knee before the great microbe hunter . . ." The minister raised his eyebrows and shrugged his shoulders.

His dramatics evoked a smile from Pasteur. "Have you been offered tea or coffee, Monsieur Minister?"

"I'm afraid I need more than refreshments from you, Doctor. The crisis increases with every hour. Let me show you what I mean."

An aide accompanying the minister unrolled a large map of the city on Pasteur's desk. Areas of the map had been outlined in red.

"The entire city has suffered influenza symptoms, but in general with few deaths, and those mostly among the very old and very young. But hundreds of deaths hitting every age group began here." The minister jabbed a finger on the map. "In this poor section above the area of the sewers you examined yesterday. And it has spread like a deadly flood." He pointed at the surrounding area.

"Staying in the poor neighborhoods." Roth stated the obvious.

"Only in poor areas," the minister repeated. "Feeding the accusations of radicals that the poor are being targeted for extinction."

"We took samples from the sewer," Dr. Pasteur said, "and received only this morning the blood and tissue samples of the deceased worker taken by Doctor Brouardel's deputy. Brouardel refused to permit us to take samples from the worker ourselves."

Pasteur's tone didn't fail to reveal that he was still rankled by the health director's attitude. The minister was well aware of the controversy between Pasteurians and the medical community. Like any good politician, he avoided the issue by raising his eyebrows and looking sympathetic while not committing himself to anything.

"What do your tests reveal?"

"We found countless microbes as would be expected in a sewer, but we are unable to isolate a particular microbe that we can identify with the Black Fever. Even if the fever microbe is too small to see with our microscopes, we should be able to detect its presence with our experiments. We did not."

"How can you detect something that you can't see?"

"By the symptoms they create when a sample taken from an infected creature is given to a healthy one. We can't see the microbe that causes even ordinary influenza, but with experiments, we know it exists and that it can be spread from person to person through air and physical contact. If there were Black Fever microbes in the samples, they should cause a reaction in laboratory animals."

"Does the fact you can't see them in any way prove the theory that miasma from the sewers is the cause? Doesn't the death of the sewer worker support the theory?"

Pasteur shook his head. "Monsieur Minister, the death of one worker among hundreds hardly confirms the theory. He could have contacted the disease anywhere. There is no doubt that sewers carry the most varied and concentrated microbes imaginable, but sewers have been with man for thousands of years. The miasma theory has been popular with certain elements because it sounds logical. Microbes breed in sewers, vapors rise from sewers, we smell and breathe them in, thus it sounds logical that we are breathing in sewer microbes."

"What do you find wrong with the theory?"

"Logic and reason are for philosophers, scientists rely upon objective tests. Many tests have been done of sewer smells and none support the theory that the disease is spread by them. Sewers spread disease in many ways, from physical contact, by contaminated drinking water, but the stench has not been found to carry disease-causing microbes."

"Frankly, Messieurs Doctors, a finding that the sewers were the cause would not be unwelcome by our government because it would rebut the baseless allegations that the fever is a plot to rid the country of its poor. But if not the sewers, then we must find the cause. Doctor Pasteur, your past services to France have been inestimable. And once again the country must call upon you. The crisis has reached new proportions because something of the most serious nature has occurred. It has spread to this area, La Poivrière."

Pasteur ran his own finger across the map. "So, it has spread across the city from the original site."

"Not *spread*, but *jumped* from one area of destitute people to another locale of the poor, passing over the more affluent areas."

Pasteur scoffed. "Microbes don't pick their victims based upon their monetary worth or social position."

"Exactly what the radicals are shouting when they accuse the government of poisoning the poor. So why has the fever bypassed the well-to-do sections and struck the poor?"

Pasteur and Roth exchanged looks. They found nothing in the samples to explain the epidemic from a scientific point of view, let alone from a study of society. Roth knew that even if Pasteur had a theory as to what was happening, he would not voice it. He was known for his reticence even to his closest associates when it came to expressing opinions prior to all the evidence being examined.

"Tell me about the sewer openings in this new area of contagion. Is there anything unusual about them?" Pasteur asked.

"The sewer facilities in the area are the same as many

thousands of others in this city of over two million. There's no reason for the Black Fever to strike lethally in one neighborhood and mildly in another. You scoff at the notion that a miasma was responsible for the outbreak. While a certain number of us in government would privately support your opinion about sewer gases, it's the only explanation that the public considers credible. What else are we to tell them? That a politically minded microbe has decided to kill off the poor of the city?"

Pasteur was silent, but his face revealed his opinion that such a theory was absurd.

The minister waved at his aide. "Give them the samples."

The aide sat a box on the desk.

"These are from Pigalle Hospital, which is where all Black Fever victims are sent. We are keeping that facility as our medical command center to reduce the possibility of further spread of the disease. I took the liberty of having Doctor Dubois at the hospital provide blood and tissue samples of the most recent victims."

"We shall examine the samples immediately. But I would have preferred to have taken them myself."

The minister looked pained. "As you know, the medical practitioners—"

"Yes, yes, but I need your assurance that these samples were taken from a person immediately after death."

"The time of death and the time the samples were taken are on each bottle. Tell me, Monsieur Doctor, are there any conclusions at all that you've arrived at? I'll be asked by the president at tomorrow's cabinet meeting."

"For certain the fever does not spontaneously generate from inside the body. Like the plague, typhoid, and other contagions, it is caused by an invasion of a person by a microbe. The culprit is a parasite that attacks the body after it enters. While it is possible that the microbe breeds in the sewers and enters our bodies through contact with air or drinking water, at this point we have not established how the contact is made or how it spreads."

"Until we know, Messieurs, you understand that we must support the miasma theory."

"I leave politics to those of you who practice that art. From a scientific point of view, the decisive proof will be to discover the presence of the microbe by examining it in a sterile culture. That is what we shall do."

PASTEUR AND ROTH retired to the laboratory with the new samples from Pigalle Hospital and immediately began testing.

Microbes were mainly aquatic creatures that had to live in liquid to survive. When the "host" they infected died and bodily fluids dried up, most microbes also died, though some of them instead went into a state of hibernation—"spores" covered by hard shells, waiting to be picked up by another host. Once they found a warm, comfortable sea to live in, such as the human bloodstream, they grew and multiplied at an inconceivable rate. Microbes that carried human disease—plague, cholera, small pox, and dozens of other ailments— found the human body a bounty of food and shelter, an ocean of plenty.

When a sample of blood and tissue was drawn from an infected person it provided a culture they could use to experiment with, enabling them to identify the microbe and learn how it spread and how to stop it.

Their first examination of the samples was the most basic possible. Using sterile utensils and sterile plates, they took a piece of each sample and examined it under the microscope looking for microbes. Blood and urine were ordinarily sterile. Even when not sterile, a common microbe, like one causing a urinary tract infection, would be recognizable to them and eliminated as a cause of the Black Fever.

Dr. Pasteur gave René and Roth precise instructions as to how he wanted the samples set up. This procedure was quite tiring—examining the samples in an undiluted state and then placing a drop of each sample in various mediums under varying conditions.

Some microbes thrived when exposed to air, others existed without oxygen. Some lived only in a vacuum, others in pure carbonic acid. Like humans, they were particular about the temperatures they could survive in—while some could survive boiling water, others perished with a few degrees change in temperature.

When an aide complained of the many tests Pasteur demanded, he told them, "Ce n'est pas la mer à boire." It's not the sea to swallow. He tolerated no malingering from his staff. Like a general leading an army, he demanded heroic efforts and was always the first to give such efforts.

Soon after becoming employed at the Institut, Roth learned that the Pasteurians were proud that they were the only laboratory in France where it was possible to properly handle microbes, exposing them to an indefinite number of successive mediums, searching for the microbe's favorite, instead of limited to just a few soups.

All had to be done carefully. Microbes were invisible killers. One could spend thousands of hours examining an invisible entity and be struck down by a single lapse in handling the specimen.

When Roth finished examining samples under the microscopes, he told Dr. Pasteur, "I'm unable to isolate a microbe."

The frown on his face showed his disappointment.

"There's no reaction from laboratory animals commiserate with what one would expect. Even if the microbe is too small to be seen under our microscopes, it is not too small to kill." Pasteur was puzzled. "We should be able to detect it in other ways."

RENÉ, WHO HAD been working in an adjoining lab, interrupted Roth with his findings. "Tomas, once again I have encountered strange results from samples sent by Doctor Dubois. The specimen is marked as taken from a Black Fever victim, but I suspect that death was caused by carbon monoxide poisoning."

Carbon monoxide deaths were common in the winter months because most heating was done with coal. Poor people in small rooms with coal braziers were most susceptible.

"Perhaps the person succumbed to poisoned air because he was weakened by the fever and couldn't get out of the room."

René shook his head.

Roth could see he was very disturbed. René knew how meticulous Pasteur was and feared making a mistake.

"This isn't the first time I haven't been able to isolate a fever microbe in specimens this doctor Dubois has sent . . . and every specimen points to other ailments as the cause of death. I am completely stumped. I haven't told Doctor Pasteur about my findings, but I feel now—"

"You're right, let me check them before you approach him. In the meantime, I'll speak to him about me contacting Dubois and see if he will let me obtain specimens directly."

29

An urgent message from the minister once again sped Pasteur and Roth from the Institut, this time to an impoverished district where an outbreak of the fever had occurred.

They proceeded behind the health department director's carriage to the tenement house they were to investigate, both of them wishing that they could make the investigation sans the company of the pompous and arrogant Doctor Brouardel and his assistant. Brouardel had no idea what science was really about or what it was capable of accomplishing.

As the carriages halted on the corrupted cobblestone street in front of the tenement, they entered into a world of prostitutes, pimps, petty criminals, and the poorest of laborers. Three police wagons were lined up, waiting for them. A crowd had gathered. The message from the minister stated that the police would be present in case of any "disturbance."

Pasteur and Roth stepped down from their carriage. A dozen street children, hollow-eyed mudlarks with dirty faces and pinched bodies followed their movements with the intensity of lab rats. There was a sad cunning in the faces of these children: only the clever survived this milieu where young girls withered into whores and boys became fodder for the guillotine.

Women who paused to note their arrival watched them with defeated eyes recessed in dark sockets; broken men, leading lives of quiet desperation, their hope crushed by the vicious trap of poverty, stared at the coaches and clothes as if they had been purchased with food taken from their children's mouths. A black flag of anarchy hung from a window of the tenement. Desperate people listened to anyone who promised them bread.

There was grumbling among those gathered. "Have you been sent to kill more of us?" a man yelled.

"That's Monsieur Doctor Pasteur," an awed voice piped in.

The crowd buzzed with the name and they parted respectfully as the scientists walked into the tenement in the accompaniment of four officers. Pasteur's relationship with the medical profession was controversial, to say the least, but to the rest of France, he was a national treasure.

The health director and his young assistant remained in their carriage, declining to step out. Cowards. They would never understand what the people were going through. Nor did they care.

The concierge greeted Pasteur and Roth at the entry. "Welcome, Messieurs, welcome."

He was a revolting creature wearing a dirty shirt whose original color was lost under a goulash of food stains and grime; heavy suspenders held up worn pants and a globular belly.

It was morning and he smelled of wine, garlic, sweat, and even less pleasant things, the likes of which got thrown into the sewer hole from chamber pots. Under a microscope, no doubt, he would have proved to possess more microbes than a barrel of sewer sludge.

"You've had a number of deaths from the fever," Pasteur said. "Has this building suffered more than others?"

"Oui. At least half the people in the building have had the fever and eighteen have died."

The tenement house covered half a city block, seven stories of smoke blackened stone, crowded around a filthy cesspool of a courtyard. The only "plumbing" fixture was a pump handle in the center of the courtyard to draw water. The sewer hole they came to inspect was in a small room on the ground floor. A metal cover that had long ago rusted opened and a trail of droppings from chamber pots were the only furnishings. Pigeons cooed from the rafters as they entered.

"Take samples," Pasteur instructed Roth.

The smell inside was worse than they had experienced in the sewer. The sewer smell was almost chemical. The room had the odor of human waste. It occurred to Roth that in many ways the sewer, where waste was periodically flushed out completely, was more sanitary than the pest hole of a room. The sewer opening was the suspected source of the miasma inhaled when people came to empty their chamber pots.

"When a family suffered the fever, did it usually begin with the person who disposes of the family's chamber pot?" Pasteur asked.

The concierge shrugged and raised his eyebrows. "Everyone gets it, Monsieur, all that God wants to have it."

"Of the people who died, how many were men, women, children?"

"Nine women, five men, four children."

Most dumping of chamber pots would be done by women and older children, exposing them more to the sewer hole. But that fact meant very little. Women were also more likely to care for the sick, and thus were more exposed to it, and children, along with old people, were most likely to perish from the fever.

"Tell me, Monsieur Concierge," Pasteur said, "is there anything about your building that is different from the others around it?"

"My building is better run and cleaner than any around."

Pasteur and Roth exchanged looks and abandoned any notion of getting information from the man. There was little difference about this tenement building, the people in it, or the way waste was disposed of, than thousands of other buildings in the city. Most private homes, except those of the very rich, lacked up-to-date plumbing. And even the rich often had less effective plumbing than was available to the Romans two thousand years ago.

During their earlier venture in the sewer, Dr. Brouardel boasted that he refused to have plumbing installed in his own home out of fear that the pipes would draw poisonous fumes into the house from the sewer. Pasteur and Roth both scoffed at the notion. Plumbing with proper traps kept out sewer fumes, but many people still maintained the notion that the pipes would let in poisonous gases.

When Roth finished gathering samples, he found Pasteur staring up at the ceiling. Pigeons were coming and going through a hole near the ceiling and nesting in the rafters.

"Pigeons," Pasteur said in almost a whisper, watching, lost in a world of his own. He had found another piece to the mystery.

The director's assistant stuck his head in the room. The fool was wearing a nosegay. "Messieurs, the Director inquires as to whether you are ready to leave." He sounded like a scared child. "A problem is mounting out here."

A much larger crowd had gathered outside and continued growing as people throughout the neighborhood became aware of their presence. Men wearing the red scarves of revolutionaries were arguing with the police officers.

"They've come to murder more poor people!" a Red yelled.

Another shouted, "All oppressors of the people must die."

The building manager was trying to sneak away when Pasteur's sharp command stopped him. "Monsieur Concierge, have you discovered any dead pigeons or other birds?"

"No, Monsieur."

"How about any dead animals? Dogs, cats, rats?"

"No. But there would be none of those."

"Why?"

"The people eat them. Pigeons, too, when they can catch them."

Pasteur continued staring up at the ceiling, oblivious to the chaos outside. Roth took his arm and hurried him toward the carriage for Roth was certain a riot was to unfold at any moment. The director had exited his carriage and walked beside them.

"What have you concluded?" he asked.

Pasteur stared at him dumbfounded. "I don't reach conclusions from staring at tea leaves, Monsieur Director."

"Are you accusing me of being a witch doctor?"

"I was speaking of my own methods, not yours. I must return to my lab and test the samples. Now, you must excuse me. I'm tired and hungry and wish to return to the Institut before I'm murdered by anarchists."

As their carriage rumbled away, Pasteur leaned back, worn and fragile. His hands were shaking from the exertion and his complexion was pale. Pasteur said something and Roth, deep in thought, didn't catch it.

"What did you say?"

Pasteur's eyes fluttered open for just a second. "Pigeons and frogs."

Pigeons and frogs. A microbe that killed humans and rats, but not pigeons and frogs. What did hot-blooded birds and cold-blooded amphibians have in common that protected them from the microbe?

30

Nellie

During the carriage ride to the Café Procope to meet Jules I decide not to tell him about the man who inquired about me at the café and the large man in the alley. Best I proceed with caution, until I know I can trust him. Besides, he may have hired the large man to spy on me. His comment about coming to Paris to kill a man still buzzes in my head.

When I enter the café and observe Jules sitting at his table writing with the ghost of Voltaire by his side, I find myself drawn to him in a romantic way. He's quite attractive with his salt-and-pepper hair, strong jawbones, and imagination—traits I've always been drawn to. I love a man with an active and intelligent mind. Like my father.

He's writing frantically, captured by an idea, perhaps another balloon journey to a mysterious island or to the bottom of the sea in a submersible. What a thrill it must be for the writer to play God, creating a world and populating it with people and places of their imagination.

I shake my head. These silly, romantic thoughts are plain out ridiculous. This is just a business arrangement, *nothing else.* I must stay focused. Besides, as my mother would tell me, he's too old for me.

The maitre d' maintains a pretense that this is the first time he's seen me as he escorts me to the table.

"Are you ready to continue your crusade, Mademoiselle?" Jules asks, putting aside foolscap and pen. "This mad passion to find this creature of your nightmares?"

My affinity with the man flies out the window.

"My crusade, Monsieur Verne? I don't mind playing Joan of Arc to *your* country, doing the work of the police, but my penchant for sacrifice falls short of being burned at the stake. Furthermore, he's not a creature of my nightmares, but of your city."

"Mademoiselle Brown," Jules stands up, "I stand corrected. I just hope I won't be burned along with you. Shall we go?"

I am amazed at how quickly this man can turn my heart around; one minute I have a deep affection toward him, the next I could strangle him, and then he's back to warming my heart. I could use a *café au lait* and a sweet roll, but I smile graciously and we leave.

"You are a crusader, Mademoiselle Brown," he says to me once we're on the street. "Who else would chase a killer around the world."

"And you, Monsieur Verne, what are you?"

"A bird that soars high above the world, never touching life. That's what an adventure writer is. We only imagine what others experience. That's why I joined you in this mad hunt. I want to peck among real people and see what I've been missing. Have you seen the Paris papers this morning?"

"No." My knees go weak. Am I on the front page?

"Your friend Doctor Dubois is quoted extensively. His hospital is where the fever patients are brought. He's quoted as saying that it's strange that the fever contagion spread to another poor district without stopping in between. He says little, but the papers read much into it."

"That the disease is being deliberately spread into poor neighborhoods?"

"Exactly."

"But how . . . and why?"

"Anarchists claim it's the doings of the rich."

"That must annoy the poor people and fuel their hatred of the wealthy."

"That is an understatement. I believe it's time I hear Dubois' thoughts on the matter myself."

"There's no mention in the papers of the woman murdered in the Pepper Pot?"

"Of course not."

Now what did he mean by that? That I was right about the cover-up? Or that it wasn't reported because it was a figment of my imagination? I bite my tongue rather than push for an answer that might cause me to explode. Besides, I have a more pressing issue weighing heavy on my thoughts—what Dubois might say to Jules about me. Last night Jules and I agreed we'd introduce him as a French relative of mine, Jules Montant. Early this morning I sent Dubois a telegram informing him that I would be dropping by with a gentleman who has offered to assist me. I also asked him not to disclose the fact that I am a reporter or anything about the police. If Dubois hasn't received the message, or doesn't cooperate, I'm a cooked goose—or whatever that expression is.

In a fiacre, Jules poses a question about the medical education of the man I knew in New York as Dr. Blum. "Many men carrying the title of doctor have not earned the right. Official appearing documents from universities are customarily taken at face value, especially if foreign institutions are involved. From what you've told me about the condition of the slasher's victims, while the person who made the cuts has some medical knowledge, they're hardly the work of a skilled surgeon."

"True, but the slashings weren't done under surgical conditions either. Most likely on a street, during a struggle, and in a great hurry. The police hypothesized that the man got a sexual thrill at opening a woman's body." I shutter to think I was almost one of his victims. "We're dealing with a really sick human being."

"I wonder . . ."

Jules is hearing me, and could repeat every word I said, but he's not really listening. "Wonder what?"

"I'm just thinking . . . what if he's looking for something when he's dissecting?"

"Looking for something?" What a strange thing to say. "What on earth could he be looking for?" Now he really has me puzzled. This remark is so unexpected from a man who is known around the world for his knowledge of science.

"Really, Jules, one would hardly imagine that in this day and age there's anything unknown about the anatomy of the human body. If a man wants to know where a woman's liver is located, he need merely consult a reference book on the matter."

At the hospital I force myself up each step. For once my feet aren't taking over and it's my mind that's forcing me forward. When we reach the top I pause and gather my nerves to once again face the terrible smells of sickness, death, and the memory of that young woman on the doctor's table.

"Are you all right?" Jules asks.

"Yes, I'm fine." No way will I let Jules know I am having a moment of "womanly weakness," as he would put it.

The hospital reception area is still crowded with poor people seeking treatment for their ails. I wonder if there is ever a moment when it's not crowded. Some of the people appear to me to be the same ones that were waiting yesterday, but I dismiss the notion. However, the smell of chemicals and sickness is the same. And the same harried clerks are at the reception station. We slip by to "cold call" the doctor.

Carrying vinegar sponges we wander through the hallways until Jules finds the doctor examining a patient in one of the large dormitory-type rooms that holds both the sick and dead. The doctor joins us in the hallway.

After introductions, Jules asks, "I understand you

have identified the source of the infection that struck the prostitute Mademoiselle Brown encountered in the graveyard."

"Ah, the newspapers, they added much to my statements. And caused me a great deal of trouble. I've been sanctioned by the medical director and forbidden to give any more statements to the press." He lowers his voice. "I suspect the fact my name was in the newspaper and not his may have ignited his ire. Mademoiselle knows I have a microscope. If my superiors find out that I'm experimenting, I will be fired."

"Isn't it a bit coincidental that so many victims are prostitutes?" I ask.

Dubois shrugs. "Prostitutes live in poor areas. Poor people are dying."

"This condition seems to kill very rapidly," Jules says, "if Mademoiselle Brown saw the victim alive and well moments before her death. Does that correspond to your examination of other victims of the fever?"

If I saw the woman alive and well? "How fast can the fever kill?" I interrupt, trying to hold my temper.

Dubois thinks for a moment. "That would depend upon many factors, ranging from the age and medical condition of the victim, to how a person is infected. We assume the fever rises from sewers and is passed most commonly through inhalation to the lungs. It can also come from touching, eating, drinking."

"Can it kill in minutes?" Jules asks.

Dubois sighs. "I don't know. Black Fever has similar symptoms as influenza. If she got a large dose of the contagion directly into her bloodstream it probably would kill her quickly, but *within minutes* . . . ?"

I've endured enough of their "ifs."

"Doctor Dubois, I realize you're having a hard time believing me, but I know she was healthy. I saw her."

"Mademoiselle, I don't doubt your word. She might have looked and appeared healthy, but obviously she wasn't. We do know of poisonous gases that can strike down a person instantly. If the contagion can kill so quickly, it would support the theory that it's caused by a poisonous miasma."

An attendant comes down the hall with a small wooden box in hand. "Doctor Dubois, you've received another package from China."

"Merci. Please put it in my office."

After the attendant passes, I ask, "Wasn't there a scratch on her upper shoulder or neck area?"

Dr. Dubois frowns and purses his lips. "I don't remember a scratch, but I was only looking for signs of significant violence. If there was, it probably came as a result of her falling when she went into a death coma."

"Is it possible to have the fever spread through a scratch or cut?"

"I can't answer that because we don't know for sure yet what causes the fever."

"What about any scratches, cuts, or unusual marks on any of the other victims of Black Fever?" Jules questions.

"*No,*" agitation fills his voice, "but again, I haven't particularly looked. Why are you so interested in scratches and cuts?"

I make my statement in a serious tone of voice, because it sounds all too incredible. "We are wondering if the fever can be deliberately passed on."

Dr. Dubois raises his eyebrows. "The contagion has spread from the steppes of Russia to Paris and is racing far beyond. Only God has such power."

32

Once we're back in the reception area, Jules takes hold of my arm and whispers, "Wait for me outside." He parts with me to speak to a clerk.

When he comes out, Jules is deep in thought. As we walk up the street I tell myself not to interrupt his thinking, but I'm too curious to wait. "What did you ask the clerk?"

"Where the doctor was from."

"Why?"

"Dubois has a slight accent. Since you're not a native French speaker, you wouldn't notice it, but it's apparent to me. The clerk believes the doctor's from Bayonne. That's near the Spanish border and could account for a regional accent. About one out of five French people can't speak the language well enough in court to testify without an interpreter. Educated foreigners often speak it better than our own provincials. How well does he fit your impression of the slasher?"

"Well, no beard, of course. And the madhouse doctor had much darker hair, although I think the thickness is the same, but not the length. They're about the same height. Same build. Age is almost the same . . . I think. It's hard to tell the age of a man who wears a full beard and hides much of the rest of his head with a hat and long hair."

I try to picture Dr. Dubois as the long-haired, heavy-bearded, tinted-spectacled Dr. Blum, but the two images will not crystallize. And I can't say this to Jules, but the hairs on the back of my neck didn't rise when I first met him at the graveyard, or at the hospital, and not even now. Dr. Dubois doesn't reek of the evil I felt with Dr. Blum. But even I must admit it would be unprofessional of me to cancel someone out just because of my gut feelings.

"I never spoke to Doctor Blum or observed him face-to-face, except for that one very brief moment in the shack. But I don't have the feeling he's Doctor Dubois. What about you, any thoughts?"

"Since only my poor, sick nephew claims to have seen the slasher . . ." he pauses for effect and I just smile, "and having never met Doctor Blum previously, I have no opinion. I will know more when I find out about the finger."

"The finger?"

"The tip of his right pinkie is missing."

How did I miss that! A sideways glance from Jules tells me that I shouldn't have—and he's right. I make a strong mental note that I have to be more observant. I am hunting down a killer and sloppiness is unacceptable.

"Perhaps a childhood accident," he continues, "or a slip of the knife while performing surgery. I will have my doctor wire medical authorities in the Bayonne region and inquire as to Doctor Dubois' physical description and credits."

He flags down a fiacre. Once we're settled in, he instructs the driver, "Institut Pasteur."

I can barely control my excitement. "Do you really think we'll be able to meet with Doctor Pasteur?"

"If he is in, I'm sure he'll receive us. I was once on a

government committee with him, some nonsense concerning public health."

"But this means you'll have to use your real name."

"Of course. Nellie, I'm not in hiding, it's just that I have no desire to let friends know I'm in the city. But Pasteur is not a sociable man. He's too involved in his work to inquire too deeply about my actions."

"Still, I can't imagine just walking in and being able to speak to Louis Pasteur."

Jules could remind me that I boldly walked into the Café Procope and dropped a murder investigation on one of the most famous writers in the world. I'm relieved he's deep in thought and doesn't appear to have picked up on my faux pas.

"We won't have a problem seeing him," Jules murmurs, almost to himself. "The Black Fever newspaper stories will have piqued his interest, if he's not already actually involved in the matter, which I suspect he is. No one on Earth knows more about microbes than Pasteur. We must get his reaction to the prostitute's death. He's a chemist, not a medical doctor, but that hasn't prevented him from delving extensively into the field of medicine."

"I know. He found a cure for rabies."

"And rabies is a medical condition. While he can concoct the rabies vaccine in his laboratory, he's not able to administer it to patients, but employs a medical doctor for that purpose. Unfortunately, the medical profession has been looking for a way to discredit Pasteur and the rabies vaccine has given them their strongest evidence."

"How could the rabies vaccine be their strongest evidence when it has saved so many lives?"

"Pasteur is very . . . how would you Americans say it . . . oh yes, ornery. He's extremely blunt in his criticism of doctors and continually accuses them of causing disease among their patients by their lack of sanitary practice. He claims that doctors should wash their hands before examining patients and sterilize their instruments, because the microbes he sees under a microscope cause diseases that are spread by doctors to their patients with their hands and instruments."

"It sounds logical, but I suspect most people are like my mother and believe that all diseases are caused by God and that there is little we can do about it."

"Fortunately, most doctors have advanced beyond that belief, but many also reject Pasteur's theories. Doctors see disease as something that arises from conditions in the body rather than spread by microbes. I suspect the truth, as it is so often when two sides take diametrically opposing viewpoints, lies somewhere in between. But Pasteur's concepts are slowly gaining respect. A noted Vienna surgeon recently proposed that doctors wash their hands before operating on a patient."

"But wasn't surgical sterilization already being performed for years by Doctor Lister in Great Britain?"

Jules looks at me in surprise and I lean closer to gently lock eyes with him in the carriage. "As I told you, Monsieur Jules Verne, I read newspapers despite the contention that such matters are not proper for a lady's mind."

He allows me a small smile before continuing. "Doctor Lister has found that cleaning a wound after an operation results in fewer infections. The Viennese surgeon is suggesting that hands be sterilized *before* surgery."

"Please, tell me a little more about the controversy between Pasteur and the doctors. What happened with the rabies vaccine?" I'm eager to learn more because an interview with Dr. Pasteur would be quite a coup.

"The accusation is that Pasteur used the rabies vaccine prematurely without proper testing and caused the deaths of two patients. They claim he was so eager to prove the effectiveness of the vaccine that he had two young people, a boy and a girl, both bitten by possibly rabid dogs, injected with the vaccine prior to proper testing of his concoction. The two young people both died."

"That's horrible."

Jules shrugs. "So is rabies if it isn't cured."

"Why do they think he administered the vaccine prematurely?"

"Pasteur's vaccine is made from rabbits infected by rabies in his lab. The children died from rabbit rabies, not the canine variety. Thus, the children died from the vaccine injected into them.

"Doctor Pasteur is a great scientist," Jules continues, "the greatest in the world. What he's done for the world should not be diminished because of human failures. If it were not for him, thousands of people would die each year from poisonous milk, wine would sour on its way to the market, and cattle and sheep all over the world would transmit a deadly disease. Pasteur cannot solve all the ills of the world with his microscope, but his discoveries will pave the way for a golden age of . . ."

Jules suddenly turns to face the window and a heavy silence ensues.

Hating silence I ask, "Is something wrong?"

A moment passes before he slowly turns back to me.

"I have a bad habit of predicting the future. Too often it is the bad things that come to light."

My instincts ring like church bells. Whatever demon Jules is fighting has popped up again. I bite my lip to keep from inquiring, but it's a losing battle with me and once again I open my mouth when I should keep it shut.

"Jules, yesterday you said something that left me in quite a state of agitation. May I ask—"

"No you may not."

His words are sharp—very sharp, and oddly they hurt. He turns to face the window once again and I look down at my hands. I really hate uncomfortable moments like this and wish we were at our destination.

33

The Institut's buildings resemble university structures—one stately red brick and the other grey. Smooth stone steps lead to a wide, imposing entryway, from which a long hallway flows the length of the building. The hallway is wide and at least twenty feet high. The atmosphere here is sober and venerable. Quiet and dignified, like a hallowed old university corridor.

Jules hands his card to the clerk at the reception desk and announces himself. "Jules Verne to see Doctor Pasteur."

The clerk looks up at him in surprise.

"Sans beard," Jules adds.

As soon as the clerk leaves, I ask him eagerly, "What did you write on the back of your card?"

"Two words. Black Fever. I should warn you, don't be surprised at the appearance of Doctor Pasteur. He's had strokes that aged him alarmingly. Although I believe he's in his sixties, he appears older. And don't be offended if he won't shake hands with you."

"I won't. He doesn't shake hands with anyone. He believes it transmits germs. However, I don't agree. It's too far-fetched, catching a cold or giving an illness to someone just by shaking hands."

Jules once again looks at me with surprise. "Mademoiselle Brown, you never cease to amaze me."

"Thank you . . . I think."

"You have an incredible range of knowledge . . . and completely unsupported opinions. But a word of advice, never rule anything out as *too* far-fetched." A veil of darkness slips across Jules' face. The same veil of darkness when he said he came to Paris to kill a man. "I have written of things I never dreamed would come true, and they did. Remember that as you look for your Doctor Blum."

I am about to respond to his "unsupported opinions" remark when the clerk returns and says Dr. Pasteur will see us.

Tall double doors near the entryway lead to Doctor Pasteur's private apartment. The walls of the inner hallway are covered with red wallpaper and trimmed with dark wood molding, all quite elegant. This hallway is much narrower than the main one we came through, but the ceiling is also a good twenty feet high and the doors themselves tower a dozen feet.

The simple but grand entrances seem symbolic of the gentleman we are about to meet. One would think that his private apartment would be nestled somewhere more isolated, but I suppose it fits a man whose entire life is wrapped up in his work. Madame Pasteur must be an obliging angel to mesh her private life with her husband's work.

The clerk asks us to wait in the living room. Being the curious cat that I am, I stick my nose everywhere while Jules explains and complains.

"I'll use a child's harness next time I take you

anywhere," he threatens, but I have a feeling he's not *that* annoyed with me.

The living room's very formal. Stuffed chairs, end tables crowded with lamps, knickknacks and art objects. Even though a large fireplace warms the room, it feels like a place for receiving guests rather than where one would kick off their shoes and relax. On one wall is a large painting of Pasteur with a small girl.

"His granddaughter, Camille." Jules says. "The painting was a gift from Jacobsen Carlsburg Brewery, the first brewery to use his pasteurization process."

Across the hallway is a very large dining room that conveys the impression it's used more for business conferences than eating. The room's dominated by a life-size, tarnished, gilt-framed portrait of Pasteur in his laboratory, holding a glass jar containing the dried spinal cord of a rabbit inflicted with rabies.

"That was painted by Edelfelt, a Finnish painter. If you notice, Pasteur's left hand is resting on a set of books. His arm became paralyzed from one of his strokes."

My respect and admiration for this man has increased even before we meet. He is so dedicated to his work even his physical incapacities do not deter him.

"Upstairs are bedrooms and a private sitting room. The downstairs is used for receiving guests."

At the end of the hallway, near the door which leads into Pasteur's office, is a large, paned window. The window glass has thin red, blue-green, and purple lines. In front of the window is an amazing statue—a woman striking a soldier with the butt of a rifle. The piece is called *Quand Même*.

"Roughly translated it means 'Even Though,'" Jules explains. "It's an Alsatian woman hitting a Prussian soldier and represents that the Germans have been occupying the Alsace-Lorraine region since 1870. Pasteur taught in Strasbourg, the largest city in the Alsace. It is a reflection of Pasteur's patriotism and the fact that France still considers the area as being held captive."

The clerk returns and shows us into Pasteur's office. "He sends his apologies, he'll be here momentarily."

Pasteur's office is not what I expect it to be. I assume a world-renowned scientist running a famous institution would have a large office, but it's rather small and reflects the fact that his interests are in the laboratory with its test tubes and microscopes and not a room full of books.

The office has dusky green walls framed by dark wood molding. Dark red velvet curtains frame the windows. The rugs on the brown wood floor have an Oriental pattern. Breaking a little of the sober ambiance is a white ceiling, too high up to cast much light down, and a tall mirror that extends from the mantel of the red marble fireplace to the ceiling.

I particularly like the elaborately carved wood mantel. On it is another piece of art, a small statue of a woman on her tiptoes facing the mirror and reaching up with one hand to grasp a rose.

Jules answers my unasked question. "The statue was presented to Pasteur by the grateful agricultural sector after he created a vaccine for the anthrax microbe that killed thousands of animals and many people each year."

On the wall behind Pasteur's desk is another piece of art, a simple ink drawing drawn by Henner of a woman in black. "And this picture?"

"It's called *Woman in Waiting* and represents a woman who is in mourning for the Alsace occupation. Pasteur returned the honors bestowed upon him by the Germans after the occupation of the Alsace area."

His writing desk is unassuming, a simple wood table unadorned with carvings, and a leather top. A plain brown leather chair sits behind the desk. On the wall across the way is an impressive green and gold porcelain clock, several feet high and wide, Louis XV style, dating from the eighteenth century.

I am in awe as Dr. Pasteur finally enters. He's old and venerable, like his building. With him is a younger man who introduces himself as Dr. Tomas Roth, Pasteur's lab assistant. He seems quite reserved.

Jules is certainly right about Pasteur's appearance. He appears weak, a wasting away that happens to some people in old age. However, I don't see any dimness in his eyes, even filtered as they are through strong lenses. Instead, I see the wonderment of a child. His eyes are bright and alive and filled with the luster of a man who not only has more years on this planet, but more paths of discovery to hack through. His failing body will not stop him.

As for his assistant, Tomas Roth, he's a sparse man with an all too serious countenance. I don't get the personal warmth from him that I do with Dr. Pasteur. He makes me feel uneasy . . . as if I'm something to be examined under a microscope and dissected.

Dr. Roth has that scientist's abstraction, as if he has emerged from a darkened lab, blinking in the sunlight. Although facial hair is all the fashion now, like Jules, his face is clean shaven. I recognize his French has a touch of accent. While I had not picked up on Dr. Dubois' accent, Dr. Roth's is easier for me to discern.

My introduction by Jules is brief. "This is Mademoiselle Brown, an American."

They slightly tip their heads, like tipping a hat, but no one offers to shake hands.

Jules addresses Pasteur, "It's good of you to see us without notice."

I sense enormous respect in his voice, which is interesting considering that Jules himself is world renowned.

Pasteur gives a nod of thanks. "Your name alone would have caused me to throw open my doors, but I must confess that cryptic message on the back of your card excited my interest. You have shaved your beard, *mon ami*. You and Tomas must be the only men in France over the age of eighteen whose faces are not covered with hair."

"Perhaps the only ones in all Europe," Jules says. "Some men would just as soon walk down the street naked than shave the hair on their face. You must know the story that has been circulating in the boulevard cafés, about the Guardsman who brandished six inches of waxed mustachios, the finest eagle wings in his regiment. He burned one while lighting his pipe. Of course he couldn't parade with his regiment or even show his face in public without his mustachios. The poor devil was so depressed he killed himself. Shot himself in the face so his shame would not be exposed by an open coffin."

The story elicits chuckles from the men. And they say women are vain. I assume the story is one of those mysterious rumors that spread like wildfire and are rarely true.

"Please Gentlemen, Mademoiselle, sit." Pasteur sits in the chair behind his desk. "I not only understand his feelings about his mustache, but when my experiments are going bad, I feel like taking my own life."

"*D'accord,*" Jules says. "As to my beard, sometimes a face is best concealed in plain sight. I have reasons important only to me as to why I've shaved my beard to disappear from the public eye."

Pasteur's eyes flicker in my direction just slightly and I feel myself redden. He obviously assumes that the reason for Jules' behavior is a liaison with me.

"I'm a Pinkerton detective from New York," I find myself announcing boldly. I don't know where these lies come from. The devil must oil my tongue.

"Not so unusual a profession for women," Jules hastily imposes, "if you recall that Vidocq used women as undercover agents for La Sûreté."

"Ah, yes," Pasteur smiles, "but those women were criminals working undercover. Mademoiselle Brown does not strike me as the criminal type."

"*Merci*, Monsieur Doctor."

"Now, my friend, what is the reason for your call in the company of a detective from America."

Jules leans foward in his chair. "Black Fever. What do the words mean to you, Doctor?"

Pasteur raises his eyebrows. "An illness that I read about in the newspapers. Some form of influenza, it appears. A most lethal and fast-acting disease accompanied with a death that can come quickly, sometimes within hours."

Sometimes within *minutes*, I want to say, but keep quiet.

"My understanding," Jules says, "is that the disease has been given its name by the young doctor at Pigalle Hospital, a Doctor Dubois, who has been at the center of the treatment of the cases that have emerged so far. Mademoiselle Brown and I have spoken to the doctor. I would be surprised if you haven't been contacted about the matter, perhaps directly by the government."

Pasteur avoids Jules' last remark and asks, "This doctor, what is he like?"

Jules thinks for a moment. "He's young, has an inquiring mind. He has a microscope, somewhat of a laboratory set up in a utility room in the hospital. A secret one—considering the opposition of the medical profession to your techniques. He admits some creedence to your theories but is cautious because he's afraid of offending those who can make or destroy a career still being molded."

Pasteur nods. "I haven't met the young man, but I know his type. There are a thousand more like him in France. The medical training he received in school conflicts with what he experiences in practice. The methods I employ in the laboratory excite him. But he stands posed between two worlds, a foot in each, not sure of which way to step."

"Mademoiselle Brown has met with the doctor twice, once with me. She actually observed the autopsied body of a woman inflicted with the disease and may be able to enlighten us on what she saw."

Pasteur looks at me with new respect. A woman attending an autopsy without fainting?

"The woman's internal organs had . . . blackened, and forgive me for using this analogy for the poor woman, but the color of her innards resembled red meat after it's been left in a warm room overnight. It even had that . . . that putrid smell, a *spoiled* meat smell . . ." my voice trails off as my heart jumps into my throat at the memory.

Dr. Roth pours me a glass of water.

"*Merci.*" I take a sip and continue, "I learned from Doctor Dubois that the victims are in decayed state from the moment of death. The smell and the putrid decay have led him to link the cause of the contagion to sewer gases."

Pasteur and Roth exchange looks. I must be giving them fresh information and it feels invigorating. I continue, "Doctor Dubois believes the sewer gases cause a rotting of the flesh and organs."

Pasteur's lips turn down at the corner. "Sewer gases. Yes, it's what the medical profession raises every time an illness erupts that they can't understand. No doubt the young doctor's conclusions have been influenced by

Doctor Brouardel. What did this young man tell you he saw under his microscope when he examined specimens from the victims?"

"Nothing. He saw no microbes."

"And you, Monsieur Verne, you who conjures up science from your imagination, what is your feeling about the affair?"

"I'm greatly bothered by it. Something strange is going on. Things I cannot explain at this time. But my feeling is that the contagion is going to get worse and that whatever the cause, the nation's—the world's—greatest microbiologist should be in the vanguard of examining this strange new disease . . ."

Pasteur shakes his head before Jules finishes talking.

"No, that is impossible, impossible, until I am invited in by the medical doctors who are handling the matter. And I am afraid that will not happen. Even before this matter, I embarrassed health department doctors when they erred diagnosing a cholera outbreak in Marseille. No, I cannot get involved in the matter."

"Then perhaps, as a Good Samaritan, you can assist us with our investigation?" Jules asks.

"And what is the nature of your investigation?"

Jules holds up his hands as if he is physically blocking the question. "Mademoiselle Brown is on a secret assignment and can't disclose the reasons for the investigation. However, I can assure you that as a son of France, there is nothing she is doing that would bring shame on our country. In all honesty what she is investigating is to the benefit of France."

Pasteur looks at Roth again, as if for confirmation. He leans back in his chair and closes his eyes for a moment. "I don't doubt your sincerity. We are both members of the Legion of Honor."

He hesitates again before going on, as if he is gathering his thoughts—and straining them through a filter. "I have, in an unofficial way, become interested in the contagion," he finally admits. "I've been given samples from some of the victims. Tests are still being performed and the origin of the contagion is still under investigation. But logically, there are two sources for the contagion to arise from. Microbes and poisonous chemicals. No chemicals have been found to date, nor has a living organism or microbe. While there is a great deal of logic to conclude sewer fumes are involved—the odor, the decay—*logic* is not science. I know of no incident in which sewer gases harmed anyone in this manner.

"What does concern me is that the symptoms of high fever and coughs are also those associated with an invasion of the body by microbes. The quick decay of organs surprises me. It must be caused by a microbe so virulent it strikes with great speed. Yet when we view the samples under a microscope, we don't see it. While our microscopes are not powerful enough to see microbes, we can detect their presence by other experiments. We have failed even at that. It's quite frustrating."

"Based upon the limited facts before you," Jules says, "is it more likely that the contagion is caused by an invasion of microbes rather than an exposure to poison?"

"Yes."

"And you don't believe the sewer system is the source?"

Pasteur hesitates a moment. "You said sewer *system*. We've been talking about sewer *gases*. For certain, microbes are lurking in sewer systems. But in terms of this condition being caused by vapors rising from the sewer, I would need further evidence to reach that conclusion."

"There are two and a half million people in Paris," I interject, "but up to now, the contagion has only appeared in a few areas. What would happen if a quick acting lethal and contagious microbe got loose in the city?"

"The same thing would happen that happened last time."

"Last time!" The surprise in my voice has everyone looking at me and I feel a little foolish . . . no, a lot foolish. I have no idea what they are talking about.

Pasteur's eyes twinkle and he gives me a kind smile. "The Black Plague was caused by a microbe, one that we have not yet even seen, although I'm certain that we will some day when microscopes are improved. It killed tens of millions in Europe, probably one out of every three people. If it happened today, over twelve million people would die in France alone. Plagues and other epidemics return periodically to attack us, though not as devastating as the one in the Middle Ages."

He stops and eyes Jules narrowly.

"Monsieur Verne, I hope you have not come here to pick my brain for one of your novels, for I can assure you that the consequences of a widespread microbe attacking the city would be much worse than even your amazing imagination could devise."

34

After Jules and I leave the Institut, we walk along the street in silence, ignoring the offers for services from passing carriages, both of us in a brown study.

My mind is spinning from the consequences Dr. Pasteur described. There are about forty million people in France, sixty million in the United States. Between the two countries alone, over thirty million people could be killed by a great plague, not to mention tens of millions more throughout Europe and the rest of the world.

"Jules, I'm confused. We went to Pasteur to find out about the microbe, what it can do, and how fast it can kill a human being. And I must say the information we received was quite frightening. But what does this have to do with the slasher's killings?"

I suspected Dr. Blum was conducting some sort of horrid experiments in his lab, but the death of millions was too much to comprehend.

"From what you have told me, he's a devil with a link to science—though not the relationship men like Pasteur enjoy. I suspect he's experimenting on his victims. Perhaps they're his lab rats."

"Human laboratory rats . . . *that's horrible* . . . using

human beings as guinea pigs? It certainly fits with the maniac's lust for dissecting his victims. But why?"

Jules shrugs. "He's conducting mad experiments on women, satisfying both his sexual perversions and aberrant science."

"My God, it sounds very much like that. But the man must be truly crazy. People aren't lab rats."

"There's no doubt that a man who cuts up women is insane. But an aberrant mentality can be a strong driving force. What we must determine is his motive. Just because he's insane doesn't mean there isn't a design to his acts. What may be twisted, perverse madness to us is logic and reason to a madman."

"I've pursued a madman with a crazed impulse to slash women. The idea that he could be using women as lab rats is even more repulsive."

"Think back, where did you first find him? In a shack, set up as a lab, at a mental hospital that really didn't ask questions when a woman went missing."

"Yes, Doctor Blum told Josephine he needed her help in a project. But I thought that to be a ruse. But it's just too crazy."

"There's no reason a scientist, if that's what he is, can't be as crazy as any other demented man. Can you imagine the harm of someone with scientific brilliance turning to alchemy and the dark side of science? Intelligence is not a gift just for the good. Some of the greatest rulers who have ever lived, men who have swayed over millions or conquered empires, were madmen. Ivan the Terrible, the Borgias, Genghis Khan, Attila the Hun, Richard III, Henry VIII, they were all blood-thirsty mass murderers. Scientists like Doctor Pasteur have saved thousands of lives. Who knows what harm a mad genius can do? There are more virulent killers in a cup of sewer water than all of the armies of the Great Khan. Turn them loose on the world and they would be an invisible army of conquerors."

"Jules, we are hunting for a man that walks on two feet, not an invisible army of germs. Besides, I came to Paris to find a killer, not to save the world." But even as I speak the words, headlines flash in my mind: *NELLIE BLY SAVES THE WORLD.*

Saving the world would not be such a bad thing. I just pray I'll live to report it.

35

Jules and I go in separate directions. He's off to have dinner with his doctor and discuss the fever outbreak in more detail. Initially, I feel slighted that I didn't get an invitation to the dinner, but I must admit it works nicely for me. I'm not through intriguing for the day.

Upon arriving at Pigalle Hospital, I give the fiacre driver an extra tip to go in and inquire at the reception desk as to the hour Dr. Dubois gets off work. He is told six o'clock. Since I have an hour to wait, I send him on his way, thanking him, and take a brisk walk to burn off nervous energy and clear my head.

When I return I decide to wait in a café-bar across from the hospital, a place where one can stand at the counter and get a cup of *café au lait*. As I sip my drink and try to fit together the pieces of Jules' insane notion about the slasher and this killer microbe, I get a glimpse of a tall and very large-built man coming out of the hospital. I almost spill my drink. From the height and bulk I am certain this is the same man who was lying in wait for me last night outside my garret.

There can't be two men in Paris with that physique. He's wearing a flowing black cape and a hat that a Musketeer would be embarrassed to don. A large golden eagle feather is slanting out of the dark purple velvet band.

Once again, I can't see the face.

He turns and goes down the street. Curious as to who he is and where he's going, I leave the café and follow him. I've gone no more than a dozen feet when he turns into a building. Hurrying after him, I enter the building, an office establishment with a pharmacy on the first floor.

He's nowhere in sight.

I ask the pharmacist, "Did a tall, *very* large man wearing a black cape come in here?"

He jerks his head toward a door. "He went to the offices."

The door he indicates leads into an entryway that has only a stairway leading to the offices above and a door that I presume takes you out to the back of the building. I start to go up the steps and pause—what's my plan? I can't go office to office asking for a huge man in a black cape with a crazy hat.

I check the time. Dr. Dubois will be leaving the hospital soon. If I continue this hunt, I will miss him. I go back to the café and wait at the coffee bar, sipping a new *café au lait* and watching the hospital steps. I can't shake that huge man from my mind. Could he have a connection to Dr. Dubois?

PROMPTLY AT SIX, Dr. Dubois comes down the front steps of the hospital and walks up the boulevard. I follow on foot, giving him a good lead. I'm surprised at the location he leads me to—a circus.

Cirque Fernando, the world's most famous circus, is not far from the Moulin Rouge. It's permanently housed in a wood building shaped like a huge circus tent. I've passed the building several times during my Montmartre ventures, but never had the time to buy a ticket and enjoy the acts that have the reputation of being the finest in the world.

He doesn't buy a ticket, but instead joins a large group of people that have formed outside next to a hot air balloon. The balloon is staked beside the main tent. Its passenger basket is big enough to transport four people. I'm familiar with both gas and hot air balloons because I rode in one at a Pittsburgh fair soon after starting my first reporting job.

The ride took us three thousand feet into the air and a fresh breeze swept us miles from Pittsburgh before setting us down in a cornfield. Swinging and bouncing in that balloon basket had been a frightful ride at the time, but in looking back it was an exciting experience. I was positive my editor would commend me for my daring feat, but instead he was annoyed. Called it *unladylike!* An expression I despise. No doubt it was invented by a man who didn't want a woman playing with his toys.

The circus balloon is a "captive" one—ropes are lashed to its basket so it won't rise more than fifty feet in the air. From the talk around me I learn the balloon will carry trapeze artists above the crowd where they'll perform death defying feats designed to motivate people to buy tickets to see more daring acts inside the tent.

The artists tonight are the Flying Lombardos, an Italian brother-sister team. A barker in a red ruffled frock coat, matching top hat and a jet-black beard atop a platform next to the balloon extols the skill and courage of the young trapeze artists.

Dark clouds loom overhead, giving an added touch to the excitement. Jules would enjoy this. Many of his most successful books have dealt with aeronauts, the daring men who defy gravity in balloons to fly like birds.

The daring duo come onto the stage-platform and the

audience gives them a thunderous ovation. They're certainly a handsome pair, about my age with red hair, pale green eyes, and complexions kissed by the sun. I suspect they're not just brother and sister but twins—with long hair and a padded chest, the brother could well pass for his sister.

As the balloon lurches up, the trapeze artists give a bow to the audience and leap from the platform onto aerial ladders hanging beneath the basket. The two young daredevils have nerves of steel. They swing from one ladder to the other. The young man, hanging from his knees, catches his sister as she leaps like a monkey from her own ladder. We gasp in horror as she slips from his hands—and scream with relief as she catches the ladder's bottom rung. I am sure all part of the act, but extremely well done.

I spot Dr. Dubois in the crowd. His face is flushed with excitement, but it's the look of a man who is aroused by more than the vicarious danger. No doubt he's smitten with the trapeze girl.

Once the balloon exhibition is over, the good doctor heads up Boulevard Clichy with me a safe distance behind him.

Night is falling and people are leaving work, some heading home, while others stop for drinks at the boulevard cafés. Dr. Dubois does the latter and enters a café called the Rat Mort. I sit on a bench nearby, unsure what to do next.

The entrance is guarded by a large woman enthroned on a high bench behind a bar. She's of some fifty years, whose swelling contours are tightly laced by belts and corsets. She seems to know everyone that enters, including the doctor. I need to figure out a way to get by her and not been seen by Dr. Dubois. I hear someone call her "Laure" and get behind another woman in line to be ushered into the salon proper. Each woman who enters cranes over the saucers on the counter and kisses Laure on the mouth with tender familiarity.*

What have I gotten myself into? If I want to get in, I'm going to have to kiss this woman on the lips! Never! As I contemplate my fate, the young woman in front of me turns and says, "Quite a bunch of old hags, aren't they?" She has a common look to her and I peg her as a shop girl.

Smiling, I murmur a listening response. I'm more concerned on how to avoid kissing the woman.

She jerks her head at the café. "I've just come by to pick up a meal and a few extra francs. I'm not of that persuasion, if you know what I mean, but these old *poules* like to have young faces to flirt with. It's better than pulling the devil by the tail."

To pull the devil by the tail is to live from hand to mouth.

"Come here often?" she asks.

"My first time."

"Well, let me show you the ropes."

"That's very kind of you. I'm Nellie."

"Rosine."

Rosine gives Laure, the gatekeeper, a kiss and I flow by with just a nod. She doesn't mind. The girl behind me is eager to kiss her.

I spot Dr. Dubois approaching a table where two people are already seated. One rises to greet the doctor—it's the big man that was lying in wait for me outside my

---

* Coincidentally, this description of the Rat Mort (Dead Rat) Café is almost the same description Émile Zola used in his 1880 risqué novel of Parisian theater life, *Nana*. The café in Zola's book might have been the Rat Mort, thinly disguised as "Laure's." We don't know how Nellie ended up with a similar passage in her journal notes. It's probable they both visited the café when Laure was there.—The Editors.

apartment building and the one I tried to follow from the hospital. The big man kisses Dr. Dubois on the lips! A long, full kiss. Good Lord, they're sodomites!

I haven't read the Krafft-Ebling study Jules mentioned, but I've heard it discussed, and I'm not a babe in the woods. I know there are liaisons between men—a medical condition called an "inversion" of sexual feelings— and that a new term, "homosexuality," is used in the German study. Strict laws are on the books almost everywhere prohibiting such couplings. In many countries the death penalty is applied. But this is bohemian Montmartre where anything goes.

The other person at Dr. Dubois' table is a woman. She never gets up. I am unable to make out her features or age because her back is to me, but the doctor also kisses her on the lips as he sits down.

At another table a young man with short curly hair is keeping a table full of middle-aged women breathlessly attentive to his slightest caprice. Further observation reveals that when the young man laughs, his bosom swells. The man is really a woman! "Boston marriages" is what the boys in the newsroom call liaisons between women.

As my escort leads me in, Dubois, the big man, and the woman, rise from their table and disappear up a stairway.

36

"Over here, Rosine, you girls join us."

The woman who beckoned us wears a man's fedora, the hat made popular by Victorien Sardou's play of the same name. Another woman sits next to her. Both have clumsy figures and so much rouge and lipstick caked on, they look like clowns. As they fawn over Rosine and eye me, they remind me of the matronly hens who cackled the loudest at church socials when I was a little girl.

To say the least, I have no interest in the women's conversation and pay no attention. I needed to know what Dubois and his big friend were doing upstairs but I couldn't just rush up the steps. I don't even notice the drink before me until I feel Rosine nudging me.

"My friends bought you a green fairy."

"*Merci.*" I take a gulp and it goes down my throat like green lava. I stop breathing. My whole body lights on fire. My eyes feel like they have swelled and are ready to burst from their sockets. Determined not to draw attention to myself, I very slowly let out a breath, sure I am expelling fire. I cough politely in a handkerchief and wipe my teary eyes. I try to breathe, but it hurts.

"All right, my dear?" The woman with the fedora gives me a sloppy grin.

"Fine," I croak. "It tastes like licorice."

Rosine takes a swig of her own drink. "You have to get used to it, of course, but once you do, you're hooked like a fish."

The three women go on with their empty café chatter as I politely force myself to slowly sip my drink. I do say, Dr. Dubois is full of surprises.

"Here, my love." Rosine places another green fairy in front of me, disrupting my thoughts. "This one will taste much better, now that you've got the burn of the first out of the way." She laughs and goes back to talking with the women.

I am leery of having another drink.

"Come on." Rosine leans close and whispers in my ear, "You don't want to insult my friends. Drink up."

I know the score when it comes to alcohol. It all boils down to mind over matter. It's really that simple. My reaction to alcohol is just a matter of mind over matter. I can surrender to the alcohol, let it take control of my mind, or I can take control of it. My choice. It makes no difference that this is my first experience with a strong drink; I will be able to handle it because I am a very determined, strong-willed, modern woman.

As I told Mr. Pulitzer before I left for Paris, we cannot be afraid of the challenges that are presented to us in our life. The only way to conquer them is to face them head on with a strong determination to conquer and win. The same goes for liquor.

Satisfied that I have this beverage well under control and feeling quite forthright, I have another and wait patiently for Dubois and his friends to reappear. As the minutes tick off, I begin to feel lightheaded. Finally I ask, "What goes on upstairs?"

Rosine puts her hand on my thigh and leans much closer than she did before, her lips brushing my ear this time as she whispers, "It's a private place for secret things. Let's leave these old cows and I'll show you."

Ah, secret things.

Exactly what I thought—the dark heart of the den of iniquity. No doubt I will catch Dubois and his friends red-handed in flagrante delicto. Excited, I gulp down the last of my third drink and lick my lips, grinning at Rosine.

"Yummy. You're right about this drink. I like it." I get up and flop back down. "Whoa! I feel dizzy."

Rosine helps me up. "Its okay, honey, you just need to get your feet under you."

"Keeping them under me is the problem." I giggle as we head for the stairs. Rosine's arm is around my waist holding me up. "Up, up, up the stairs, one, two, three—up we go."

"*Shhh,*" she laughs, "you're attracting attention."

"That won't do," I cackle. My head is so light; I could have flown up the stairs.

"*Shhh.*"

"Rosine," I try to whisper, "do you know why it's called a green fairy?"

She shakes her head no and laughs. "Please tell me."

"It's because it makes you as light as a fairy."

We both break out giggling, making it harder for us to get up the steps. At the top of the stairs we enter a smoky room that smells sweet.

"Over there, I want a dark corner." I steer her to a small table hidden in a dark corner. Once seated, I look around the room, trying to spot my prey. Rosine snuggles very, very, close to me. Her hand goes onto my thigh, while her lips kiss my cheek, then my ear. I pay no attention, for I am on a mission.

In the haze of smoke I see the big man, Dr. Dubois,

and the woman. Dr. Dubois appears to be pointing at something.

"That's them," I say, frowning at the group. I stare at them and finally realize it's *me* Dr. Dubois is pointing at.

"You surprise me . . ." Rosine whispers in my ear as her hand moves way up inside my dress and pushes between my thighs. "I didn't take you for one who wanted fun."

I turn to her to respond and *she gives me a full kiss on the mouth!*

In a flash she wraps one hand around my shoulder holding me tight, while the other fondles my breasts. The room starts to spin—faster than a merry-go-round. And even though I try, I can't pull away from her. Finally she stops.

"Wha—!" is all that comes out of my mouth. I shove her away from me, sending her and her chair flying onto the floor. As I stand up, the little table goes over.

My head continues to swirl and swirl and I collapse back down, but the swirling won't stop. It becomes a maelstrom, like the terrible black whirlpool Jules Verne traveled to the Arctic Circle to witness.

A wave of vertigo engulfs my mind and then there is nothing.

37

Tomas Roth

While Roth was in the laboratory studying his notes, Émile Duclaux, Dr. Pasteur's second in command of the facility, poked his head in and instructed Roth to meet Pasteur in the rabies lab. As Roth got up to wash his hands and follow him out, Duclaux pointed down at something on the floor. "Isn't that René's cap?"

"Why, yes. He must have dropped it on his way out." Roth picked up the yarmulke knitted by René's wife and tossed it on the counter.

Roth's job as Pasteur's assistant did not include the highly specialized rabies work, but he was not surprised that he was instructed to meet Pasteur there. Inflammatory accusations about the Black Fever outbreak were on the front pages of last evening's newspapers. No doubt the Minister of the Interior made another visit to the Institut.

Duclaux read Roth's thoughts as they walked down the corridor. "Last night it was the minister again. Next time I believe it will be the President himself pleading for help."

"Perhaps the Institut should give classes to politicians on how to use a microscope."

Duclaux gave him a look of disapproval that said humor was not appreciated with the city in a crisis.

Immediately upon entering the rabies laboratory, Roth rolled up his sleeves to wash his hands at a sink with an overhanging spigot and deep basin. Hand washing was mandatory for each person who entered or left a laboratory—a fixed ritual established by Dr. Pasteur. One began by washing the bar of soap itself, rinsing away the outer layer, then lathering hands and wrists, rinsing a layer off the soap again before returning it to its dish.

"The laboratory is a zoo with many exotic and dangerous animals," Pasteur told Roth when he had come to work at the Institut. "You must take care none of them bite you."

Roth had even seen Pasteur unconsciously wiping his water glass, plate, and utensil with his napkin during Institut lunches. The man was a fanatic about cleanliness, but one could not blame Pasteur after what he had discovered under the microscope and was always reminded of the horrible deaths these unseen creatures did to his family and close friends, not to mention society.

Dr. Pasteur was standing by, deep in thought, while a rabies assistant examined a rabbit's spinal cord. Roth didn't dare disturb Pasteur with questions or suggestions. Rising at dawn, Pasteur was completely engrossed in his work throughout the day, spending most of his waking hours in the laboratories. In the evening, to save his eyesight from the ravages of gaslights and oil lamps, Madame Pasteur read the day's newspapers to him in their private apartment. That was his life, a life that did not include the opera or even family picnics.

Pasteur was dedicated, determined. Roth agreed that it was the only way to be if one wanted to accomplish anything of importance in life. He also thought the opera and family picnics were trivial and boring.

Dr. Grancher, the medical doctor who performed Dr. Pasteur's medical procedures, appeared at Roth's side. Pasteur gave a little start, as if he was suddenly aware that he was not alone in the universe. Roth believed no one, other than himself, had such concentration.

"The children from America, have they arrived?" he asked Grancher.

"A few minutes ago."

Three children, two boys and a girl, each about nine or ten years old, had been bitten by a rabid fox in a rural area south of Boston. A Boston newspaper paid passage for the children across the Atlantic, sending along a reporter to wire accounts of the race to get the children to Institut Pasteur before they were driven mad and died from the loathsome disease.

Rolls of sterilized flasks held marrow infected with rabies—nerve tissue of a rabid rabbit that was mixed with veal broth and inoculated into bitten victims. After Pasteur made arrangements with Dr. Grancher to initiate treatment to the American children, Roth followed him to the sink where they washed their hands before leaving the lab.

"What are the results of the tests you and René have been conducting?" Pasteur inquired.

"The same. We've been unable to see the microbe under the microscope or isolate it and transfer it to another host."

"*Mon Dieu*, could the microbe actually die immediately upon the death of the host? Certainly we would expect the invaders to die after they've used up all the nourishment in the body, but can that happen so quickly? And leaving no trace?"

"Perhaps the creature has an extremely short life span."

"Not that short, it has to live to be passed to others,

otherwise it wouldn't be infectious. And René, where is he? I need his results."

"I believe he went home. But I can check and see if he is in the lab next door."

Pasteur picked up the pad Roth recorded lab notes on. "I'm sure he hasn't gone home. He knows never to leave without going over his results with me first." There was a slight irritation in his voice. "When you find him, please ask him to see me."

Roth went to the lab where René ran his tests. As he opened the door an obvious odor prevailed. After a moment, he closed the door and returned to Dr. Pasteur. Pasteur was engrossed in reading Roth's notes and Roth gently placed his hand on Pasteur's arm to get his attention.

"Monsieur Doctor, we have a serious problem."

His liquid greyish-green eyes found Roth's.

"What is it?"

"René is dead. The microbe is loose in the Institut."

38

Nellie

I awake slowly, struggling out of a deep well of sleep. My head is heavy. I lie perfectly still, surrounded by darkness, slowly letting each of my senses come awake. A strange sound finds my ears—a harsh, rumbling noise, but I can't identify the sound or my whereabouts. Light is coming from some source and I automatically turn my head—not a good move. I can't believe how my head hurts.

Things around me begin to come into focus. I'm in my own room, in bed, fully clothed and completely confused. How did I get here? And what is the source of that strange noise? Not knowing which will be the lesser evil—sitting up or moving my head—I choose to slowly twist my neck and follow the sound to its source.

Good God—the large man I saw kissing Dr. Dubois is sprawled on my floor! He's sound asleep and snoring.

I jerk awake. My head forgets about its pain. I feel under the pillow for the long-barreled .44. It's not loaded, but the big man won't know that. Clutching the gun, I carefully climb out of bed so not to wake him. Once I'm standing over him with the gun pointed straight at his head, I command in a loud voice, "Put up your hands!"

Nothing. I kick his foot. It merely makes a bump in his snoring. Kneeling down, I stick the gun in his face. Holding it with two hands, I pull back the hammer. Annie Oakly told me the tell-tale click of a gun cocking is the loudest little sound in the world. She was right. The snoring came to a rumbling halt and the man's eyes flutter open.

"Put up your hands." I demand.

He blinks at me. "Why?"

"So I don't shoot you."

He seems to be mystified by the threat, as if he's puzzled by the notion I would shoot him.

"Dear girl, why would you shoot me after I helped you?" His voice is very British.

"Helped me?"

"Why yes. How do you think you got from the café to your room?"

How indeed? He starts to sit up and I shove the gun muzzle against his nose. He carefully pushes it aside, but I still keep it pointed at his face.

"I carried you. And wasn't your concierge a regular Medusa. That's what you called her, you know, quite accurately, a regular Medusa she is, and fortunately unable to understand your English."

I back off as he rises on an elbow, keeping the gun pointed straight at him. "I don't remember any such thing."

"Of course not, you were quite sponged . . . slept through the night and the whole day."

"What?"

"Obviously, you're not well acquainted with the green fairy. Absinthe has a very high alcohol content, 136 proof, and will knock you silly if you're not careful."

I start to defend myself, but have nothing to say, so I let him continue. He seems to have plenty to say.

"Happens to all of us in the beginning. I picked you off the floor and carried you back here."

"Let's get down to basics. Tell me why you've been following me and what you have to do with the slasher."

He giggles. In an unconscious gesture he puts his hand to his mouth to hide rather greenish teeth that protrude unattractively from coarse lips. He has two huge rings on his fingers—a ruby and a rough block of silver with a design from Greek antiquity. It isn't often you see a grown man giggling so, but this huge man does, and rather girlishly. If I wasn't so confused and angry, I believe I would have giggled along with him—or at him. Finally he stops and clears his throat.

"My dear girl, do I appear to be someone who would be in league with a killer?"

His voice is cultured and haughty, as only an overeducated Brit can be. And it's melodious, like a finely tuned musical instrument. He speaks as if he enjoys the sound of his own voice.

Giving the man the once over, I can't decide exactly how I would place him in a civilized society. He dresses as he speaks, from several ages of history. His clothes are of the oddest sort, street clothes that are little less provocative than the costumes at carnival time.

A full overcoat . . . no, more a cloak that he's using as a blanket, comes down to his ankles. It's dark green with black fur trim that matches his hat and black breeches. The breeches come to the top of his knees where black silk stockings flow down to low cut black patent shoes with a shiny silver buckle.

Under the overcoat is a black velvet jacket; a china blue shirt matches the color of his eyes. The wide Lord Byron collar is opened to expose the hair of his chest, the only manly attribute to this person of somewhat dubious sex.

He appears to be in the worst physical condition, striking me as someone who gets his exercise *talking*. With his skin as pale as a winter moon and eyes as blue as the sea, he reminds me of a great white whale—big, flabby, and sluggish. How he carried me up the steps without a coronary is a mystery.

"I was only too glad to be of assistance when you became, shall we say inconvenienced, at the café. It was the luck of the seven Japanese gods of good fortune that I happened along at the right moment."

"Nonsense. I was drugged at that den of iniquity. And it wasn't luck that you were there, I followed Doctor Dubois."

"Naturally, I had deduced that, but being the gentleman I am, I avoided mentioning it to save feelings all around."

"If you want to save more than your feelings, you better tell me what you and the good doctor are up to. I took shooting lessons from Annie Oakly and my finger gets an itch to pull the trigger after a while. So, let's start by putting a name to you."

"Oscar Jones of London, at your service." If he could have bowed, he would have.

"My trigger finger doesn't like that name. Try another."

"I beg your—"

I adjust my grip on the gun.

"Yes, yes, of course. Well, my dear girl, if you must know, I am Oscar Wilde."

It wasn't a statement, but an announcement, perhaps even a proclamation. The sort of thing one might expect shouted from the gates of Buckingham Palace.

"Not *the* Oscar Wilde?"

He glows. "There is only one and that is gift enough for the world."

"Never heard of you," I tell him truthfully. "You better talk fast, Mister Wilde, because I don't know how much longer my little fingers can keep this big gun from going off and blowing another hole in your face as big as your mouth."

He looks more pained by the fact that I didn't recognize his name than frightened by the gun.

"I'm from London. Rather well known in all the literary circles. I've even been to America, but obviously you missed me."

"Obviously. You write books?"

"I have several planned, but I'm also a poet and playwright. And, until very recently, editor of *Woman's World* magazine. If you will forgive my lack of modesty, while my name may not be spoken on the streets, people in correct society know it. I am anxiously solicited as a dinner guest for my wit and wisdom."

He has one of those cultured English voices of the upper class who precisely enunciate their words with an almost lyrical rhythm. The way he speaks to you, even with a gun in his face, makes you feel he is talking down to you.

"Toured your fine country, spoke about art, even out West. Even went out to a boomtown called Leadville and lectured roughneck miners about Florentine art. That's where I learned about revolvers, exactly like the one you're holding. The miners consider bad art worthy of the penalty of death—at one saloon, there is a sign which says *Please don't shoot the pianist, he's doing his best.*"

He gives me a coy look with a carnal grin and once again his hand goes up to hide his teeth.

I look at the gun I'm holding. He's knows the gun is empty. If it was loaded you'd see the bullets in the revolving chamber. I let it drop into my lap. It's getting way too heavy to keep pointing anyway.

"Okay, if you're so famous for talking, go right ahead. Tell me what you were doing with the doctor."

"I'm investigating a murder," he says rapidly. "I'm a detective, in a manner of speaking."

"You mean the self-appointed sort of detective?" It's obviously a profession I am familiar with.

"Well . . . yes, in a manner of speaking. Though I can assure you, I've read up on the subject." He's telling the truth, I know it. The man can exaggerate, but not lie. He thinks his words are too important to be false.

"Keep talking. Who was murdered?"

He takes a moment, as if it's hard for him to answer. "A dear friend of mine . . . Jean-Jacque Telney."

I honestly feel he's trying to gain his composure. It's the same reaction I have when I talk about Josephine. "I'm sorry."

"Thank you, my dear." He has true pain in his eyes. "He was a poet. You've heard of him?"

"No . . . I'm sorry. I've heard of Verlaine."

"Ah, a voice of the gods. As a poet myself, I can attest to that."

"Do you have any idea who murdered your friend?"

"That's what Doctor Dubois and I are trying to find out." Oscar sits up and fans his face with a red silk handkerchief, sending a whiff of perfume my direction.

"Was Jean-Jacque a sodomite like you and Doctor Dubois?"

The handkerchief flaps like he is shooing flies away from his face. "My dear, that's hardly a proper way for a lady to talk."

"I'll take that as a yes. Now, would you mind telling me how your friend died?"

Oscar bends his head down for a second before

answering and I realize the question came out too bluntly. "I'm sorry."

"A madman brutally cut him."

His voice cracks as he answers and agony fills his eyes. Again, memories of Josephine flood my mind and I can't help but reach out and touch his arm. We sit silent, each feeling our grief for someone we cared for and now gone.

"Please forgive me for asking, but I must. How did he cut him? Can you describe the wounds?"

He makes a cutting motion across his abdomen. "Here. Severely. And lower." His fat lips tremble with emotion and his eyes tear. "Like they do animals in slaughter-houses. How could anybody do that to another person? And to someone as kind and gentle as Jean-Jacque."

This makes no sense. The slasher has never attacked a *man*.

"I've studied detecting." Oscar fills the brief void with his words, a very soothing voice at that. "I dined just last month in London with Doctor Doyle who writes those tales about Sherlock Holmes, a consulting detective who uses science and deductive reasoning to solve crimes. I've read him thoroughly and also spent an afternoon with a Scotland Yard inspector who is a friend of my father. But frankly, despite my intellect and expertise, I am finding this mystery to be a singularly difficult one to fathom."*

---

* For a man who had written only two plays, and highly criticized poetry, Oscar managed to get an attractive offer during that dinner to write a book. Arthur Conan Doyle sold the publisher his second Sherlock Holmes story, *The Sign of Four*. Wilde sold the publisher the concept of a book that ultimately became *The Picture of Dorian Gray*, which was published in 1890. The publisher asked Oscar for 100,000 word book and got a much shorter one—and the reply that "There are not 100,000 beautiful words in the English language." The Dorian book essentially launched Oscar's career as a brilliant writer.—The Editors.

"What does Doctor Dubois have to do with this matter?"

"Luc Dubois is my friend."

"Your friend, that's all?"

"Why . . . yes."

"It's just that when I saw the two of you last night, I thought . . ."

"No, no, my dear. He was, however, on intimate terms with Jean-Jacque. When we took up the investigation after poor Jean-Jacque was butchered, we reasoned that a maniac who kills so bizarrely once, will kill again. Luc volunteered to be the police surgeon for Montmartre so he can be called to the scene of the murders. He came into contact with you at the cemetery where that horrible Black Fever victim was found. The officer questioning you at the scene revealed to Luc your theory that the dead woman had been a victim of the slasher. Naturally, that piqued our interest, but we didn't know how to contact you until you presented yourself at the hospital."

"What did you expect to accomplish?"

"Why, to gain your confidence, dear girl, and get you to tell me what you know about this unusual affair."

"Why didn't you just ask me? Especially since I went to Doctor Dubois with questions. You would think after I told him my situation, *he* would have asked me. Why didn't he? And why were you hiding outside my garret?"

He starts to say something, then closes his mouth. No doubt one of those rare times he is at a loss for words.

"Too difficult to answer?"

"Don't be insolent now. I had a plan worked out that even Zeus would have approved. And I wasn't stalking you. I was waiting for you to come home. Then I was going to approach you, in a gentlemanly manner. But then that damn dog chased me. He almost bit me!"

"Too bad."

"Wha—?"

"Continue."

"Luc says you believe the slasher stalks prostitutes. I have a friend, a painter, who knows more prostitutes than anyone in Paris. Like myself, he's also an anarchist."

"A famous painter?"

"Oh, no. No one you've heard of. His paintings aren't even bought for wallpaper. He hangs them in cafés because he can't get respectable showings."

"Why does he know so many prostitutes?"

"He likes to paint them. To get truly informed about his subjects, he is presently living in a house of prostitution. Really quite an interesting chap. Toulouse is welcomed everywhere and men whisper secrets to him that they would never divulge to their mistress."

He delicately pats the sweat on his forehead. The sweet scent of lilacs evokes an image of the café scene where men and women gather to practice their unconventional views of sex, sojourning from their day's work at a place where they can let down their hair—or in the case of women, perhaps push it up under a cap. With that image came an insight into why Jean-Jacque, a man, was murdered, and I jump up from the floor.

"Your friend, Jean-Jacque, was a cross-dresser, wasn't he? He dressed as a woman. Am I right?"

Wilde's eyes pop. "How did you know that?"

I lean back against the railing post on the step and let out a great sigh. "Elementary, my dear Mister Wilde, elementary."

We find the faces of
all Lautrec's friends in the
backgrounds of his pictures . . .
In the oils and pastels we can see the
madams offering young and more or
less unspoiled girls to old, thickly painted
gentlemen dressed in grand but slightly soiled
clothes and ready for any kind of liaison. To
others they are pointing out those whose
specialty is whipping, the English vice, who can be
recognized by their stern looks. Then there are the
lesbians, knowing quite well that the girls often like
to forget in their arms the men who keep them. The
young pimps are usually brilliant dancers, launching
their sisters into the world while overseeing the two
or three women who work for them; and, more
sinister, the tanned, scarred face and probably
tattooed body of the pimp come back from Biribi,
the military prison, and ready to become the
"terror" of a *quartier.*

—Philippe Jullian,
Montmartre

39

"Yes, I've heard of the man," Jules says.

He wrinkles his nose as if thinking about Oscar Wilde is malodorous. The rocking of the carriage sends me brushing against him. His scent is masculine and very appealing. I straighten up.

Jules continues. "A café intellectual, a society wit, a self-appointed arbiter of literature who fancies comedies of manners. His name appears occasionally on the society page. His literary credits always appear vague, some volumes of poetry, I believe."

"And a couple plays. I'm not sure both were even produced. But he does know people, like this artist we're going to see." I wonder what it is about Oscar that has made Jules so disturbed—especially when he's never met the man. I dare not ask for fear he'll just bite my head off.

"I can't believe you talked me into meeting this creature and his artist friend at a house of prostitution. If I'm seen . . ."

I can't guarantee he won't be recognized, so I put a positive reason on why we are going there. "Oscar tells me this man knows more about what happens in Mont-

martre than the nosiest concierge. He might have knowledge of the slasher."

"Humph," he utters.

"I also understand he's from a noble family, his father's a count or something."

"A count? A count's son lives in a house of prostitution and paints whores? Are you certain that your friend
Oscar isn't a lotus-eater!?"

"A lotus-eater . . . really . . ."

Jules just gives me a look like I've lost my head. Maybe
I have—I mean, for a young woman to travel unaccom-
panied to a foreign country to stop a mad killer . . . I
must be the one eating lotus!

"In all honesty, I don't care what he eats, who he is,
and who he associates with. All that matters is finding the
slasher. If I have to, I'll use the devil himself to help me."

Jules takes a long, deep breath and then slowly turns
and looks at me with those intense brown eyes of his.
Here it comes—how impetuous I am, how I don't think
of the consequences, and I'm such an American
woman . . .

"You're right . . . and the devil may prove to be your
strongest ally."

He goes back to staring out his window as if his whole
life is passing by. Jules obviously needs time to work on
the devil that's eating away at him. I respect his wish for
privacy and turn and look out my window. As the coach
travels down a dark street, I can't help but observe him
in the light of the passing gaslights. I try to be discreet
by watching him from the corner of my eye.

The more I deal with him, the more I find him com-
plicated, intriguing, and I must admit . . . a handsome
puzzle. I just wish I could put my finger on the name of
the demon that sometimes possesses him—slipping past
his composure and exposing anger, even rage, beneath

his calm exterior. He has the potential for violence—he did tell me he came to Paris to kill a man. Then I had a horrible thought: could my attraction to him be clouding my judgment? Many intelligent women made fools of themselves because they became blinded by love.

"You actually pointed a gun at the man?" Jules stares at me with a mixture of interest . . . and disbelief.

"Only at his face."

He shakes his head and shudders. "I guess that can be expected from a woman raised in a country where cultural conflicts are battles between cowboys and Indians."

"There's more to America than—"

"Yes, yes, Americans are very inventive; it will be a great country someday, if it ever stops to realize it's only one part of a big world."

That's it, nothing I say will change his mind about Americans so I steer him back to the subject at hand. "Oscar's important to the investigation. If for no other reason than he can make himself a pest."

I don't mention Oscar knows I'm wanted by the police and that I'm an investigative reporter. I swore Oscar to secrecy before we parted this morning. "Mum's the word," he assured me. Unfortunately, Oscar has such a love to talk I fear it's going to be hard for him to keep his word. But life is full of surprises.

"Fine. But we should investigate Wilde before sharing any secrets with him. I have a friend who covers the boulevard cafés for a newspaper. We'll consult with him about the man."

"If that makes you feel better. In the meantime, did I tell you that Oscar said the artist is an anarchist? This is good, since I suspect the slasher is one."

Another huff emerges from Jules. "People like your friend Oscar are café anarchists. They argue radical change over a glass of absinthe, but sleep in their comfortable beds while the poor shiver under Seine bridges. They would take their turn on the guillotine if their distorted political theories actually got implemented."

He leans back and half shuts his eyes. "Please pardon me. Part of it is old age, the spite of the old against the spirit of youth. It has been eons since I sat in a café and debated social change. And partly it's anger. I am the best-known author in France, possibly in the entire world. The most prestigious award given to a French author is membership in the Academy. To a writer, it's the equivalent of being knighted. My membership has always been blocked by people Oscar Wilde personifies— literary butterflies who *ooh* and *aah* over silly comedies of manners, boring stories of the affairs of the upper classes while denigrating my tales of science and adventure that are read all over the world."

He turns to me, his eyes dark. "If I should pull the sword from my cane and plunge it into your friend's heart, please understand that my bitterness is not personal."

"Understood . . . but Jules, you must know that they are the real losers. Do you realize that you are in the exact situation as Doctor Pasteur?"

"What in heaven are you talking about?"

"Doctor Pasteur is hated by the doctors and banned from working with them and he would give anything to be accepted and more importantly acknowledged by them. You're not accepted by your peers because you don't write what they think is high brow. They're envious and jealous of you because your books are loved all over the world. Ignore them. You've already won. So what if you don't have membership to the Academy. What would it really give you that you don't already have?"

Still, I understand how much it makes your blood boil

when you work hard to prove you're just as worthy and are still not accepted. At least Jules isn't patted on the head like a good little girl and then sent off to cover society weddings.

"Mademoiselle Brown, you never cease to amaze me. Thank you for your wise and kind words."

"You're welcome." If I could have puffed up like a peacock, I would have.

"MADAME POMPOUR'S IS the best house of pleasure in the area," Oscar informs us as we stand in front of the establishment. "That's Toulouse's opinion and he's legendary about his knowledge of such things."

"Is that his first or last name?" I ask.

"Henri Toulouse-Lautrec. His family is of the old nobility, but his father, the Count of Toulouse, severed ties with him because he chooses to paint real-life prostitutes and cancan girls, and the men who gawk at them. He's still trying to find an audience and appreciation for his work."

"Unusual subject matters for someone who wants to have his art appreciated," I note. "I can't imagine buying a piece of it to display in a drawing room."

"My dear, every artist must listen to the muse whispering in his ear. You'll see that Toulouse is an unusual person. His choice to paint the peculiar rather than the mundane is part of his nature. He occasionally lives in a house of pleasure to study the girls. And I suppose in a queer way he identifies with them."

"He identifies with prostitutes?" Jules asks.

"Not their sex life, but the fact that they're outcasts. Toulouse was born under an unpropitious star. The gods have not played fair with him personally, but they gave him second sight into his fellow mortals. In his paintings, he portrays the underworld of prostitutes for the brutal, cynical place that it is, rejecting the sentimentality and glamour that so many other artists and people place on it. In showing the crudeness and vulgarity of a brothel, he tells us something about every one of us, as if the brothel is a reflection of all of our lives."

"Interesting," I say, but that is not how I feel. This painter sounds like a queer fellow.

Oscar continues, "Toulouse can find out very quickly whether this madman we seek is hanging about houses of prostitution in the Montmartre. The girls trust him and will reveal things to him that they would never reveal to us. Not to mention the danger involved in asking too many questions at one of these establishments. The proprietors, including Madame Pompour, tend to get nasty if there's any trouble or their affairs are brought to the attention of the police. Naturally, they're not averse to having a head knocked if they feel the need. Shall we go in?"

Flaming torches are posted at the gate to Madame Pompour's villa. A big man in a billowing scarlet robe, a white turban, and a scimitar in his fist, greets us with a grin as broad as his blade.

"Welcome, Messieurs, Mademoiselle, to the Garden of Delights where all of your pleasures will be fulfilled." He bows profusely and mutters some gibberish that we're to assume is a language of the Orient.

We follow him down a path lined with torches and cross a courtyard filled with exotic jungle flowers and large palm trees. Considering the weather in Paris, one may presume that the vegetation is fake. To the left is a large heart-shaped fountain with white lilies floating in the water. In the center is a statue of a naked man and woman intertwined with each other, all body parts quite vivid.

The entrance is two massive doors with an elaborate Turkish-looking copper *façade* imprinted with a design of men with women in sexual positions I could have never imagined.

"We are entering the Arabian Nights," Oscar proclaims.

"More like the cave of Ali Baba and the forty thieves," Jules mutters.

Inside we're immediately attacked by a pungent sweet scent. Beyond the foyer is a large room dominated by a circular couch of red velvet that has a huge fountain in the center with a marble statue of *Venus de Milo*. Heart-shaped red flowers adorn the water. Five women lounge around the sofa. Two other women are off to the side laughing and appear to be having an enjoyable time drinking with a male guest. The women's dresses are of different modes of fashion, from harem silks to fancy ball gowns. While the style of the clothing differs, it all exposes an excessive amount of décolletage.

Every woman in the room looks at us, no doubt measuring the girth of the men's wallets with greater authority than a pickpocket. Their stares at me reveal they're wondering who—or what—I am.

Sitting across the room cross-legged on the floor near the bar is a turbaned "native" wearing a white loin-cloth, and smoking a water pipe. He gives me a grin. The blank area for his missing two front teeth show black. He waves the mouthpiece of the water pipe like a snake beckoning its next victim.

Opium. The dream maker is legal in most countries. This isn't a smell unfamiliar to me. I wrote an exposé on an opium den that imports teenage Chinese girls for immoral use by its customers. My editor so feared the tong who ran it that the paper hired George J. Sullivan, the boxing champion, as my bodyguard for a month.

A door behind the bar opens and out steps a large

woman mummified in gaudy layers of makeup and wrapped in pink, purple, and green silky harem sheers. This has to be Madame Pompour—a bejeweled and perfumed water buffalo draped in silk.

"Welcome, my friends, to my Garden of Delight."

Oscar makes brief introductions. "We're here to see that rascal Toulouse. Is he still demanding the girls pay him with their services for inclusion in his paintings?"

"If they did, it would be the first thing he'd make off of his paintings. Toulouse is in the conservatory, but be quick with your hellos. The early bird gets the best choice of my lovely girls."

The woman gives me an appraising look as if she wonders what my *profession* is.

A woman from the bar comes by holding onto a man's arm; she waves to Jules as they head for the upstairs. "So good to see you again, Monsieur." Jules turns red and mutters, "The woman must be mistaken; I've never seen her before in my life."

I smile. "Of course."

We follow Oscar into a room dominated by an elegant white grand piano. A young woman is playing a melancholy tune while a man wearing a paint-smudged smock sits before an easel and pigment tray, painting.

His model is a woman draped in a cloth that has fallen off her shoulder, exposing full breasts with very pink nipples. Embarrassed, I try not to look, but I can't help notice that she's thickset and has lost her youthful look, not at all what one would imagine to find in a high-class establishment.

"A professional model," Oscar stage whispers. "Toulouse is showing what the poor girls go through each fortnight when they lift their dresses to have their private parts inspected by a doctor in order to keep their prostitute's card."

That must be the *fille en carte* Detective Lussac mentioned. I eye the painting taking shape on the easel. I don't consider myself an art critic, but do fancy myself art *educated*. While I have endeavored to help prostitutes because of their sad fall from grace, I find capturing the pathos on canvas repugnant. It's encouraging their destitute lives by glamorizing their immoral and self-harmful occupation.

Off to the side, leaning against the wall is another painting, one still in progress, a street scene with a street girl kicking her leg high, exposing her lace doing the cancan for a crowd of men. He does capture the moment, but why? Who'd hang a painting of a cancandancer in their home?

As the artist turns to greet us, I'm thrown off guard and quickly look back at the model to hide my surprise. He's not sitting down—he's actually a very short man *standing up*.

The odd thing about his height is that he's proportioned normally other than stumps for legs. This is what Oscar meant about the gods giving him a bad turn. His lips, full and dark-bloody red and turned outward, give him a rather hideous, almost clownish, expression to his features. His eyes are intelligent and cynical, both bold and unpitying, as if to say he recognizes the ugliness in himself.

"Still up to your old tricks, Toulouse? Pretending you have an interest in painting ladies of the night so you can sample their wares?"

"Exactly, my friend. But I must hire real models. These brothel girls expect me to pay them as much for sitting for me as they get for lying on their backs. But I ask you, where else can I find such earthy pulchritude?"

We take a seat at a table and I whisper to Jules while Toulouse is thanking the model for her efforts and paying her for the session. "Someone should tell him that he'll never achieve artistic acclaim painting prostitutes and dancing girls."

Jules shrugs. "Who knows? This is Montmartre. It wouldn't surprise me if your friend Wilde and the little man both become famous. A dog can become famous on the Butte if you teach it to bark in harmony." *

The woman playing the piano leaves her stool and Jules roams over to examine the fine instrument. She takes a drink of water from a pitcher at our table and asks me, "Do any of you desire company?"

From her look and tone I realize that she is including me in the question and my backbone stiffens. "We're here on business."

She gives a saucy grin. "So am I."

"Are you also one of Monsieur Toulouse's models?"

She utters a French vulgarism, one that I don't quite understand, although I recognize there's reference to the private parts of a man's lower extremities.

"Only when I'm hungry. These artists have little money and share less with their models, although Toulouse is better than most. Too many are swine who want you to sit for hours for a few sous and fuck you afterward without paying a sou more. At least he pays."

My face burns and I hide my reaction behind my handkerchief.

She takes out a compact mirror and resets the front strands of her hair with her fingers. "With Toulouse, it is not his money that's the problem, but his tool. The girls call him Coffee Pot because his cock's as big as one."

I continue to bury my face in my handkerchief. She

---

* Oscar got his first taste of real literary appreciation with the Dorian book the following year. Toulouse-Lautrec's Moulin Rouge poster started him on the road to fame the next year, 1891.—The Editors.

smiles coyly at me and leans over, seductively whispering in my ear. "Come upstairs and I will kiss both sets of your lips."

"I—I—"

Jules comes over as the woman leaves to find a less reluctant customer. He raises his eyebrows. "Birds of a feather . . . ?"

"Why you—"

"Toulouse has some information for us!" Oscar beams, saving Jules from getting a piece of my mind. "May I present His Excellency Viscount Toulouse-Lautrec, Mademoiselle Nellie Brown and Monsieur Jules Morant." Oscar makes the introduction with a grand sweep of his hand.

"Please ignore this buffoon," Toulouse says. "My father took the title away from me after I failed the family on all levels. My height, of course, is the most obvious. Rather hard on my father to have an only son and heir to an ancient noble title whose feet can't reach the spurs."

Oscar claps his hands. "Tell them about the slasher."

"I know nothing of the slasher, but I've heard talk about a man who approaches girls with a proposition."

"What kind of proposition?" I'm excited. We could finally have a real lead.

"A street girl was asked to accompany a man to another place. That's what is strange about the proposition. The street girls usually take a man to *their* place. A man who can afford a carriage and a place to take a prostitute is unlikely to pick up a streetwalker. Not only can he get a much higher quality girl in a house like this one, it involves much less risk of getting the big pox."

The big pox he is referring to is syphilis, a raging epidemic everywhere, including Paris, where it's said one out of every five men has it. So many men carry it home to their wives, Britain's Lady Cook suggested that men with syphilis be branded so their innocent wives don't get the loathsome disease.

"Do you know how we can contact this girl?" I ask.

"She's been missing ever since she accepted the assignation. Her sister was complaining to the woman I spoke to that she hasn't been seen since she left with the man."

"Missing . . ." He's killed her. "Did she go to the police?"

"Yes, to no avail. Who cares about another street girl? They end up in the Seine or the woman's prison at Saint-Lazare anyway."

"How can we contact the sister?"

"She died from the influenza yesterday."

"Well, what about this woman you spoke to?"

"She knows nothing more. I was curious about the incident because of the London Ripper activities last year and I asked a number of questions. That was all she knew."

"None of the women have complained about other strange requests, not sexual, but anything that seems odd to them?"

"Not that I've heard, but I haven't been seeking out the stories either."

"Would you mind asking the others about strange requests, any missing women?"

"The prostitutes I know are mostly house girls, but I can ask them to talk to the street girls they know."

Never one to be left out of a conversation for too long, Oscar pipes in. "Nellie believes the man committing these atrocious acts might also be an anarchist."

"He wears black clothes and a red anarchist scarf," I explain.

The painter nods. "Like the followers and admirers of Louise Michel."

"Yes, when I saw her speaking yesterday she was wearing all black, except for a red scarf. I realize it must be her trademark, but why is that?"

"She began wearing black after the murder of a young journalist, Victor Noir," Jules explains. "Noir was sent by another journalist to deliver a challenge to a duel to Prince Pierre-Napoléon, a cousin of Napoléon III. The prince shot him. After the prince was found not guilty by a court of inquiry, Louise wore black to the funeral and has done so ever since."*

"So the slasher must be a follower of the Red Virgin?" I ask him.

"Not necessarily. Thousands have adopted the fashion."

"If you want to ask the Red Virgin about any suspicious anarchists," Toulouse says, "you'll need to ask Aristide where she's hiding."

"Who's Aristide?"

"The owner of Le Mirliton, a café. It's up the street, on Bou' Rochechouart."

I stand up. "We must talk with this gentleman immediately."

"But of course!" Toulouse agrees. "I am thirsty and need a green fairy to help me find my soul."

---

* In a bizarre twist to this Victor Noir story, Jules' publisher purchased a manuscript from a man named "André Laurie" who was actually Paschal Grousset, the radical who sent Noir to challenge the prince to a duel. Jules worked over the story and it was published under his name. Laurie was the pen name of Grousset, who went into exile after being a Commune leader.—The Editors.

40

Jules and I follow Oscar and the painter. As we come up the street, they disappear into a doorway at 84 Boulevard Rochechouart. The establishment appears closed, but a man dressed as refined as a ragpicker eyes us contemptuously when we approach the door.

"You are perhaps on the wrong street, Monsieur, Madame. Possibly you are looking for a La Roquerre café."

The reference is to an area known for its criminals. I look to Jules, expecting to see that famous temper of his flare, but his features are unreadable.

"We wish to enter," Jules says in a flat tone.

"Enter?" He gestures disrespectfully at me. "You, and this . . . person? We shall see." He beats heavily upon the door with his fist and a large judas door opens. A villainous face glares out. "What'd you want!"

"These two ask to enter."

"And?"

The ragpicker shrugs. "They appear harmless." He glances at us. "Perhaps a little stupid."

The sound of a large bolt being shoved back comes from the other side and the door swings open.

A better dressed man, but just as vile in temperament,

greets us. His dress and carriage is odd and flamboyant at the same time. He is not tall, but has powerful, dominating features and piercing black eyes. Long, straight, black hair falls from under a floppy purple velvet hat that has a romantic flair to it, the sort of hat one might expect Lord Byron to have worn when he fought in the Greek revolution. His hunting jacket has metal buttons. Black velvet pants billow around his boots. But his most interesting item of clothing is the blood-red scarf of revolutionaries—his is wrapped around his neck and falls down his back in cape-like fashion. Like Jules, he's clean shaven.

"Welcome to Mont*merde*, Monsieur, Madame. How many children of the poor did you crush under your carriage wheels on your way here?"

I realize the creature had just welcomed us to a mountain of . . . excrement and he's being facetiously rude, but I still don't like it and have to bite my tongue.

"We're with Toulouse," Jules says matter-of-factly.

"Toulouse? You mean that pig of a count who paints dirty pictures of poor prostitutes while he lives off the francs his family has stolen from the poor for five hundred years?"

"That very person."

"Then come in, see your friend before he loses his head in the next revolution!"

The salon is dark and crowded. Haze from cigarettes, cigars, and pipes have assembled among the dust and cobwebs in the heavy beams of the ceiling. It's a wonder anyone can breathe in the place.

Black wrought-iron gas lanterns cast pale and gloomy light upon the time-stained, brown shade of the walls and floor. Paintings and sketches hug the walls. I recognize the hand of Toulouse in two paintings I pass.

Everywhere, on the walls, overhead beams, fireplace

mantle, are odds and ends of the queerest sort—snarling grotesque heads, leering gargoyles, twisted figures of man and beast, Turkish swords and other strange bric-a-brac. The place had been decorated by a drunken satyr. Surprisingly, the tables are plain bare wood, not at all cleverly finished, and the seating mostly hard benches.

The host, if that is what he is, marches us to Toulouse's table. A piano player springs into life and the crowd sings.

"Sit!" the host commands, slamming his walking stick on the table.

Toulouse grabs his drink and greets us with a friendly smile. He and Jules immediately huddle in conversation while I examine my surroundings. I hear the name "Aristide" called by a patron and the unpleasant man who seated us responds. So, this is the man we came to talk with—a strange name for a strange man. Abruptly, Aristide leaps upon a table and points his stick in our direction.

"Did you see what entered?!" He proceeds to bang the table with his stick. "*Quiet!* Quiet, you swine!"

When the noise subsides, he again points at our table. "Did you see what kind of fish just entered?" He didn't wait for his trained minions to answer. "A sturgeon. A big, old sturgeon, full of bourgeois pomp."

Jules and Toulouse are deep in conversation, totally oblivious to what is going on. I tap Jules' arm. "He called you a bourgeois sturgeon."

"Yes, fine."

This Aristide creature then points directly at me. "And look, look my friends at what swims behind him. A little minnow. *Un fleu du feu*, young enough to be his daughter. I take my hat off to the man. He may be beardless on his chin, but he obviously has plenty of *beard* where it counts."

The audience roars and my face grows hot. *Oh, if I*

ARISTIDE BRUANT RECITING ONE OF HIS VERSES

was in New York with a couple of my buddy boys from
the Bowery detail . . . I know the whole thing is a joke,
that people pay to come to this cabaret to be insulted by
this crude man, but I personally don't like to be the butt
of jokes by a bully.

"I wonder where the big fish got the little minnow?
Could it be at Saint-Lazare? Is she one of these nuns

who are not married to God but to any man who could buy her time for a few sous?"

That does it! Saint-Lazare is a woman's prison. As the audience shrieks with laughter, I get up and march across the room. Jules calls after me, but I do not falter from my path. The audience grows quiet with anticipation as I approach Aristide. He stands still atop the table. Arms are akimbo, grinning evilly. These are the moments he lives for—another fish has been hooked and will be humiliated. I stop in front of the table and look up at him.

"Monsieur Aristide, my father has brought me here to discover what you will do about the baby."

"The baby?"

"Yes, the baby, Aristide. Little Pierre who you gave me as a present when you stayed at our inn when I was twelve years old and lured me into your room under the pretense—"

Jules pulls me away, but I have the pleasure of hearing Aristide's habitués laugh at him for once and they applaud. I'm tempted to turn around and bow, but Jules is pulling too hard.

As we go back to the table, our host belts out a song about a street apache and the working-class girl who was sentenced to Saint-Lazare because of him, while Oscar floats around the room like a colorful butterfly, distributing his verbal favors.

"Aristide considers himself a champion of the poor," Jules tells me, "but he's the most bourgeois of any of us. He hurts the poor with his songs of thieves and prostitutes, instructing us that poverty and moral corruption are two sides of the same coin."

"Well done, Mademoiselle, few people win a round with Bruant," Toulouse says, after we are seated. "His humor's crude, his songs cruder. I'm sure they're sung even in the cafés of New York."

I nod. I've never heard of Mr. Bruant or his songs, but I don't want Toulouse to think I'm ignorant of such things, or that New Yorkers are not aware of what goes on in Paris. One is expected to be aware of what is happening in Paris, no matter where one lives.

Toulouse is already drawing, making a pencil sketch of Bruant that will no doubt someday appear on his easel. I feel like grabbing the little man, shaking him and telling him that he's wasting his time with these scenes from the seedier side of life. What possible value could a painting of Aristide Bruant ever be?

A poet, one of the hanger-ons guarding the piano, gets up and spiels some verse, more street talk by bourgeois revolutionaries. Everyone in France seems to be a revolutionary. At least in cafés.

"I spoke briefly to Aristide," Toulouse speaks as he continues drawing. "He won't disclose the Red Virgin's location to you because he's worried you are police spies, but he told me to ask at a café called Le Couteau."

Le Couteau—The Knife, a proper name for an anarchist café.

"It's under the rubble of an old mill near Moulin de la Galette that got knocked down from the shelling during the Commune. Legay, the owner, got out of prison with the amnesty of the Commune fighters and opened a café in the basement—a seedy place that serves apaches and anarchists. He provides them a place to plot assassinations over cheap beer and build bombs in the backroom. Even Aristide hesitates to go there unless Louise Michel is there. I went there once, but feared for my wallet and my throat. Legay got half his face shot off and the other half is even uglier."

The poet by the piano starts circulating around the room with a tin cup to collect money for his presentation. Anyone who refuses is cursed. I excuse myself to go to the convenience room. I've been bad-mouthed enough for the night.

The wall on the way to the toilets is filled with paintings from Montmartre artists who, like Toulouse, will never gain fame because they refuse to paint pleasing scenes. A country scene is deliberately made *blurry*. What is it with these Montmartre painters? Why would this artist, one Vincent van Gogh, imagine that he could actually sell this type of work?*

As I turn the corner to the hallway that leads down to the convenience room, I recognize another painting with Toulouse's style. The scene is of two women doing the cancan in a crowded café, not professional dancers but of women who do an impromptu dance, to the cheers of a roomful of men. I don't believe it. I grab the painting off the wall and take it back to our table.

"*Look!*"

Toulouse is instantly excited. "You like it? One hundred francs. But for you, Mademoiselle, fifty."

"It's him," I tell them.

Three men are in the painting, at a table, watching women dance. The two men in the center face forward. One of them has a heavy beard, rose-tinted glasses, and a box hat. He wears a red scarf and a black suit.

"A coincidence perhaps," Jules states in a "calm down" tone.

"No, *it's him*. There's no mistake. Who's this man, Toulouse?"

Toulouse, showing his disgust that I am not interested in buying his painting, has buried his face in a tall glass of absinthe. He daintily wipes his forehead with his

---

* One must not judge Nellie's artistic judgment too harshly. Van Gogh shot himself the following year near Paris, dying at the age of 37 after having sold only one painting in his lifetime.—The Editors.

handkerchief before looking back at the picture. He's a real gentleman, even if he paints tawdry pictures.

"An anarchist."

"How do you know he's a real anarchist?"

He shrugs. "He has the clothes, scarf."

"What's his name?"

"He's a face in a painting. Give him whatever name his features conjure up for you. Perhaps he's a Jean . . . or a Pierre."

"How long ago did you do this painting?" Jules is now interested.

Toulouse examines it. "Two, three years ago."

"It fits. That's when the killings began in Paris."

"Do you recognize the other two men?" Jules asks Toulouse.

He shakes his head. "Just café patrons. They have a reason to be together at the same table, but they are not friends."

"How do you know that?" I ask.

Toulouse gestures at the picture. "Look at their clothes. Two are conservatively dressed, not expensively, or fashionably, but as professional men dress—perhaps even less fashionably than that, more like college professors or mid-level government officials. They're not bohemian, not men of the arts or literature, and definitely not anarchists, completely unlike him. His companions have a drink after work and go home to their families. He lingers at underground cafés until late at night and argues with comrades whether the French government will fall if the President is killed."

I'm impressed. "Toulouse, you should have been a detective. This café scene, is it another salon here at Le Mirliton?"

"No, I did this at the Le Chat Noir. You should ask Salis, the owner, about the men. They might be regulars."

"May we borrow the picture?"

"I would prefer you buy it, but it seems to be my lot in life to paint what people shun like the pox."

As Jules and I leave, I spot a bouquet of flowers in a vase at a nearby table. I grab them and place them before Toulouse. "Paint flowers instead of cancan girls," I advise him, "and you will find the world at your door."

I hurry to catch up with Jules, leaving Toulouse staring dumfounded at the vase of flowers.

While I'm not ordinarily free with my advice, believing that self-improvement comes from within, I'm very grateful to the odd little man for capturing the slasher on canvas and feel I should give him the benefit of my artistic knowledge. It's the least I can do.

Dear Oscar is too busy playing the social butterfly to notice our exit, but Aristide Bruant stands on top a table and queries his corps of waiters, "What do we think of the customers?"

"The customers are pigs!" the waiters chorus in unison.

I can't help but turn around and bow before exiting.

41

"I hope this next cabaret is more pleasant than Le Mirliton."

Jules chuckles at my statement. "You will be more charmed by Rodolphe Salis. He's Bruant's father—professionally speaking. Le Mirliton occupies the quarters abandoned by Le Chat Noir a few years ago. Most of the bizarre odds and ends scattered around Le Mirliton were abandoned by Salis in the move. There is even one famous chair, forgotten during the move. When Salis came back to get it, Bruant refused to turn it over. He hung it on a wall and points it out to customers when he roasts Salis in his monologues."

"Bruant worked for Salis?"

"Yes, when Le Chat Noir was at the Rochechouart location. He wrote the Chat Noir theme song that Salis still uses. Salis has something of the same approach toward customers."

"Oh, this should be a wonderful visit."

"No, it won't be as bad. He's not as vulgar and considers himself more of a friend of the arts than a revolutionary."

At the entrance to Le Chat Noir a man in the uniform of

a Swiss Guard asks our names. Swiss Guards were the palace guards massacred by a mob when they tried to protect their king and queen during the French Revolution.

He tells Jules that Salis is handling a mutiny of galley slaves and will not be available for a few minutes and then proceeds to pound three times on the floor to announce our entrance, "Monsieur Morant and Mademoiselle Brown."

As Le Mirliton tried to capture the spirit of the streets, Le Chat Noir is a fantasy world decorated in a mixture of ancient, medieval, Renaissance, and the Louies of France. Added all around are bits of the macabre and bizarre— Oriental fire masks, cups said to have graced the lips of Voltaire and Charlemagne, the skull and shin bones of the fifteenth-century vagabond poet François Villon, a clock telling time with two tails of a cat, and a menagerie of art and junk, though most of the outrageous pieces appear to have been left behind at Le Mirliton.

As we walk through a dining room called Salle du Conseil, the Council Room, there are people drinking beer and eating French fries with their fingers while they listen to a winsome young woman with a sad face accompanied by a piano singing:

> I seek my fortune at the Black Cat in the moonlight of Montmartre.
>
> I seek my fortune at the Black Cat of Montmartre, in the evening.

"Have you seen a shadow play?" Jules asks me.

"Yes. A puppet show when I was a child."

"Le Chat Noir's shadow theater isn't child's play. It's the state of the art in mechanical moving pictures, presented by Rivière and Robida. Let's take a look at it while we wait for Salis. I've heard it's a good one."

Jules leads me to a dark, crowded room called Salles des Fêtes on the next floor. A strange creature hangs from the ceiling, perhaps a large fish with the head of a snarling dog. On the far wall is a peculiar oval-shaped mantel framing a large, bright, "white screen" composed of fine cloth back lit by bright lanterns. A courtly piece above it displays a fierce cat-like griffin, winged and snarling, held up by roles of dramatic heads, laughing, crying, frightened—all the emotions of the theater. Naturally, there's a stalking cat or two.

On the screen enemy airships, great balloon-like flying machines rigged with cannons and machine guns, drop bombs on Paris while French aeronauts battle them from their own balloons. The airships move across the sky, bombs fall, explosives rip the city's silhouetted skyline, flames shoot up from burning buildings, screams and shouts cry out along with the sound of fierce wind and destruction.

I wish I could go backstage and see how the stage crew is creating the realistic atmosphere; it's far beyond the typical washtub "thunder" of stage plays. I turn to Jules to ask if it would be possible, but he is completely engrossed in the play. To my surprise, he appears tense, even angered at the war scenes.

"Monsieur, Mademoiselle."

A waiter dressed as a university don snaps us to attention.

"Monsieur Salis will see you now."

On our way back downstairs, Jules says, "It'll come."

"What?"

"Airships battling over great cities."

Fortunately for the world, Jules' imagination is far-fetched. If everything he imagined came true, we'd live in a world in which people fly between cities in airships, are carried up very tall buildings by moving stairs, rockets will race to the moon, moving pictures will be mechanical rather than done as shadow plays, and in everyone's homes there will be telephones and electric lights. *What a crazy world that would be.*

"Welcome to Le Chat Noir."

Monsieur Salis is a well-nourished man with red hair and beard. He's dressed in a brocade waistcoat that would have looked appropriate at a king's coronation . . . when worn by the king. He stares a little quizzically at Jules, as if he should recognize him. Jules ignores his look and instead diverts Monsieur Salis's attention to the painting we brought.

"We have this painting by Toulouse-Lautrec."

Salis leans the painting against the back of a chair. "Yes . . . I've seen this one before. Toulouse offered it to me and hung it at Bruant's when I rejected it. Someone saw it in a toilet, I believe. Of course, the whole place is a toilet."

"We're interested in the identity of these men."

"Why would I know their identity? And more important, I have a restaurant to run. I suggest you ask Toulouse."

He starts to turn away and I stop him.

"The man with the red scarf is my husband. He has left me with three small children to feed and has gone with another woman, changing his name. I need to find him. It could happen to any of your daughters."

"Could happen? Mademoiselle, it happens to them every day." He points at one of his waiters. "He has two daughters and their husbands are all like that scoundrel in the picture, café revolutionaries who are too proud to work but not too proud to have an old man labor to stuff their bellies."

He examines the painting again, then picks it up and holds it out arm's length. He turns it this way and that way, squinting, and then scrunching his nose like a rabbit.

"No . . . I don't know him. Obviously one of the Red Virgin's followers. They spend half of their time plotting assassinations and the other half in prison. No, I'm sorry, I don't know the man's name or his whereabouts."

"*Merci*, Monsieur."

Jules takes the painting and as we turn to leave Salis poses a question that stops us.

"Why don't you ask his friends?"

We both stare stupidly at the café owner.

"His friends?" I ask.

"The ones from the institute."

"What institute?"

"Institut Pasteur, of course. I'm sure these men are Pasteurians. I've seen them at times with other members of the Institut, celebrating a birthday or a promotion at work."

I take the picture from Jules and look at it again more carefully. "I can't believe we didn't see that."

"See what?" Jules is still puzzled.

"Pasteur's assistant. That's Tomas Roth." I didn't recognize the other "Pasteurian."

Stunned, Jules and I stare at each other. Pasteur's staff at a café with the slasher? As we leave, the sad-but-comely young woman sings one of those songs of the streets that the bourgeois Parisians love to be teased with.

Stray dogs have their holes, murders have their prisons,
but a poor old worker like me, doesn't have a home . . .

42

Pasteur's associates with a Red Virgin anarchist?" This is all so crazy. "Members of the Institut at a so- cial gathering with the slasher? What do you make of it?"

Jules stops and faces me. "We don't know it's the slasher."

"True, but it's still a radical anarchist with Pasteur's people. We must talk to these people immediately."

His face becomes stern. He hasn't been in a good mood since we watched the shadow play.

"It's nearly midnight, hardly a time to call on Dr. Pas- teur, though I'm sure that would be of little concern to you."

I can't believe how unkind he can be at times, but he's right. It's late. "You're right, I forgot what time it is. How- ever, it's the perfect time to check out this anarchist café, Le Couteau. I bet the Red Virgin is there right now."

"And be murdered? Has that brain fever you're so sus- ceptible to attacked you again?"

I bite my tongue and take a deep breath. "I don't think—"

"Exactly, Mademoiselle, I couldn't have put it better."

"And you—you can go straight to Hades, Jules Verne!"

"I'm already there."

"Then stay there and boil in whatever self-pity is gripping you. I have a killer to catch. Goodnight."

I abruptly turn around and march purposefully down the street leaving Jules in my dust. Damn him! Who does he think he is? How dare he be so rude to me? Frenchmen! Forget about any romantic ideas I had about him. He's right, I do have brain fever, but it has nothing to do with the slasher; it's Jules. He drives me crazy.

I'm around a corner and halfway down the street when I realize Jules still has the picture. Rats! I should have taken it and dropped it off at my garret. Heaven knows what might happen to it in his hands. But the die is cast. Besides, after that outburst I've probably lost Jules as a partner—but as the French say, *"C'est la vie."*

Tomorrow I'll just storm into the Procope and retrieve the picture from him. But that's tomorrow and this is now. Nothing will stop me. Not even the chilly night or the brooding black clouds driven on the breath of an icy wind that appears unending in the sky. Then, as if the gods are trying to warn me, in the distance comes a long, deep rumble. A storm is brewing.

I know I'm not acting rationally. I'm still heated from anger and I have to admit I'm also angry at myself for once again I have put my foot in my mouth and placed myself in a bad situation. But what's done is done. I basically know were the Moulin de la Galette is located— at the top of the Butte. Once up there, I should be able to locate the café . . . I hope.

The path I have to climb in order to talk with the Red Virgin looks singularly uninviting. The dark night shrouds the top of the steps—a steep, twisting stone way bordered by a wall. Vines, blackened by freezing nights, droop listlessly over the wall like wilted, old fingers waiting for some poor, unexpected soul to walk by so they can snatch them up. Okay, this is no time for my crazy imagination to act up. It's important I remain calm and clear headed.

I cautiously follow the stone steps. Hidden behind the walls on each side of the steps are small white cottages with wooden shutters tightly shut and gardens forgotten for the winter. Their red tile roofs accent the dark of the night. When they abruptly end I am confronted with a dirt path and an endless pasture. The tinny clang of a goat's bell comes from somewhere in the pasture. Thunder rumbles again, long and deep. Only this time it's closer, a definite threat to drench me with cold rain. Scattered about are small, thorny-like bushes and little mounds of barren dirt. An empty wooden cart with a broken wheel has been stranded on the side of the path.

Near the top of the hill stands a large somber tree, its branches stripped and showing a purplish color when the storm lights up the sky. For a split second as the lightning flashes I see a figure under the tree. It disappears when darkness falls again.

My feet drag to a halt.

Why would someone be waiting under a tree on a rough night? Is it a man I see? My man in black? Or is it the dark night playing tricks on me? I don't know what to think, but the impression of a man standing under that tree stays with me. I'm positive I saw a figure. Am I to face the slasher again . . . *alone*?

I stand rooted, unsure of what to do, as my fears duel with my pride. I finally decide what I saw was nothing but branches being tossed about in the wind, playing a trick on me. I force my reluctant feet forward. They drag as if they know something I should.

Thunder rumbles overhead and lightning ignites the sky again.

A person *is* under the tree.

I stop in my tracks, my heart racing. There's no doubt in my mind. Someone is out there waiting in this dark night. Another flash and the figure is gone. I strain to look, but I can't see anyone. Then the figure emerges.

It's walking toward me.

My instincts scream for me to run, but my feet are cemented to the ground. Thunder breaks my trance and I turn, running back down the hill. As I reach the steps I glance back.

The person is still coming toward me.

Gathering the bottom of my dress in hand, I take the steps two at a time. My foot turns on something and I stumble, suddenly free-falling.

43

"*Nellie!*" It's Jules. "What are you doing?"

"I'm sitting here, enjoying the beautiful night," I snap at him. "What does it look like I'm doing?" I don't add that my pride is broken. "What are *you* doing?"

"I thought you'd try something stupid, so I came after you. Are you hurt?"

"No, just a little bruised. How did you get ahead of me?"

"I know the area."

"You scared the life out of me."

"I know, I'm sorry, but I didn't know it was you. I came closer to get a look and you ran. I don't blame you for being frightened. You've faced this madman alone and you know how dangerous he is."

There he goes again, saying something thoughtful and very kind that melts my anger away, so I permit him to help me up.

"I was unfair to you," he continues. "That shadow play turned my stomach. I know it's only men behind the screen manipulating objects of war, but—"

I wait for him to finish. When he doesn't, I pipe in.

"It's somehow connected to that strange remark you made about being in Paris to kill someone."

We lock eyes. I don't see anger, but something else. Before I can formulate what, I'm in his arms, his lips pressing against mine. They are warm and lush and I meet them eagerly, my chest hard against his. When the kiss is over I don't move. I finally get my wits about me and remember my duty of modesty and break away.

"My apologies," he says.

Like a lost child, I stupidly look down at the ground. He, thank goodness, gently takes me by the arm and helps me up the hill.

"Is it far to the café?"

"Not far. Let's find it before we're murdered."

As we crest the hill, the Church of the Sacré-Coeur stands off to our right. Stately, but unfinished, scaffolding clings to it like a spiderweb. We have passed no one along the way and continue on in silence, navigating a maze of stony passageways wedged between walls of dark gardens going this way and that way.

"Jules, are we lost?"

He gives me a grunt of irritation, which leads me to believe we're lost. There is no longer even the pretense of street lighting and the houses become less cared for as we progress. Then I hear music. "Where's the music coming from?"

"It's not music. It's the blades of a windmill, sadly, the last of them. For centuries windmills ground the flour for the bakers of Paris. What you hear is the last one crying out because they're no longer wanted or needed."

"How sad."

"I'm being cynical."

"Really . . ."

He ignores me and for a moment we stand looking at a tall dark structure near the top of some stone steps, a strange and uncanny cenotaph against the moonlit horizon. It's an old giant filled with memories. Happy, spirited music comes from inside as we get closer.

"Le Moulin de la Galette," Jules says deflated. "We'll drop in and get our bearings."

Bright lanterns led the way to the windmill which has taken up a different profession than grinding flour. While Jules is getting directions from a ticket taker, I sneak up the passageway to get a peek inside the dance hall. An old woman is collecting coats in a vestiary. I hand her fifty sous "to take a look" and she waves me inside.

Like the Moulin Rouge, the Galette's dance hall is very large, with a band of only trumpets and trombones on an elevated stage at the far end. Some of the musicians are sitting on stools, some standing, while others are sitting on the edge of the stage. The music is loud, the clothes of the dancers bright as a rainbow. The center floor is crowded with young men and women, stepping, swirling, laughing. Grins cover the face of every man and it's no wonder—the girls are showing considerable leg, and sometimes a bit of thigh.

Unlike the "ladies" who visit the cabarets on the boulevards below, stepping out of carriages in tall hats and bellowing silk dresses, these women are hatless and the clothes are simple—mostly white blouses and black skirts. A bow pinned here and there adds some variety to their simple outfits. As for the men, there are no top hats and tails here. Their faces are red from the exertion of the dances, their caps mounted at a rakish slant, their trousers fitted tight at the knees.

I recognize the young people in the hall because I was once one of them: shop girls, messenger boys, and factory workers. They work six long days, from daybreak to nightfall and Sunday is the only day they can rest and enjoy themselves. They're the kind of people I knew in Pittsburgh; people I worked with shoulder to shoulder.

The Moulin Rouge and cabarets of Montmartre are for the middle and upper classes. The Galette is a place of the worker, the kind I was raised with and for which I have fond memories.

A group of shop girls come swirling by and one of them grabs my arm and suddenly I'm swept off onto the dance floor. I'm a little awkward at first because I don't know exactly what to do, but I mimic the girls and quickly find myself kicking up my heels, laughing.

It's wonderful! I feel free—free of all worries and cares. And I can't stop laughing. I'm a young woman just having fun. A hand grabs me and as quickly as I joined the dancing I am off the dance floor and into Jules' arms . . . again. He holds me close and we just stare into each other's eyes.

I want him to kiss me and I know from his eyes it's what he wants. But instead he gently brushes a strand of hair off my cheek. "Time to go." With a sigh I turn from my past and follow him to an underground café, Le Couteau, run by a felon and named for a deadly instrument.

Across the street from the Galette, men are loitering about. Our clothes get us hard, sullen stares. Jules expertly maneuvers me to his left arm, keeping his right arm free if he needs to swing his walking stick.

"This was one of the last stands of the Commune defenders," Jules tells me. He gestures at the neighborhood. "Even the police are not enthused about straying here. They occasionally raid it for suspects in political crimes, and when they do, they come in force. Don't look, but off to our right there is a man in the second floor of a building across from the mill."

"Why don't you want me to look?"

"We don't want him to think we're spying him out."

As we get closer to the building, damage inflicted by the battles fought between the government troops and Commune soldiers almost two decades ago is still visible. The entire left wall is gone, leaving a pile of rubble; the back wall fronting the cliff side of the hill, is also rubble. The other two walls are standing, but pockmarks are evidence that a blaze of small-arms fire left its imprint.

A dim gaslight, not bright or friendly, flickers at the top of a stone stairway leading down to a basement café. A crudely painted sign is attached to a post at the top of the stairs. No name is inscribed, only the image of a bloody knife.

I'm glad Jules is with me. It was foolish of me to think I could come here alone.

Two men are sitting at the top of the stairs playing a dice game. Each has a bottle of wine beside him and one has a cigarette dangling from his lips. They make room for us to pass, but insolently. At the bottom of the steps another surly looking devil is sitting on a stool next to the door and smoking a cigarette. He says nothing as Jules opens the door and holds it for me, but his look is contemptuous.

The café is as unfriendly inside as it is out. A layer of grey tobacco haze hangs in the air and the place reeks of cheap beer—a smell not totally unfamiliar. My stepfather wore it quite often. There are a dozen tables and several times that many men. None are university types or even the working class of the Galette. Frankly, they are common criminals to my eye, with perhaps an alcoholic poet or two thrown in.

Only three or four women are in the room and I find them especially interesting. The world is full of tough men, but these women—they're a rare breed of *hard women.* It takes me a moment to place them in the scheme of how I categorize things in my mind, and when I do I am surprised by the conclusion. Soldiers. This is how I think of these women even though all of them are too old for any army. They remind me of the withered hags seen in paintings of the French Revolution, women shouting for blood when victims of the Terror were paraded through the streets.

I wonder if we have not come to the wrong place. Then I see Montmartre's legend at the back of the room, at a table with three men. There is no mistaking the Red Virgin—her sharp, narrow features, high forehead, and raven hair give her an American Indian look, despite her pale skin. She is wearing her trademark black clothes and red scarf.

I start for her table, but Jules takes my arm and directs me to another table.

"There is a certain protocol in approaching revolutionaries who are wanted by the police," he whispers.

Jules writes a note on a piece of foolscap and signals for a waiter.

An ancient creature that looks like he belongs on a pirate's boat hobbles over to us on a leg and a stump. There is no question that this is Legay. And Salis was correct—the scars on his face improved his looks. His neck bears the scar of a collar or rope.

"For Mademoiselle Michel."

As he reaches for the note and coin, another scar is exposed on his wrist. After the man hobbles away, Jules says, "The wrist scar is from being shackled to an oar. He spent time on a prison galley in his early years for theft, murder, and revolutionary activities, no doubt."

"That seems to sum up all the clientele in this place. What did you say in your note?"

"That we wish to speak to her about the death of innocent women. And I identified myself and my companion as Nellie Brown."

"You signed it Jules Verne?"

"We came up to this den of anarchists murders in the dead of the night. It would be unproductive to risk getting our throats cut because Louise Michel is unwilling to talk to strangers."

"You've met her?"

"No, but I have a rather unusual connection to her."

"And that is what?"

Slurred exclamations come from the table to our right as an old derelict lifts his head for a moment to mutter something before collapsing back down on the table. My mother would describe his condition as pickled.

Jules nods at him. "The gentleman who appears to have just crawled from the gutter is Paul Verlaine, the poet laureate of France's bohemians. He's a drunk and a derelict, but both attributes merely enhance his standing with the rest of the degenerates of the arts. He has never been the same since he shot his lover."

"A younger poet I believe . . . Arthur Rimbaud."

"Yes . . ." Jules looks at me completely surprised.

I continue. "What is so sad is just a few years ago he was instrumental in publishing Rimbaud's *Illuminations*, but here he sits alone and completely wasted. His wife wants nothing to do with him and he has little if no contact with his son, George. I heard one tale that the bullet struck his wrist, and another that it went into his derrière. Verlaine served a two-year sentence at Mons. The Belgians are less tolerant about shooting one's lover than you are . . . the French, I mean."

"Mademoiselle Brown—"

"I know . . . you are amazed at my wealth of knowledge, but what I don't know and I would like to know—"

I'm unable to finish my question to Jules about his connection to the Red Virgin because the old murderer, revolutionary, or whatever the waiter is, taps Jules on the shoulder and jerks his thumb toward the table where Louise sits.

Jules and I rise and make our way, in the haze, back to her table. The men at the table strike me as the type who should be doing time on a prison galley, if such things still exit.

"*Bonsoir*, Mademoiselle, Messieurs." Jules bows.

"It's a great honor to meet you," I tell the Red Virgin truthfully.

No one says a word as we take seats, not even a response to our greetings. Since formality is obviously not needed, or wanted, I plow right in, speaking directly to Louise Michel.

"I'm an American. My sister was murdered by a maniac in New York. I have followed the madman's trail to Paris. I need your help in finding him so he can be brought to justice."

Jules sinks down a little in his chair, as if he is cringing from my speech. Louise and her male companions all stare at me as if I climbed out of one of Jules' moon rockets. Louise starts to say something and stops as her attention is directed behind me.

To my surprise it's the trapeze act from the circus, the handsome and daring brother and sister team that mesmerized Dr. Dubois. They're dressed in street clothes— the young man in a well-cut Italian suit of dark linen and silk, and the girl in a forest green dress with yellow trim. The only jewelry the girl wears is a black pendant in the shape of a horse, not a typical horse but one with a rough and ancient look, carved perhaps from ebony or some other dark stone. It's quite striking.

Like us, they don't fit in this place.

Greetings are exchanged and a look passes between Louise and the newcomers, a look that I interpret as a signal they're not to sit at our table—at least not now, not while we are here. They move on. Interesting. Dubois had shown an interest in the two and they have a connection to the city's most notorious anarchist.

"Why are you telling me this?" the Red Virgin asks me.

"I believe the killer's an anarchist."

The man on Louise's right attacks me. "The only way to bring justice to the people is to destroy the governments and businesses that oppress them. The only way to destroy them is to kill them! If your sister was killed by an anarchist, it was for the good of all."

He's a brute with a mean countenance. He purposely glares, daring me to oppose him. I've encountered bullies like him before. They love to see women squirm. My father taught me a trick. Look back at them square in the eye—*just one eye*. This way their stare will not unnerve you. I do not falter when I answer him.

"Perhaps you wouldn't be so generous about death if it was your own life." I then turn to Louise. "My sister wasn't killed for political reasons. The killer is a maniac who preys on women, a vicious animal who butchers women for his own demented cravings."

She raises her eyebrows. "Do you expect to find your killer here? No doubt there are a few killers among us," she smiles and looks to the man on her right who had lashed out at me, "but they go after bigger game than women."

The men laugh. I'm tempted to stand up and give them all a piece of my mind, but I'll get nowhere except thrown out, so I control myself and continue.

"The man I seek murders the poorest and most defenseless women, social outcasts who have no protection from the law. He rips the life from prostitutes with a knife." I'm certain that the reference to attacks on the dredges of society will appeal to her sense of justice.

"You still haven't told us why you have come to this café and approach me with your story. This is a political café, not an institute for the criminally insane."

"I told you the murderer is an anarchist—*a Montmartre anarchist*."

I might as well have called the pope a debaucher at a convention of Catholics. The two men at the table stiffen and frown darkly and Louise raises an eyebrow. I have definitely hit a nerve and hurry to get the rest of my story out.

"The man may have been involved in Chicago's Haymarket bombing. When I encountered him in New York he was pretending to be a doctor and used his position to murder prostitutes at a madhouse. I tracked him to London where he killed more prostitutes and now to Paris where he's continuing his dirty tricks. If we don't stop him he will continue the slaughter, moving from city to city to keep the police off guard."

"You seek help from us to turn a comrade over to the police?" The speaker is the man on Louise's left. He looks as mean spirited as the other man. "We're not police spies." He then spits on the floor.

"The man's a murderer, not of kings and politicians, but of helpless women. Women you are fighting to free," I retort.

"Whores? What's a few less whores if the yoke of capitalism and tyranny is thrown off?"

Once again, the men laugh and to my surprise so does Louise. That's it! My blood rises and I stand up. I feel Jules cautioning hand on my arm, but I'm too angry to obey.

"I'm not here to talk politics, but humanity. Something I thought," I look directly into Louise's eye, "*you* would understand. Obviously I'm wrong."

"Why do you believe this man is an anarchist?" Louise asks me.

"He wears the red scarf and black clothes you've made famous."

"There are hundreds of thousands of followers of anarchy in France, millions around the world. You say he's not even French. Why would you think we could help?"

"I heard you talk at Place Blanche. I know you are admired everywhere. You may not know the man yourself, but you can put the word out to others that—"

"Didn't you hear us, woman!"

The big man on her right gets to his feet snarling, knocking his chair over backward. Jules tenses beside me.

"You're trying to make us police spies! Get out of here or you'll end up on a meat hook!"

Jules springs to his feet. "That's a foul thing to say to a lady. Apologize or I'll—"

"Please, please, sit down, François, Mademoiselle Brown, you too Monsieur Verne."

When we are all back in our seats, Louise gives Verne an amused look. "Have you stolen any more of my ideas, Monsieur Verne?"

"I'm afraid, Mademoiselle, that I haven't come across any more of your ideas to steal. All the worse for my writing, since *Twenty Thousand Leagues Under the Sea* is one of my most popular works."

"I'm afraid you and your spirited friend have made an unprofitable trip all the way up here. While I don't condone the death of innocent people, my friend is correct when he says we're not police spies. We have no interest in your problem. Though I'm sorry you lost a sister," she says to me.

I stand up again. "I'm sure that will console the family of the next innocent woman who's murdered by this fiend. I'm sorry to bother you. When I was a factory girl, a pamphlet with one of your speeches fell into my hands and changed my life. It's too bad the woman who wrote those words doesn't live up to her own legend."

I was out the front door before Jules caught up with me.

"I'm sorry. I couldn't keep my mouth shut."

"It's all right."

Never have I felt so deflated. Louise Michel is a person I have admired and tried to emulate. And now, for the moment, all that came crashing down. I was hit with a harsh reality of life—when you put a person on a pedestal, you will be disappointed. It's the nature of the beast. I just had a dose of reality and right now it stinks.

As we came closer to my garret, I can't help but ask about the Red Virgin's remark. "What did she mean about you stealing her novel? Is that the connection you mentioned beforehand?"

Jules shakes his head. "A ridiculous rumor that spread all over Paris like wildfire. Following the collapse of the Commune, Louise was sent to a jungle prison in the South Pacific. While there, she discovered a mollusk, a type of sea snail and named it 'nautilus,' the same name as the submarine in my novel. From that fact, scandalous allegations erupted that I had purchased the tale of Captain Nemo and his *Nautilus* submarine from her for a mere hundred francs, and the saint that she is, she donated the money to the poor. Of course, the gossip ignored the fact that my book was published a year before she was sent to New Caledonia and that I named my submarine after the *Nautilus* submergible built by the American Robert Fulton many years before." He shakes his head again. "Where do such stories come from?"

"Stupid people."

Jules looks at me in amusement.

"I was shocked at the attitude of Louise Michel and her two thug friends. They are willing to protect a murderer just because he's an anarchist." I stop and turn to Jules. "If we had said he was bourgeois, they would have enlisted every man in the café to find him. Doesn't she care that he is killing innocent women?"

"Who knows what a fanatic values? You and I put a high price on every life. To the radical a thousand lives, a million, are merely martyrs for their cause. Look at the bombs anarchists use to kill—for every politician or industrialist killed, a dozen innocent people die."

"It's all so insane . . . did you notice the look that passed between the two from the circus and Louise Michel? They must be anarchists."

Jules' cane taps a steady rhythm on the sidewalk as we walk. "Yes, but that doesn't surprise me. Italy is a hotbed of anarchism, even more so than France. The question is Doctor Dubois' interest in them. Is he enthralled with their performances—or their politics?"

My impression is that the young doctor is more enthralled with their bodies, especially the brother's, but it would have been unladylike for me to suggest such a thing.

"I also found the horse pendants interesting," Jules says. "The girl wearing one on a chain, the brother and the two thugs, as you put it, had them pinned to their lapels. The horses were not highly noticeable because of the dark color of their clothes."

I didn't notice the horses on the men and I can kick myself for it. Jules was being polite and making excuses about the dark color of their clothes, but I should have noticed them. Instead, I was too busy arguing and standing my ground.

Jules purses his lips. "I'm just wondering if the pendants are a membership badge for an anarchist group. I find Dr. Dubois' connection to all of this provocative. I shall be highly interested in the results of the background check I've initiated on him."

As we arrive at the point where the passageway to my apartment leads up the hillside, Jules starts to wave down a fiacre to go back to his own place then stops.

"With everything you've been through, I think it prudent of me to walk you to your garret."

"Jules . . . how gallant of you. But, I'll be fine. Besides, it will be impossible for you to obtain a fiacre on my street." I suddenly remembered the painting. "What did you do with Toulouse's painting?"

"I left it at the Le Chat Noir. I'll pick it up tomorrow. Goodnight Mademoiselle. And thank you for such an entertaining evening."

"No, I'm the one who should thank you. I have to admit I wouldn't have survived on my own. *Merci.*"

"You're welcome, but I don't underestimate your ability to handle things. You are full of surprises."

For a moment we stand staring at each other—that awkward pause where no one knows what to do or say.

"Let's meet at the Institut Pasteur tomorrow at two o'clock." Jules breaks the spell, but as he stands looking down at my face, I hold my breath hoping he'll kiss me. But instead he speaks again.

"And I'll make sure to have the painting."

"Oh . . . okay."

I don't know what else to say. Obviously I read the

tone of his voice wrongly, so I hold out my hand, not so much to shake his, but to give his hand a sentimental squeeze. I realize that shaking hands with a woman is not the custom of men and my gesture catches him by surprise. I give his hand a good hard squeeze.

"Not used to shaking hands with a woman, are you?"

He smiles sheepishly. "If you're an example of the future of women in a man's world, I believe there are many surprises in store for men. Perhaps, someday, women will even wear pants, drive their own carriages, and heaven forbid, vote."

We laugh. He doesn't let go of my hand.

My heart feels like it's going to burst out of my chest and my knees tremble at the thought that he might take me into his arms and kiss me again. I need to ground myself, so I say something . . .

"Oh, I believe woman will do much more than that."

"I believe you do. But what *more* is there?"

"Run a company, and who knows, maybe a *country*."

"Mademoiselle Brown, now that is radical thinking. Louise Michel would be proud of you."

"Yes, but it's not radical thinking. I'm as capable with a set of reins in my hand as most men, so why can't we vote, or be a president of a company or country—it's only fair, don't you think?" I give him my most charming smile.

He lets go of my hand and bows. "The way you ask, a man can only respond in agreement. I suppose you're an example of what men have in store for them when there are more women like you."

"I am not an example of anything. As long as men are frightened of losing their power, they will keep women oppressed—"

"Nonsense, there's a few mindless suffrages, mostly Lesbos—"

"Is that your idea of what thinking women are—lesbians?"

"You assume that I consider any woman a 'thinker.'"

"Mister Verne—"

"Monsieur Verne, you keep lapsing into English. And I'm just joking." He suddenly becomes serious. "But it was foolish of me to have taken a woman into that den of fanatics—especially you. If anything had happened to you . . ."

He grabs me up in his arms and kisses me.

When he lets go, I kiss him back.

"That's what you can expect from the *new* modern women." And then I abruptly turn and hurry on my way, waving to him as I run up the dark alley.

44

Perun

"Mademoiselle Michel." Perun approaches the Red Virgin's table with Dr. Dubois by his side. "I see you've met the impetuous young reporter from America."

"Perun . . . and Doctor Dubois," Louise Michel forces a smile, "what brings you here? I thought we discussed everything the other day."

Perun grabs a chair and sits down across from her. "I've made an important change in our plan and thought you should know. What was she doing here?"

"What change? Dubois, you might as well sit down."

The brother of the circus trapeze stands up and puts a chair for Dubois between himself and his sister.

"Do you know who the woman is who accompanied Jules Verne?" Perun asks.

The Red Virgin nods. "I saw her picture once. She's an American reporter. Her name is Nellie Bly."

"Why did she come to see you?"

"To solicit help."

"What help?"

She raises her eyebrows. "Have you joined the prosecutor's office, Monsieur? Is that what gives you the right to cross-examine me?"

LE MOULIN DE LA GALETTE

"Pardon. I ask as a brother of the black flag."

"There's a mad killer, as she puts it, here, in Montmarte, butchering prostitutes and she knows how I feel about women being murdered. She believes he's an anarchist and she wanted me to help her find him. He killed her sister."

"And . . ."

"I refused."

"Interesting . . . what did she tell you about this killer?"

"Only that this man is possibly of Eastern European heritage. She encountered him in New York. He was pretending to be a doctor and used his position to murder prostitutes at a madhouse. He's since killed prostitutes in London and now she believes him to be in Paris. Why the interest in her?"

"A newspaper reporter can be dangerous to our cause. One has to be careful." Perun's voice reeks with an underlying threat, but the Red Virgin doesn't cower. Dubois unconsciously rubs his pinkie.

"Dubois," Louise looks over to him, "what happened to your finger?"

"Oh . . . just an accident, I was careless during an operation."

"Hate to see what happened to the patient."

Everyone laughs. Louise meets Perun's eye again. He is not laughing. "Is there anything else I can help you with, Perun?"

"No." Perun stands up. "You were smart to not help her. Luc . . ."

45

Nellie

Once safely back in my garret, I flop on my bed and take a deep breath. I kissed Jules. I kissed him! I've never kissed a man. What I mean is that I've always let the man kiss me, but for me to purposely kiss a man—*never*. What in heaven has gotten into me?

What is it about this man that has me acting so irrationally and thinking about silly things—the feel of my breasts against his chest, the taste of his lips, the warmth and strength of his body, and the yearning that swept over me when he took me in his arms?

My word! I need to stop these foolish thoughts. Sleep will be impossible, so I might as well see if I can figure out who my man in black is. Maybe if I write down all my information he will materialize.

After a long tedious time of compiling notes, all I have is a headache. Exhausted, I crawl into bed. Bright side—I won't have any problem falling asleep.

I sit up in a dead stupor. I'm not sure, but I think a sound is coming from my door. A piece of paper slowly materializes from under the door and I stare at it dumb-founded. Groggily I force myself up.

The paper contains a single line: *Notre Dame. Ten o'clock*. No signature. The handwriting is a feminine scrawl. But who?

"Louise Michel." It has to be.

The paper's cheap, torn off the type of tablet kept at the cashier counters of cafés. And the handwriting is large and aggressive, as I image Louise Michel's would be. The secretiveness and abruptness smacks of her. Who else could it be?

But why is the Red Virgin asking me to meet with her? She already told me she won't help. And why a church? Especially the Notre Dame. It's not just a church, but one of the most beautiful cathedrals in Christendom.

Is this a trap?

I quickly take a sponge bath. I have to hurry if I'm to make it by ten o'clock this morning. I hope the sender didn't expect me to show up at the gargoyle-haunted cathedral at ten o'clock tonight!

NOTRE DAME.

One can't view Notre Dame, which is French for "Our Lady," without experiencing awe and reverence. Not only is it hard to believe something so magnificent can exist, but the power and glory of the cathedral never fail to raise goose flesh on my soul.

Notre Dame is a symbol of not just Paris, but all France. They built her on the eastern end of the *Île de la Cité*, a small ship-shaped island on the Seine. Settled in the heart of Paris, it's surrounded by grand old buildings. As I cross the *Pont Neuf* I remember the fact the island harbors both the Police Judiciaries and Police Prefecture.

Could I be walking into a trap set by a bloodthirsty anarchist? Clamped in irons by a police inspector? Either scenario is not too difficult to imagine and I question whether I was foolish to come alone. However, Jules and I weren't to meet until two in the afternoon and I don't know how to contact him.

As I stand mesmerized by the eerie *façade* of the cathedral, I experience the strongest desire to leave when a priest who could have stepped right off the pages of Victor Hugo's great novel, *The Hunchback of Notre Dame*, approaches me.

He's short and hunched from age and whatever burdens he carries. His face is small and wrinkled, deeply etched with the lines of a monkey, ugly, cynical, and amused, all at the same time. In a dusty brown habit, he appears less like a priest than the dried mummified remains of a medieval monk, found in the corner of a forgotten cell in an ancient monastery.

"Mademoiselle, please follow me."

For the first time my belief that I'm to meet with the Red Virgin is shaken—she considers the Church as great a tyrant as the government and would hardly hide in one with a priest as a guide.

What have I gotten myself into?

WE ASCEND STAIRS in the north tower and cross over to the south tower, encountering gargoyles and carved monsters, not the least of which is the infamous striga—a kind of vampire who gazes unrelenting over the city, his chin resting on his hands.

A "vast symphony in stone" is what the incomparable Victor Hugo called the cathedral. In this sinister stone forest populated with creatures from nightmares, vicious dogs, serpents, and monsters, I sense a dark and haunted symphony written in blood with the quill of Edgar Allan Poe. A gothic tale with its mysterious subterranean passages, dark battlements, hidden panels, and trapdoors—one leading to Victor Frankenstein's secret laboratory where he pieces together his modern Prometheus, and behind another, the strange matter involving *Dr. Jekyll and Mr. Hyde.*

As my imagination rages on, we enter a chamber in the south tower housing a great bell, the thirteen-ton monster rung only on special occasions by Quasimodo, the beloved hunchback who made his first appearance in literary life on the foundling shelf.

A priest who has been reading by candlelight rises to his feet and permits the hood of his habit to fall to his shoulders. Instead of a man, Louise Michel smiles at me.

I raise my eyebrows at her priestly garb. "Didn't you try to burn this very cathedral to the ground?"

She sighs and looks around a bit mournfully, as if my question could raise the very encasements against her.

"In the heat of passions roused by injustice, injustice itself can occur. No, I didn't personally make the bonfire of choir chairs that very nearly took the life of Our Lady of Stone. Actually, I was busy handing out cans of petrol to others to create a wall of fire in the city and slow down the advance of the Versailles troops. When some of my comrades began to panic and flee, I began loading and firing a cannon myself."

"Louise La Petroleuse," the old priest mutters, as he shuffles away to leave us alone. I haven't heard the name applied to her before and with my crude French, I translate it as best I'm able to, "Louise the Firestarter." I nod after the priest. "Strange bedfellows? Or is he in disguise to plant an anarchist bomb?"

"He's a real priest, but he's also the one who thought of burning the choir chairs. He occasionally finds himself torn between his devotion to God and his sense of justice."

"I certainly admire your choice of hiding places."

"My comrades chose the sewers. Frankly, I would bed with the pope rather than face those damp environs."

I take a seat on a stool and fold my hands in my lap. "After our last meeting, I had the impression you and your friends would rather murder me than talk to me."

"If your death can further the cause to unchain the slaves of the bourgeoisie, I would drive a stake through your heart myself, Mademoiselle Bly."

"That's comforting to know. How did you find out my name?" The only person in Paris who knows my real identity is the slasher.

"I recognized you. Your picture once appeared in a radical French newspaper. The story claimed you are a fine example for women."

"From your tone of voice, you don't agree."

"You haven't started a revolution, you've joined the enemy. You work for a rich newspaper owner whose mercantile soul is rented by the sweatshop owners with their advertising. You write about crimes on the streets but not about the crimes governments commit by oppressing the people."

"That's not fair. I *am* a revolutionary, not with cannons, but by example. I've worked hard to get a position never held before by a woman. Other women have obtained newspaper jobs because of my performance, thousands more have been inspired to go into other trades and most importantly, millions of women now know it's possible to be something besides a household slave. It's only a beginning but most revolutions start with just a few people."

"You can do more. You can turn your pen into a sword. The world is changing—here and in your country. The Revolution has started, *demoiselle*. Your country won't escape it. Millions of American workers slave in mines and mills for starvation wages, while a few fat pigs get fatter off their sweat."

"Progress is slow," I continue to defend myself, "but the day will come when women will have the right to vote and be educated, when men and women injured on the job or laid off won't face starvation. Just because I refuse to resort to violence doesn't mean I haven't turned my pen into a sword. It might be slow, but it's permanent. Violence doesn't bring change faster; it retards it."

She shrugs. "I learned a bitter lesson when the Commune was overwhelmed. Thousands of my comrades were summarily executed on the streets. Blood flowed in the gutters and mass graves were dug to handle all the victims. We hadn't dealt with the opposition in that manner. We fought when attacked, but never massacred. Now I adhere to the doctrine of propaganda by the deed. The killing of key leaders who keep the proletariat enslaved is just and desirable."

"The man I seek doesn't attack leaders, he murders innocent women."

"That's what you said, and that's why I'm meeting with you. I'm not just an anarchist, but an advocate of the rights of women. I'd never condone the acts you spoke of. When we organized to fight the Versailles troops, Montmartre women, as well as men, took up arms. Prostitutes joined as willingly as did seamstresses and schoolteachers. When others objected to permitting prostitutes to fight for the Commune, I rose and argued that they were as much victims of exploitation as the poor and insisted they be allowed to join. When we women covered the cannons with our bodies and refused to move when Versailles officers ordered their soldiers to shoot, there were prostitutes among us."

"Then you're willing to help me bring this madman to bay?"

"I can offer little help, for many reasons. People make a mistake in assuming that anarchists are all part of a unitary organization, but that's not true. Anarchy is a social philosophy shared by millions of people. And there are hundreds, if not thousands, of different anarchy organizations. I have no more knowledge or control over a fellow anarchist planting a bomb under the carriage of a cabinet minister than I do about what you have for breakfast this morning. And I have another, more pressing problem. I have to return to England and continue the fight from there. The bourgeois swine who runs my wonderful France has decided to imprison me in a madhouse if they catch me."

I start to say something and she holds up a forefinger, like the schoolmarm she once was.

"But I do hear rumors."

"What sort of rumors?"

"All sorts. Some true, some false, some exaggerated. The man you seek may be Russian."

"Russian, yes, that would fit. We called him the German doctor, but in America, many foreigners get labeled 'German' simply because there are so many different immigrants from Central and Eastern Europe. What—"

"That's all I can tell you. You could put me on the rack and gouge my eyes with hot pinchers and I could tell you no more. You have to seek your answers elsewhere. Here." She hands me a piece of paper with writing on it.

S. I. Chernov, 292 Rue Antoine-Joseph

"Who's this?"

"A bourgeois swine—a Russian who spies for the

czar's Third Section, the Russian political police. The revolutionaries that they don't murder, or imprison to torture, are kept track of by the political police."

"What will he tell me?"

"If the man you seek is Russian and he is in Paris, this man will know."

"Louise, I—"

"Don't thank me, I'd rather cut off both my arms and legs and blind myself than be an informant. I do this not for you or your exploitative employers. You see this scarf?" She pulls open the monk's robe to reveal her black clothes and red scarf. "Some of the blood that makes this scarf red belongs to the prostitutes of Montmartre. When the stand was made at the barricades in Place Blanche they fought bravely and died defending the square. Not one was shot in the back."

Anger has made her features strong and defiant. "Gilles de Rais. That's who you are dealing with. Now leave before I change my mind."

As I get up she speaks, "Mademoiselle Bly, if this man is what you say, he has no heart, no conscience, and he will kill you. And if he is an anarchist, the men you met last night at my table will kill you before you can stop him. To them you are a bourgeois swine. He is their comrade."

I nod my head and leave. I'm not sure if she was trying to warn me or scare the life out of me—either way, she succeeded. Unfortunately I wasn't paying attention to the route the priest used to bring me here. So, I will use the logic that if I stay on these cold, stone steps going down, they will eventually bring me to the bottom.

I can't help wonder . . . why did she have me leave alone first? She knows I don't know my way. I understand that she's torn by conflicting emotions and loyalties. Her duty to the cause of anarchism and her sense of outrage that a madman is killing women are in conflict, but she also bluntly expressed her disapproval of me and my ways to help society. And what did she mean by *before I change my mind*?

Never have I've been so eager to leave a church. I believe I held my breath the whole time. Yet if I had to do it again I would for now I know the name of the slasher—*Gilles de Rais*.

46

An inquiry in the telegraph office across the bridge reveals there's no telephone for the Procope where I'm to meet Jules in a couple of hours, so I send a telegram to the café with the Chernov information and advising Jules I'm going there.

Since we were going to the Institut I call there and ask for Pasteur's assistant, Monsieur Roth. I'm told that Roth is in a lab in a building without a phone. I decide to leave the same information as the telegram, with a message asking Roth to pass it on to Jules.

THE ADDRESS FOR S. I. Chernov is a two-story wood house on a street that's little more than an alley.

The house is modest, needs a little paint and care, but it's not a derelict. An older man answers the door, a gentleman perhaps in his early sixties, short, stumpy, bald, a cannonball with arms and legs.

"*Bonjour*, Mademoiselle." His lifted eyebrows pose a question.

I suddenly realize I hadn't given thought about what

to say to the man and stand there tongue-tied, searching for one of those lies that come so easy to me.

"Perhaps you are at the wrong house?"

"Monsieur Chernov?"

"Yes."

"Monsieur . . . what I'm about to say to you will sound strange, but I beg you to hear me through because of the singular importance of the matter."

His eyebrows go up even higher. "It is still morning, Mademoiselle. I usually find strangeness hides its head until after dark."

"I'm sorry. I realize this is very abrupt and I haven't even introduced myself. I'm an American newspaper reporter, Nellie Bly. I'm in Paris, doing a story about a series of killings. I've come to suspect that the killings are the work of an anarchist, perhaps a Russian one. I was given your name as an agent of the Russian police in the hopes that you might assist my investigation."

My words fly at him without spaces between them. After the last word hits him, I keep my lips tightly shut and pray he'll talk with me.

He stares at me, his own mouth a little agape. He blinks a couple of times. His eyes are large and brown and they look at me hard. Very hard. He seems to be on the brink of ordering me from his premises or . . . ?

"Tea, Mademoiselle?"

I let out a deep sigh. "Yes, thank you."

We pass into a foyer and through a living room.

The living room is sparsely furnished—a comfortable couch, a rocking chair, a straight back chair, and two small end tables. Newspapers and magazines are everywhere, in tall piles in the middle of the room, stacked up against the walls, covering the tables, and the two chairs. The fireplace mantle has a single picture on it, that of a woman and two small children.

I follow him into a kitchen breakfast nook that has a window to a rose garden. Three of the four chairs in the nook are covered with newspapers and there's a stack on the table. He appears to read every radical paper in the city. *L'Venger*, one of the main anarchist rags, is unfolded next to a cup of tea.

He quickly cleans off the table and a chair for me. After he puts on water for tea, he joins me.

"You must think I'm insane," I say.

"For a certainty, Mademoiselle, for a certainty. Which newspaper do you work for?"

"Mister Pulitzer's *New York World*."

"I have heard of the newspaper, but unfortunately, despite having been to America, my English is very bad."

"Monsieur Chernov, I—"

"Who sent you to me?"

"I'm not at liberty to share the name."

"Russian?"

"French."

He grunted. "In the government?"

I laugh. "Not hardly."

"Ah, a radical. Communist? Other Socialist? Anarchist?"

"No doubt all of those."

"What were you told about me?"

"That you work for something called the Third Section, some sort of Russian secret police."

"*Nyet*," he shakes his head vigorously like a dog shaking off water, "it can't be that secret if word of it is passed around like Italian ices. What did the person say I would do for you?"

"Nothing. I was simply given your name as an expert on Russian radicals. I believe the man is a radical, probably an anarchist."

"Who do you seek?"

"A man by the name of Gilles de Rais?"

He shakes his head. "That is not a Russian name. Perhaps French, Belgian, Spanish, something, but not Russian."

"I've been told he's Russian."

"Really . . ."

He gets up and makes the tea and pours me a cup before sitting back down. He clasps his hands across his big belly and smiles. "Start at the beginning. Tell me everything. Please avoid lying . . . too much."

I sigh. And start at the beginning in the madhouse at Blackwell's Island.

He listens with a quiet intensity. But is most interested in my description of the man I came to call the German doctor. Unfortunately, a man with a beard and long hair would fit millions of men in France alone. I stop the narration at the graveyard.

He purses his lips, drawing them together not in disapproval of me but of the man who kills women. He mutters something dark in Russian and then reverts to French.

"Your French, you speak it much better than me, you have hardly any accent. Have you been in France long?"

"No. Russia has a special affinity with France. My own education in French came as a result of a French tutor in the noble household where I was raised. Many young men from wealthy Russian families go to university in France. French is the second language of educated Russians, French literature, clothes, food . . . one is not considered educated or sophisticated in Moscow or St. Petersburg if one is not as French as *frites*."

It occurs to me that it would be easier for a Russian raised in the French tradition to assimilate without suspicion in Paris than New York.

He reads my mind. "Yes, it is easier for Russians here in Paris than any other city. Not only because we Russians ape the French, but Paris is the most international of all cities. It is also the most politically open. Revolutionary ideas simmer in Paris like a political stew. Occasionally the pot boils over."

"From my tale, is there anything you can tell me about the anarchist I believe is responsible for these killings?"

"One fact you already know. His appearance fits the description of almost every anarchist in Paris. If you're asking me about whether I specifically know of a Russian anarchist who murders women, the answer is no. If I did, I would have informed the French police."

He purses his lips again. "But perhaps we can sift through the facts and arrive at a list of suspects. You've told me about the manifestations you have observed about this man—his actions in New York, London, and now Paris. To link your suspicions to a Russian anarchist, you need to know something about that type of person."

"Yes, of course."

"Are you familiar with the movement?"

"A little. I know that anarchists consider government as inherently tyrannical and believe they can destroy governments and free the people through acts of violence, especially by killing off a country's political leaders."

"I'm sure you know that not all anarchists believe in the path of violence. In Paris and London, it is considered fashionable among the writers, artists, and other intelligentsia to advocate radical views. These people don't believe in the path of violence, the so-called 'propaganda by the deed.' It's the Italian and Russian anarchists who have proven the most aggressive practitioners of violence. I'll give you a cast of characters of Russian anarchism, Mademoiselle, and we shall see if we recognize the creature you seek."

In a low, grave voice, he begins. "Have you ever heard of the Society of the Pale Horse?"

I start to shake my head no, but then remember Jules' remark about the horse pendants on the circus performers and the two thugs at the anarchist café.

"I've seen horse pendants on anarchists. Are they membership badges for an anarchist group?"

"Yes, but we will come back to that society. To understand Russia and violence, you must appreciate the vastness, harsh climate, and isolation. France is a large country in Europe in terms of its area, but *forty* Frances would fit in Russia. There are wolves in Russia, not just four-legged ones, but hunger, blizzards, violence. A Russian must not only learn to work with one hand but be prepared to battle wolves snarling at him with the other. It's natural that the people who advocate change in the country would resort to violent acts to accomplish it.

"It was an Italian anarchist, Enrico Malatesta, who spread the doctrine of propaganda by the deed. Russian revolutionaries adopted it wholeheartedly. They believed that if they killed the head of the government, the people would rise up against the nobility and rich landowners who exploit the common man. Initially, the person standing in their way was Czar Alexander II.

"The czar had freed the serfs and planned to give some constitutional rights to the people, but he moved slowly, and the reforms did not go far enough for the radicals who claimed the serfs got an unfair share of the land distributed, and had to pay an exorbitant price. Incredibly, the conspiracy to kill the czar began over two decades ago and took about fifteen years to accomplish.

"The czar had an uncanny ability to avoid assassination, and his flaunting of death was legendary. The attempts began when a radical, one Karakozof, saw the czar standing by his coach. He drew a pistol from his clothes and raised it to fire, but his aim was spoiled by a bystander who rushed him. Two years later, right here in Paris, the czar was riding in an open coach with Emperor Napoléon III when Berezowski, a Polish fanatic, fired two shots and missed him.

"Besides the attempts on the czar himself, there were officials targeted. In one of the most bizarre incidents, a young woman of twenty-six, Vera Zasulich, stood in a line of petitioners appearing before General Trepof, the Governor of St. Petersburg. When it came her turn to present her petition to Trepof, she calmly took out a gun and shot him. She was, luckily for Trepof, a poor shot and only wounded him. What was most bizarre about the incident was that a jury refused to convict her for the shooting."

I remember Oscar telling me that Vera Zasulich was the heroine of a play he wrote, a play which was actually produced, but closed after a few performances. "My recollection is that the government decided that no more radicals were to be tried before juries."

"Yes, that is correct." He clicks his tongue and goes on. "That same year, other high officials were attacked." He uses a handkerchief to smother a cough before continuing. "This rabid murder lust gets more and more incredible. And insane. The radical Solovy shoots at the czar, again in St. Petersburg, as the czar is walking along a public quay. His Majesty dodges both bullets. The assassin loses his nerve and runs. A passing milk woman tackles him. A rather ignominious end to an attempt to kill the world's most powerful monarch.

"About ten years ago, the attempts to kill Alexander became the life's work of two young radicals, Sofia Perovskaya and her lover, Andrei Zhelyabov. Sofia was the driving force behind the attempts. She gathered around her a small, clandestine group of young intellectuals who swore a willingness to give their lives in the cause of regicide.

"They broke off from the Populist Party and formed the Narodnaya Volya, the People's Will—a terrorist organization of anarchists, nihilists, and other radicals with the objective of murdering the leaders of Russia. They began by attempting to blow up the czar's train. Andrei placed a homemade nitroglycerin-based bomb on the tracks where the czar's special train was to pass in the Ukaine. It missed the train. Sofia launched an attempt to blow up the train as it was nearing Moscow. She blew up the wrong train."

He gets up and paces the kitchen for a moment, then sits back down. "These are only the opening scenes of unusual and diabolical attempts to kill the czar. One of their adherents, Stefan Chalturin, a carpenter, got a job in the Winter Palace. Over a period of time he smuggled in explosives under his clothes. He built a bomb and placed it beneath the dining room. At a time when the czar was scheduled to dine, he set off the bomb. People were killed."

Chernov looks at me and shrugs. "The czar was late for dinner and didn't suffer a scratch."

I shake my head in wonderment. "It wasn't his time to die. So far, from your narrative, only Andrei Zhelyabov, Sofia's lover, and Stefan Chalturin, the carpenter, might be the man I seek."

"Not unless they rose from the grave. But there's one whose name has not been mentioned but who was a part of every attempt. You say that the man you seek has a laboratory. That would make him a chemist."

"Or he might be a medical doctor."

"Why? Because he said he's a medical doctor? The new biological chemistry of practitioners like Doctor

Pasteur and Germany's Doctor Koch go hand-in-hand with the medical profession. In Russia, many chemists, like Koch, are also medical doctors. Medicine is how they earn their living because there's little market for the work of a chemist. Except among anarchists."

"For explosives?"

"Exactly. Dynamite, that invention of Monsieur Nobel in Sweden, is expensive in Russia and hard to smuggle in. But the formula for dynamite and its more powerful and dangerous brother, nitroglycerin, are well known. Any good chemist could make the compounds. And that's where Perun comes in."

"Perun?"

"Perun is the chief god of the ancient Russian pantheon, a pagan god whose traits were similar to the mighty Thor of Norse legend. He's a god of thunder and lightning, violence and war. An ax was his symbol. The radical organization that set out to kill the czar called itself the Society of the Ax, after Nechayev's movement, possibly to throw suspicion on the already jailed radical. The man who became their chief chemist, who made the explosives, was known outside the inner circle of conspirators only by the code name Perun."

"What's his real name?"

"I don't have that information. But the name doesn't matter."

"He's dead?"

"Unfortunately not. But whatever name he was born with, is not the name he bears today. For our purposes, let's simply refer to him as Perun, since that is the name he operates under. Our information is that his family background is that of poor tenant farmers, what we call serfs."

"Isn't that typical of revolutionaries?"

"Not of Russian ones. Kropotkin, the foremost anarchist theorist, is a prince, Bakunin the son of a landowner,

Vera Zasulich the daughter of a nobleman, Sofia Perovskaya's father was a general. We believe Perun was the son of serfs but orphaned at an early age. He ultimately was taken in by a chemist who provided him a generous education."

"Including speaking French?"

"Most certainly. Perun's interests ran toward science and he became a chemistry student in St. Petersburg. Scientific interest is not the typical background for the young revolutionaries of my country. Most radicals were nurtured in law school or the teaching profession. One can assume Perun's student condition was a step above poverty and starvation, which is the general condition of all but the children of the wealthy and aristocracy. Because of his need for money, he took odd jobs. One such job appeared quite innocent: he picked up printing at night from a print shop and delivered it to an apartment house, leaving it in a box outside. One night he was arrested by the Third Section and the printing materials, radical pamphlets calling for the people to rise and tear down the government, were seized."

"Was he aware of what he was carrying?"

"Probably not, at least he didn't confess to it after he was arrested and put to the question."

"Put to the question . . . tortured?"

Chernov shrugs. "I wasn't present, but physical persuasion is not unheard of in cases involving radicals. But I'm told that he was also the victim of a carnal act that occasionally occurs to men in jail."

"He was attacked by other prisoners?"

"Perhaps by an interrogator," he says evasively. "It was ultimately concluded that Perun was innocently involved in the delivery of the pamphlets and he was finally released. We can assume he was a bitter and angry young man."

"Ripe for revolution."

"Exactly. Many of these young revolutionaries become 'converted' in an almost religious sense after they experience an injustice. In fact, his co-conspirator, Andrei, also from a family of *de facto* serfs, swore vengeance of the bourgeoisie in his childhood after his favorite aunt was raped by a large landowner who escaped prosecution. Perun joined the conspiratorial group led by Sofia and Andrei, and prepared the bombs that they tried to kill the czar with.

"One of their compatriots was captured and they knew he would ultimately identify them under torture. They also knew the czar was regularly driven through the streets of St. Petersburg over certain roads. They came up with a grand scheme to rent a store on the street, mine under the road, and place explosives to ignite when the carriage arrived. Perun had also designed hand-held nitro bombs, resembling snow balls that exploded on impact.

"Andrei was arrested. He boasted to the police that the czar would be dead within three days. The chief of police begged the czar to stay out of harm's way for a few days until they could arrest the other conspirators, but the czar refused to be intimidated by a group of young radicals. The radicals attacked the czar's carriage. The street explosives failed and even the nitro bombs, thrown at the carriage by terrorists under the command of Sofia, didn't harm the czar, though some of his guards were wounded.

"Because so many attempts to kill him had failed, perhaps the czar himself had begun to believe in his own invincibility. Refusing to heed his protectors after the attack, he insisted upon returning to the scene where his guards were wounded. He was on foot, inspecting the wounded, when a revolutionary ran up to him and threw a nitro bomb at his feet, killing himself and the czar."

"And Perun?"

"Most of the conspirators were found, arrested and executed, including both Andrei and Sofia. Perun and others escaped and made their way to France, Italy, and Switzerland. Those groups have close ties with radicals still in Russia. As you may have heard, revolutionaries have also tried to assassinate Alexander III." *

"Is that why you're in Paris? Because the revolutionary movement in Russia is supported by radicals here?"

"I'm in Paris for personal reasons." He hesitates and then rises from his chair and goes into the other room. He returns with the picture of the woman and two children I'd seen on the fireplace mantel. His eyes are moist and his voice impassioned as he shows me the picture. "My wife, Natasha, son, Sergo, and daughter, Natalia.

"They were on the train bound for Moscow that Sofia blew up. She called herself an intellectual, but could not read a train schedule. I was a policeman, a supervisor in St. Petersburg at the time. My wife had taken the train so our children could visit with their grandparents." His voice shakes.

"There were seven conspirators involved in that train explosion. Five of them were arrested and executed after the assassination of the czar. One I tracked to Switzerland. He met an untimely death." Chernov's big hands squeeze open and shut.

I shudder, imagining that the man's "untimely death" occurred between those two big paws.

"Perun was there, too, involved in another conspiratorial assassin group. But I missed him. I heard he left for America."

---

* One of the radicals hanged for the assassination attempt on Alexander III was the brother of Lenin, the founder of the Russian Communist Party and first leader of the Soviet Union. —The Editors.

"America! He might be my man. When did this happen?"

"I followed the trail to America. It ended at the Haymarket Square in Chicago, about three years ago."

"The bombing!"

He nods. "Someone turned an otherwise peaceful anarchist rally into a nightmare by throwing a bomb that killed seven policemen."

"I followed the trial. No one knows who threw the bomb. The police simply arrested eight anarchist labor leaders who had organized the rally and tried them for murder. Four were hanged, one committed suicide, before Governor Altgeld courageously pardoned the other three awaiting execution."

"My investigation revealed that the bomb was thrown because the anarchists involved in the American labor movement were not considered violent enough by an international group of anarchists operating out of Switzerland."

"So they sent Perun, to America, to stir up trouble." I shake my head. "Just as they stirred up trouble when the czar was getting too lenient."

"Exactly. I lost track of Perun after Chicago. I returned to Europe and ultimately to Paris because the Swiss were getting tired of being a home for exiled anarchists and many moved on to Paris. I hoped to find Perun here. I receive a small stipend from my government for keeping them advised on anarchists in general. But I'd be retired on a nice pension in St. Petersburg today, with my family, if Perun had not mixed a bomb that took away everyone in the world that I loved." He pauses, to get control of his emotions. "Awhile ago, I asked if you'd heard of the Society of the Pale Horse. That is what this clandestine cell of fanatics call themselves."

"The Fourth Horseman," I whisper.

"Yes, the one that would kill with a sword, hunger, and the beasts of the earth. 'And his name was Death and Hell followed him,' is how the Bible reads."

I get goosebumps. "Such madness . . . such murderous madness. What does Perun look like?"

"I don't know."

"You don't know! How have you been tracking him?"

"By name and deed—almost the same way you have been tracking your doctor. It's easy for a man to change one's appearance when it is equally fashionable to have hair, beard, and mustache of any length or be clean shaven. He's known in the movement simply as Perun. His real name isn't known outside the small core of fanatical anarchists and possibly the upper echelon of police in St. Petersburg."

"Do you know where Perun is now?"

"Here in Paris."

"Are you certain?"

"I have a source that's proven reliable in the past. Something *big* is being planned here in Paris."

We hear a knock.

"I hope you don't mind, but I'm expecting a friend," I tell Chernov.

"Not at all. However, it may be the woman who comes for my laundry."

He leaves the table. I get up and pace the little breakfast nook, trying to contain my excitement and digest all that he has said. There's no proof that Perun is my maniac from the madhouse, but my intuition is screaming he is.

I hear Chernov opening the front door and an exclamation. An explosion erupts that knocks me off my feet.

I sit on the floor, stunned, my ears ringing.

Smoke, a burned, bitter, chemical smell, pours through the doorway from the living room. Struggling to my feet I lurch to the doorway. The living room is full of smoke.

The front part of the house is ripped wide open and on fire. Mr. Chernov is on his back, on the living room floor. There's nothing to be done for him—what's on the floor is hardly recognizable.

I cough my way to the kitchen door and stagger into the garden. A gate leads out of the garden to the alley-street at the rear of the house.

I cry uncontrollably. Poor Mr. Chernov is dead.

47

I stumble coming out of the alley and onto the street. My hearing's stunned, my eyes sting, tears blur my vision. There's great commotion around me, people shouting, running, but it's all a fog. What is clear is that I have to get away before I'm detained by the police. A woman touches my arm and says something. I think she is asking if I'm injured. I mumble "no" and just keep walking—moving myself away from the turmoil, from poor Mr. Chernov, back in the direction I had come.

Tears keep coming, not just because of the sting from the smoke, but for Mr. Chernov. I hope he's at peace and has joined his wife and children. Fire trucks rumble by, bells ring, the heavy hooves of the horses pounding the cobblestones. Slowly my hearing starts to come back. Someone else, a man, asks if I need help. I shake my head no and keep walking.

"Nellie!"

A carriage pulls up beside me. Jules opens the door and jumps down.

"You're hurt!"

"No, no, not hurt. Just . . ." I couldn't finish. My tears become sobs.

He puts his arm around me and assists me into the coach.

TWO HOURS LATER we are sitting in a café and talking. Jules had taken me home to change and freshen up. My clothes and face were blackened by smoke. Entering the building, Madame Malon stepped out of her flat to glare at me and quickly fled back inside, slamming the door behind her, after Jules gave her a menacing look and tapped his cane aggressively. He escorted me to the door of my garret and then went back down to give me privacy.

I told him how I had received a note from Louise Michel and that she directed me to the czarist agent.

"I returned to Monsieur Chernov's while you were cleaning up. A bomb blew out the front of the house. What saved you were the walls between you and the blast."

I shudder at the thought of being ripped to pieces.

"I spoke to the officers on the scene. A neighbor returning to her home spotted a man near the apartment a moment before the blast, but was not able to give a description."

"It was Gilles de Rais, who is also known as Perun."

Jules gave me a look not unlike the one he gave me when I told him I'd been an inmate in a madhouse. "Why do you say that?"

"Louise Michel said the killer's name is Gilles de Rais. He's Russian and apparently he speaks fluid French. Monsieur Chernov said the man's code name in the Russian anarchist underground is Perun. My guess is that he's using the Gilles name in Paris as a cover."

"Perun. Some sort of Slavic god."

"The god of thunder and—and that sort of thing."

"Do you think that the Red Virgin deliberately sent you to the Russian's house to be murdered?"

"Of course not. She could have had me killed in the alley outside my room or a thousand other places. Not to mention Notre Dame. But I won't doubt her anarchist friends tipped off the bomber that I was going there. This Gilles person doesn't want me to trace him back to Russia."

Jules rubs his chin, thoughtful. "I agree. Killing someone with a bomb isn't Louise Michel's style. If she wanted you dead, she would more likely hand you a knife and fight you one-to-one with her own knife."

"Jules, I don't understand. You don't seem pleased by my information. We have a name for the killer. There can't be more than one Gilles de Rais in Paris. We can now track him down."

"Nellie, Gilles de Rais has been dead for at least the last four hundred years. He was a baron and marshal of France back in the 1400s. He had a distinguished military career, rode with Joan of Arc, and fought several battles at her side. He rose to be one of the richest and most powerful men in the country, maintaining a court that was more lavish than the king's.

"Unfortunately, he was also quite mad. He became fascinated with black alchemy, certain that he could invoke the power of the devil and make himself master of the world. To achieve this end, he murdered many people—abducting, torturing, and murdering over a hundred children alone."

"Good God."

"His end came at a relatively young age, in his early thirties I believe, he was arrested, tried and hanged."

"Louise tricked me . . . but why?"

"No, I don't think that was her intent. I believe that she was truly aroused by your accusation that an anarchist was killing prostitutes. I suspect she didn't call him Gilles de Rais to identify him, but was commenting upon his murderous character—just as a person in London might refer to an anonymous slasher as 'Jack the Ripper.' "

I felt completely deflated. "And I thought I'd broken the case."

"Perhaps you have, perhaps you have," he murmured.

"How? I thought Gilles de Rais was Perun, but he's dead—long dead. I assumed he followed me to poor Mister Chernov's and blew him up to keep me from knowing his identity. It looks like I was simply in the wrong place at the wrong time—an anarchist deciding to do away with a policeman. Or maybe . . . Jules?"

He looks at me with that faraway look, as if he is staring beyond the now and into a book of secrets, but I decide to continue even though I know he's not really listening.

"Maybe this Perun person, whoever he is, *was* trying to blow both of us up because he's the slasher. He knew I would discover who he was once I talked to Chernov and he couldn't have that happen. I was just plain lucky to escape. But, if I take into consideration what Chernov said about Perun, his profile might not fit the slasher's."

Jules comes out of his brown study pursing his lips. "Louise steered you to Chernov because she learned a Russian is involved. So, why can't this anarchist Perun be the slasher?"

"Chernov told me Perun is an idealistic anarchist who is killing government leaders. The slasher is a homicidal maniac who kills women for pleasure. They don't match up. Chernov also said something big is planned here in Paris and he's certain Perun is behind it—as he was with the Haymarket bombings in Chicago. I don't see the slasher being involved in an elaborate scheme to blow up the government. It just doesn't fit his profile. He's here to kill women, just like he did in New York and London."

"You're wrong."

"Excuse me?"

"There is no reason the slasher cannot be a homicidal maniac and an anarchist terrorist. He could be killing women for his perverted pleasure while maintaining his anarchist activities to satisfy his political views."

I look at Jules long and hard. "Ok . . . I have to admit that after Chernov told me about Perun, my intuition screamed he's the slasher. But, when I look at the whole picture, I must say it's too bizarre, too far-fetched."

"Maybe not. I have found that when nothing makes complete sense, there's usually a clever mind behind it. I think it is time we spoke to Doctor Pasteur about Toulouse's painting. I'll take you back to your room while I go to the Institut. You're in no condition to make a trip to Pasteur's."

Men. Why do they believe when a woman experiences any kind of traumatic situation they need rest? I'm positive even a man would need rest after what I experienced. Well, this is my hunt and he is not going to pursue it without me. It took every ounce of my strength to stand up and say, "Let's get a fiacre and be on our way. I'm going with you. And that's final."

48

At the Institut, we're admitted into Pasteur's private office shortly after requesting to see both Dr. Pasteur and his young assistant, Tomas Roth. The two men join us minutes later. Pasteur looks older and more stressed than the last time I saw him. Jules stares at him with concern.

"Monsieur Doctor," Jules says, "I'm sorry to intrude on such short notice. Should we come another time?"

"No, no. It's just that this is a sad occasion." Pasteur is not only downhearted, but troubled. "One of our young assistants died from an exposure to a microbe, perhaps the Black Fever contagion. The authorities removed his body just hours ago. If it had been anyone but you, Monsieur Verne, they would have been turned away at the door. The entire Institut is concerned about our colleague's death."

Jules and I both murmur our condolences.

"I do apologize, but the matter that brings us to you concerns this painting and also deals with life and death." Jules unwraps it and sits it on the desk.

Both men stare curiously at the painting.

"A café artist," Jules continues, "painted this at Le Chat Noir several years ago. You appear surprised, Doctor

Roth, but we've been led to believe that this man is you and that the others are from the Institut."

"It certainly appears to be me."

I don't know if it's just me, but he seems to be slightly agitated about the picture. I glance at Jules. He's poker-faced as Tomas continues talking.

"I did work briefly for the Institut a few years ago, before taking on another task. I returned months ago. I do remember the café incident, though I didn't know we were being painted." He raises his eyebrows. "I suppose an artist would make a pencil sketch and then paint the rest from memory, since we didn't sit for him."

"We're interested in the identity of this man." Jules points at the man wearing the red scarf. "Do you gentlemen recognize him?"

"Yes, that's Doctor Leon Nurep, a Russian chemist that worked here briefly."

"How is that spelled?" Jules asks.

"N-u-r-e-p."

"What is this about, Monsieur Verne?" Pasteur asks.

Jules hesitates. "The man may be involved in murder."

"Murder!" Pasteur is shocked.

Dr. Roth shakes his head, but he doesn't look anywhere as shocked as Dr. Pasteur. "Perhaps so, perhaps so."

I'm curious as to his response and ask Dr. Roth, "You're not surprised at the charge, Doctor?"

"Nurep is both an anarchist and a Russian, which, as everyone knows, is an explosive combination."

"Do you know where he is?" Jules directs his question to Dr. Roth.

"No, I haven't seen him in several years. In fact, not since the night we attended Le Chat Noir for dinner. The event was a farewell gathering for him, dinner earlier and then the cabaret antics. Nurep had been associated with us briefly in work we were doing for his employer.

We terminated the work when we discovered that the nature of the work had been misrepresented to us."

"Who was he working for?" I ask.

Rather than answering me, Dr. Roth looks to Pasteur.

Jules speaks directly to Dr. Pasteur. "It is a matter of great importance. You know that I'm a great admirer of your work. I assure you that we have no information that the Institut is in any manner involved in this affair. We're not seeking scandal, only justice."

"I believe you because I know you are a patriot of France and would not be involved in a lark," Dr. Pasteur says to Jules, but gives me a grave look.

I bite my tongue, for I instantly want to defend myself.

"I vouch for Mademoiselle. She's not only completely trustworthy, but she is the chief foe and investigator of a criminal scheme that bodes the most severe consequences to France."

I glow in the light of Jules' praise.

Pasteur sighs. I have the feeling that nothing short of the earth opening and swallowing Paris would draw him from his work. But now he has a death at the Institut and our strange visit that implies the two might be intertwined. The poor man is torn and tired and would probably like nothing better than to go to his lab and bury himself in his experiments.

"He was working for the Comte d'Artigas."

"*Artigas.*" Jules' face goes dark as he repeats the name. I ask, "The munitions manufacturer?"

"Yes," Roth replies, "I'm certain you know of his reputation even in America."

"His reputation has indeed reached America. He is a cannon king like Krupp in Germany."

"A warmonger is what he is. He'd sell poisoned candy to babies if he could profit from it." Jules does not hide his anger.

Pasteur nods in agreement. "Exactly. He is not a person we would be associated with—ever. He approached me with a project concerning weapons and when I flatly turned him away, he employed Nurep to come to us under false pretenses. Nurep told us he was working on a new type of agricultural fertilizer, a product to help farmers. When I discovered he was working for Artigas, I immediately terminated the relationship. Not that there was much of a relationship, it only lasted a few months. I personally have no recollection of having met Nurep myself. He met with Doctor Roth a few times. They conducted some experiments regarding a chemical compound."

"What was this compound?" Jules turns to Roth.

"I am afraid, Monsieur, that even though I am not well disposed toward the gentlemen for their falsehoods, I will not disclose their secrets."

Dr. Pasteur noted assent to his assistant's position.

"Doctor Nurep, was he a strange one? By that, I mean, did he have any queer sort of ideas—besides his politics? Perhaps in regard to the way he, uh, thought of women?"

Pasteur looks at me quite puzzled, but Dr. Roth answers my question as if I asked what time of day it is—very matter of fact.

"If he did, it was not disclosed to us. Nor was his politics. We wouldn't associate with a radical. I only worked with him briefly in a laboratory environment and didn't socialize with him except that one night at Le Chat Noir. Dr. Pasteur suggested we at least give him a farewell dinner when he was forbidden to work further at the Institut. That was the first time he wore the red scarf of a revolutionary in our presence. At first we thought he was simply being amusing. As you know, most revolutions are café table talk. But Nurep became very verbose about his political beliefs that night. I can assure you we cut the evening short."

"What did he say?"

"I really don't remember. Something about how the wealthy want to keep the people poor and the only way to stop this abuse of power was to get rid of these people—take their wealth and distribute it evenly among everyone. We were quite surprised."

"Oh . . ." It's not what I wanted to hear, it's too generic, so I decide to take a chance and probe further. "Did he ever mention the Society of the Pale Horse?"

"No. As I said, we didn't encourage his radical conversation and cut the evening short."

"Can you tell me what sort of man he was to work with?"

"I found him competent in the laboratory. Quite a brilliant researcher as a matter of fact. Not as up to date on techniques and literature in the field as one would expect, but I suspect that innovations are slow to reach Russia."

"How was his French?"

Roth smiles. "Much better than yours and mine, Mademoiselle. He would not be taken for a Parisian, but like many educated Russians, he speaks official French better and with no more accent than provincials."

"What is your accent, if I may ask?" Jules asks.

"Alsatian."

"I am lucky to have obtained Doctor Roth as my assistant," Doctor Pasteur speaks up. "He was offered a position by Koch in Berlin, but his Alsatian soul is French, not Prussian."

"When was the last time you saw Nurep?" I ask.

Roth raises his hands in a frustrated gesture. "Mademoiselle, as I have told you—that night at Le Chat Noir."

"Did anyone else at the Institut work with him?

Someone who might know something more about him?"

"Only me."

"And the other man in the painting." Pasteur corrects Roth. A shadow passes across his face. "But he will not be able to help you. He's René Grousset, the young man who died of fever. He was a student helper then, not a full-time employee."

Silence lay heavy in the air. As always I am the one to break the silence. "What was Nurep's field of work?"

"Explosives." The response came from Jules. "A chemical weapon, if I know Artigas. The devil is trying to devise some weapon of horror to make war even more terrible than it already is. He counts lives in terms of how many francs he can make exterminating them."

Pasteur and Roth confirm Jules' theory by the expressions on their faces.

I am surprised at Jules' tone. There is anger in his voice. Not the wrath one expresses against abstract injustices, but anger that is personal—and violent.

49

We left Toulouse's painting for safekeeping at the Institut because Jules called his newspaper friend and arranged for us to meet him at a café before meeting Oscar at the Procope.

"Aurélien Scholl is an old friend," Jules says as a fiacre takes us to the Café de la Paix across from the Opera. "He's one of those rare newspapermen whose sword is mightier than his pen. As is his dueling pistol. He periodically fights duels to defend his articles, and being something of a café lover, a duel to defend his life against a jealous husband is occasionally necessary."

I change the subject because a more important issue has been gnawing away at my brain.

"I didn't find the conversation with Pasteur and Roth very satisfying. Don't you find it odd that a member of the Institut who had dealings with this man Nurep is dead of the fever? I mean, how convenient can that be? And Roth . . . he puzzles me. Something's not right. I feel it, and it's eating away at me. I didn't like him refusing to tell us what Nurep and his boss were concocting. Didn't you find the whole conversation a bit . . . I don't know . . . off?"

"I'm not quite sure what you mean by *off*, but it definitely wasn't satisfying. I do agree that Roth seemed a little bit vague about Nurep, but maybe he knew there was nothing really to tell. In regard to Artigas, I believe Roth is just like Pasteur—projects are confidential. Pasteur was obviously both stressed and reluctant to provide further information about his employee's death." Jules pauses and meets my eye. "But, at least we were able to confirm that this Nurep is the same man the czarist agent sought."

"We were? Just because, Perun and Nurep are both Russians—Oh my goodness—*It's the same name, spelled backward.*"

"Yes. Your czarist agent was correct, the anarchist Perun is in Paris. But whether he is your slasher remains to be seen."

Another issue weighs heavily on my brain as we get close to the café—that of revealing to Jules' newspaper friend my slasher information. If he broke the story, I'd be out cold after all my work.

"I'm a little wary of telling the slasher story to the newspaper reporter. If something ended up prematurely in the news, the slasher would probably leave the city and carry his ghastly crimes elsewhere." Brilliant. Even I amaze myself sometimes. "And for the first time, I feel like I am getting close to catching him, really close and nothing is going to get in my way or . . ." I almost say, "take my story."

"Don't worry, this slasher business is not the type of story he'd be interested in. Still, you're probably right, we shouldn't bring it up. I won't lie to him, but perhaps we can tell him part of the truth. You shouldn't have difficulty with that."

He goes on, cutting off my rebuttal before it slips off my tongue.

"We'll tell him that you're chasing a murder suspect,

a violent anarchist who set off a bomb in America that killed your sister. And that we suspect the man, a Russian, who has worked for Artigas in the past, is here in Paris. Is that vague enough for you?"

"Yes, and to add another dose of credibility to it, we can tell him that the anarchist was involved in the Haymarket incident in Chicago. The bombing is still a controversial subject in America, but would have little interest to the French."

"Excellent." He comes out of his grave reserve to give me a small smile. "Your ability to lie at any moment, on any subject, is quite astonishing."

I do a little curtsy, as best as I can sitting down. "Thank you, Monsieur Verne. Coming from a man who has thrilled the world with his works of *fiction*, that is indeed a heady compliment. You say Scholl has to defend his articles with duels. Isn't there a law protecting freedom of the press?"

"Of course there is, but a man's honor rises above the law. As difficult as it is for a woman to understand, if a man is insulted or called out, he must meet on the dueling field or hide his head in shame."

"Naturally, we poor, backward women wouldn't understand honor."

He suddenly chuckles. It's a warm and cuddly chuckle and I want to hug him.

"You're right. Duels are often the work of men who are really small boys. I recall an incident in which two young reporters meeting on the dueling field with swords were so frightened that *both* of them vomited."

"I hope they put away their swords and went home friends."

"Actually, they were both so embarrassed they hacked unmercifully, but thankfully amateurishly, at each other."

"Why are you so angry at that man Artigas?" I blurted

it out. My curiosity about his reaction to Artigas has been aching to be satisfied and the timing seemed right— Jules is in a better mood. And I've never been one to let sleeping dogs lie, however, as I watch his fists clench and his face redden, I fear I have gone too far.

"*He's a cannibal who ate my brains.*"

He then turns to the window again, refusing to say more.

SCHOLL IS UNLIKE any reporter I've ever met. He reminds me of a lone predator, a jungle cat that doesn't share his kills. But while a rough-and-tumble American reporter would be an alley cat with scuffed shoes and wrinkled raincoat, Scholl—monocle and dressed impeccably—is a haughty and cultured king of beasts. He has a scar on the side of his face and I wonder if it is a memento from a duel.

We sit with him at a sidewalk table. I would have preferred an inside table, it's a bit cool, but the sun is out and the *café au lait* warms me. As Jules explains our quest for information, Scholl slips a glance at me, examining me through his monocle. From his look, I can see he's decided that there's more between Jules and me than the investigation. I find myself wishing he was right.

"A monster," Scholl says, when Jules asks about Count Artigas, "a giant squid from *Twenty Thousand Leagues Under the Sea*. He swallows everything that comes near him. He makes munitions, of course, sells his guns to the highest bidder. Then he turns around and sells them to his customer's enemies. He has no allegiance to anyone but the franc. Gold is his lover and his god." Scholl grins at me. "Something like American businessmen. Only the count sells death."

"Is he old aristocracy?" I decide to ignore his sarcasm, this time.

"Purchased the title during the Second Empire."

"What kind of munitions does he sell?"

"Anything that will kill. Small arms, artillery, hand bombs, whatever will do the job. He sells to anyone with the money—to rebels fighting the Turks in the Balkans and to the Turks to use against the rebels. He has agents in the trouble spots of the world. It's said that he hires *agents provocateurs* to start wars by stirring up trouble when business is slow. Some years ago he was even selling to warring Indian tribes through his agents in Québec."

"Have you ever heard of a Doctor Leon Nurep?" Jules asks. "He apparently worked for Artigas a couple years ago. It's Perun spelled backward."

Scholl shakes his head. "No. Is that your suspect?"

"At this stage we're not certain, but he fits the description."

"Is he a medical doctor?"

"A chemist."

The newspaperman retrieves his attaché case from an adjoining chair. "When you called and asked to discuss Artigas, I grabbed my file on him. There are several pictures of him and some of his employees. Let's take a look and see if your chemist is among them."

He sets out pictures that include Artigas and what appears to be a group of executives and workers in front of a factory. Artigas is a short, thin, bald man that looks more like a nervous accountant than a cannon king. I don't see anyone I take to be Perun.

"If you're going to deal with the count, you had better watch your step. This man," Scholl points at a large man, an unpleasant sort with a large pug nose and quarrelsome mouth, "Jacque Malliot—he's a former policeman who is technically one of Artigas's assistants. I've heard he provides Artigas with the type of assistance that is more of a physical nature."

"An enforcer?" Jules asks.

"Maybe worse. A killer. He has provoked duels a couple of times with Artigas's competitors. One man he killed, another he seriously wounded. More than one throat has been slit in a less gentlemanly fashion than dueling for owing money to Artigas or being a disloyal employee."

I peer closer at the picture. "Is Malliot's right hand missing?"

"Yes, I've heard it was cut off by an opposing gang. What you see in place of the hand is a steel ball, about fist size, quite a nasty thing to get hit by. More than one man's jaw—or brain—has been shattered from that iron fist."

"Is Perun missing a hand?" Jules asks me.

"No, not that I know of, I was just curious." I can hardly tell him that this Malliot might have been seeking information about me and the pamphlets I am passing out. Why is Artigas interested in me? "Artigas and Malliot sound like little more than criminals."

"Murderous criminals at that. I've heard café talk that Malliot is a member of the Haute Pègre. Are you familiar with the organization, Mademoiselle?"

"No."

"Perhaps organization is too strong a word. It is an association, perhaps even a caste, of criminals—not street apaches or pickpockets, but criminals who control vices and illicit activities of every nature."

"They call ordinary thieves *chifonniers*—ragpickers," Jules interjects.

"Yes, and the *gens comme il faut*, the upper echelon of

the conspirators, live like princes at the top of a criminal conspiracy that has its own set of rules, soldiers, and weapons. In the old days the police only had to worry about the Romanichel, the Gypsy bands of murderers and thieves. But the Haute Pègre operates like organized military units of pègres, underworld criminals. Have you ever heard the story of the attempt to rob the Duke of Brunswick?" The question is directed at Jules.

Jules shakes his head no.

"Quite the eccentric, this English lord. He settled in Paris and set up residence at a queer sort of house that resembled a strongbox. Appropriate, because he kept a great hoard of diamonds in the house, fifteen to twenty million francs worth. This princely fellow with the wealth of kings was said to be so miserly that he avoided eating meat daily because of the cost. I saw this strange creature many years ago at a lesser café. When he rose to leave, his body made a rattling sound, the clatter of bones when the wind sets a skeleton in motion.

"The Haute Pègre decided to separate the duke from his diamonds. They managed to get one of their tribe into his employ as a servant. The man discovered that mi'lord kept the diamonds in a strongbox hidden in a wolf hole behind his bed. When the duke was out of the house, the thief used an iron bar to break into the wolf hole." Scholl smiles. He apparently likes this part of the story. "One must be more cautious of separating a miser from his gems than a nun from her own jewel. As the thief grabbed the strongbox, he was shot ten times. The duke had a rack of loaded pistols, connected to electric wires, set to fire when the strongbox was touched."

As Scholl clips the end of a cigar and prepares to light up, Jules asks, "Is Artigas involved in the Haute Pègre?"

"No one knows." He blows foul smoke. "But there

have been rumors. More to the point is Jacque Malliot. The duke's deceased servant was also named Malliot." Scholl shrugged. "An uncle, cousin, brother, father? I suspect a relationship. The Haute Pègre is a close-knit family."

Jules says, "If men like Artigas practiced their traits on the street, we would call them thieves and murderers and send them to the guillotine. But when they wear fashionable suits and pay someone else to use the knife, we call them businessmen and admire them. There is indeed a thin line between the hand that makes a gun that has no purpose but to kill a human being and the hand that pulls the trigger."

Scholl puts away the pictures. "If you want to know more about this chemist, why don't you ask Artigas himself? I hear he's in Paris for the Exposition. His company has an exhibit in the Palais de Machinery."

"A munitions manufacturer showing off his wares of death at the Exposition? *Outrageous.*" Jules' anger is about to explode.

"The power of money. The Exposition directors denied his application for an exhibit permit, but soon after some deputies in the Chamber and other high officials began to receive an extra source of income. When enough graft was paid, the Expo directors were told that France should demonstrate its military power to the world. As you know, the army and navy have exhibits also, but Artigas's is at least inconspicuous."

"Artigas represents the dirty side of France's military power."

"Exactly. Anyway, a compromise was reached and a small building was built at the back of the Palais de Machinery. The excuse was that for safety and secrecy reasons, the armaments should not be in the main hall, but the real reason is that the directors did not want the exhibit in plain sight." He pauses for a moment. "I heard another dirty rumor about Artigas. Artigas hired a chemist to develop a new type of artillery shell—"

"I'm familiar with the story," Jules interrupts. His tone causes me to glance at him.

"Then you're aware that a chemist involved tried to secretly sell the compound to a foreign power and ended up floating in the Seine?"

"Yes, a man from Marseille. I have another question for you," Jules says, "this time about an Irishman, one Oscar Wilde."

Scholl laughs. "Ah, you go from the sinister to the ridiculous. Have you met this prince of the boulevard cafés?"

"I've had the doubtful pleasure."

"The Britisher is an incredible café and dinner phenomena. Never has one man created so much attention in the dining room world of the arts with having done so little. The man's most significant contribution to the arts is his wagging tongue. And he has a habit of borrowing his ideas from others."

"Borrowing?" I ask. "You mean plagiarizing?"

"Sometimes taken outright, more often adapted. In fifteen minutes of café oratory at the Café Royale, I've heard him espouse the ideas of Plato, Cicero, Descartes, and Karl Marx without giving any of them credit."

"Marx?" Jules eyebrows go up. "Is Wilde a Communist?"

"An anarchist, I think is what he calls himself, and a socialist. He even wrote a play about that woman, what was her name, the Russian . . . Vera, Vera something . . ."

"Vera Zasulich."

Both Jules and Scholl look at me in surprise. "She tried to kill General Trepov, the Governor of St. Petersburg, but only wounded him. The play was called *The Nihilist*. Nihilists are a type of anarchists, if memory serves me correct. However, the play closed after a few performances."

I swear I will never stop being amazed at how men are so shocked to find that a woman has any knowledge about politics. I lift my chin a notch higher.

Jules asks Scholl, "This Oscar Wilde is an anarchist and a nihilist?"

"Wilde is a talker, not a doer. He's at his best in cafés among people who find the green fairy and white angel more stimulating than wine. He'd faint if someone asked him to throw a bomb. He's not really a political theorist, but a café orator who wraps words in bright paper and tosses them at people as if he's a king throwing coins to peasants. He says he is an anarchist at heart, but I suspect that his heart is solely dedicated to hearing himself talk and wearing the green carnation." Scholl shoots a glance at me to see if I am offended by his reference to Wilde's homosexual orientation.

I flutter my eyes ladylike. "I know the green fairy is absinthe, but what's the white angel?"

"Cocaine. Wilde, by the way, frequents this café. He claims he once saw an angel fluttering over the square. I image what he saw flying was one of the stone angels from atop the Opera across the street. No doubt he saw the image after partaking of cocaine and absinthe."

A man enters with a woman on his arm and they sit nearby. Scholl and the man exchange greetings before the man sits. The man is generously built and rather handsome in a brooding sort of way. There's a bit of gloom about him. Jules moves his chair slightly so the newcomers cannot get a direct look at his face.

Scholl nods in their direction. "Guy de Maupassant and his newest la fem, the wife of Lapointe, the banker."

I lift my eyebrows and Scholl leans closer and whispers, "It's all right, Mademoiselle, she loves her husband. She loves him so much, she uses the husbands of other women in order not to wear out her own."

Scholl and Jules have a good laugh.

"I think I've heard his name. He's a writer, isn't he?" I ask.

"Yes," Scholl says surprised again.

Once again I show off only because it really ruffles my feathers the way men think of woman. "Before I left for Paris, I read a short story of his called, 'Boule de suif,' Ball of Fat. The tale brought both tears and anger from me. It concerns a prostitute traveling by coach during the Franco-Prussian War. She is well treated by her fellow French passengers, who want to share her provision of food. A German officer stops the coach and refuses to let it proceed unless she has sex with him. The other passengers, anxious to be on their way, induce her to satisfy him. After the deed is done on their behalf, they ostracize her for the rest of the journey."

Scholl looks at me with new respect, "That was one of his best."

"Yes. I think it was a brilliant piece of writing—sad, but brilliant." Had I not been wanted by the Paris police, I would have gotten up and commended Maupassant for his genius.

Scholl smiles. "Well, the woman with him does not know what she is getting into. Maupassant has boasted that he is going to take vengeance on women for giving him the big pox by passing it onto any woman who will sleep with him." *

---

* Guy de Maupassant's brother died in 1889 and Guy went into deep depression. In 1892 he tried suicide by cutting his own throat and was institutionalized. He died the following year at the age of 42. Part of his mental problems were the result of advanced syphilis. The brother of Edmond Goncourt, who satirized Oscar Wilde in his *Journal*, also died of the big pox.—The Editors.

50

After we leave Scholl at the café, Jules and I walk down Avenue de l'Opera in the direction of the Seine. We're early for our meeting with Wilde and decide to walk off some of the time before grabbing a carriage. My head is swirling with questions and theories, and I'm eager to address them to Jules, but from his grave countenance it's obvious he's not in the mood to talk. I really have to bite my tongue.

There are two issues that perplex me. As a reporter I learned that there are no innocent coincidences. Malliot has to be the ex-policeman who asked about me at the café where I checked on the prostitutes. Now the question is *why?* Why does the cannon king care about what I am investigating? I wish I could discuss this with Jules, but then he'd start asking me questions I don't want to answer.

Besides, this raises another question about Jules. What is the connection between him and Artigas? Obviously there's bad blood between the two. But what? My mind is volcanic and ready to explode. I can't take it. I need answers.

"Jules, I'm beginning to suspect that you've been with-holding information from me. As my mother would say, every time this man Artigas' name is mentioned, you dance like a cat in a frying pan."

"A cat in a frying pan?"

"It's an old American expression." Actually, I'd only heard my mother use it, but it sounds old to me. The tapping of his cane becomes more aggressive; I've hit a nerve.

"There's another old expression, American and French. It's called sticking your nose in places where you shouldn't."

Amazing. He talks about how he came to Paris to kill a man and cannibals eating his brains and he thinks I should ignore it? Impossible.

"Excuse me for saying this Jules, but I don't think—"

"Strange." His mind is talking aloud, as my mother would say when I interrupted her in mid sentence.

"What's strange?"

"That Perun would associate with the likes of Artigas. They're enemies. In the eyes of an anarchist, Artigas is a capitalistic enslaver of the common man, the very sort of moneyed plunderer the anarchist wants to kill. And anarchists are the greatest threat to men of Artigas' ilk. They live in fear and surround themselves with bodyguards because they know any one of them may be the next victim of the radicals."

"Then why would Perun work for Artigas?"

"Maybe," Jules muses, "he isn't working for him. Maybe he's working *with* him. Or even better, Perun could be spying. Perhaps Artigas is developing a new killing weapon, the sort of thing an anarchist group would love to get their hands on."

As I give this idea a bit of thought, Jules' walking stick continues to tap the ground with a thoughtful, almost nervous cadence that I have observed occurs when he is engrossed in solving a problem.

"Jules, whenever Artigas' name is mentioned, you become rather, uh, disconcerted. You react as if there is bad blood between you. We're conducting an investigation together and this man suddenly fits into it. Don't you think it would be unfair for you to withhold information from me?"

"Keep information from you?" He laughs. "Mademoiselle, dealing with you is like peeling an onion that changes each time a layer is exposed. If you told me it's daytime, I would have to check to see if the sun is in the sky."

Obviously, this is not the time to discuss Artigas with him.

51

At the Procope we find Oscar surrounded by a group of people, including waiters. They have gathered by his table listening to him expound on the subject of aesthetics, which I think has something to do with the philosophy that only beautiful things matter. It is not brains or hearts that count, but surface beauty. If a woman is not beautiful, if a flower is not lovely, they are worthless. Apparently no one has told Oscar that beauty is only skin deep ... and that his surface skin is not so very pretty. But, I must admit, his voice is beautiful.

Oscar doesn't talk, he sings phrases, his tongue is a conductor's baton that brings together ideas and sounds from a dozen different parts of his brain at the same time. There is something grotesque and yet appealing about this huge creature who expresses himself with extravagant gestures and poetic license. I have to admit that he is a strange bird, but the more I am around him, the more I find to admire and adore. Deep down I believe he has a heart of gold. The only way to place him in a scheme of killing prostitutes would be if they were talked to death.

"Ask your friend to meet us outside. I have some questions I didn't get the opportunity to ask him last night."

I don't need to know the reason why Jules doesn't want to be seen with Oscar in the Procope. The man is a verbose peacock anywhere in public. He draws attention like a naked woman.

At my signal Oscar joins us outside, walking through the crowd as if it is the Red Sea parting for him. He beams at Jules. "I heard a waiter refer to you as Jules Verne. How delightful to meet the man who wrote those books of my childhood about balloon trips and projectiles to the moon. Why, I thought you were dead!"

"After making your acquaintance, Monsieur, I'm certain that I have died and gone to hell."

So much for camaraderie. We start walking to a café a few blocks away.

Oscar has exchanged his green overcoat for a deep purple, almost black cape that falls to his shoe tops. Under the cape he wears a forest green velvet coat, lilac shirt, dark grey beeches, white stockings, and patent leather shoes. His hat is oversize and extravagant, a chevalier's hat, the same lilac as his shirt and with a red feather stuck in it. All in all, he looks as inconspicuous as a P. T. Barnum parade.

"Your friend who was murdered, did he ever mention having a Russian friend?" Jules voice is gruff, as if he would prefer to shake the information out of Oscar.

"Russian? No, is this mad killer Russian?"

"We're not certain." The gruffness in Jules' voice doesn't subside. "Did he ever mention a chemist? Or someone involved in science in any manner."

"No Russians, no chemists, although a Russian contact would not have been surprising, there's quite a few Russian students in Paris. Isn't Paris rather the institute of higher learning for the Russian upper classes."

It isn't a question, but it throws me for a moment.

Oscar's use of an Irish colloquial sentence structure is just his way of showing his ability to talk like the lower classes. In other words, another way for him to dazzle a listener by making them think about what he's saying. He starts a dissertation on the Russian university system and Jules interrupts.

"I'm sure your café acquaintances will find that information fascinating. As to your friend whose life was taken, describe the circumstances of the crime."

Oscar sighs, in pain from the memory. I don't believe he's faking. He is simply a dramatic person—melodramatic at that. Maybe it's his way to handle the hurt.

"Jean-Jacque was found still dressed in his female attire in a small, dark alley off of Boulevard de Clichy. His abdomen had been laid open, but there was so little evidence of bleeding in the alley. The police surmised he had been murdered elsewhere and his body was dropped in the alley afterward."

"Does he live near the alley?"

"Heavens no, Jean-Jacque was a person of breeding. The area where his body was found houses the poor and other of God's unfortunates."

Jules taps the sidewalk with his cane. "Interesting. How did his body get placed in that alley? Even on the Butte, one would not drag a body down the street. I wonder . . . why did the killer find it necessary to transport the body in some manner to that spot?"

"To discourage a police investigation," I suggest. "He's always struck in poor areas and chose victims whose death would raise less of an outcry than the deaths of respectable people. He may have met Jean-Jacque at Place Blanche or anywhere, even across town at Boulevard Saint-Michel and lured her—him."

"Lured to where? To the killer's dwelling? Does that mean the killer lives in an area near the alley?"

"The crime could have been committed in a fiacre on the way there," Oscar offers.

"The fiacre would have been bathed in blood and reported to the police. The killer could have had his own private carriage, but that would involve an accomplice since a driver would probably be needed." Jules turns to me. "I agree that the motive for leaving the body in an alley would be to discourage a thorough police investigation. But the body would have had to be transported there in some manner. We can hardly assume that the killer threw the body over his shoulder and carried it there or took a fiacre with a dead body. It's easy to conceal a dead body in a carriage driven by a coachman, but less so in a small self-driven rig. He either has a carriage—"

"Or, as you suggested, lives in the area," I interrupt. "But, if he has a carriage, we can assume he's a person of considerable means. If that's so, why would he live in a poor area?"

"Easier to hide his evil doings," Jules says.

The remark stops me dead cold. "Yes. He must live very near the alley. Transporting a dead person more than a few feet is very difficult. We have to go immediately and take a look at this location."

Jules grabs my arm. "After we finish with Artigas at the Exposition."

"We're going to the Exposition." Oscar smiles with delight.

"*We* don't all have to—"

"Since Artigas has such an evil reputation, perhaps the three of us should go together," I suggest, in the hopes of maintaining peace.

"Not Count Artigas himself, you say. I've seen the man around the Café de la Paix. Rather an unpleasant sort, no culture really, isn't he just a bag of money. How is he mixed up in all this?"

I fill Oscar in on what we learned about Toulouse's picture.

"Louis Pasteur? The scientist? So the old fossil's still with us. Found a cure for dog bite a few years ago, didn't he. Perhaps someone should be searching for a cure for man's bite."

He beams at us, no doubt in the hopes of getting a pat for his witticism. Jules looks to the heavens as if he is expecting—or hoping—for divine intervention, perhaps a strike of lightning.

"When we get to the Exposition," Jules turns and looks at me with pleading eyes, "perhaps you and Monsieur Wilde would care to look at the exhibits while I talk to Artigas."

"No, no, wouldn't hear of it," Oscar says, echoing my sentiments exactly. "I'm not going to be dallying about while you are working. I shall be right there, shoulder to shoulder, comrades in arms, and all that. Besides, I've already seen the chocolate *Venus de Milo*."

Only the French would think of advertising chocolate as a work of art. With bare breasts.

"The Tower of Babel" . . .

The undersigned citizens, being artists, painters, sculptors, architects, and others devoted to and desirous preserving the amenities of Paris, wish to protest, in the name of our national good taste, against such an erection in the very heart of our city, as the monstrous and useless Eiffel Tower, already christened . . . "The Tower of Babel" . . .

How much longer is the City of Paris to be a play-ground for these barbarous and sordid imaginations which disfigure and dishonor her? For the Eiffel Tower, which even commercially minded America rejected, is a public dishonor to our city. All our historic buildings, our monuments of rare and appealing beauty, are dwarfed and humiliated by this monstrous apotheosis of the factory chimney whose odious shadow will lie over the city . . .

—Plea to
the Exposition Director
in opposition to the Eiffel Tower,
signed by artists and writers
and published in
Le Temps, 1887

52

The Paris World Fair, L'Exposition, spread over two hundred and twenty-eight acres. "What a dazzling sight." Oscar waves his arms, as if a squire showing his domain. "There is something for just about everyone in the world. Industry and the arts on the Champs de Mars, horticulture on the Trocadéro, agriculture on the Quai d'Orsay, colonial exhibits, evil military rubbish, health and social welfare on the Esplanade des Invalides. At one end of the Champs de Mars is the largest structure at the Exposition, the Palace of Machines. On the other end you have the world's tallest structure, the Eiffel Tower. It's truly wonderful," Oscar sings in his melodramatic voice.

As we make our way down the Champs de Mars we pass structures that house attractions. Eastward along the Quay are the food products and agricultural exhibits from all over the world. Most impressive is a huge oak wine barrel capable of holding the equivalent of 200,000 bottles, elaborately carved and gilded with coats of arms of the wineries of Champagne.

Cafés along the way are crowded and overflowing.

People are eating wherever they can find an empty spot. Sprawled all over the lawns and steps of exhibit halls are picnics of cold meat, cheese, fruit, and wine.

On the Esplanade des Invalides, the most colorful and aromatic exhibits come from colonial pavilions: smells of Oriental spices, North African couscous, the beat of tom-toms, Polynesian flutes, the cry of a muezzin from a min-aret, the concussion of a copper drum at a Cambodian temple.

I have to agree with Oscar; the exposition is nothing like I've seen before. While Jules stops for a moment to enjoy the nubile young women from Java and Tahiti per-form exotic native dances with authenticity that no doubt offends prim and proper ladies, I am fascinated with Rue du Cairo, a reproduction of a Cairo street: swiveling belly dancers, including Aiousche, the top attraction, beggars demanding baksheesh, carpet sellers hawking their wares, donkeys braying stubbornly, Turkish delight sweets, hot mint tea, and bitter coffee.

"You must see Buffalo Bill's Wild West Show starring Annie Oakley at the Neuilly Hippodrome," Oscar tells us. "I was out West once, boomtowns, cowboys, Indi-ans, all that sort of thing."

"Perhaps another time," I murmur. We are definitely not going to see Bill and Annie. Thank goodness Oscar has forgotten I told him I got shooting lessons when I wrote a story about their show. The moment Annie sees me she'll scream my name and run to me.

As we approach the Palais de Machines it looms up as a grey colossal volume. Unlike the rest of the exposi-tion the enormous structure, at first sight, has a cold ambience—plain and austere. But the closer we get, the extensive detail with decorative moldings, ornamental pedestals, and arches embellished with different shades of variegated foliage becomes apparent. At the eastern entrance stand two nude sculptures representing Steam by Henri-Michel-Antoire Chapu, and Electricity by Louis-Ernest Barrias.

Jules says, "You can get a bird's-eye view of the hall by riding on an electrically operated platform high above the machinery. It carries visitors across the length of the building at a height of twenty-two feet."

There's pride in Jules' voice and I realize why. A number of the machines in this vast hall, including a "moving sidewalk," made their first appearance on the pages of his books.

"Isn't there a horseless carriage with an engine powered not by steam, but gasoline?" I ask Jules.

"Yes. It is called a Benz. There's great potential for such a machine."

"Really? I heard it's a big toy for a rich man. Why anyone would want to drive a carriage powered by a noisy, smoking, smelly engine when they can drive one drawn by a horse? Besides, these horseless carriages will do nothing but pollute our air, create noise and havoc in the streets, and probably incur unnecessary cost."

"Indeed." For a moment I believe I have left Jules speechless. "Look, Thomas Edison has all of his inventions on display. The phonograph is my favorite. I believe this is one invention you can't condemn."

A large crowd has gathered at the exhibit; some people have on earpieces to listen to recordings.

"These . . . these mechanical monsters," Oscar says, waving his walking stick at the rolls of machinery, "are slavers of man, not his liberator. They are distractions, not *provocateurs* of great ideas. Without them—"

"All this," Jules waves his walking stick at the rows of exhibits, "is the work of mere lice, parasites on this great living planet hurtling through the heavens. We believe we are so important in the cosmic scheme, but in reality we are insignificant parasites on Mother Earth, bloodsuckers that may some day be shaken off."

When Jules finishes being philosophical, Oscar stops and pulls out a piece of foolscap from his pocket and makes a note.

I edge closer to Jules. "You know he's going to repeat your words in a boulevard café by night's end."

A small satisfied smile teases the corners of his mouth. "I read that tripe in this morning's newspaper. They are the words of Henri Vallance, the philosopher. Everyone who hears our friend will know he stole the thought."

"As I was saying," Oscar expounds, "man has been enslaved by his own unbridled urge to invent machines—"

"And without them those shiny shoes you wear would be gone and you would be walking barefoot," Jules retorts. "The extravagant clothes on your back would be replaced by animal skins, and instead of taking a train and boat back to London, you would have to walk and swim and kill your food along the way." He points his walking stick to our right. "Artigas' exhibit entrance is in this direction. Perhaps you can keep in abeyance your quibbles on the evils of the Industrial Age until after we have dealt with one of its worse offenders."

We go through an exhibit hall housing French military artillery pieces and machine guns that make modern warfare so deadly.

Oscar waves a generous hand at the killing machines. "These toys of grown men in uniform are not the future of war. Someday each side will send a single chemist onto the field of battle carrying a bottle containing a compound so lethal it will wipe away whole armies."*

---

* This statement about the future of war, which has a Jules Verne futuristic flavor to it, was first made by Oscar at the lunch he had with the creator of Sherlock Holmes, Arthur Conan Doyle, and the American

Jules stops and stares at Oscar. "Where did you hear that?"

Jules' body language is so abrupt, Oscar is taken back. "Why, I suppose I deduced it from what is going on in the world." His eyebrows shoot up. "My good man, no doubt I've been influenced by your books, the ones from my youth and the ones my wife is already putting away for my own sons. Captain Nemo and his terrible killing machine, the *Nautilus*, rockets to the moon, the city-killing weapons in *The Begum's Fortune*—"

"My books were written to entertain, not terrify."

"And they certainly accomplished the purpose of entertaining. Captain Nemo is an interesting villain, certainly not an Othello or Cesare Borgia, but nonetheless a knave with many facets. He has the mind and soul of an anarchist, a staunch defender of personal liberty, and while the terrible means by which he extracts justice and vengeance are not ones most of us would condone, he is truly a revolutionary, a man who on the one hand wavers between love and hate, pity and revenge, but on the other is above such petty human weaknesses."

Jules retorts defensively, "Nemo does not attack. He defends when he is attacked."

"But there's violence in him, he's an archangel of vengeance for the deaths of his family and those of his comrades, yet," Oscar waves his hands in the air as if he's conducting a symphony of his words, "this sometimes cruel tyrant of the deep is devoting his life to battling the tyranny of nations who put great warships on seas. And

---

publisher in September 1889, two months before he attended the world fair with Nellie and Jules. In his own autobiography, Conan Doyle reported Oscar's comment as, "A chemist on each side will approach the frontier with a bottle." A. Conan Doyle, *Memories and Adventures.*—The Editors.

despite his sailors, Nemo is a man all alone. Ultimately, there is just him and the sea."

Oscar's comments give me pause to think as the two carry on their discussion. I'd never thought of Captain Nemo as an anarchist and self-appointed vigilante, but as I think of him this way—I believe Oscar is correct, and it helps me understand the undercurrent of anger and violence I've felt coming from Jules.

THE ENTRANCE TO Artigas' exhibit is in a far corner of the great hall.

Scholl was right. It is inconspicuous, hidden in plain sight, merely a wood podium with a simple brass plaque on the front bearing the baron's name and his coat of arms, which gives me an epiphany—what if the slasher has been hiding in plain sight right in front of me? This intriguing thought teases me as we approach the entrance.

A uniformed attendant stands behind a podium by an unmarked door, which I believe I can correctly assume is the door to the lion's den.

"We're here to see Artigas," Jules states.

I note that he doesn't use the count's title.

The attendant opens a guest book. "Do you have an appointment, Monsieur?"

"No. Tell him Jules Verne wishes to speak with him." He hands the man his calling card.

The man adjusts his eyeglasses to look at the card and then stares at Jules.

"The beard is gone, but the name is the same. Please tell Artigas I'm here."

"One moment, Monsieur."

While the attendant is gone, I try to read Jules' features out of the corner of my eye. I sense powerful emotions beneath the surface.

The attendant returns and escorts us in. The high-domed main room displays lethal-looking weapons, its centerpiece being an armored, horse-drawn cart that bristles with an artillery piece and two machine guns that appeare similar to the Maxim guns I've seen in the States. Count Artigas and his man, Malliot, are in a small office. I wonder if they, or at least Malliot, will recognize me.

The office is too small for all of us and Oscar politely takes his large frame over to examine weaponry while Jules and I enter. I'm leery, but most curious to meet the men who have been interested in my doings. I just hope that if they do recognize me, they won't acknowledge it.

In person, Artigas looks more like a wolf in man's clothing—very expensive clothing—than the account-ant type that Scholl's pictures portrayed. He has cold black hair, a short black beard, and an extravagant black mustache, without a stitch of grey in any of it. He either has an ample supply of bootblack or he manages to deny nature and keep the color of his youth when he is at least in his sixtieth year.

He has that broad, expansive waistline favored by men of wealth all over the world. His black frock coat, grey pants, and white spats are of the finest quality. His cravat is yellow and sports an enormous diamond stick-pin that is no doubt worth the national budget of a small country. The most distinguishing feature about him is his eyes—looking at them is like looking down cannon barrels, round and black and lethal. Artigas stands up and offers his hand to Jules.

"This is an honor, Monsieur Verne. I am a great ad-mirer of yours."

Jules hesitates a brief moment before shaking his hand. I suspect he realizes to refuse to shake will immediately terminate the interview. Both Artigas and Malliot give me a long look when Jules introduces me as Mademoiselle Brown. I'm sure they recognize me.

"To what do I owe the pleasure of your company and this lovely lady?" Artigas asks.

"Mademoiselle Brown is trying to find a man who once worked for you. Leon Nurep," Jules says in a flat tone.

Artigas' gaze is steady. "Nurep, Nurep, I'm not certain I recall the name. And why is Mademoiselle seeking this man?"

"She's a Pinkerton agent from America."

Jules' answer shocks me and I flinch in surprise, but maintain my composure. The story we'd agreed upon at Le Chat Noir was that the man had abandoned his wife and family.

"Did you hear that, Jacque, a Pinkerton detective who is a woman."

Artigas and Malliot exchange raised eyebrows and look at me. I keep my expression blank.

Jules smiles. "Come now, Artigas, you must know that women have been involved in criminal detection since the days when Vidocq used them to track down the criminal underworld. But then, Monsieur," Jules nods at Malliot, "perhaps it's you who would know something of the criminal underworld."

A dark look from Malliot confirms he does not miss the innuendo.

"But the women Vidocq used for the Sûreté were of a different sort than this young woman," Artigas answers smoothly. "Perhaps someday we will have the opportunity to find out more about her background." His comment carries as much meaning as Jules'. "In the meantime, Mademoiselle, what crimes and misdemeanors did this person commit that brings you across an ocean to find him?"

"Murder," I state flatly. "He's an anarchist who we believe was involved in a bombing."

"The Haymarket bombing?"

"Yes. How did you know that?"

Artigas shrugs. "It's the most famous anarchist bombing in your country. What is the latest information you have about Monsieur Nurep's whereabouts?"

"That's why we have come to you, Count. My information is that he worked for you."

"I now do recall a man by that name in my employ. But it was for a short time, quite awhile ago, and the work he did was of no consequence."

"Then why are you looking for him?" The question just shot out of my mouth. But it suddenly hit me—*that was why they were following me.*

Malliot says, "He didn't say he was looking for him."

"Let's stop chasing cats in the dark." Anger erupts from Jules' voice. It's obvious he's losing patience. "We want Nurep, you want him. I don't know why you're after him, but knowing where your heart is, there must be money at the bottom of it. Mademoiselle Brown is not here for money, but justice."

Malliot starts to say something but Artigas holds up a hand to stop him and addresses Jules.

"I take offense at your words and your tone. It's painful for me to receive such abuse from a man whom I admire. You may not believe this, but your fascinating stories have provided considerable inspiration for me in my business affairs."

"Monsieur, I find it grossly insulting that my writing has encouraged you to carry on a business as heinous as yours. With that sort of inspiration, I'll gladly give up the pen and bide my time growing lettuce." Jules abruptly turns and walks out of the room.

I politely smile at the men. "I concur." And I join Jules in the main room.

"He's a swine who will burn in hell for his crimes," Jules says.

Malliot comes out of the room right behind us—sullen and dangerous. The steel ball on the end of his arm looks deadly. Jules turns to him, holding his cane with both hands as if he will draw a blade from it.

Oscar is suddenly between them.

Malliot stops short, surprised by the big man.

"I say, perhaps you can help me," the Irishman says frustrated. He's holding a round steel ball, the size of a soccer ball. "I turned the knob on this thing and now it's ticking."

Malliot stares at the object. "My God, it's a marine mine. You've armed it!"

"Oh my!" Oscar instantly shoves it into the man's arm. "Please take care of it."

We quickly retreat out of the room leaving Malliot holding the ball, looking completely lost as to what to do.

Once out of the pavilion, I give Oscar an appraising look. If I'm not mistaken, he's not at all the babbling fool he appears to be.

"I appreciate your intervention." Jules genuinely pats Oscar on his shoulder.

"Intervention?" The big man shrugs. "Purely accidental, I can assure you."

Neither of us believe him.

"Let's hope they're able to disarm that sea mine," I say.

Oscar chuckles. "Not a problem, my dear girl. A man explaining the equipment told me the explosive charges have been removed from the display items."

An explosion sounds behind us and we whip around. Firework rockets explode above the pavilion. We break down and have a good laugh.

WE PART WITH Oscar at the Port D'Iéna. As we walk, Jules' features are stoic, but I know he is thinking about how nice it would be to drive a stake through Artigas' heart.

"Did you notice the count's teeth?" I say to make conversation. "Unlike the incisors of ordinary human beings, he appears to have a mouth full of rip-and-tear canines. I think I've seen tamer smiles on vicious dogs."

"You have my apology."

"For what?"

"I permitted my hatred of that man to affect our investigation."

"Perhaps if you told me why you dislike the man so much," I murmur. I suspect Jules heard, but chooses not to answer, and we just continue to walk.

Once off the bridge we stop. The sky has cleared and a full moon shines down. Lovers are walking on the river quay as romantic violin music comes from a café. I find myself wishing Jules would ask me to his hotel.

"Would you like to come back to my hotel for a drink?"

For a moment I just look at him not believing what I heard and wishing I could say yes. "Yes, but no."

Without warning he takes me in his arms, kisses me, and then abruptly turns and leaves. I come very close to running after him, but that stupid code of morality for women rears its ugly head and slaps me in the face. But I must admit, there is another reason I can't go to his hotel. I already scheduled a secret meeting with Oscar.

I only pray it's worth it.

53

I'm deep in thought about my feeling for Jules when Oscar shows up.

"Nellie, my dear, I hope you haven't been waiting long? I was unfortunately detained by an old friend I hadn't seen for quite sometime . . ."

Oscar doesn't want an answer from me, he just goes on and on as he escorts me through Le Passage and down alleys and stairs to Boulevard Rochechouart. How does he have time to breathe? He's in good humor—laughing, talking away.

"I've arranged a meeting at a café with André, a friend of my Jean-Jacque." He pauses a moment, as to give him respect, and then continues. "The café is walking distance on Bou' Clichy across from the circus. La Taverne du Bagne. I sent André a telegram this morning asking him to meet us."

"You really think he can help?"

"Of course, my dear, why else would I arrange for a meeting?"

"Okay, but why do you think he can help us?"

"Because," Oscar pauses dramatically, "he was the last person to be with Jean-Jacque before . . ."

"Oh . . ."

For a moment we walk in horrible silence.

"Oscar, I realize this is hard for you and I want you to know I really appreciate your help . . ."

"It's quite all right, my dear, anything to catch this ghastly beast."

"So, André and Jean-Jacque were . . . close?"

"Oh! Heavens no. One could not get close to Jean-Jacque anymore than one could fondle an angel. André was a friend. Whatever small affection André had for Jean-Jacque was purely ephemeral. I shouldered him from Jean-Jacque's heart."

"Hmmm . . ."

Oscar gives me a sideways glance.

"This tavern we are going to, is the English translation something like the Labor Tavern?"

"Partly. But the reference is to hard labor, the kind you do in prison."

"Why would one use a prison term to name a café?"

He chuckles. "One of the loveliest things about Paris is its imagination. While London has might and majesty, Paris has art and mystery. Here, you can travel to the far reaches of the earth and always have the Seine nearby. Tonight you will visit Devil's Island. Lisbonne, the owner, like Louise Michel, was a Communard who was sent to prison. His café recalls those days as a convict. Some of the waiters are friends from the Commune."

Entering La Taverne du Bagne, the first person we encounter is a waiter dressed as a convict.

"Pierre," Oscar whispers to me, "is an actual ex-convict."

"Another hero of the Commune?" I'm finding Communard heroes are as common as mice in Montmartre.

"No. Actually a nonpolitical felon—he caught his lover cheating and cut off his penis."

Oscar is an immediate source of attention. It makes

no difference that he's not a particularly handsome man, in the manner of which men are judged; this unique giant with bad teeth and a voice that could coach the gods from Olympus, is admired.

"Nellie, my dear." Oscar takes me by the hand and introduces me to a Japanese person just before he is swept away. "Miki, we're here to meet André. Would you mind telling my friend Nellie about poor Jean-Jacque until he gets here."

Miki has white powder on her skin, mysterious Oriental eyes, red lips, red rouge on her cheeks, and hair up in a bun with a jeweled ivory comb through it. I feel awkward. I don't know if Miki is male or female. She was talking to a man when Oscar interrupted.

"Please, don't let me interrupt," I say. As I wait for Miki to finish her conversation with her friend, all I can hear in my head is Alice's conversation with the Cheshire Cat:

> "But I don't want to go among mad people," Alice remarked. "Oh, you can't help that," replied the Cat, "we're all mad here. I'm mad. You're mad." "How do you know I'm mad?" said Alice. "You must be," said the Cat, "or you wouldn't have come here."

Her friend gives her airy cheek kisses and moves away to another group.

"He recently returned from the Pacific islands." Miki takes a puff from her cigarette. It's held by a long, ivory cigarette holder. Her voice is soft and as exotic as her looks. Her French is noticeably accented, even to me. I give up trying to figure out her sex. Whatever it is, she is a lovely representation of the East. And strangely enough, I can understand a man falling for her.

"Oscar tells me that Jean-Jacque and André were friends."

"No, my darling, they were lovers. Oscar doesn't like to admit it. I suppose Oscar also told you Jean-Jacque was one of God's fondest angels."

"Something like that."

"Don't believe it. Jean-Jacque had most people fooled. Oscar cares for a man's mind as well as his body, but when it came to Jean-Jacque, well . . . I'm afraid it was Jean-Jacque's jade stock that was the greatest temptation."

I wish I had Miki's Oriental fan to hide my face.

"It was famous, of course."

"Pardon?"

"Jean-Jacque's jade stock. Everyone talked about it. Ten inches, straight as an arrow with a knob on the end that felt like soft, smooth marble."

I take a long sip of my drink hoping it will mask my flushed face. The door bursts open behind us and a messenger boy in the blue uniform and cap of a British General Postal Office struts in singing, "Telegram for Lord Somerset! Telegram for Lord Somerset!"

I welcome the interruption. A tall man is talking to Oscar and the boy heads directly for him. The man, who is almost as tall as Oscar, is bald, but has an erect, athletic military bearing and sports a wide, thick handlebar mustache.

"Do you know who he is?" Miki asks.

"Oh yes, indeed I do. Lord Arthur Somerset is the son of a duke. For the past several months he has been very prominently mentioned in the New York papers."

"Why?"

"He fled England in September to avoid prosecution for buggery arising from the Cleveland Street scandal. The scandal erupted when a postal supervisor became suspicious of one of the messengers who delivered telegraphs in the city. Like everyone else, the British love the

speed and convenience of telegrams. A number of young
men employed in the deliveries became involved with a
house on Cleveland Street in London where they engaged
in sex acts with other men, reporting that they earned
more than a week's wages for less than an hour's work.
Lord Somerset was identified as the man who engaged
the messenger boys for what the newspapers called gamahuching."

She clapped with delight. It's obvious I don't need to
explain "gamahuching" to Miki. The twinkle in her eye
is priceless, so I continue.

"What gave the New York papers a field day was the
fact that Somerset, who is a drinking companion of the
Prince of Wales and a member of the prince's own club,
had been given advanced warning to get out of the
country when charges were to be brought."*

"My, my . . ." was all Miki could say.

Once across the room, the "messenger boy" delivers
his telegraph—he pulls down his pants, exposing the
message, "frig me" on his rear.

Oscar returns to me as laughter fills the room.

"Sorry, my dear . . . on several counts. André sent a
message. He's off to Lyons to care for a sick aunt, so we
won't be seeing him tonight. As for the crude demonstra-
tion, one good thing came out of it. I was being forced
to listen to Lord Somerset about horses. The man has
nothing to say and says it."

---

* Lord Somerset spent the rest of his life in exile in France. His lawyer
back in London went to jail for bribing witnesses to flee the country.
The inclination toward manly love ran in the family. One of Somerset's brothers was divorced by his wife on the grounds that he had
abandoned her for a man.—The Editors.

54

I awake that morning eager to meet Jules.

As I step outside, I recognize a yawning girl on her way into the sewing shop. I saw her last night strolling by cafés, subtly letting men know she's available. She must be what Sûreté Detective Lussac calls a "casual girl"—a laundress or shop girl who must resort to part-time prostitution to make ends meet. It's sad. There are too many of these girls. To my surprise, coming up the street toward me is Dr. Dubois. He politely tips his hat.

"Bonjour, Mademoiselle. Discovering you on my walk to work is a pleasant surprise. I seldom take this route. Tell me, have you found a solution to your *polar*?" He speaks in bad English, which is as difficult for me to understand as I'm sure my French is for him.

"*Polar*?"

"Ah, an American would say a mystery, a *whodunit*."

"No, I still don't know—*whodunit*. I have more questions and fewer answers than when I started. I didn't realize you spoke English."

"Yes, a little, I spent a year in England. At school."

Dubois appears a bit disheveled, his collar is a little off-kilter, and his eyes are red. He doesn't look as if he had a good night's sleep. He forces a smile for my benefit.

"So, no luck in finding *le meurtrier*, the killer?"

"No, not yet, but I do believe I'm getting close."

"Really? What evidence have you acquired?"

I regret my foolish boast. I only made it to see his reaction. "It's nothing I can talk about."

He stares past me. "Yes, I know what you mean, so many secrets, the fever . . ."

"Secrets?"

"Yes, you know, things that must be kept from the public." His answer is as forced as his smile, as if he's covering up a slip of the tongue. He's nervous, fidgety.

"How goes the fight against the fever outbreak?" I ask.

"Splendidly—if you're on the side of the malady. It's all coming to a head."

"The outbreak?"

"Yes, of course the outbreak. What do you think I mean?" He's almost rude. "My superiors will not be pleased if they discover I've spoken to you. I'll be fired." He lifts his eyebrows again. "Perhaps arrested."

"Well, I think it's been very courageous of you to help. We both owe it to the women of this city to do our best to track down this crazed killer."

"I would feel better about my not revealing to the police you've contacted me if I knew you are making progress."

"A doctor performing laboratory work is involved in the death of prostitutes. We're working closely with Doctor Pasteur concerning the matter." What a golden tongue I have! I said everything and nothing.

"Is there anything else you can tell me?"

I decide to test the waters. "He's Russian." Did I see him blink when I made my pronouncement?

"A Russian—that would make sense." He rubs the stub of his severed pinkie.

"Why?"

"Why?" He raises his hands in a particularly French gesture. I have the impression he is backpedaling, trying to cover for his reaction. "Russians are violent and crazy. Did you hear about the explosion at the Café Momus?"

"No."

"It happened late last night. The café's popular with newspapermen, usually those of a conservative bent. Someone placed a bomb on a window ledge and walked away. It blew out the front of the café, injuring several people. Strange enough, the only person seriously hurt was a leftist reporter, a man with anarchist sympathies, who was dining with a friend." He leans closer to me. "The police suspect there is a connection between the bomber and the fever."

"Why?"

"The bomber left a note claiming he set the bomb to revenge attacks on the poor."

"Is there any progress on finding a cure for the influenza?"

"None, but the best medical doctors in the city are dealing with the problem."

"If Doctor Pasteur had—"

"He has everything he needs. The hospital's director assigned me to provide the samples that are sent to Doctor Pasteur. There's nothing else he needs." He looks around. "I'm risking not just my job, but my career talking to you."

"You're right." I squeeze his arm. "I'm sorry. You have been very cooperative with me."

He pulls out his pocket watch and presses it open to check the time. "If you see my friend Oscar, would you please tell him I will meet him later at the café?"

"Certainly." I don't ask what restaurant. I assume it

to be the Rat Mort. As he turns to leave I say, "He's an anarchist, you know."

"Oscar?"

"The slasher." Once again, just a subtle reaction by him. But I decide to continue. "An anarchist. And he's made mistakes, or I wouldn't be so hot on his trail."

"What mistakes?"

"I'm not really in a position to reveal that. Let's just say he's left a trail."

"Mistakes that leave a trail . . . Yes, of course, we all make mistakes. You can do everything right and then be brought down by one little mistake." He speaks as if he is talking to himself.

"Doctor Dubois?"

"Please pardon me. I must go."

I stare at his back as he hurries away. Now what was that conversation about? If I'm not wrong, the young doctor has had a very traumatic experience. Or a terrible fright. Very strange. My suspicion of him, waylaid by Oscar's endorsement of his good character, is boiling over again.

JULES LOOKS READY to put a bomb down Oscar's throat as they await me at a café on Boulevard de Clichy. It's a chilly morning and they're seated inside. Oscar is talking. And talking and talking. Jules looks like he's being roasted over a hot fire . . . very slowly, his flesh scorching, fat dripping from his body feeding the flames.

I take my place at the table and immediately give them a summary of my conversation with Dr. Dubois. It doesn't make Oscar happy.

"You think my friend Luc is a homicidal maniac."

"I'm not saying that, I'm just saying I'm wondering about him. I don't know what to think. He acted so strangely. I have the impression he was seeking information."

Oscar strokes his chin. "There is one thing. Luc's route to the hospital is nowhere near your garret. To the contrary, he lives in exactly the opposite direction."

"You should look further into your friend's activities," Jules suggests a little too eagerly.

"So I shall."

"And you can put your detective skills to good stead in other ways. The police have not investigated properly the whole affair involving Jean-Jacque. You should go underground, perhaps even in disguise and work as a consulting detective does."

Oscar's eyes light up like the revolving torch atop the Tour Eiffel. "A consulting detective, yes, like my friend Doyle's Sherlock Holmes."

"Don't forget Poe—"

"Of course, there must be French editions of "The Murders in the Rue Morgue" in the bookstalls along the Seine. I shall have to review them for methodology. I'll look into it immediately!"

"And don't forget your disguise. Perhaps a black cape and—"

"Of course! A large black hat, one with a broad rim. A lilac shirt—"

"And knee-high boots," I interject.

Before Oscar rushes off to prepare for his disguise, I give him the message from Dubois. Jules and I share a laugh after he leaves.

"Very clever," I tell Jules. "That should keep him occupied for a day or two."

"It will take him a week just to prepare his disguise. Hopefully, after that he will run into your slasher in a dark alley and be cut into little pieces."

"Jules! What a horrid thing to say."

"Mademoiselle, if I tied you to a chair and forced you to listen to this pompous, self-proclaimed paradigm of wit and social manners—"

"I would cut my own throat."

"I will join you if I have to listen to Monsieur Wilde again today. But before we suffer that fate, we must go to the Institut. As I was leaving the hotel a messenger arrived from Doctor Pasteur stating that he had information concerning the matter we discussed."

Leaving the café, Jules makes another observation. "It's interesting that Luc Dubois appears to be under stress at the very time we seem to be making progress in the investigation. And then there is Oscar acting the fool."

"Does Oscar strike you as a fool?"

"Not at all. Perhaps a god from Mount Olympus cast down for some great sin—or to punish us for our sins."

AT THE INSTITUT we are immediately shown into Dr. Pasteur's office. His assistant, Tomas Roth, is at his side. The elderly scientist is apologetic.

"I was not aware when we spoke that the Institut did in fact have a more recent contact with this man Nurep, or whatever his name is. Two months ago he ordered soups for the preparation of cultures."

"Soups?" I'm lost.

"A sterilized medium used to grow microbes in. It may be distilled water or rainwater, animal blood, any number of broths, such as chicken broth, or even solids."

"Did Peru . . . Doctor Nurep say what he was working on?"

"There were no discussions. The soups were ordered by post and shipped to a train depot."

"Is that the total contact with the man?" Jules asks. "A written communication?"

"The letter simply stated the type and number of soups and the delivery address. We no longer have it, but my clerk showed it to me to obtain approval for the shipment. I'm afraid I'd forgotten about it."

"How was payment arranged?" I ask.

"Sufficient francs were enclosed in the communication."

"Can the type of soups ordered tell you anything about the nature of his work?" I am hoping we can get some insight in Perun.

"Nothing, except that it involves microbes. He ordered a number of different soups and could be experimenting with almost any type of bacterium."

"So there is nothing about the request that gives us any clue about Nurep's activities?"

"It tells you that several months ago he lacked basic laboratory equipment to prepare his own mediums. Because experimenters usually prepare their own mediums, we found his request unusual. Had there not been a prior relationship with the Institut, we would not have filled the request." Pasteur smiles a little shyly. "I am a detective only in regard to the crimes of microbes, but from the nature of the request, I would deduce that Nurep was only at the locale where we sent the soups for a short time and had not yet set up a proper lab."

"Where were the materials shipped to?" Jules questions.

"A train depot in the Normandie region. Doctor Roth will provide you the information."

"What's the status on the Black Fever research?" I ask Dr. Pasteur.

"We are in the same situation as before."

"You mean the research is still being hampered by controversy with the medical doctors."

Dr. Pasteur says nothing, but his features tell me he doesn't disagree.

I decide to tell him about Dubois' visit. "I had a discussion this morning with Doctor Dubois, the man who sends you the fever samples."

"Yes, the young doctor at Pigalle Hospital, I believe."

"Then you don't know him?"

"No, his samples arrive by messenger." Pasteur turns to Roth. "Has he ever been at the Institut?"

Roth shakes his head. "No. The samples come by messenger."

"We only hope that he is competent in his task of taking samples." Pasteur adjusts his glasses and peers narrowly at me. "I sense a question in your mind about this Doctor Dubois."

"Frankly, I found our discussion unsettling. I have the impression that he's in some sort of difficulty and was seeking information from me."

"Information?" Pasteur appears intrigued.

"Yes. I think about the murders we're investigating."

"But what can this young doctor have to do with the crimes?"

"We don't know," Jules interjects, "but we intend to find out. Other than the fact he's been deputized to provide you with samples, do you know anything else about Doctor Dubois?"

"Nothing. I assume he's one of Brouardel's young trainees." Pasteur shakes his head. "Microbes are so much easier to understand than humans. They either benefit or harm you. But no microbe, not even the Black Plague, tries to harm you, not even ones that kill."

"A microbe that kills doesn't intend to?" I ask.

"If they kill you, they are destroying their host. They kill only inadvertently." Once again he shakes his head. "But humans . . . they are so much more premeditated."

55

"S ince the soups had been shipped to Normandy, I must travel there immediately," Jules announces as we walk away from the Institut.

I try to suppress that rush of anger that surges in me when I am being left out—especially when I realize the reason is because I am a woman. "I'm going with you." As soon as I spoke, Jules does exactly what I expect. He objects.

"It's no job for a lady."

I stop, take a hold of his arm so he also has to stop, and look him square in the eyes. "Neither is chasing a mad killer halfway around the world."

"You will just be in the way."

"Funny, Monsieur Verne, I was just thinking the same about you."

"I know you have accomplished a great deal for a woman, but you don't understand that there is an excellent probability of real danger."

"And being chased by the slasher in a graveyard wasn't? Or my coming within a hairsbreadth of being killed by him in the dead of night on Blackwell's Island?"

"Mademoiselle—"

"I am going with or without your consent. And you can't stop me."

He looks at me like a father would glare at a stubborn daughter. "The station is two hours by train. An overnight stay will be necessary. Since it is impossible for a woman to travel more than an hour from home without sufficient luggage to equip an entire division of the French army—"

"I could travel around the world with a single valise."

"You may recall, I wrote a book about a trip around the world. The quickest it can be done is in eighty days. And several large trunks would be necessary to maintain even the most minimal comportment of respectability for a woman."

I tap his chest with my finger. "I am going with you whether you like it or not."

"Fine. But keep in mind, Mademoiselle, this is a sparsely populated area. I doubt if there is more than an inn or two. If there is only one room available . . ." He shrugs and fails to suppress a smirk.

If he thinks this will stop me, he doesn't realize he is dealing with a modern woman—sexual innuendos will not frighten me off.

"If there is only one room, you can sleep in the stable. It was once good enough for our Lord and most certainly must be good enough for a mere writer."

His smirk turns into a frown.

Finally we agree to meet at Gare Saint-Lazare at one o'clock this afternoon.

56

Dubois

After work Luc Dubois went to the barge. Perun is not pleased to see him.

"You were told not to come here except late at night."

"I'm sorry, but I have important information. I spoke with the American woman. She is getting very close to identifying you."

Perun shrugs. "So?"

Dubois stares at the anarchist leader. "But—if she does . . . what would happen to our rebellion?"

Perun suddenly steps closer and Dubois backs up, knocking against the table, causing a copper vial of liquid to spill. "Sorry." Dubois holds the vial against the edge of the table. Using the side of his hand as a scraper, he pushes liquid from the metal table top into the vial. "I'm sorry. What is it?"

"Black plague."

"My God!" Dubois drops the vial and steps back, violently shaking his wet hand.

"It's water for the cat, you fool. Pick it up and refill it."

He avoids Perun's glare as he goes to the sink. He thought the man wanted to know when that woman was getting close to discovering him.

"I told you to stay away from the woman."

"I—I kn—know, I know, I'm sorry."

"Why did you disobey me?"

"I didn't mean to, I'm . . . I'm confused."

"What are you confused about?"

As he stands at the sink with his back to Perun, Dubois' right knee shakes. "I don't know, just confused. We're getting so close . . ."

"I see. We're finally getting ready to deliver a blow that will be heard around the world . . . and you're confused? Could it be that you're apprehensive about our goal?"

Dubois forces himself to turn and face him. "No, of course not." His voice sounds hollow and false even to his own ears.

"Are you our comrade? A man of action who is willing to demonstrate his loyalty by deeds? To kill for the cause . . . to die yourself if need be?"

"Of course I am!"

"You failed me once before . . ."

"He—he was a friend."

"He was a bourgeois, an enemy of the people."

"Yes, yes you're right, he had to die. I'll make it up to you, I promise." Dubois steps closer. "I just want to share things with you. You know how I feel about you." He reaches out to touch Perun and jerks his hand back at the look on the man's face.

Perun whispers, "The problem is not with how you feel. It's what others would think if you told them."

"I would never tell them about us."

Perun raises his eyebrows. "*Us?* You have never really understood. There is only *one of us* . . . and I am the one." He steps into the galley where Vlad, a fellow Russian who serves as his overseer with other workers, is drinking coffee and smoking. He speaks to Vlad before the two men enter the laboratory.

Perun jerks his head at Dubois. "Suit him up."

Dubois gapes. "What? I don't know anything about that."

"That" is work in the walk-in incubators were the colonies of microbes are grown and harvested.

"You said you wanted to help."

"I meant with experiments, using the microscope—"

"You don't want to work alongside your comrades? Physical labor is too good for him," Perun tells Vlad.

"No—no—that's not it. I just wouldn't know what to do."

"You know how to use a broom and a dust pan, don't you? A wake from a big boat rocked us earlier and colony trays flew out because the cupboard wasn't latched properly. It's just dust that needs to be swept up and put back in the trays."

Dubois knows that the "dust" is heavily infected with microbes.

"Well, comrade, are you too bourgeoisie to sweep a floor?"

Dubois clears his throat. The thought of going into the incubator is terrifying. "No, of course not."

"Suit him up," Perun says again.

Dubois follows Vlad through the galley and down a back corridor where the diving suits are stored. He knows the diving suits are not perfect because they've lost workers to the invisible enemies.

"They're so tiny, they get in sometimes . . . don't they?" he asks Vlad.

"You know what the leader always tells us, don't you? They're just sleeping. When they wake up inside you, they're hungry. And we are their meat." He howls with laughter as he unhooks a hanging suit.

Dubois' throat is dry, his heart pounding. He wants to

run and hide, but he knows he would not make it to the quay alive. His hands go into the sleeves of the suit. His pinkie throbs and he can't massage it. "What kind of bacteria is in the incubator?" he asks.

Vlad shrugs and ignores the question. The spore colonies are numbered—and only Perun knows which species of bacteria correspond to a number. The one thing for certain is that they are all deadly.

The large, round brass helmet is the last to go on. It's heavy and claustrophobic. Vlad leaves the porthole open in front of the helmet so Dubois can breathe while the helmet is being sealed to the body suit.

"We usually pump air into the suit through a hose, but the opening where the hose is attached in the room is contaminated."

"How will I breathe?" Dubois is sweating. The metal helmet feels like a big rock on his head.

"With the bladder."

The "bladder" appears to Dubois to be a bulging leather bag. "What is that?"

"A gold beater's bag—a cow's intestine." Vlad laughs again. "It's filled with oxygen. Aeronauts use them when they go so high there isn't enough air to breathe. The oxygen bag will be connected to your helmet with the hose. You carry the bag in with you and can set it down to work. The hose is long enough to reach wherever you go in the room." He showed him how to adjust the circulation.

After he's suited up, Vlad attaches a chain around his waist.

"What's that for?"

"The end gets attached through a hole in the door we keep sealed. Sometimes a worker can't make it back. We use the chain to pull him out."

Dubois starts to say something and Vlad cuts him off

by shutting the helmet porthole. He guides Dubois to a door that opens into a small alcove. Inside the alcove is another airtight door leading to the incubator. Once Dubois is in the alcove, Vlad shuts the outer door and Dubois enters the incubator.

Trays are scattered on the floor. The dust harboring billions of invisible deadly microbes is so fine it goes airborne with every step he takes in the heavy suit. He stands in the middle of the small room and stares around helpless, not really knowing what to do. He realizes Vlad had not given him either a broom or a dust pan. He's breathing heavy and his courage snaps. He goes back to the airtight door. It is locked. He jerks the handle and bangs on the door.

Dripping with sweat, he feels entombed in the suit and breathing comes hard. He turns and sees Perun and Vlad. They are in the laboratory, watching from the safe side of the glass wall. Perun stares at him stonily. Vlad is laughing.

He can't breathe! He adjusts the oxygen regulator but it gives no relief. He stares at the air bag. It's going flat. A hole had been sliced in it, allowing his life's air to leak out. He staggers toward the window and jerks to a stop. *The chain.* It won't let him go any farther. He tries to get it off but it's locked on. And Vlad has the key.

He understands.

The chain was put on him so he couldn't break out through the glass window to the laboratory. He screams and waves at Perun. "I know!" he screams.

Perun can't hear him. But he can see Dubois' anguished, twisted features through the helmet porthole.

Vlad says, "He's trying to tell us he can't breathe."

"He can breathe. All he has to do is take off the helmet, take it off." Perun taps his head. He speaks the words slowly, mouthing them so Dubois can understand.

Dubois' thoughts are convulsing and he struggles to understand what Perun means. Tapping his head was the real clue. Take it off? If he takes off the helmet to breathe, he will inhale bacteria.

What did Vlad say about the microbes when they get inside you . . . they wake up hungry.

57

Nellie & Jules

I am waiting on the platform when Jules arrives with a porter pushing a cart loaded with two very large bags.

"Ready for an adventure into the French countryside?" Jules asks with such delight, it makes me wonder what he's up to.

"I usually find my investigations are trips through Dante's Inferno at the time I experience them. They only become 'adventures' when I am warm and safe and describing them to friends . . . *afterward*."

"You are a very interesting woman, Nellie. Someday I will use you as a character in a book."

I beam. Sometimes Jules says things that warm the cockles of my heart.

"We had better board." He offers me his arm. "Where's your luggage?"

I hold up my valise. "This is it." I enjoy watching him look at his own heap of bags and back at my single valise. "Don't you recall, Monsieur Verne, that Phileas Fogg launched his trip around the world with only a carpetbag containing two shirts, three pairs of stockings, and a lot of money?"

"Do you know what I like about you, Nellie?"

I beam even more. "What?"

"Nothing. Nothing at all."

THE RAILWAY CARRIAGE is uncomfortably warm and the steady rhythm of its wheels lures me into a gentle sleep. When I awake, Jules is still sitting in the exact same position as when we departed, smoking his pipe and reading.

Not far from the city of Paris, the French countryside unfolds in a series of rolling hills. Thatched roof-huts and oxen pulling plows give the scene a European Currier & Ives feel. I was raised in Pennsylvania countryside not too unsimilar to these scenes. Even though the rustic area is picturesque and charmingly cozy, behind the quaint exterior is a great deal of hard work, sometimes from daybreak to nightfall in the foulest weather. And poverty. Few small farmers have more than two coins to rub together. The clothes on their backs are usually handmade and the food on their dinner tables grown on the farm. It is a hard life, sometimes a cruel one. Poor farmers are not often better off than slavish factory workers.

As I STEP off the train, a cool, soft breeze brushes my cheek. The fresh air is a welcomed relief from the stuffy train car. Other than an office for selling tickets, the railroad station consists of nothing but a narrow wood platform open to the elements.

Jules speaks to the ticket seller. After a few minutes he returns.

"We need to hurry. I arranged passage with that coach." He points across the road. "It's the only one serving the station. The village is about an hour from here and the driver expects rain. We have to get there before the road becomes unpassable."

Listening to Jules and the driver converse, I realize what Jules meant when he said many people in the country do not speak French good enough to testify in court without an interpreter. I'm able to follow only the general drift of the driver's remarks.

In the privacy of the carriage, I ask Jules, "What made you pick this village we're going to?"

"Our driver has transported a man that fits Perun's description back and forth from the village a number of times. He hasn't seen him since he took him to the train station several months ago, soon after carrying to the village a package from Institut Pasteur. He's carried other deliveries to Perun, but remembers this one package in particular because of Pasteur's name on it."

"What does he say the man looks like?"

"His description is as vague as yours—perhaps in his thirties or forties, with a heavy beard and long hair. No red scarf, but wearing the scarf of a revolutionary outside of Paris would probably attract more attention than the man wants. Someone at the village has to know our man."

"If they're willing to talk."

"With a few francs most people will talk."

Dark clouds gather as daylight is slipping away. The road is a series of ruts and the going is much slower. Tall, unkempt hedges used as fencing are on both sides of the road.

"There's one more thing," Jules says. I can tell by the lift in his voice and the twinkle in his eyes whatever he has to say amuses him. "The village we are going to is very small and poor. There is only one inn, one room for rent."

"Really . . . you telegraphed the inn?"

"The driver told me. *One room*. And it's available because he has not taken anyone out to the village since Perun left."

"There's only *one* room in the whole village?"

"Yes . . . one small inn, one small room." He purses his lips and contrives a studious expression. "There's one other thing."

"Yes . . ."

"We shall have to register as husband and wife. Otherwise they will not rent us the room."

Poor Jules, he is expecting—no, I believe eagerly waiting for some sort of womanly shock from me. Instead, I bat my eyes demurely. "That will be fine, dear." I let that sink in and then expose my cruel streak. "But, you will get awfully wet if they don't have a stable."

POVERTY IS PERVASIVE in the countryside we cross. People are smaller than in the city, as if their growth has been stunted. I say as much to Jules.

"Most French farmers are as prosperous as their British or American counterparts. But you're right, this is a poor area and the people here must scrape for bare subsistence. They probably enjoy meat only on holy feast days."

Outside a mud hut, I see a girl, probably no more than fourteen or fifteen, pretty as young girls are, but already looking haggard. She probably has not had a bath in her life nor owns a change of clothes.

"She probably sleeps on a bed of leaves," Jules says, following my gaze, "and will be ancient by the age of twenty-five—if she survives ten pregnancies between now and then."

"These people are still in the medieval age. I can see why the revolutionaries want to have a new social order."

"There are regions in America where people are as poor as these. Do you advocate revolution in America, too?"

IT'S DRIZZLING BY the time we approach a narrow, wooden bridge leading into the village. In the dusk it appears barely wide enough to hold our carriage. I hold my breath as we cross.

The village is a cluster of mud and straw houses with thatched roofs. Candlelight flickers in some windows, but most are dark. Cows and goats stand wet and motionless in the pastures, while a scarecrow hops around, ignoring the drizzle as he pokes at things on the ground. A few horses raise their heads to see what is coming. Scattered about are enormously large oak trees.

Planted at the end of the dirt road, like an afterthought, is an inn. It's small, lacking in any grace, and as uninviting as its environs. Music filters out from the tavern as the door opens and a man staggers out. He takes the steps with drunken grace and sloshes in a mud puddle as he walks away. Peering from the windows are faces. The windows are dirty. So are the faces. About a dozen plain, drab cement headstones are stuck in the ground off the road to the right.

"Charming," is all I can muster as I step down from the carriage and into the mud.

Off on a hill to the left, barely visible through the mist, are the ruins of what appears to be a medieval tower, built by some knight to defend this miserable little realm. The crumbling stone edifice is a gloomy sentinel looking down on the village.

I inch closer to Jules. "We should have gone back with the carriage and returned in the morning. This place looks like it fell out of the pages of Mary Shelley's *Frankenstein*."

"He'll be back to get us at noon tomorrow."

"That might be too late."

"It'll give us a chance to investigate the matter thoroughly."

"That's what I'm afraid of."

It starts raining and I awkwardly step over Jules' bags that were deposited on the porch and enter. The smells of musty wine, moldy food, and dirt hit me. Seven or eight men are inside, a couple at the short bar and others around the two tables. The men are dull-faced, numb appearing, as if they have lost life's battles and are now prisoners without hope. I regret to say that some of them appear rather dense, if not downright stupid. I suppose Mr. Darwin would say centuries of intermarriage is responsible for developing less than desirable specimens. Perhaps their brains have suffered the same malady from inbreeding as did the legs of Toulouse.

No one offers to help bring the bags in, or acknowledges we have entered—except to silently stare.

The innkeeper comes out from behind the bar, wiping his hands on his apron. He shouldn't have bothered. The apron is fouler than his hands. He has a fat head, almost no neck, and eyes and lips that are lost in the heavy wrinkles of his face. His arms are short, like overstuffed sausages, and his stomach is as wide as it is long. A replica, about eighteen, I take to be his son, stands nearby pouring a mug of wine.

Jules enters and begins negotiations for the room. I have seen cows sold with less discussion. I meet the stare of three men at a nearby table. They're lifeless. I smile politely. The lips of one of them quiver, but are unable to form a smile. I feel sorry for these people in this village without cheer.

Finally, we follow the innkeeper up a gloomy flight of stairs to a door at the top. He pushes it open and heads back down, brushing by, squeezing me between him and the wall. I gag from the smell of garlic and sour wine. He murmurs something that I take to be an apology. Poor Jules, he must follow him to retrieve the luggage . . . if it is still there.

"No dinner will be necessary," Jules says to the man as they are going down the stairs. "We had a late lunch."

That's a big lie. My stomach is well aware that we had an early lunch. However, the thought of what might pass as food in this place, well . . . I'd rather starve.

Our room is small, with a single tiny window. I would open it to get the dank, musty smell out, but rain savagely beats upon it. A yellowish, brown stuffed chair, frayed and stained, sits by the window. I cringe at the thought of sitting in it. A small round table is next to it. A cockroach—creatures I hate—walks across it. I decide to continue holding my valise as I examine the bed. The mattress is frumpy, stuffed with rags and hay. What color the bedding might have once been is a mystery. I choose not to even think when it was last washed. I know it's ridiculous, but I sense bedbugs looking up at me, licking their lips—tiny vampires starving for fresh blood—*my blood*.

I will not sleep on that bed or use their dirty lice-infested gray blankets. Nor will I sit on that chair. I'll stand up all night if I have to. I fight down a heat of anger starting to boil in me.

It was poor planning on Jules part to bring us into this disgusting place so late we have to stay the night. He should have known how primitive it might be. But I must keep my temper in control. I close my eyes, take a deep breath and start coughing to death. I must have inhaled a billion little dust bugs! No need for dinner, I think I just had mine.

Reluctantly, I set my valise on the floor and open the

dirty window. Fresh air should change my mood—
besides this room needs a wash.

From the window I see the innkeeper's son hurrying
toward a barn. He comes out riding a skinny, swayback
old nag that looks like a candidate for a glue factory.
The boy and horse head off in the direction of the rail
station. They're stopped by an old woman. I can't make
out the words, but from the body language the old
woman appears to be pleading with him. He shakes his
head no and urges the horse to pass her. When she turns
toward me, I'm positive she's crying. The door bangs
open and I jump back startled.

"Sorry. I didn't mean to frighten you." Jules is huffing
from carrying both pieces of luggage up the stairs.

"I'm going downstairs and insist upon clean blankets."

Jules has the bad grace to laugh. My jaw sets and I
clinch my fists.

"Do you really think that creature downstairs would
understand the meaning of fresh linen? Or have such a
thing?"

He's right. I'm deflated and with no place to sit down.

"I, on the other hand, Mademoiselle, am a seasoned
traveler." Jules opens one of his suitcases. Inside are clean,
fresh, soft white blankets bearing the embroidered name
of his hotel and two beautiful pillows.

"*Jules!* You're a genius!" I clap my hands with delight.
"I don't suppose you have dinner in the other bag?"

"A loaf of bread, a jug of wine, a little cheese, some
sausage, and thou."

"And I see you have fresh towels and a bar of soap."
I've never been so happy. I curtsy. "Monsieur, you are
truly a man for all seasons. I am forever in your debt."

He comes so close I can feel his male aura. "Yes, you
are . . ." He gently straightens the collar on my dress.

I look into his eyes and see a man that I know I want to love.

His arms go round me and his lips meet mine. I find myself wanting more. I wrap my arms around his neck, pulling him closer, deeper into me. I've lost all thought and senses. All I know and feel is this kiss—this incredible kiss that I never want to end. I feel his hands on my cheeks and he slowly pulls us apart. Our breath mingles with each other's.

"Jules . . ."

"Hush . . ." He gently caresses my cheek and then kisses my lips again. As his lips caress my neck, my breathing becomes labored, my body ignites. Oh, I do want him. His hands separate my clothing from my breasts and I find myself shuddering from delight as his tongue wraps around my nipple. I want more and find myself bending down and kissing the top of his head as he sucks my nipples.

My knees go weak and he gently holds me and brings me down to the floor. I don't know when or how he had done it, but one of the soft white blankets is laid out on the floor—ready for me. That's when I guess one could say, "my senses came to," and a phrase my mother repeated many times shrieks in my brain as if to snap me to attention. "Remember, Pink, making love is making babies." But, much to my surprise, I find myself pushing aside all those years of indoctrinated rules. *I want Jules to make love to me.*

Jules brushes a piece of hair away from my face. "Nellie . . ."

For what seems like forever we lock into each other's eyes—he, searching for an answer from me, while I battle with desire and morals, and the consequences it will bring.

"I don't think you're ready."

Tears start pouring down my cheeks. He was right. "Love makes babies," echoed in my head. I want to . . . but I can't.

"Nellie . . . it's okay."

Jules gently puts a pillow under my head and takes the other blanket and covers me and then starts to get up, but I grab his hand, "Please, lie here with me . . ."

He gets the other pillow and joins me under the blanket.

"Hold me."

His strong arms embrace me and I nuzzle my cheek into his chest and wrap my arms around him. I can feel his chest rise and fall and hear the beating of his heart. His heart is beating rapidly against mine—what could be more beautiful. We hold each other tight and I feel as if we are melting into one. That's when I kiss him and look deep into his eyes—*consequences be damned*.

58

I awake in the morning to find Jules gone and a note laying on his pillow, "*I've gone for a walk to mingle (if that's possible) with the town folk.—Jules.*" I smile and snuggle deeper into the blanket. I'm grateful to Jules for not being here when I awoke. This is all so new to me—I need time alone to think, digest what happened.

I gave myself to him last night.

It encompasses so much—I am now a woman. I am no longer a young girl or a virgin. I made love to a man and I'm not married. Oh my . . . I sit straight up in our floor bed. I really hate it when reality strikes me in the face. I could be pregnant. And my dear mother . . . what will she think?! But what is surprising me, in all honesty, is that I'm not ashamed.

"*I'm not ashamed,*" blurts out of my mouth and I start laughing. "I'm not ashamed."

It's a wonderful relief, nothing like I thought I would experience. I had all these ideas on when it was going to happen and how I would feel. And I must say this scenario never entered my thoughts—especially with a married man. Why don't I feel guilty and embarrassed and all those horrible things the church says I should feel if I made love out of wedlock? Because my heart tells me otherwise.

My father was right. He told me always to listen to your heart. You can never go wrong. I take the pocket watch my father gave me and hold it tight. Even though I listened to my heart and feel okay about this, I have a funny feeling when I see Jules . . . just the thought of seeing him sends a thousand butterflies in my stomach. What I need to do is stop thinking, get up, get dressed, and pay the piper. And pray to God, I don't act like a fool.

OUTSIDE, I FIND the sun desperately trying to brighten up this dreary little village, but too many clouds block its way. I had hoped with the light of day the village would transform into a quaint, charming place. It doesn't. The place is as bleak as it was on a rainy night.

As I walk along the dirt path that leads through the village I spot Jules ahead talking to a man plowing a field and my heart takes off. I slow down my pace—way down. What do I say? How do I act? I didn't think through how I was going to act when I saw him. I'll just be myself. But my mind starts to act like I'm one of those girls that become silly because a man made love to her. I don't want to be like that. I'm an intelligent, modern woman—no guilt, no consequence, no commitment. I lift my chin and plow through any of inhibitions and doubts I have toward Jules.

He's muttering to himself about something "strange," and starts when he suddenly realizes I'm there.

"I'm sorry. I didn't mean to startle you. So, what's strange?" I ask.

"These people won't talk about their visitor. They're not just tight-lipped, but get angry when I persist on asking questions. Even when I tell them I'm willing to pay for information. I offered the innkeeper as much money as he probably makes in a month and all I got in return was a blank stare. He says our room will not be available tonight. Not that we planned on staying, but he didn't know that."

"Maybe he's expecting someone?"

"No. My guess is that he doesn't want us around, not at any price. Nor do the other townspeople. There's only one thing that would keep a poor man from accepting money."

"Sex?" So much for focusing on today's issues.

"Fear. I see it in their eyes. They falter at the very mention of their strange guest. One farmer did mention that an 'agricultural inspector' had been at the village."

"Come again?"

"I suspect that was Perun's cover story, that he was doing agricultural experiments for the government. The farmer said they have a 'cursed field' that you can't graze animals on. Something, perhaps some poisonous plant, kills them, but it's been a village problem for decades."

As our steps carry us out of the village, the old woman I saw last night talking to the innkeeper's son comes toward us. Her head is down and she's talking to herself—more like arguing, agitated, waving her hands widely about. She's almost upon us before she realizes we are in her path. She looks up with a start.

"Madame," I say, "do you know where we can find the inspector?" It's a shot in the dark, but it hits bull's-eye.

She starts babbling. "My daughter, she's missing, gone, she'd never leave me. She went with him."

"With who?"

"The inspector. Up there." She turns and points up at the ruins of the tower.

"*Mannette!*"

The shout comes from behind us. The innkeeper and

two of the village men have come up from behind us. One is holding a sledgehammer. None of them look pleasant.

"Come, Madame Courtoise," the innkeeper says in a curt tone, "your daughter is waiting for you."

"Oh dear God, you've found her!" The poor crazy old thing rushes by us.

I put my hand out to stop her and Jules grabs it. "They're lying," I whisper.

"Forget it. Let's take a look at the tower." He pulls me away.

"They're lying to that woman. Something terrible has happened to her daughter. Why are they lying to her?"

Jules keeps a firm grip on my arm as he starts to lead me up the hill. "Something terrible has happened here and there are a hundred frightened people who don't want their secrets exposed. When we get back to Paris we will report the matter to the authorities. But until then, let's make sure we get back in one piece."

He has a point. I go along like a lamb—a scared one. We won't be able to get away from the village until the coach returns.

Hundreds of years ago the tower was a protective battlement for a medieval knight who ruled the land. It wouldn't have seen the wars of nations, it is too small for that, but of the petty fighting between knights and barons and the murderous raids of maundering bands. I just hope it hasn't been stained by the blood of the old woman's daughter at the hands of Perun.

Once atop the hill, the ruin is larger than it appears below. The tower itself has crumbled to half its original size, but there are also lower walls still standing, almost completely covered by ivy and brush.

"I think there's a room down there." Jules is on his hands and knees looking down a gaping hole.

"Over here, there's a stairway," I say.

Stone steps erupted by roots and vines lead down. In the not too distant past vegetation had been cleared.

Once below we enter a small, damp room—no bigger than the bedroom at the inn, but much darker. Cobwebs hang from the ceiling. Rats scramble into holes at our approach. It's as quiet as a crypt. Without light, we cannot see into the dark corners.

"He hung lanterns," Jules says, pointing out soot stains. "And he had this area for a workbench." The workbench, a long and fairly wide stone ledge, is bare. "These stains were no doubt caused by chemicals."

More of the room comes into focus as our eyes adjust to the dark. Jules carefully examines every detail. It won't surprise me if he pulls out a magnifying glass and crawls in the dirt looking for clues like a consulting detective. I admit I am more of an idea person than one occupied with details. I look to the overall situation for inspiration, not soot and cobwebs.

"Odd," Jules says.

"What?"

"This dirt." He indicates the dirt near the workbench that is darker than the dirt on the rest of the floor. "It doesn't belong here. There's even some grass mixed in. He must have dug it somewhere in the fields and brought it here to examine. And see this buildup on the floor against the workbench. It appears he worked with the dirt, even shifted some of it with a screen because it's a fine powder. Why would Perun be interested in dirt from the fields? Is it possible that the man who stayed here was actually an agriculture inspector and not Perun?"

"No." I shiver. "The man who worked in this place is the slasher. He killed that poor woman's daughter."

"Female intuition?"

"Not at all. As I told you, I once had the misfortune to see for myself what the man does to women in a laboratory. Look here." I push a mound of ashes with my shoe. "Something was burned here."

Jules squats and examines the fire debris. "He burned a piece of crate." He holds up a piece that didn't completely burn.

"It's got Chinese writing on it," I say. "I saw a crate with Chinese writing on it in Doctor Dubois' hospital lab. It wouldn't be the same crate, but one Dubois sent months ago."

"It didn't necessarily come from Dubois."

"No, of course not, people involved in this investigation probably get crates from China everyday."

He clears his throat, probably unable to come up with a proper retort. "Let's take a look at that cursed field the farmer told me about." He wraps the charred piece of wood in a handkerchief and puts it in his inside pocket.

From the top of the hill, I see something that causes me to stop and catch my breath.

"What's the matter?"

"Over there . . . in that field . . . there's an open grave."

He follows my gaze. "That's the one they called cursed. Let's take a look."

Sure, why not. I'm used to open graves. I almost blurt out that bit of frightened sarcasm, but hold my tongue.

The villagers have fenced off the cursed field with a thorny hedge and we enter through a crude wooden gate. Jules walks smartly. I, on the other hand, hang back as we approach the grave. Dirt has been piled up along one side. Jules stops at the edge and stares down.

"It's a grave all right." He looks back at me. "But not what you think. Come here."

I do a double take when I look in. "A cow?"

"Yes, a long dead one, mostly just hide and bone left, which means it's been dead a lot longer than a few months ago. It may have been dug up months ago, but it was buried years ago."

"Why would someone dig up a dead cow?"

"I don't know." He squats down. "Give me your handkerchief."

I do so. "What are you doing?"

"Whoever dug up the cow took samples of the hide. You can tell pieces have been cut off. And we also know he took dirt samples." He looks up at me. "I'm afraid I'll need your coin purse to put some dirt in."

"You can have it, but only if you promise not to try and convince me that the man who dug up this cow was an agricultural inspector. I don't know why Perun would do such a thing, but the hairs on the back of my neck are screaming that we have discovered a major clue."

"When your short hairs reveal why a dead cow is a clue to a man who slashes women, please let me know."

AN UNPLEASANT SURPRISE is awaiting us when reach the bottom of the hill. The innkeeper, his son, and his two friends have been joined by three other village men. One looks like a blacksmith—stout with thick, bulging arms. Their dark expressions suggest more of a lynch mob than a reception committee.

"Stay behind me," Jules voice is stern.

"The cavalry has come."

Jules looks at me puzzled.

I nod my head toward the bridge. Coming into the village is the carriage to take us back to the train station.

RETRACING OUR RIDE across the countryside, I find myself once again unable to keep from asking a question that had been puzzling me since I met Jules.

"Jules . . . is Count Artigas the person you came to Paris to kill?"

He stiffens beside me and his cane begins a cadence on the carriage floor that tells me my question has hit a sore spot. "That issue is none of your business. I regret ever having made the remark. Had I known your inability to let a matter drop . . ."

My mother always said you get more from a person with honey than vinegar, so I squeeze his arm and speak softly. "We're conducting an investigation. Don't you think it's unfair to withhold information from me?"

I realize it's the wrong approach the moment I open my mouth. The last time I made the same point he compared my degree of candor to peeling an onion. I brace myself for an explosion.

"You're right," he says.

"I am?"

"You deserve an answer. And you already know part of it—Artigas is the man I swore to kill. I knew the man only by reputation, but I had seen his handiwork a year ago when I took my sailing yacht on a Mèditerranean cruise. We sailed along the coast of North Africa, dropping anchor in Tangiers and Algiers before setting a course for Tunis. We hit a blow off the coast and put into the cove of a small market town not realizing that the town had just hours before been the scene of a power struggle between rival tribal leaders. Coming ashore in our tender, we found the terrible consequence of the tribal dispute. Men, women, and children, dead in the streets."

"How ghastly."

"Worse than you can imagine because these people did not die from bullets. Some were killed from the shrapnel but most had suffered painfully from poisonous gas the shells contained."

"Poisonous gas in an artillery shell?"

"Upon impact, the shells put out a deadly gas of carbolic acid that fried a person's lungs. The people killed by the explosions were the lucky ones. The unlucky had breathed in the gas and they would die slowly, some over the years, as their lungs gave them less and less air."

"Artigas was the monster who sold them the shells?"

"His company manufactured a weapon of war that not only killed combatants, but was certain to spread death over a large area and kill the innocent."

"That's horrible. What maniac thought up such a terrible weapon?"

"They took it from one of my books. *And used the idea to kill people.*"

59

We spoke little on the return trip and arrive back at Gare Saint-Lazare in the late afternoon. Both of us are tired. My feelings about Jules weigh heavily on my mind and I suspect that he is not completely indisposed to thinking about me. I dare not probe anymore about the incident in North Africa. It's his personal demon.

One thing I'm certain about: neither one of us wants to admit or acknowledge that things have changed between us. For now it is easier to set aside our feelings and concentrate on what brought us together—catching Perun. But as we stand at the train station waiting for a fiacre, there is an awkward silence between us.

"Nellie . . ." Jules, for once, breaks the silence. He looks stressed. "I owe you an apology. I know I haven't addressed last night—"

"Right now we have to stop this devil before he strikes again."

I must have said the correct thing because Jules smiles—just a "thank you" kind-of smile.

"Mademoiselle Brown, have I told you what I like about you?"

I laugh. "As a matter of fact you have."

"Well, I stand corrected and I want to make it up to you. Since I have a running bath, why don't you come to my hotel and freshen up. Afterward, we'll go to Pasteur with our findings."

"That's a *very* tempting offer, but I need fresh clothes."

"Are you sure? I can have your clothes cleaned."

"Thank you, but I think it best I go to my place." I was lying, but I needed time alone . . . to think.

"All right. But after we see Doctor Pasteur, I insist on taking you to dinner."

"That, I won't refuse. But, don't you think we should meet with Oscar before dinner? We can have drinks at the Rat Mort. He can give us a report of his activities as a consulting detective and who knows, maybe he's discovered something."

"A meeting with your friend will only give me indigestion and destroy any chance of enjoying dinner. Please think twice about your idea."

A fiacre pulls up and Jules insists I take it. I squeeze his hand after he helps me in and he squeezes it back. "See you at Pasteur's in three hours."

"All right." And I wave my assent as my fiacre pulls away from the curb.

As I COME trudging up Le Passage, I find Oscar sitting on a stone bench in front of the apartment building. I'm too tired to deal with energy-charged witticisms. And I'm in desperate need to order a bath and just soak. He spots me and gains his feet.

"Nellie!" He looks grave. "I've been waiting for hours."

"Sorry. The train was late. What's the matter, Oscar? You look like you lost your best friend." I don't know why I said that, but from the shocked look on Oscar's face I realize something close to it happened.

"You heard." His tone and look changes to drama—a woman relating that her lover died in battle.

"Heard what?"

"He's dead."

"Who's dead?"

"Luc."

"Doctor Dubois is dead?"

"Yes . . ."

"But . . . how?"

"Black Fever."

"Oh, no . . ." I sit down on the stone bench. Oscar joins me.

"They found him in an alley in the wee hours this morning. I got the news from his concierge, a message at my hotel. Luc instructed the man to give me something if anything happened to him. I didn't have the strength to talk to the concierge, but instead came over here in the hopes you will go there with me."

Poor Oscar. He's truly miserable. I give him a hug. "I'm sorry." Unfortunately, I've had so many black thoughts about Luc Dubois that at this moment I'm only sorry he died before I could trap him into a confession.

"He must have contacted the fever at the hospital. I told him it was risky dealing with fever victims, but he was so intent on finding Jacque's killer."

"No, he was murdered. Probably by his anarchist friend."

He nods slowly. "I think that, too, but I was hoping for a more heroic death."

"He was up to his neck in this thing. We found evidence at a countryside lab that implicates Luc sent a crate there. And more evidence of murders."

"The . . . the slasher?"

"Yes," I sigh wearily, "the one and only. Did you talk to Luc before he died?"

Oscar shakes his head. "I tried. I even went to the hospital, but he wouldn't see me. Naturally, that provoked my suspicions, ones I've tried to suppress even after hearing your damnation of him. I asked our friends and was told he had grown more and more distant from them for the past few months. Lately he's been withdrawn and depressed."

"Is that all you know about his death—found in an alley, stricken down by Black Fever?"

"That's all the concierge's message stated, along with the fact he's holding something for me."

"You don't know what it is?"

"No clue. I know it's my duty to find out, but I don't have the strength to go alone."

"It's okay. Let's both do your duty. Take me to this concierge."

THE CONCIERGE IS a pleasant, courteous older man with a mop of thick white hair and rosy cheeks. Showing concern and remorse for the passing of Luc Dubois, he could give Madame Malon lessons in concierge-ship. He's surprised to see us and gives us startling news.

"But, Monsieur, the doctor's uncle gathered the package an hour ago."

"His uncle?"

"He said you asked him to pick it up when he came by to gather things."

"When the uncle came, did he specifically ask for Monsieur Wilde's package?" I ask.

"Yes, of course, he said he was here to gather his nephew's family memoirs."

I exchange looks with Oscar. It's obvious that the man who took Oscar's package didn't come specifically for it. The concierge volunteered it, despite what he's telling us.

"Can we have the uncle's address?" I ask.

"He didn't give it."

"His name?"

"I don't know that either, I never saw the man before this morning."

"Never saw him before—then how did you know he's Luc's uncle?" Oscar's upset.

"Because he said so."

"Did he take anything else from Luc's room?" I ask.

He shrugs. "I don't know, but if he did, it couldn't have been much or I would have helped him because of his hand."

"His hand?"

"Yes, he has only one."

"Malliot," I tell Oscar.

"Good, you know him." The concierge is relieved. "For a moment I thought he might be a thief."

"May we see Luc's room?" I ask. "Oscar wishes to say good-bye to his friend there."

"But of course. On the second floor, second door from the stairs."

"Is it locked?"

"Locked? Of course not, my tenants are all honest people."

"I wonder what was in the package?" I ask Oscar as we are going up the stairs. "I guess we'll have to ask Uncle Malliot."

"He will probably cut our throats as an answer. Isn't he the clever one. Coming here to clean out Luc's things."

"I believe they call that destroying evidence."

I push open the door to the flat and pause. "We know the reason for Malliot's visit. He was searching for something. Now the question is, *what?*"

Books were thrown on the floor, knickknacks were

broken into pieces, clothing was emptied from drawers, bedding tossed, mattresses overturned, and even the food goods were opened and dumped.

Oscar sighs. "Wasn't it a thorough search." He pushes a pile of flour near the sink with his foot. "What can one hide in flour?"

"Plenty. My mother used to hide grocery money in it. Who knows? Luc may have feared for his life and tried to get evidence into your hands to protect himself."

"Or name his killers."

I shrug. "It could be anything or . . . nothing. Malliot may have been looking for a clue to the whereabouts of the man they know as Perun."

"Doesn't it also mean Malliot was involved in Luc's death?"

I shake my head. "I don't know, maybe. But if Luc was killed last night and Malliot didn't show up until an hour ago, it's not likely."

Oscar pulls his cape tight. "Nellie girl . . . Luc died of the fever. Doctor Pasteur's little killers could be crawling toward us right now, ready to eat us."

"Don't worry, I don't think there's been anything accidental about the people who've been struck down by the fever. Luc was involved in the chicanery, of that I am certain. But where he fits into the scheme is as murky as the purpose of the machinations."

Oscar starts to say something, but his eyes water and he turns from me.

To me, Luc Dubois is a villain, but I have to remember that he was Oscar's friend and probably his lover. And something I've discovered about Oscar—besides the fact he's no fool, he's also no phony. His bigger-than-life emotions come from the fact he's bigger-than-life himself. He's a bear of a man in size, but is more emotionally sensitive than a wronged woman in a penny-dreadful novel. I take his arm and lead him out of the flat. I'm sure Malliot had not left anything for us to find.

I SEND OSCAR back to his hotel to rest, though I suspect he will end up at a café with friends and drinks. He is not the type to suffer alone. As we part he says, "I'll contact André and arrange a meeting."

"All right." What I really want to say is, why? He has several times said he would arrange a meeting with the cross-dresser, but there has always been a reason why André can't join us. But it's probably good for Oscar—gives him something to do.

I SEND A message to Jules at his hotel, telling him I need to speak to him urgently and send another wire to the carriage driver at the Normandy train depot asking questions we had both forgotten to ask when he transported us. I request an immediate response from the coachman directed to Jules' hotel. It's waiting for me when I arrive. I read it to Jules in the fiacre carrying us to the Institut Pasteur: "*The day before you. A man with one hand.*"

"I am humbled before you, Nellie. I completely missed it."

"We both did."

We had not asked about *other* men the taciturn carriage driver had taken out to the village.

"Artigas' felon has been one step ahead of us." Jules is disgusted. And angry at himself.

"Light years ahead."

"This Russian chemist must be developing the goose that lays golden eggs for Artigas. The count is a man who deals with heads of state and can stir up war between nations. Nothing short of gold sufficient to bedazzle Croesus would keep Artigas' interest for several years. I wonder if Malliot found anything at the village that would have helped our investigation."

I shake my head. "Something's not right."

"Not right? Is there anything right about this situation?"

"I mean, it's just not adding up. It was difficult enough searching for a mad doctor. Now it seems there's a powerful industrialist and the Lord only knows who else is leaving muddy boot marks on top of my clues."

"I must give you credit for something, Nellie. Wiring that carriage driver was very clever. You are a great detective. Perhaps you should be writing detective stories."

I have to bite my tongue to keep from telling him I just finished writing one—*The Mystery of Central Park*.* It appeared in the bookstores just before I left for Paris.

---

* *The Mystery of Central Park*, published October 12, 1889. Her detective, Penelope Howard, solved a murder in Central Park.—The Editors.

60

We wait only a few minutes in Doctor Pasteur's office before he and Dr. Roth join us.

"Gentlemen," Jules does a polite nod with his head, "have you heard about Doctor Dubois' death?"

They look at each other in surprise.

"He died of the Black Fever."

Dr. Pasteur is genuinely shocked. "*Mon Dieu*, can it be? First poor René, and now another young doctor investigating the contagion. It is carelessness, my own fault. I should have had stricter controls for handling the beast here and been more aggressive about warning other researchers to avoid infection when handling deadly microbes."

I am genuinely touched by Dr. Pasteur's strong compassion for his assistant and Dubois. Jules and I had agreed not to slander Dubois' name until we have solid evidence.

Jules pulls the piece of wood crate from his bag. "We brought back a couple of items from the area where Perun apparently had a laboratory. This crate bears shipping marks that indicate it was sent from China. When we met with Doctor Dubois at the hospital he received what the clerk called *another* package from China."

"Why is a crate from China in the countryside?" Pasteur asks.

"Perhaps for something devious and sinister."

"Sinister? Devious?" Pasteur turns to Roth who's standing by his chair. "I have lived too long if such words have entered the technical jargon of science."

Jules shakes his head. "I also have lived too long, my friend, long enough to see so many of the terrible things I imagined come to fruition. But be as it may, does this type of crate have any significance to you?" Jules hands Pasteur the piece of crate.

The elderly scientist examines it before handing it to Roth. "It says it's from the Yunnan region of China."

"Is that of importance?" I ask.

"Perhaps it's nothing, but that region has been battling the plague for several decades."

I ask, "Is the plague and Black Fever the same?"

"The symptoms are not the same." Pasteur is grave. "We considered whether it was a form of the plague and it may well be, but while we can at least detect the existence of the plague microbe in laboratory tests, we have neither seen nor even detected the fever bacterium."

"Did I mention previously that the first time I was in Dubois' office I also saw a crate shipped from Alexandria, Egypt?"

Pasteur looks to Roth again, lifting his eyebrows. "There's a cholera epidemic in Alexandria, still raging after many years. I sent three of my staff to Egypt to investigate the outbreak. It appears to have come out of Mecca, traveling the routes of the pilgrims back to their homelands, ultimately making its way to Europe. Poor Thuillier, one of my brightest scientists, succumbed to the contagion and died in Alexandria."

I'm puzzled. "What could a plague in China and the cholera in Egypt have to do with Doctor Dubois and this man Perun?"

Pasteur shrugs and spreads his hands on his desk. "Perhaps they obtained samples of the two diseases to compare to this Black Fever, perhaps believing that the fever is a mutated form of one of these known diseases. There are an infinite number of maladies inflicting mankind. Unfortunately, until we have better weapons on our side, we can find and destroy only a few of them."

"Was this piece of crate the only evidence of laboratory experiments you found in the village?" Roth directs his question to Jules.

"We found the burned out remains of a laboratory and picked up some of the ash debris in the hopes you can analyze it."

Roth is already shaking his head. "Unlikely we'd find microbes that survived a fire."

His remark depresses me. "That's all we came up with, the crate and the ashes. And a handful of dirt from some cursed fields."

Pasteur reacts as if he'd been slapped. "Cursed fields? What do you mean, cursed fields?"

"A farmer at the village told us that animals die if they graze there. It appears Perun dug up a dead cow buried there. We took a soil sample." I study Pasteur's face. His eyes are ablaze. "Is this important?"

"The soil sample, do you have it with you?"

"Yes." Jules hands the bag containing the sample to Roth.

"Have you touched the materials?" Pasteur asked.

Jules shakes his head. "I was careful not to."

"Is it just dirt?" Pasteur seems anxious. "Are any of the cow's remains included?"

"There's a piece of cow hide in the sample, and perhaps a worm or two."

"You found worms at the site." Pasteur gets up, excited. "Just as I thought. Wait while we take a preliminary look at the samples."

As we wait, we have tea with Madame Pasteur—a quiet, unassuming woman who strikes me as a perfect match for the great scientist devoted to his work. I have a hard time making polite talk with Madame Pasteur because I'm dying of curiosity about Pasteur's reaction to my cursed fields comment. When Madame Pasteur politely excuses herself to leave the room, I ask Jules, "What do you think is so important about the worms?"

He whispers back, "Perun has been experimenting with them to create a giant worm that will eat the world."

An hour later, we follow Roth back into the office where Pasteur is already seated. The elderly scientist's face is drawn and pale, but his eyes are bright and powerful.

"Anthrax," Pasteur states.

"Anthrax?" I look to see if Jules understands. He does.

"I can understand if you've never heard of this microbe, Mademoiselle, it is known mostly in the sheep and cattle industry. It's commonly called the woolgatherer's disease because it mostly affects people who work with animal hides."

"Is it a significant disease?"

"It is if you own cattle or sheep, or work with hides, but it usually isn't as highly contagious a disease as the Black Death. Anthrax spreads mostly by touch to an open cut, though it can be inhaled from dust brushed from infected animals. The more contagious diseases are inhaled from infected persons. However, anthrax is extremely deadly. If inhaled, it is almost always fatal."

"Doctor Pasteur developed the vaccination that protects animals from anthrax," Roth says. "It saved sheep and cattle raisers millions of francs each year. But that discovery came at great risk to the doctor's reputation as a scientist, especially after others, who thought they knew a better answer, had thrown down the gauntlet."

Pasteur waves aside Roth's praise as if discovering a vaccination for a dreaded disease is just something he does on a daily basis.

"I was most fortunate—and had a similar experience to the one you had in the village. Animals were dying from an epidemic of anthrax and workers were getting the condition. I spoke to farmers who said there were certain fields that were particularly dangerous to animals; that more than an ordinary number of animals died when grazed there. They also spoke of these fields as being cursed, damned by God. While walking in such a field, I saw that the farmers had buried the dead animals on the spot where they died. I kicked up dirt on one such burial mound and noticed worms. From those worms, I realized how the contagion was spread from animal to animal."

He pauses and takes a drink of water. "It's the process of feeding that spread the disease. The farmers buried the diseased animals in the ground. There, worms would feast upon their flesh. Some of the worms would make their way to the surface, where they are eaten by cattle nibbling grass. Those cattle die from the infection, then are buried and provide more fodder for the worms."

I shake my head. "Incredible. But wouldn't it stop and the fields be useful again if they dug up the dead animals and properly disposed of them?"

"It's not that simple, Mademoiselle. Anthrax is one of the most durable microbes I have studied. The microbes are known to last for decades in affected ground. And, because they're too small to see with the naked eye and have already been spread by the worms, just removing the dead animals won't get rid of them. There are billions of them in a single shovelful of dirt."

Jules says to Pasteur, "The actions of this Perun person is getting stranger and stranger. What possible experiments can he be doing that would involve the plague, cholera, and anthrax? Do you draw any conclusions from these facts?"

"I draw no conclusions that cannot be confirmed in my laboratory. I have a question for the two of you. What is it exactly you believe this man Perun has been doing? What are these dark deeds you hint at?"

A look from Jules tells me to field the question. "I believe Perun has murdered women by somehow injecting them or otherwise infecting them with horrid diseases."

"*What!*" Pasteur bangs his hand on his desk. "A scientist using his science to kill? *Mon Dieu*, I truly have lived too long. Why would he do such a thing?"

"I suspect he's mad as a hatter. It may give him the same sort of thrill that another man gets riding a fast horse or shooting a lion or tiger."

"How does Doctor Dubois fit into this madness?"

"Like you, we have more questions than answers. It may be nothing more than Dubois provided him samples for his experiments. Or that Dubois was somehow involved in it. I rather suspected the latter."

"Is it possible that Dubois was the killer you sought?" That came from Roth.

"I don't believe so." I take a deep breath. "I've seen the killer—the man we believe is Perun, at least from a distance. Dubois' body language was much different, slower and gentler, you could say. No, I'm sure Dubois was not my man."

When I finish, those penetrating eyes of Pasteur are past me, no doubt seeing eons ahead of us poor mortals.

"First the frogs and rats, and now the worms. And the birds . . . I must not forget the birds." Pasteur is lost in very deep thoughts.

"Frogs, rats, worms, and birds?" I raise my eyebrows. "I don't know about frogs and things, but I do know a woman died from the fever literally before my eyes."

My statement awakens Pasteur from his thoughts, "Tell me about her again. Tell me *everything* you saw."

I describe in great detail what happened that night before the graveyard incident and afterward, meeting Dubois, and what I saw the next day at the hospital. The great man taps a pencil on his desk as he sees beyond anything we can envision. An absolute stillness grips the room. I'm afraid to even move—afraid I will break the spell. Finally, he leans back in his chair and expels a great sigh.

"There is an inconsistency, one that bothers me a great deal."

"And that is?" I have to ask.

"The condition of the woman you saw being autopsied by Doctor Dubois. You described her blood as thick and black. Is that correct?"

"Yes, that's how I remember it."

"Even the innards you saw were blackened."

"Yes."

"Doctor Dubois told you that they were typical symptoms of the Black Fever. Yes?"

"Correct. Is that a problem?"

"Black blood in the viscera can be caused by an invasion of the anthrax bacteria. Anthrax can only grow and multiply in the presence of oxygen. Oxygen gives blood its bright color; anthrax consumes the oxygen and turns blood blackish."

"Perun's been infecting women with anthrax!" I can't believe it.

"No. Anthrax is a quick-acting contagion, but not something that kills in minutes."

"She could have been infected earlier."

Pasteur shakes his head. "The deterioration was too fast to have simply been anthrax."

"If not anthrax, then what?"

Instead of answering my question, Pasteur looks up to Roth who is still standing beside his chair. "It's not consistent. You see that, don't you? What we were provided with is not consistent."

"Yes, I do see that."

"What do you see?" I can't stand it. I'm on the edge of my seat.

Pasteur waves his hand, as if pushing away a nuisance. "The samples we received from Dubois. You say the woman had blackened blood and that's typical of the fever. I was told that the fever came from some black spots on the flesh that soon disappeared after death. The samples of blood and flesh I've been provided have been red."

Jules interjects. "Red, meaning they have not lost their oxygen."

"Yes."

"Dubois gave you false samples." I say the obvious and silence follows. Thoughts dribble down from my brain and out my mouth. "It's more than just the women. There are many people sick in the city, people dying. Dubois has hindered the research on the influenza outbreak to let people die. Why?"

Pasteur grimaces. "Mademoiselle, hundreds of thousands of people have died across Europe and North America from the contagion, and those are just the ones counted in the so-called civilized countries where such statistics are maintained. I thought of the Black Fever as a strand of the less deadly influenza. Now I must wonder if it is not even related to the general malady. We are not just talking about a man who stalks women in the night. We may be dealing with a killer that stalks civilization itself. I don't know what's killing those people, but I must find out."

"What are we to do?"

"I must conduct more tests. Everything we have talked about is nothing but the most severe speculation. It must be proven. I must have laboratory results that are irrefutable. No one will listen if I cannot come forward with objective results. I need legitimate samples. We must begin negotiations with the minister." He looks to Roth. "He must intercede to provide me legitimate samples."

"Are you talking about a government official?" I ask.

"Yes."

"That could take a long time." Those thoughts were not dribbling down from my brain anymore, they were gushing. "I may be able to get you samples in a matter of hours."

"How?"

"It just happens that the uncle of a victim of the fever is a close friend of mine. I'm sure I can get him to have the body released to me quite quickly."

JULES AND I are outside the Institut before he asks me the obvious question, with much dread in his voice.

"Tell me that you're not planning to have Malliot pretend to be Dubois' uncle and get us the body. That would be ridiculous. The man would never agree."

"I'm not planning to have Malliot pretend to be Dubois' uncle."

"Thank God. I'm relieved."

"I'm planning to have *you* be his uncle."

61

We are all so sad over Doctor Dubois' death," the nurse says. "He was an example for all of us. We don't know what we shall do without him. Are you also a doctor, Monsieur Uncle?"

Jules grumbles something to the nurse that sounds like "no" as we march down the hospital corridor. He looks more like a man being twisted on a rack in a medieval dungeon than a grieving relative. He's hopeless as an actor. The only saving grace is that there is no reason for the nurse to be suspicious. No one in their right mind would claim the body of a Black Fever victim unless they were a close relative.

Dubois' body has been keep in a walk-in icebox next to the loading ramp at the back of the hospital. On the way to the hospital, we arranged for a mortuary wagon to pick up the body and wired Pasteur to meet us at the mortuary within an hour.

"I'm so glad that he has close relatives," the nurse continues, talking through a vinegar sponge. "We all thought he was an orphan. Do you live in Paris?"

"Occasionally," is all Jules says.

We go out the backdoor and onto the loading dock, depositing our sponges in a tub by the door.

"You both look familiar. Have you ever visited Doctor Dubois here?"

"On occasion." Jules glances at me with concern.

"Then that must be it."

The mortuary wagon driver gets off his rig and comes onto the dock. While the nurse has the driver sign papers, Jules and I stand on the dock and try to look like grieving relatives.

"It's strange, isn't it," I say to Jules, "after you pass, you are no longer a person but a thing. It's no longer Doctor Dubois, but his body."

"That's because his spirit has fled the dead and decaying mass."

"That's a comforting thought. Everything's going well, don't you think?" I spoke too soon. A man I take to be a doctor hurries across the dock to us.

"*Bonjour.* I am Doctor Brouardel, the Director of Health. Doctor Dubois was one of my assistants." He shakes hands with Jules, squinting at him and adjusting his pince-nez to get a better look. "Have we met, Monsieur?"

Jules clears his throat. "I don't believe we've had the pleasure of meeting." He looks as innocent as a fox caught in the chicken coop.

It suddenly occurs to me that the Director of Health may have been on the same government health community that Jules served on with Pasteur.

"You and your . . ." Brouardel looks to me.

"This is Doctor Dubois' fiancée, Mademoiselle Carré."

The health director is as surprised as me to learn Dubois had a fiancée. I put my handkerchief to my face to hide my grief and murmur something unintelligible, hoping to hide my foreign accent.

"I'm quite surprised. I never knew Luc had family or a fiancée. Why, I had even heard—well, never mind that. Again, I wish to offer both of you my condolences. When will the funeral be? Naturally, I'll want to attend."

"Ah, that's still being planned. We shall notify you," Jules says quickly.

Dr. Brouardel removes his hat. "There he is now."

A hospital morgue attendant wheels out a body wrapped in a black sheet. I walk away, handkerchief to my face, to give the impression of grief. Truthfully, I am affected. Whatever Dr. Dubois was, I am still affected by the sight of his body as it's being loaded into the back of the mortuary wagon.

Behind me Jules and Dr. Brouardel exchange good-byes, then Jules quickly joins me. Our fiacre is waiting across the street from the dock and I have to tell my feet not to break into a run. At the carriage, I look back and see Dr. Brouardel turning from a discussion with a morgue attendant to the nurse who had shown us to the loading dock. The nurse gestures behind her rather frantically and on to the landing comes a familiar figure—a man with one hand.

"Oh my God. The cat's out of the frying pan."

Jules looks back as he assists me into the carriage. "Another uncle has arrived. That should give Brouardel some pause. I thought he was going to recognize me—he served on the same health committee as Pasteur and I."

"What do you think will happen?"

He shakes his head and shrugs. "Brouardel could turn the police on us. We would be arrested, imprisoned, and guillotined. But in fact, probably nothing will happen because Maillot will not dare blow his own cover by exposing us."

A dreadful thought occurs to me. I grab Jules arm. "Jules, what if Maillot really is Dubois' uncle?"

Instead of answering, he stares out the carriage window at the passing buildings.

"The cat's out of the bag."

"What?"

"The cat's out of the bag, not the frying pan. I heard it during a trip to America. You have the expression wrong."

"Either way, our cat is cooked."

62

On the way to the mortuary, we pass one of those terribly poor neighborhoods that breed prostitution, thievery, and misery. Children with dirty faces and skinny frames play in the gutter as we sweep by in the carriage.

"Did she really say that?" I ask.

Jules is silent for a moment. "Did *whom* really say *what*?"

"Marie Antoinette. Did she really say, 'let them eat cake' when the poor were shouting for bread?"

"I've heard an anecdote that one of her children asked, 'why don't they eat cake' when he heard shouts for bread, but I would not swear to the veracity of the tale. For certain, the queen never said it."

"We live in strange times, don't we, Jules. Anarchists are not only planting bombs, but willingly using their own bodies as vehicles to set off the bomb, hoping to kill as many people as possible. People are going to bed starving in many countries. And I hate to admit that even in America we have greedy businessmen like Artigas who don't care who gets hurt as long as they profit. They say you can predict the future. Will the world ever change?"

"It's a certainty that the world will change. The question is, will people change and stop hating each other?"

DOCTORS PASTEUR AND Roth are waiting at the mortuary with a case full of laboratory equipment. They will take blood and flesh samples from the corpse and check them immediately. The mortician gives me a piece of his mind while the body is being unloaded.

"This is most unusual, Mademoiselle. We do not permit such procedures on our premises, nor would I have agreed to it if I had known the deceased is a fever victim."

"You should feel proud," I tell the skinny little man, "one of the greatest men of France has chosen your establishment to conduct a test that will save the city, maybe even your life or the life of one of your family members. You will be rewarded in heaven for your assistance."

He rubs his hands and gives me a look that only morticians and snake oil salesmen can conjure. "I am afraid I shall require a more Earthly reward. Shall we say twice the agreed fee?"

"The root of all evil," I tell Jules, after I pay the man.

"Money?"

"*Greed.*"

AFTER AN HOUR with no word from the scientists in the embalming room, I suggest to Jules that we take a walk and get some fresh air. "I need to walk or I'll start screaming."

I find myself taking a hold of his arm. It makes me feel safer with him at my side. To my pleasure he re- ⌐nds by moving closer to me. I really have no desire to talk and it appears neither does Jules. All I want to do is forget everything that has happened and what I'm afraid will happen, so I image how I would like things to be right now with Jules and me . . . tonight, we are a married couple out for an evening stroll in a beautiful section of Paris. It's late fall and the leaves are changing colors. Later we will join friends at Maxim's for dinner. The air is crisp and—

"Nellie." Jules interrupts my dreaming. "A police wagon just came around the corner."

"Just keep walking," I tell Jules.

We go only a few paces when I come face-to-face with someone from the past.

"You!"

I smile, "*Bonjour*, Detective Lussac. We have been waiting for you. Isn't it nice," I turn to Jules, "we just called the police and here they are."

Jules looks puzzled, but says nothing.

Detective Lussac's companion is a man in his fifties. His face is long and there is no humor in his eyes or mouth. I recognize him as the man I passed the night I fled the police station.

"You have led us on a fine chase, Mademoiselle Bly. I am Chief Inspector Morant. You will find that the police of Paris are more than willing to reward your devious activities with time in jail."

Jules steps forward. "Nellie has been uncovering a plot so serious to the fate of our city she will be rewarded membership in the Legion of Honor rather than a jail cell."

"And who may I ask are you, Monsieur? For if you have been conspiring with this woman," he points a long, Ichabod Crane-like finger at Jules, "I will need your name for the police blotter."

"I am Jules Verne."

"Nonsense. You look nothing like Jules Verne."

"I look precisely like Jules Verne without a beard."

"Monsieur, you look like a madman, with or without a beard."

The mortuary door opens and Dr. Pasteur steps out, basically muttering to himself, "It is a calamity."

Inspector Morant grins. "I suppose you will tell me that that is Phileas Fogg."

"No, Monsieur Inspector. That is *Louis Pasteur*."

The police inspector guffaws so hard he bends over. When he straightens, the humor is gone. "Put these two in irons. And that old man, also. We will have them all transported to a prison hospital for mental examination."

Detective Lussac stares at Pasteur and then at Jules. "Inspector. I think we have a problem."

63

"A truly fiendish scheme," Dr. Pasteur informs us.

We are in a conference room at the headquarters of the Sûreté. In attendance besides myself are Jules, Pasteur, Roth, Inspector Morant, Detective Lussac, the Minister of Interior, and the Prefect of Police.

"Anthrax," Pasteur says, "cholera, botulism, probably the bubonic plague, typhoid fever, even a strain of influenza, God only knows what's in the bomb."

"A bomb?" The Minister of Interior is completely puzzled.

"A *microbe* bomb." Pasteur shakes his head. "The contents of the compound are more obvious in examining the body and viscera with the naked eye than under a microscope. You see the fever rash typical of typhoid, black marks on the skin from the buboes, blotches and boils of plague, a report that the body was still twitching still hours after death with the spasms of cholera . . . I can't tell what all is in the compound, only that a drop of it is the most lethal poison on earth."

The Minister of the Interior stares up at the ceiling for a moment, pursing his lips tightly together. "You say a scientist actually mixed all these—these poisonous microbes together?"

"Unfortunately, yes. But it's not that simple. To the contrary, it would be extremely difficult to develop a culture that different microbes can live in all at the same time. It would take years of experimentation. And we don't know if it is in liquid or solid form."

"He's had years." Everyone looks at me. "I have been hunting him for the last two years, Artigas employed him three years ago. And he's had plenty of human lab animals to experiment upon."

Pasteur nodded. "That may be true, but I suspect he has only recently developed the compound that Dubois was infected with. I draw this conclusion for a couple of reasons. First, Dubois' symptoms are much more varied than what I've been told other Black Fever victims have experienced, inferring that the compound given him is more complex than earlier ones. And secondly, there are the birds and the frogs."

"The birds and the frog?" the Minister asks.

"And the rats. I should have suspected anthrax immediately because the frogs and birds were not affected by the contagion and the rats were. Anthrax, like all other life forms, survives and multiples only in a specified environment. The blood of frogs and birds are not hospitable environments for this particular microbe. The frog's blood is too cold, the bird's too hot, but the rat, like humans, has a temperature in the right range. I now believe that the contagion that struck the tenement I personally inspected was heavy with anthrax, more than what appears to have struck Dubois. I suspect that this madman has been experimenting with different deadly microbe combinations and only recently developed this complex combination."

"A microbe cocktail." I'm amazed. "He's going to un-
ndora's box on Paris."

"But how is he spreading it?" Inspector Morant asks. "Thousands of people have contracted the disease."

"All the microbes in the compound are highly contagious," Pasteur shakes his head. "Once he has one person infected, it will spread like wildfire to others. But I suspect that he has also been experimenting with methods of spreading the microbes to large numbers of people at the same time. The easiest way would be by infecting what they breathe, eat, or drink."

"Absolute insanity." The Minister gets up and paces the room. "We must find this madman before others die. Inspector Morant, I want you to put all the men you can spare into finding this fiend."

"That won't do. You're not dealing with crime—this is war."

The statement comes from me. Jules looks across the table at me. He has been particularly silent toward me since we were taken by the police. I know the reason.

"Yes, she's right," he says, "you must prepare for war."

Jules has interceded because the men around the table are not used to hearing the ideas of a woman in matters of national security. I am only in the room because Dr. Pasteur said I had important information. The fact that I was the one who uncovered the heinous plot is irrelevant. To the French officials, I am still a foreign reporter who can embarrass the government. Worse, I'm a woman poking her nose in their business.

Jules continues. "The city is under siege, invisible bombs will be exploded in our midst at any moment. You must muster the army itself into service."

"Monsieur Verne, while I respect your imagination, I don't believe a single madman—"

"He's not a single madman, he's an anarchist, a fanatical and murderous one. And he has a weapon so deadly it has almost inconceivable destructive force. From what

Dr. Pasteur has said, if this deadly compound is spread all over the city, Paris will be a ghost town for decades."

Inspector Morant gawks at Jules. "Are you proposing that it's possible for this madman to kill everyone in this city? With these invisible animals, creatures you can't even see without a microscope? That it can turn Paris into a deserted city? You expect us to believe that?"

"Yes." Pasteur is quite grave. "It's definitely possible. Some of these microbes, the anthrax and botulism for example, can lie dormant for decades on the ground, waiting to be inhaled or otherwise enter the bloodstream where they suddenly come alive and begin to multiply when they receive nourishment."

"How has it been spread so far?" Inspector Morant demands. "People are not eating worms. Has our food been contaminated? Our water? Air? What?"

"Perhaps all three, air at one place, water another, as he searches for the most effective way to spread the contagion. The man is an excellent scientist, even if he is lower than a worm as a human being. *Mon Dieu*, what Mademoiselle thought was simply an insane slashing of women may have been a perverse and perverted method of autopsy."

"Checking the progress of the disease in his human lab rats." Jules sighs.

The Minister of the Interior rubs his forehead. "This is insane. How can he spread it, this microbe mixture, bomb, or whatever it is to be called?"

Pasteur answers. "First he will have to produce the compound in sufficient quantity to be spread. We can assume that at this point he has developed a soup rich in killing power. To make large quantities of the soup is very simple. The difficult part is preventing the person who prepares the substance from being infected himself, but as a scientist, he is no doubt adept at handling deadly microbes in the laboratory. After he has the compound, he must choose how it is to be spread. A liquid could only be widely spread by putting it into water—perhaps a river or lake." Pasteur bows his head down as if in prayer.

"The Seine," Jules whispers.

"A dry compound might be spread by throwing it in water," Pasteur says, "but it can also be put in food, or in a dust form in the air."

"From a high point." Jules' mind is on a roll. "The Eiffel Tower on a windy day?"

There is general murmuring of assent around the table. It occurs to me that a scheme in which a madman drops deadly dust from a high place like the Eiffel Tower is the type of story Jules writes. The Minister rises from the table. He takes a deep breath and holds his head back for a moment, closing his eyes. Finally, he opens them and looks around the table.

"Messieurs and Mademoiselle, please correct me if I am wrong. An anarchist, possibly a Russian, is conspiring with other anarchists, this group known as the Pale Horse Society," he nods in my direction, "to destroy Paris. The French nation, in fact. And after that . . . the world, perhaps?

"He began his experiments on individuals, prostitutes, and has graduated to the stage where he is able to spread the calamity over a large area. From a high place, or a river, this anarchist could unleash a deadly contagion that will kill thousands. The microbe spores in the dust can remain lethal for decades, making Paris, in effect, uninhabitable for generations." He looks around the table. "Does that define what we are up against?"

"I would only add one thing," the Prefect of Police says. "The economy in France, and throughout Europe, is in deep depression. If Paris is destroyed or disabled, untold misery will spread throughout the country."

"Giving the anarchists exactly the condition of economic and political chaos they want," the Minister concludes.

"There is one other factor you need to consider," I tell the Minister.

"Mademoiselle?"

"*Time.* You don't have any. There hasn't been a new outbreak in days. And the ones that have occurred have been eminently successful. We must assume that he is producing his deadly brew in great quantities, or that he already has stockpiled it and has just been testing ways to spread it."

The Minister directs a question to the Prefect of Police. "What measures can you take?"

"Arrest and question every known violent anarchist in the city. We have informers everywhere and can spread the word that a large reward will be granted for information concerning this matter. All police vacations and days off will be canceled and all reserve units activated. We'll immediately post officers at Eiffel's tower and put the tower through a serious search."

"How about high buildings?" Jules interjects.

"We must post men atop tall buildings throughout the city." The Prefect looks back to the Minister. "We'll try to maintain secrecy to keep from creating a general panic, but how much of a barrage of activity can be kept secret is yet to be seen."

"The army—" Jules starts to say.

"Yes," the Minister says, "the army must do what it can. I will speak immediately to the President."

"The Seine is the obvious target," Inspector Morant says. "It will be the easiest to poison. From there the contagion can spread throughout the city in drinking water and fish."

Something is wrong. I can feel it. Perun is too smart

for the obvious. I meet Jules eyes across the room. There is neutrality in his eyes toward me, as if I am a stranger on a street corner asking for directions. Behind the neutral stare must be anger—anger at me. Naturally for good reason—Chief Inspector Morant let the cat out of the bag when he called me "Mademoiselle Bly." He is too well read not to know that Nellie Bly is the world's first woman investigative reporter. Now Jules knows I betrayed him. I need to talk with him.

But, first I must get my feelings across to the men around the table. They are sitting on a powder keg big enough to blow the roof off of one of the greatest cities of the world, and they neither will solicit nor tolerate an opinion from someone who is of the wrong sex, nationality, and occupation. But my instincts are *screaming* that there is a piece to the puzzle missing. Unfortunately, everyone has decided what they believe must be done, so the meeting breaks up. I rise to leave. Two officers suddenly flank me as I start to follow Jules and Dr. Pasteur out.

"You're arresting me?" I ask the Prefect.

"Protective custody. Only until the crisis is over. To insure that you are safe from this maniac."

"This is a rotten way to repay someone who's trying to save your city."

"Mademoiselle, when this is over I will personally recommend you be granted a medal for your efforts. Until then, you will be held for your many crimes, not the least of which is escaping police custody."

I look to Jules for help. He says nothing, but speaks to Dr. Pasteur. Pasteur is nodding his head in agreement when an out-of-breath officer bursts in, desiring to speak to the Prefect. After a whispered conversation, the Prefect turns to us.

"We have been advised by an anonymous source that a man we suspect is both an anarchist and a doctor is hiding out at an apartment building in the quarter where the latest contagion broke out. My men are already encircling the place. Because of the importance of this matter, I need to be present. And I will invite doctors Pasteur and Roth to attend, in case their advice concerning any substance is needed. And of course, Monsieur Verne. In case we need any advice on how to deal with this madman."

I speak loudly. "You are deliberately ignoring the one and *only* person who has had an encounter with the slasher . . . me."

He turns his back on me to leave and I blurt out, "It's a ruse."

"A ruse?"

Everyone looks at me like I have lost my head. But I know I'm right.

"Mademoiselle, what you are saying is preposterous!"

"No, it's not. You gentlemen seem to forget I have been hunting this man for the past two years, while you have become involved only in the last few hours. This is a decoy to distract your attention so he can release Pandora's Box."

The Prefect is flabbergasted. "Mademoiselle, we appreciate all you have done, but this is not in your field of expertise. You have nothing to back your theory of this being a ruse—"

"Yes, I do. When I first discovered him, a shack burned at Blackwell's Island and concealed his crimes. He learned from it. A year later in England, a Scotland Yard Inspector received an anonymous tip that the doctor would be working in his lab in an apartment building in a bad neighborhood. We no sooner arrived when an explosion rocked the building and a fire roared. Once again the police announced all evidence went up in smoke, along with the slasher. Don't you think it's a co-incidence that your police receive an anonymous tip he's in a building? He's going to blow it up. You'll think he's dead. And then he can go off and do his horrible deed."

Silence fills the room. From the looks on their faces, I think they were trying to find a way around my logic and facts.

"Mademoiselle, I don't think you realize the amount of strain you have endured." Dr. Roth says softly. "You need rest."

I start to rebut him, but he puts up a hand to stop me. "Don't you agree, Monsieur Verne?"

Everyone looks to him.

"Well . . . she has endured a lot of stress . . ."

"Yes, Doctor Roth is correct, we have wasted enough valuable time." The Prefect clears his throat. "Mademoi-selle, you will stay here where we can provide you with the utmost protection."

I wait until the door is opened before I give them the *coup de grâce*, the finishing blow the French call the stroke of mercy.

"Monsieur Prefect, you are able to identify this mad-man, aren't you?"

There is a pause at the door and a huddled conference between the Prefect and his aides. The conference breaks up and the Prefect smiles with all the sincerity a politi-cian can muster.

"Once again, Mademoiselle, France needs your ser-vices."

I take his hand, smiling.

64

Paris knows something is amiss.

No matter how the police try to hide their presence, they can't. A bartender in the Bowery once told me that he could smell a copper, claiming that all the flatfoots in New York used the same brand of cheap cologne given out free by the company that sells them uniforms.

As we roll through the streets in three carriages—black, unmarked vehicles—the people look at us with suspicion. Even the plainclothes officers driving the rigs smack of police—short, freshly trimmed hair, neat mustaches, inexpensive suits cut in a faded fashion, and the body language—sharp-eyed, straight back, and authoritative. No, the only people we are fooling are ourselves.

I share a carriage with Jules and two police officers. The police are not in the carriage to watch Jules. I'm not pleased with my status as a prisoner of war when I am the only one winning battles. Without my determination, Paris might already be a ghost city. The silence between Jules and I works on me till I finally cannot stand it any more.

"Yes, it was me who passed out the handbills with your likeness. I deceived you. I am a terrible person. But

I did it for a good cause." There. I confessed my last foul deception.

He examines me with half-closed eyes. "I read the Paris edition of foreign newspapers."

I give that some thought. My reporting occasionally appears in the French edition of the *World*. "You've known who I am from the very beginning!"

"When you stormed out of the Procope, tossing behind Gaston's name as a threat, you naturally piqued my interest. Since you identified yourself to the maitre d' as Nellie Brown from New York, I contacted a newspaper friend of mine—"

"Scholl . . . he knew, too."

"Yes. He contacted the Paris office of the New York paper and found out from the *World* that Nellie Bly was in the city. Having read some of your escapades—"

"*You deceived me!*"

That causes his jaw to drop. I quickly squeeze his hand. "However, I'm going to forgive you. But Jules, I think there is something wrong with the police's theory about the slasher's plans. They're going about it in a logical manner."

"And?"

"Perun is a madman. He may be in fact a brilliant scientist, but as you have pointed out, that's not a testament to his sanity. His actions up to now have not been logical nor reasonable, therefore we should not expect him to act the same way we would."

"What do you think he's up to?"

"I don't know. But I'm positive this is just another ruse to throw us off his trail and give him more time. The police talk about Perun poisoning the Seine. Don't you agree that's a futile act? The river will wash itself clean." I don't wait for his answer, I keep on going. "Or releasing dust from a tall building, something that would have little effect. No ... Perun is a *mad genius*. He will do something insanely spectacular. I just know it."

"You might be right, but until we come up with information about his plans, I have to agree with Doctor Roth. We must act on the possibilities we are confronted with. As you pointed out, the microbe bomb he has concocted is truly Pandora's Box. However, the story of Pandora has a twist that most of us forget."

"Which is?"

"When Pandora opened the box, releasing evils and miseries upon the world, she slammed the lid shut before the goddess Hope could escape. Hope is still there ready to use her magic when we release her."

THE QUARTER WHERE the suspected anarchist doctor is hiding is in chaos. Policemen on horse and foot are trying to contain a large crowd behind barricades. A building is on fire, the very one that the doctor is believed to be hiding in. Behind us arrive fire trucks with clanging bells.

"The people are quarantined," an officer says. "They want out. Rumors have spread that the government is planning to kill them, part of the process of getting rid of the poor."

Rocks fly and mounted officers urge their horses against the crowd. In my mind, neither side is handling the situation well, but I put the biggest blame on the police.

"These people are frightened. The Prefect should address their fears."

"I think he is about to do that in his own way." Jules looks down the street. A phalanx of helmeted police with shields and clubs attack the crowd at the Prefect's command. I turn my eyes from the violence.

Someone shouts, "There he is!" A man breaks through

the police lines and runs. Shots ring out and he stumbles and falls. I lose sight of him as a dozen officers converge on his prone figure. Moments later I'm called over to look at the man. He's dead.

"It's not Perun," I proclaim sadly. The man is much too tall and skinny.

"I recognize him," an officer says. "He's wanted for the murder of his wife. That's why he tried to escape."

I ask one of my custodians to carry a message to the Prefect. "Tell him it would be nice if we find Perun and ask him some questions *before* we shoot him." When the man trots off to deliver the message, I turn to Jules. "When I was arrested, why didn't you come to my defense?"

"I only want to keep you safe. Besides, they're not going to let you loose, no matter what."

After the crowd is beaten back, Jules and I accompany a squad of police to the burning building. Firefighters have brought the situation under control.

"Someone started fires," a fire captain tells Detective Lussac, "on different floors, trying to burn the place down. Because the walls are stone, only the wooden innards caught fire. However, we're still working localizing fires throughout the building. You must be very careful."

"Yes, yes, we will." Detective Lussac turns to me. "The Prefect asks that we hurry. We'll follow the officers in so you can identify this man Perun. He's said to be on the fourth floor. There'll be no shooting unless absolutely necessary. The Prefect says we must take him alive."

"Smart man," I mutter as I fall in with Jules at the rear of the contingent. The officers ahead of us enter each floor before we reach it, knocking down doors they find locked. The higher we go in the building, the thicker the smoke becomes. It is thickest when we reach the fourth floor.

"Stay here," Lussac tells us. "You'll be safe from bullets."

We are on the stairs near the fourth-floor landing. I keep a wet cloth to my nose and mouth, but it helps very little in filtering out the smoke. The police break open a door on the fourth floor. A moment later Lussac is at the top of the stairs, coughing.

"We found him, he's dead. See if you can identify the body. It's not pretty. His face has been badly burned."

As we enter the apartment, Jules suddenly grabs my arm. "*Quiet!* Stand still!" He listens intently. I hear it. A ticking sound. Like a clock. My blood turns cold.

"*Out!*" Jules yells.

He grabs my arm, rushing me to the door, the others behind us. We are going down the steps when the bomb explodes. I am knocked off of my feet and would be crushed by those coming down behind me if Jules didn't act as a shield. When the concussion of the explosion is over, an ominous creaking sound emits.

"*The stairway's going!*" Jules shouts.

I roll onto my feet. We reach the third-floor landing as the stairway collapses behind us. The bomb ignited the fire and flames are roaring out of control by the time we reach the ground floor and stagger outside, choking and coughing.

"He set a bomb, started a fire, and blew himself up," Lussac tells the Prefect of Police outside. "Like a good anarchist, he intended to take as many of us with him as he could."

"It wasn't him," I announce.

"You got a good look at him?" the Prefect asks.

"I didn't have to. As I tried to explain to you before, Perun set the bomb and fire to make us believe he's dead. It's all too pat."

"What proof do you have?"

"I've investigated this man on two continents. I know

his twisted mind. You have to think like him to understand his actions. He's playing with you, making a fool out of all of you."

FOR WHATEVER REASON, I find my popularity with the police is always in question. I barely get the smoke out of my lungs and my breath back when the Prefect orders two policemen to take me back into custody.

"I am truly sorry you are being treated this way," Jules says to me, but lifts neither hand nor objection to my arrest. His idea of keeping me safe.

My dress is torn in several places. My face is black from smoke and soot. And I am being arrested. To say the least, I'm livid about the lack of appreciation I've gotten for all my efforts.

"There is no justice in this world," I inform Jules as they take me away.

A POLICE MATRON takes me to a cell that is barely a notch up from a jail cell that I occupied when I had myself arrested in New York as a "thief" to do an exposé on jail conditions. I am still inspecting the cot for bedbugs and other undesirable things when Jules is let in. He seems excited.

"The police are moving fast. They found the location where Perun mixed his deadly concoction."

"Where?"

He leans forward and whispers, "This must be kept in strict confidence."

I whisper back, "Who can I tell? The rats in this dungeon?"

Jules clears his throat. Apparently, I'm a woman who doesn't know her place.

"The poisonous microbe dust is in a barge on the Seine. Perun planned to release the dust into the river as soon as he had enough. He was on the verge of making the release when he killed himself."

"They found the body?"

"No, it burned up—"

"The police are making an assumption that he's a common criminal. They don't realize the man has something you possess in abundance."

"What?" Jules asks.

"*Imagination*. He's posed as a medical doctor, a scientist, and revolutionary. The world's greatest scientist believed he was a dedicated biochemist, and he fooled France's cannon king into believing he was a faithful employee. He's helped kill an emperor and God only knows how many others. No one really knows what he looks like. Now ask yourself, if you were writing this character in a book, would he kill himself? Or would he leave the impression that he was dead to fool the police?"

"Nellie, I'm not the only one in this room who has an overabundance of imagination. But I'm able to keep a rein on my fantasies. You must understand that the best police and military minds of France are dealing with this problem."

"The same ones who have me locked up?"

"Nellie, the barge was rented by Dubois. The police have been watching the barge and have observed known anarchists come and go, along with the type of supplies and equipment needed to create large quantities of microbes."

"Did they also see a sign saying that it's an anarchist hideout?"

He squeezes my hand. "I don't blame you for being frustrated. You haven't been treated as you deserve, but that situation is only temporary."

"What are the police going to do about the barge?"

"With anarchists involved, we suspect it will also be loaded with explosives. That means it can't be stormed by ordinary means. We're trying to devise a way to get aboard quickly, so the anarchists have no time to react. Because of that imagination you claim I have, the police are consulting me."

"The next thing you're going to tell me is that you plan to attack the barge with a submarine."

His mouth hangs open. "A submarine?"

"You know, like *Twenty Thousand Leagues*—"

He draws back as if I had struck him.

"That's it! There's a submarine already in the Seine, the one being exhibited by Zédé for the Exposition."

"What?"

"We can gain entry underwater. I know exactly how it can be done." He rushes from the cell.

I shake my head. What have I started?

65

Nellie & Oscar

Early the next morning, Dr. Roth comes to my cell. His face is drawn and I fear the worst for Jules.

"Your friend Oscar has succumbed to the fever. He's at Pigalle Hospital, clinging to life."

"Oh, dear God, no." I'd forgotten all about the Irish poet. The thought of him suffering the horrible symptoms of Black Fever is too much to bear.

"I've gotten permission from the Prefect to take you to the hospital. I assured him that you would be on your honor and return here voluntarily after your visit. He agreed after I told him Doctor Pasteur and I would vouch for you."

"Thank you."

ROTH HAS A carriage waiting at the curb for us. As I enter, I gasp.

"Welcome aboard, my dear Nellie."

"Oscar!"

He laughs with delight as I climb in and take the seat beside him. Once Roth is inside, the carriage gets underway. I give Oscar a big hug and a kiss on the cheek. "You had me terribly worried."

He beams with delight. "You didn't think that I would leave you in the hands of those Huns, did you? We're taking you to the station for the Le Havre train. I've already booked you passage on the boat-train to London. From there, you can book to New York. I shall be your traveling companion, of course. After aiding in your escape, I will be persona non grata in Paris."

I shake my head in wonderment. "I can't believe you got me out."

"Actually, my dear, I am only a common soldier in the endeavor. André is the tactical genius who came up with the plan." As Oscar speaks, he nods across to Tomas Roth.

"André?"

"Yes! André. My friend I always wanted you to meet." Oscar rubs his hands together with glee. "Isn't it wonderful? I always knew André was a superb actor. He played the role of an assistant to Pasteur to get you released. We must get out of French territory before the Prefect discovers our little hoax."

The man I know as Tomas Roth locks eyes with me.

"André." The name sticks in my throat. Oscar knows him as André. Pasteur calls him Roth. But add a heavy beard, eyeglasses, and long hair covered by a pulled down box hat and Perun, the man in black, would materialize.

Oscar stares at me as the carriage is coming to a halt. "Why, what's the matter dear girl, you look pale. Don't worry, André won't be arrested, he's coming with us."

The door opens. A man with a steel ball for a hand boards. He has a pistol in his other hand.

André grins at us. "I believe you've met Monsieur Malliott."

Oscar stares at me. "Nellie . . . what—"

"You're right, Oscar, your friend André is a good actor." I shake my head. "You must be a great one to have fooled Pasteur."

André shrugs. "It wasn't difficult. Pasteur is focused completely on his work—and I complemented his work. I'm a better scientist than anyone at the Institut except Pasteur himself. And I tapped into his one great passion besides science."

That passion had been obvious from the art in Pasteur's office. "The German thing. All that artwork about freeing the territory the Germans took from France."

André claps. "Very good. Some borrowed credentials from an Alsatian researcher in the captured territory, and the accent I already had as a foreigner speaking French, and Pasteur was more than eager to permit me to work at the institute. But I must give myself credit. Once inside, I impressed him with my skills." André smiles at Oscar. "You look positively ill. Good Lord, maybe you are coming down with the fever. What do you think, Mademoiselle Bly? Does the situation look terminal to you?"

For once I am speechless and deep down I have to admit—the situation does look terminal.

"Oh, Nellie, the gods have given me almost everything." Oscar sighs. "I have genius, a distinguished name, high social position. Unfortunately, I'm afraid that being able to detect the deception of a friend is not a talent willed to me from Olympus."

"It's all right." I pat Oscar's arm. "He fooled a lot of people." I ask André, "How did you manage to be in the picture as Tomas Roth and as the radical Nurep the café artist Toulouse painted?" I'm talking to keep from panicking. My instinct is to throw myself at the carriage door but the gun in Malliot's hand dissuades me.

He chuckles. "It's really quite simple. Pasteur never

actually met me in my role as Nurep. I did my work outside the Institut and dealt only face-to-face with a member of his staff. That man fortuitously went off to Egypt and died in an outbreak, leaving a position open for me. He was the only one who actually saw me—and that was with beard and glasses. I took along René because he had never met Nurep. And had Luc Dubois hide behind the disguise I'd created."

I nod my head as if it's a fascinating revelation to me when I'd rather scream and jump from the carriage. "The beard and glasses, the hat pulled down over long hair, a disguise all along. I never really saw what you looked like. I just kept focusing on a man with a heavy beard and glasses. Since you've known who I am for a long time, why did you keep letting me investigate you?"

"Because you were considerably useful to me. While you've been running around antagonizing the police and directing them reluctantly toward a slasher, I've been able to put my plan into effect. But, of course now . . ." he shrugs, "your usefulness has ended."

I lean slightly toward him. Despite my fear, this is the man who murdered Josephine and took the lives of other women. I really hate him. "You know, you are quite mad. You're a sick hu—, no I was about to call you a human being, but you are an animal. Worse, you are a wild, crazy, mindless beast from the pit of hell."

For a moment something most foul and preternatural is exposed in the man's eyes and he truly scares me, but I don't move an inch. I refuse to give him the satisfaction of knowing how frightened I am. He takes his hand out of his pocket and a switchblade flicks open.

Oscar grabs me and pulls me back against the seat to protect me. "I might be a man of poor judgment, but I'll not allow you to hurt a woman, especially this one."

André dismisses Oscar's gallant gesture with a wave

of his knife. "I'm not going to hurt her . . . yet. I've saved her for another reason."

He smiles and sits back and I resume breathing, but then he suddenly lunges at me, his face so close I can feel his breath and the sharp, cold metal blade on my neck. "I'm saving you for myself. I want the pleasure of looking into your eyes as I slowly cut you open."

Both Oscar and I sit frozen.

André leans back as if nothing had transpired, his knife no longer in sight, but I can still feel the cold blade on my throat. He plans to kill me the way he killed Josephine. And all I can do is sit here. And poor Oscar. The man who dazzled gunslingers and rough-and-ready miners in the dust of Leadville, stares at me with his mouth open and empty of brilliant words.

"It's okay." Once again, I pat his arm.

Tears well in his eyes. "I'm so sorry, Nellie." He glares at André. "Playing the role of my friend, you did more than trick me. You murdered two people I loved. Luc and Jean-Jacque were angels and you took their lives."

André raises his eyebrows and shakes his head. "They were fools. Like you, they were café radicals, men who talk revolution but are unwilling to back up their ideals with actions. Jean-Jacque made the mistake of getting too curious about my activities—he spied on me. I ordered Luc to kill him and Luc failed me. Ultimately, I had to take care of both problems."

I realize that being part of Oscar's social circles was a perfect choice for André, Roth, Perun, whatever he calls himself. Not only did the group have the same sexual and political orientation as he, but because their personal activities are wrong in the eyes of the law, they tend to congregate and socialize more in secret than other groups of friends. And dear Oscar—I can see the rage building inside him, turning his face as mauve as his shirt. He's a big man with a gentle soul, but I have no doubt that if Malliot didn't have a gun on us, Oscar would have gone for André's throat. I decide to address André, to divert any rash and futile act of bravery on Oscar's part.

"What do we call you—André, Roth, or Perun?"

He just looks at me smug. I believe he doesn't care what we call him. He's in control and that's all he cares about. I also don't know how the count's henchman got involved with the anarchists, but there are only two possible answers—money, or Malliot's an anarchist himself.

"How could you work with the count when he's precisely the sort of rich industrialist your anarchist movement hates?"

"I didn't work with him. I used him—to fund my research, to pay Pasteur's Institut to permit me access to their work."

"With your friend here," I nod at Malliot, "paving the way. You know, that the police are onto you. If you stop at this point—"

He howls with laughter and Malliot joins him. Ugly laughs. He's pure evil. "You forget, I'm helping them plan my capture. There's a barge on the river that houses my laboratory. They're going to have a delightful surprise when they attack it. But, don't worry . . . at least they'll die faster than you two."

Still using words to beat down my panic, I take a deep breath to control myself and direct my verbal attack at Malliot. "You have no regret, do you, that you took the salary your employer provided and betrayed him?"

"I'm afraid the count is not a long-term employment prospect," Perun says. "He'll die with everyone else in the city very soon. But your friend Verne will go even sooner."

"Verne? You've set a trap for him?"

"Of course. One that Verne himself will trigger."

I raise my eyebrows to Malliot. "Your friend has a habit of disposing of his help once he's through with them—as he did with Dubois." I continue looking at Malliot, but direct my remark to Perun. "What about it, Monsieur, do you plan to do away with Monsieur Malliot when you no longer need him?"

"But of course. There will be no one named Malliot in existence when we finish."

They both get a good laugh at his remark.

Perun sneers at me with contempt. "Malliot and I have sworn to bring about a revolution at any cost. Unlike others, we're willing to give our lives."

"A thing is not necessarily true because a man is willing to die for it," Oscar says.

Perun's face darkens. "You're like the boyars who bleed the people of Russia. The sweat of others earns the bread you stuff in your ugly face. When I kill you, I'm going to do it carefully and precisely, twisting the knife in your gut, your groin, on the bottom of your feet, plucking out your eyes, then carving a hole from ear-to-ear."

66

Jules

"Reduce speed three quarters," Captain Zédé tells his engineer. "We are coming up to the barge."

Nellie's chance remark about using a submarine sent Jules racing off to the Prefect and Inspector Morant. Accompanied by officers of the law, Jules went to the submarine moored at a quay along the Seine near the entrance to the exposition and had the police commandeer the *Sangsue*. Designed to make underwater repairs to ships, the front of the submersible creates a watertight attachment to the hull at a point where repair is needed. Once attached, workers inside the front of the sub have access to the area of the hull needing repair.

Zédé's engineer-captain explains the *Sangsue* is equipped with a circular saw capable of cutting a hole big enough for a man to crawl through.

"I know the barge you speak of. It's wood, rotted, and barely keeps afloat. Once we are attached to its side, this circular saw can create the hole in seconds. Your men can be inside before anyone on the barge realizes what's happened. And poof! You kill everyone on board." The captain has a savage glint in his eye as he speaks.

"The attack will be orchestrated from both land and

underwater. When the hole is cut, we will raise the periscope to signal we're entering. At that point the attack from the street will begin as our men attack from inside. If anything goes wrong, we will lower the periscope to warn the gendarmes to stay clear."

Concern is voiced by the Prefect that the barge might be so damaged in the attack that it sinks, sending deadly microbes into the river water. But it is a risk that must be taken. There are no other options.

WITH JULES, MORANT, three officers, and a three-man crew crowded into the submarine, it's hot, cramped, and claustrophobic in the *Sangsue*. And dark. Only two lights for the whole length of the craft and neither has more power than that of a single candle.

The air is warm and stuffy and tastes stale to Jules. An officer coughs and Jules puts a handkerchief over his nose and mouth—the man might have the fever.

"Men, steady your self," the captain yells, "we are about to hit the barge and there will be a jolt."

There's a small thump as the craft attaches and the forward bulkhead door is opened. Craning his neck Jules can see the captain with a bull's-eye lantern, crawling into the nose of the submarine. In next to no time sounds of a saw ripping into wood erupts. Smoke from the saw and sawdust fill the submarine and soon there's general coughing.

The captain yells "done" and Jules, armed with a revolver, crawls forward with the officers. His lungs fouled by saw smoke and dust, legs aching from the crouching and knees poked bloody by rivets, Nellie's comment that she calls dangerous activities "adventures" only after she survives them, flashes in his mind.

His turn comes to crawl through the hole in the barge's hull and into a dark room. Police officers are lined up at a bulkhead door when he gets to his feet. A strange looking contraption is attached to the door.

Jules stares at it in the light of the lantern, realizing the object is something he's written about.

67

Nellie, Oscar, & Perun

The carriage takes us up the hill to Montmartre. We leave it at an alley too narrow for the coach to traverse. Perun leads, while Malliot is behind us with his trusty gun. Any attempt to escape would result in instant death. When we reach the end of the alley there is a long flight of stairs, followed by another. I'm certain I took some of these same steps on the night Jules and I went to the tavern where an old criminal serves stale beer to anarchists.

At the top of the second set of steps, the two Italian trapeze artists and other conspirators are waiting for us. From what I can ascertain from the talk between Perun and the trapeze girl, Oscar and myself were kidnapped to be used as hostages.

As we leave the stairs and take a footpath, Oscar confides to me in a strained whisper, "Their plan is about to be executed and they will need us only for a short time."

"That's a comforting thought."

Within a short distance we come to an entrance that's boarded-up. The door easily swings open for Perun and we enter a tunnel lit with lanterns. As we proceed down the tunnel, Perun's men pick up small wood crates stacked just inside the tunnel and bring them along. From the delicate way the crates are handled, I wonder if they hold the microbe-bomb-mixture Perun has concocted. I debate on whether to whisper my thoughts to Oscar. He looks as devastated as I feel.

"Nellie." Oscar's voice is edgy. "Do you realize we have entered an old gypsum mine?" He doesn't wait for a response from me, he needs to talk, and the words pour out in a gush. "It's the source of plaster of Paris. You know, of course, that many of the world's great art works are painted on thin layers of plaster, Michelangelo's Sistine Chapel scenes among them. I must say it's clever on Perun's part to choose an old gypsum mine not only in terms of concealment, but it has a double meaning: the bodies of thousands of anarchists and other Communards killed during the attack on the Butte were thrown into these abandoned mines. I just hope we don't join them."

The girl trapeze artist turns around and pokes a rifle in Oscar's chest. "Shut your mouth."

Oscar opens his mouth and then shuts it. I gently pat him on the back and we all continue through what seems like a never-ending, winding tunnel. To make matters worse, the further we go the smaller and smaller the tunnel becomes until even I have to stoop. Poor Oscar is nearly on his knees. Finally we come to another door—this one is made of steel. I would have never dreamed what was on the other side—we're in the sewers.

I've never been inside the sewers and am surprised by the smell. It's nothing like I thought—not that horrible smell of waste, just a damp, musty smell. I feel like I've entered my coffin.

The men stack the crates near a ladder to a manhole.

"Careful," Perun tells them. "If one of these goes off, we're all dead and so is all our work."

Oscar and I exchange looks. The crates are bombs. And considering Perun's line of work, they're filled with a deadly concoction. We put kerchiefs to our noses but the others don't bother to cover their faces—they are fanatics willing to give their lives for their cause.

Perun goes up the ladder and opens the manhole, revealing a large hot air balloon hovering at almost ground level.

I catch Oscar's eye and nod at the crates and balloon. He nods back. He understands. They are going to drop their ghastly bombs from the sky, high above the city.

PERUN, MALLIOT, AND the other men busy themselves doing what they call "arming" the crates and gingerly taking them up a ladder and through the manhole.

The trapeze girl is posted as our guard. She's only a few feet away from us, leaning back against a sewer wall, with her rifle in hand ready to use. I don't doubt that she would hesitate to kill us.

Oscar indicates the stack of crates. "Bombs of deadly microbes?"

She answers proudly—taunting us. "An army of deadly little animals in a fine dust. When the crates are dropped over the city, a small nitro charge will blow them open and scatter the dust. The whole city will be destroyed."

"And you along with it," I say. "The wind will carry it up to the people in the balloon's basket."

"We are willing to give our lives for the cause. Besides, we'll have masks to protect us."

In a corner on the other side of the tunnel are rifles leaning against the wall. Next to the weapons is an open box holding three balls, looking much like small cannonballs.

"Nitro hand bombs," Oscar says quietly. "What they

killed the czar with. No doubt for use against the police if they show up. An anarchist friend showed me one when I was researching my play about Vera."

I shake my head in amazement at the audacity of the plan. "Their plan is unimaginably sick and brutal."

"Madness knows no bounds," he says.

"Be quiet, both of you."

I frown at her. "You serve revolutionary ideals in a strange manner. Your leader is a mentally deranged killer who enjoys mutilating women. Your scheme will kill tens of thousands of innocent children, women, and helpless elderly. Are you so callous that the death of so many innocents will not damn your soul and haunt you in hell?"

Not even the bat of an eye from this woman. Her face reveals no anger, concern, or amusement. Her complete reticence in the face of this most heinous scheme is evidence that behind her pretty face is a snarling she-devil.

Oscar takes a step, slowly stretching his big body.

"Stand still!" she snaps to him.

"Mademoiselle, I don't care for your tone of voice."

She stands tall, with the rifle point-blank at his large midsection. "Stop moving or I'll kill you."

"Oscar, stand still." I grab his arm.

He pushes my hand away. "Do you realize that the rifle being pointed at me is of an extremely powerful caliber? At this range, the bullet would easily go through me and ricochet. What would it hit?" He takes a step toward her.

"Move any closer and I'll shoot!"

"Oscar, stop!"

"What's going on down there?" Perun calls down.

The woman yells to Perun, "He's—*put that down!*"

Oscar has picked up a wood crate. He looks at her with a puzzled expression. "All right, I'll drop it."

"*No!*"

I decide this is a good time to distract her. "When that dust is spilled over the city, small babies, little boys and girls, their mothers and fathers, grandparents, will all die horribly. You're not just destroying a city or a government. You're going to *kill* the very people you claim you want to help."

Oscar shakes his head. "Don't bother, dear girl, your pleas are falling into a bottomless pit. Besides, our four-legged brother, *Rattus norvegicus*, will soon take care of the problem."

"Rattus what?" I ask.

"Perhaps you know the gentleman by his more common name of 'sewer rat.' That big ugly fellow over there who is about to bite off our friend's nose."

"*Aaak!*"

The scream erupts from me. A huge, brown, ugly rat is on a ledge a foot from the girl's head. She turns her head and comes face-to-face with the rat. She recoils back from it, stumbling. Oscar's foot sweeps out and trips her. She slams against the wall and the gun goes off. A bullet zings pass me and ricochetes off the sewer wall.

Perun leans through the opening. "Put down the container," he tells Oscar.

"Never."

He points a pistol at me. "The container won't blow if dropped. It's not armed. And this gun won't ricochet like the rifle bullet. Put down the container or I'll kill Nellie."

He's smart. He knows Oscar. Oscar sets down the container.

"Now get up here, the both of you."

Oscar follows me up the ladder with the girl bringing up the rear. We're surrounded by a wall of canvas that's been put up to keep the loading of the balloon's basket concealed. Crates are stacked next to the balloon basket waiting to be loaded. One of the support cables that holds the basket to the balloon has broken loose. Both Malliot, who's in the basket, and the trapeze brother standing on a barrel next to the balloon, are working on the cable.

Perun puts a folded coat in front of his pistol and once again points it at me. I stare at it curiously, realizing that he's planning to muffle the sound of the shot that will kill me.

"Tsk, tsk, don't get impetuous, old man." Oscar grins at Perun. "I must tell you that the balance of power has shifted."

Perun gasps. Oscar has a nitro bomb in his hand. He tosses it a foot into the air and catches it. "Something I picked up during the scuffle."

Perun shouts, "*Stop!* Put . . . it . . . down. On the ground. If you do, I'll let you go."

Oscar tosses the bomb again and catches it. "Sorry, old man, but I can't do that. A gentleman doesn't walk away from confrontation with evil."

"Give it to me!"

"Why don't you give it to him, Oscar," I pipe in. "Drop it at his feet like they did to the czar."

"You two are crazy!" Malliot yells from the basket.

68

Jules

Jules joins Morant and his men before the barge's bulkhead door—a door booby-trapped with a nitro bomb. Not anticipating the police attack would come from below the waterline, the door was set to explode when opened from the other side. A signal is sent to stop police on the street from attacking. If this door was booby-trapped, others would be, too.

"I've written many times about such devices in the hands of madmen," Jules tells Morant. "I know how to disarm it."

An officer follows his instructions to remove the wire that would trip the bomb when the door is opened.

"We'll have to move slowly through the barge," Morant says. "Hopefully, we'll be able to disarm the bombs before one trips."

After the door bomb is disarmed, Jules follows the officers through the barge as they disarm other bombs. When they reach the upper deck, they realize no one had been aboard.

Out on deck, Jules leans wearily against the railing, feeling old and tired . . . and disappointed. The anarchists knew they would come to the barge, just as Nellie had deduced. That meant they plan to launch their attack from another vantage point—but where? Not the Eiffel Tower, it's presently surrounded by police. Even the elevator to the top has been disabled.

What did that mad Russian anarchist leader have in mind?

A carriage races around the corner and pulls to a stop beside the barge. It's Lussac. The detective reports to Morant. "Nellie Bly, with the help of Oscar Wilde and Doctor Roth, has escaped." He explains the Black Fever ruse.

"That makes no sense," Jules says. "Roth would never get involved in such a scheme." He stares at the two officers. "My God. What do we really know about the man?"

"He's Pasteur's assistant—"

Jules shakes his head. "A post acquired only recently. That doesn't mean he can't be an anarchist. We know that Dubois tampered with the samples. No doubt Roth did, also. And that death at the Institut, a young assistant named René. Was he really killed by the fever? Now Nellie's been kidnapped."

"No." Lussac shakes. "She went willingly with Roth and Wilde. They're probably helping her escape back to America."

"Or Roth could be delivering Nellie to Perun."

"That's preposterous!" Morant interjects. "Perun is dead. You seem to forget, we have a corpse to prove it."

"No, you don't. The exploding building, the burned body, this barge, Nellie warned me it was all a ruse, and she was right. And I ignored her because I was too excited about using the submarine. We're been tricked. Something else is being planned."

Morant nodded. "You may be right." He instructs Lussac, "Tell the Prefect that we must redouble our efforts to watch the roofs of all large buildings. These anarchists don't have wings. If they can't get to Eiffel's Tower, or pour their concoction into the river, a tall building would be their most advantageous position." He looks north, toward Montmartre. "The Butte's an anarchist nest and it's tall enough, but it would not serve them. They would need powerful winds to spread their contagion around the city."

Jules follow his gaze to the Butte. "That's it!"

"What?"

Jules point at the hill. "*The balloon!* The one the Italian circus aeronauts perform with. It's up there."

"What are you saying?"

"The balloonists are anarchists, part of Perun's secret group."

Morant shakes his head. "You're not saying they'd use the balloon . . ."

"Of course they would. They're experienced aeronauts. They would just wait until the wind blew in the right direction, then guide the balloon over the city and release the microbes. We have to get up there. Nellie and Oscar are there—if they are still alive."

As they move into action, Jules stops. "We need to distract their attention, make them think their plan to kill us worked."

Once again his unbridled imagination goes to work.

69

An explosion rumbles from the direction of the Seine. Malliot yells in triumph. "We got them! The barge has gone up with them inside. The fools walked right into our trap."

Jules. They've killed him. I start for Perun. I don't care if he is pointing a gun at me. Oscar grabs my arm and I struggle to break free.

"He killed Jules!"

Oscar keeps an iron grip on my arm. "Steady, girl. We have a city to save."

He's right, but if I had the bomb in my hand, I would have killed Perun with it.

"Your comrade is right," I shout at Perun, *"we're crazy!* Crazy enough to give our lives to stop animals like you from killing thousands of people. Do you understand that? You're not going to win. You bastard! How do you like that? *We're going to beat you!"*

I take an involuntary step back as Perun's features twists and his body shakes. He's like a wild animal that's tasted the whip and now wants to leap and rip open my throat.

Oscar shows him the nitro bomb again. "One move and this entire place goes up."

It's a standoff—but for how long? They can't move . . . but neither can we. The bomb would likely set off a chain reaction and scatter some microbic dust locally and kill people, but it's unlikely to cause the catastrophic, city-killing effect these madmen have worked for years to achieve.

We look at each other, anarchists willing to die for their cause but who know if they rush us their long-laid plans may be destroyed. And two innocents, neither of whom know how to deal with violence, though of the two of us, Oscar has kept his head and taken the lead.

So, we stand—staring at each other as Malliot ignores us and again starts loading the balloon basket with microbe-bombs.

"They're not going to do anything," Malliot tells Perun. "They don't want to die." He jerks his head at Oscar. "You can step over and take that bomb from that British fool."

Perun hesitates but my instinct is that he's going to charge.

I look at Oscar. "Throw the bomb." My voice quivers and my knees are melting but I say it again.

Oscar lifts the bomb higher. "Just because you're willing to give your life for something doesn't mean the cause is right. But sometimes it is."

From the distance comes the sound of clanging bells.

We all freeze again.

Perun suddenly laughs. "They're wasting their time. That barge is a burning inferno. No one will survive."

"*No!*" Malliot yells. "It's police wagons! They're coming here!"

Two men who are helping load the crates bolt and scramble down the sewer opening.

"Traitors!" the male trapeze artist yells after them.

Perun barely glances at the fleeing men. His attention is back on Oscar, who is once again shaking the bomb.

"Doesn't nitro explode just shaking it." Oscar says.

It's not a facetious question but that odd way Oscar has of making a statement. His voice is oddly calm.

The girl trapeze artist stares intently at Oscar with the burning eyes of a fanatic. Like Perun, she looks ready to leap.

Malliot is the only one taking action, unhooking the netting from the balloon basket as if we were not there . . . completely ignoring the bomb in Oscar's hand.

Perun is suddenly calm. "Get aboard," he tells the brother and sister team.

"Too much weight," Malliot shouts down. "We'll rise too slowly. As good comrades, they know what they have to do."

"He expects you to die for the cause while they escape," I tell the trapeze team.

The boy stares at me; unlike his sister, he looks both scared and confused but the girl hisses—making a sound like the jungle cat she reminded me of.

"You have your orders," Perun tells them. "Kill both of them and use the remaining bombs to explode the crates."

As Perun climbs aboard, Oscar takes a step forward. "I'm sorry, but I can't let you do that. If you try to take off, I will toss this bomb into the basket."

"If you do, you'll be killed, too."

"That may be so, but I must tell you that I've considered the risks and in my opinion that sacrifice will be a far better result than permitting you to take off and destroy the entire city."

Drawn to the verbal duel between Oscar and the anarchist, I only catch the movement out of the corner of my eye as the girl pounces on Oscar.

He stumbles backward, going down on his rear as the bomb goes up in the air and the girl falls with him.

I grab the bomb, getting it with both hands, but fly forward over a crate as the girl's brother comes alive and slams into me.

I carry the bomb down with me, but as I hit the pavement it slips out of my hands.

The trapeze artist's momentum carried him over the same crate and he adroitly twists in midair to avoid falling on me.

Screaming, I roll over on my stomach and grab my head with both hands to protect myself from the explosion. My ears are ringing and I realize what I hear are the police wagon bells. And not an explosion.

I raise my head and look around, my mouth gaped open. Everyone has frozen in place again. Oscar is on his rear, staring at me. The girl is straddling his legs. Her brother to my left still looks confused and scared.

Perun is halfway into the basket. He pauses for only a second and makes up his mind to go for the hand bomb rather than get into the basket.

Police wagons can now be heard loud and clear, rolling into the area. As I rise to get up Oscar knocks the girl off his lap with a blow to her head.

As Perun leaps for the bomb I scramble for it on hands and knees. He kicks me, his foot catching me in the side and sending me over onto my back with a cry of pain.

Perun stops and points his pistol down at me. "Die, bitch."

Oscar is suddenly on him. The big man literally picks Perun up and carries him, slamming him against the side of the basket, knocking the breath from the man. He wrestles the gun from the man's hand as Malliot leans out of the basket and swings at Oscar, catching the side of his head with a glancing blow from his steel fist.

The gun goes off as Oscar stumbles backward, the bullet hitting the rigging and ricocheting harmless into the wood of the basket.

Malliot casts the ropes off from inside the basket as Perun bellies into it. The trapeze brother starts to board and Malliot hits him in the face with his steel fist, knocking him off.

"Too much weight," Malliot shouts.

Screaming like a wild animal, the trapeze girl jumps over me and grabs the hand bomb off the ground. As she straightens up, Oscar's big arms go around her, grabbing the wrist of the hand holding the bomb so she is unable to throw it. He raises her in the air and pitches her forward, slamming her down on top of her brother.

An explosion sends me reeling backward as I'm struck by stinging bits of debris.

It takes me a second to realize that I'm still in one piece. Stunned, in shock, but on my feet.

The shadow of the balloon falls across me as it rises and I look up, expecting to see Perun's taunting sneer or a gun pointed at me.

I can't see either Perun or Malliot. Shots are fired from behind me. The two anarchists must be ducking down in the basket to avoid the police fire.

Over the din of shouted commands and guns firing, I hear Jules' urgent plea, "Shoot the balloon, don't shoot at the basket!"

Oscar is lying next to me. He's covered in blood.

70

How bittersweet life can be. I have a train to catch and my head is buzzing with conflicting emotions—I want to get back to America and my work, but I don't want to leave Jules. But I must. And even though the French government thanked me profusely for my assistance, they declared me persona non grata because the fair is still running and made me, and my partners in crime, swear to secrecy about the incident.

Police bullets had damaged the balloon, but it had kept rising, spinning out of control. The saving grace was the wind—it carried the balloon away from the city where it crashed south of the city in a river.

Malliot's body was recovered. He had taken a police bullet in the head as the balloon rose. Perun's body was not recovered, but the police were satisfied the anarchist leader had met his just end.

"No one could have survived the balloon crash," Inspector Morant had told us.

I hope he's right. Perun seems to have more lives than a cat.

And dear-sweet Oscar. He was only covered in what he named "malevolent blood" . . . the blood of the two trapeze artists. They didn't survive, but the girl's body had protected Oscar from the blast. At least she did one good thing in her life.

Jules and Oscar are my companions and guards, escorting me to the train station in a grand carriage sent by the Chief Inspector himself . . . making me wonder whether the carriage driver was there to see I actually got onto the train.

Since my mother raised me to always be a lady and constantly drilled into my head, "a lady never kisses and tells," I have nothing to say about my last night in Paris—except, never did I image a night could be so romantically beautiful and a morning so bittersweet.

Jules asked me during breakfast to stay a few days longer. Never in my life did I want to say "yes" so badly, but I knew the longer I stayed the more painful it would be to leave. Jules has a life I can never really adapt to. And I have a career I love and want to continue. I have to go back to America. I almost ask Jules not to accompany me to the train station. The thought of him standing there waving good-bye . . .

That morning I did something I normally don't do. It's not in my character. I cried. Mind you, not in front of Jules. As I was getting ready in the bathroom, I cried. I had to splash my face with cold water because my eyes were so red.

Thank goodness for Oscar. Having him along saved me from another cry. Who could be melancholy when the songbird of the spoken word sits across from you in a carriage?

"WELL, HERE WE are." Oscar looks out of the carriage.

I sigh silently. We have arrived. I have only a fleeting moment left with my friends. I take a deep breath and force a smile, while Jules takes out his pocket watch. I smile because it reminds me of that rocky time at the café the first time we spoke. I had pleaded for his help as he kept looking at his watch and acting as if I was a madwoman.

Tears start to well in my eyes and I scramble to get out of the carriage.

"Hold on. Not so fast, Nellie girl." Oscar pulls out a bottle of champagne. "We're early, I made sure of that. We can't leave without having a toast to you . . . to Nellie, a grand gal who will always be in our hearts."

As we lift our glasses, Jules says, "I want to add that she is a woman of indelible courage and resourcefulness. I never knew a woman could function so well in a man's world. Not only will she live in our hearts, but someday I will immortalize her in print."*

"I'm speechless . . . and honored. I only have one request."

"Yes?"

Oscar leans over to Jules, "Be prepared. Remember, this is a very *modern* woman."

"Make her the main character. You have never had a woman as the main character in your stories. And I've been meaning to ask you, why?"

"Because, my dear Nellie, women are not capable of performing the feats my heroes have to do."

"That's not true. Women can do anything a man can do. She just has to put her mind to it."

Jules scoffs and says to Oscar. "Can you imagine a woman making it around the world in eighty days as Phileas Fogg did?"

"Now you listen—"

---

* Jules kept his word. Mrs. Branican, in Verne's book of the same name, was inspired by Nellie's will and determination.—The Editors.

"The train's leaving!" Oscar grabs my glass of champagne as I struggle with my temper.

Jules once again takes out that damn pocket watch of his. "He's right. Let's go."

I hurry out of the carriage and walk away, fighting to keep from showing unladylike temper on this parting that should be poignant, not blistery. Oscar races to keep up with me.

The whistle blows and I stop right at the boarding steps. I fought hard to not cry. This was really it. I was leaving.

"Nellie," Oscar turns me around and gives me a warm hug. I have learned that this big bear who talks and dresses as no ordinary human being on the planet has the courage of a lion. "I'm really going to miss you. You saved my life."

"No, it was *you* who really saved my life." I can't help but hug him again.

Jules pats Oscar on the back. "And for that I will always be grateful. Not to mention your astounding courage in the face of the enemy."

Oscar gives him a look that questions whether Jules really means it.

"I absolutely mean it. I'm impressed not only with your intelligence and physical bravery, but your moral courage."

Ah . . . moral courage. During breakfast we had a discussion about Oscar. I pointed out to the conservative Frenchman that Oscar has the courage not only to dress and talk as he pleases, but to suffer the stings and arrows of people who condemn his sexual preferences as immoral. "Who are we to throw the first stone?" I asked him.

Jules had shook his head and advised me, "*Slings*, Nellie, not stings. 'The slings and arrows of outrageous fortune.'

It's from *Hamlet*. Slings, like arrows, were medieval weapons. And in the Bible, stones were cast, not thrown."

"*Last call! All aboard! All aboard! Last call!*"

A porter takes my valise and as I start to step onto the boarding steps Jules grabs my arm and gives me a hug. I hugged him back. I believe neither of us wanted to let go.

"*Last call! All aboard! All aboard! Last call!*"

"Good-bye Jules. Thank you for . . ."

"No, it is I who must thank you, Nellie Bly. You brought me back to life."

As I board the steps, Jules smiles to Oscar and speaks loud enough for me to hear, "She's quite a woman, but as I said a woman could never make it around the world in eighty days as Phileas Fogg did."

I can't believe I heard what I heard. How dare he say that again about women after I followed a killer halfway around the world and exposed the most heinous anarchist plot imaginable? I can't leave without expressing my ire. Thank goodness Jules and Oscar are still on the platform in yelling range.

"*Jules!*" I shout at the top of my lungs.

Jules has turned away and Oscar taps him on the shoulder and points to me.

I shout, "Why did you choose eighty days for Phileas Fogg's trip around the world?" Having read the book, I already knew the answer.

"I timed it! That's the fastest any *man* can do it."

As the train moves, I yell, "That's right, that's the fastest any *man* could do. But I'm a woman and I'm going to do it in less time! Do you hear me? I'm going to beat Phileas Fogg's record! *Do you hear me?*"

Oscar waves his bright orange handkerchief, while Jules just stands there with an enormous grin on his face as my train gains speed.

I shake my head. "Oh, if only I were on that platform, Jules Verne, you wouldn't be so smug."

"YOU PUZZLE ME, old boy." Oscar continues waving good-bye, as he speaks to Jules. "Why did you say such a thing to Nellie? You know by now how she will react. To her it's a slap across the face, a red flag to a bull."

"It's my best book and it can use another run with the public. Can you imagine how many copies will sell if that wonderful young woman takes up the challenge? Besides, France will be in her path and we'll see her again."

"YOU DON'T FOOL me, Jules Verne. You *do* want to see me again."

"Mademoiselle . . . ?"

A conductor addresses me cautiously. I'm sure he's from the school who thinks that people who stand at the window of a moving train and hold a conversation with themselves belong in an insane asylum.

"May I show you to your compartment?"

"Thank you. I'll—" I stop and gawk at a man standing at the end of the platform as the train rolls by.

"Is something the matter?" the conductor asks.

"Did you see that man on the platform?"

"What man?"

"The bearded man dressed all in black, wearing a red scarf. He's on the platform. *Stop the train!*"

"What?"

"*We've got to stop the train!*"

"Stop the train?"

"*Yes!* Stop the train. We have to catch that man."

"That is impossible." He stands erect, his backbone stiffening. "Mademoiselle. Follow me immediately to your compartment. You need to lie down and rest."

I look back at the platform. The man is gone.

I get my breathing back into order. I have to calm down and not let my imagination run wild. The inspector said no one could have survived the balloon crash.

He is dead and that's that.

I just hope he stays dead.

POSTSCRIPT

FROM

The Editors

IT SHOULD COME as a surprise to no one that Nellie Bly took up the challenge Jules threw at her.

Back in New York, she proposed a race around the world to beat Phileas Fogg's eighty days record to Pulitzer. Once again he told her that what she proposed was no job for a lady . . .

That was all he had to say to ignite a storm. It took her all of three days to plan the trip, throw a few things into a small valise, and start a race around the world on ships, trains, and carriages.

She stopped in France, of course, to say hello to old friends. And later wrote a book about her adventure: *Around the World in Seventy-Two Days*.

Although she received international acclaim for her incredible feat, to prevent worldwide panic she was forced to omit from the book certain strange and mysterious events that occurred when she went around the world in those seventy-two days.

However, the editors are pleased to announce that they have obtained Nellie's original manuscript and it will soon be ready for public viewing.

CAROL MCCLEARY AT NELLIE BLY'S GRAVE
2009

Turn the page for a preview of

THE
ILLUSION
OF
MURDER

Carol McCleary

*Available in April 2011 from
Tom Doherty Associates*

A FORGE HARDCOVER   ISBN 978-0-7653-2204-3

19th Dynasty Burial Chamber
Ancient site of Tanis
Egypt, 1889

I discovered that Egypt is a land of both mystery and magic, an exotic place where trees talk and men turn staffs into snakes, so it should not have come as such a surprise that death would also be mysterious in this ancient, haunted land of pyramids, mummies, and the eternal Nile.

That I could suffer a bizarre death in this strange land had not occurred to me until now, as I stand cold to the bone, staring down at the long black snake I've stepped on.

I don't dare lift my foot, I can't even breathe; I just stand stiffly in place, the toe of my shoe pressing down on the serpent as it thrashes and tries to coil.

Darkness is closing in as a burning torch on the dirt a few feet from me fades. When the bundle of sticks burns out, there'll be just me and the snake—in the dark.

In the dark where? A burial chamber, for sure. A sarcophagus is off to my right and I can make out on a wall a scene from the *Egyptian Book of the Dead*—the aged painting of a boat that has the head of a lion, a tail and clawed feet at the stern; aboard are wailing women, some with hands outstretched, others covering their faces—mourners for the dead.

The stone coffin, pillars, and faded hieroglyphics are the only remnants of what was perhaps the magnificent tomb of some long-dead pharaoh. Once filled with unimaginable treasures, it now has dust and cobwebs; thieves have taken everything but the ghosts.

Shouting for help will do no good. No one knows I'm here except the person who imprisoned me; someone with murder in their heart I've yet to put a name or face to, but who knows I'm trying to flush them out.

The snake's tail whips against the side of my leg and I nearly jump out of my skin.

I have no idea of what kind of snake it is, but the country is famous for its asps—deadly horned vipers and cobras. Cleopatra tested their venom on condemned prisoners to find out which killed the fastest and most painlessly before she had one bite her.

How I came to be imprisoned in an ancient tomb with one foot on a snake and the other on my own grave has me wondering how I've so quickly managed to offend the gods of this ancient land. A mystifying artifact of Egyptian black magic is the source of my troubles and I had been forewarned—possession of it has already caused blood to soak into the primordial dust of the Nile valley.

It is not the first time I've stepped into a snake pit, so to speak, but never before so literally; it's at times like this that I wonder if there is something about me that attracts the strange and the dangerous.

My name is Nellie Bly and I'm a reporter for Mr. Joseph Pulitzer's *New York World*. With too much boldness for my own good, I bullied and bluffed my way into having the newspaper send me on a race around the world in which I must beat the "record" set by Phileas Fogg in Jules Verne's novel *Around the World in Eighty Days*.

That it was the thirteenth day of my journey when I made landfall in Egypt should have also told me that this was not an auspicious time to visit a place where priests once made people eternal with dark magic and the land blistered under ten plagues hurtled by the almighty Jehovah.

The snake twists and thrashes violently and I press harder—at least I think I do. My body is blue cold, I can't feel my toes and my knee is shaking wildly as if it has a life of its own.

Did something move at the sarcophagus?

I'm sure I saw something move.

Dear God, let it be a trick of the light.

The fading torchlight is casting eerie shadows. There couldn't be anything in the stone coffin, not something alive, unless it's true that Egyptian priests could embalm in a way that preserved life for aeons.

More snakes?

The thought of being in the dark with snakes, and scorpions, and spiders, and God knows whatever else lurks in ancient tombs causes the shaking in my knee to work its way up to my hip, and my whole body trembles. I want to cry but I can't spare the strength and instead press down harder on the snake—or maybe I just think I am pressing harder. My foot is so numb I can't feel anything under it.

The torch flickers and hisses as if it's burning through the last of the pitch. I have to get to it and somehow keep it going until I can find my way out of this nightmare. There has to be a door somewhere.

My knees and my courage are turning to mush and I keep imagining I'm letting up the pressure on the struggling serpent. Or maybe I'm not imagining it.

I know I can't keep this awkward stance any longer. I have to do something now before the darkness completely embraces me.

The creature underfoot thrashes violently, whipping its whole body. It starts slipping out from under my shoe and I scream as I push down on it again, my heart pounding so hard that I'm breathless and sway dizzily, almost losing my footing.

Shutting my eyes tightly, I ask God for help. I don't think He will listen; unfortunately I'm one of those people who never talks to Him unless I'm up to my neck in alligators, but I try anyway, though I don't think that the Good Lord would approve of my present association with the dark side of Egyptian magic.

I can't be left blind in the darkness with a deadly snake. I need to get both feet on the snake and jump up and down until I'm sure it can't harm me and get to the torch before it dies.

I start to bring up my other foot up as I look down.

It's gone.

The snake has slipped out from under my foot.

Mortified, I can't move, can't breathe. It could strike at any second.

Mother of God, how did I get myself into this mess? Ancient curses, magic amulets, esoteric mysteries from the *Egyptian Book of the Dead*, murder and fanaticism—it's all insanely bizarre for a young woman from Cochran Mills, Pennsylvania, population exactly 534.

As the darkness closes in on me and my breathing takes on the hoarse rasp of a death rattle, I ask myself what I could have done differently when I decided to flush out a killer in a land blessed by the sun and damned by ancient curses.